LYCAN 1

RISE OF THE

MARK TUFO

CreateSpace Edition
Copyright 2013 Mark Tufo

Discover other titles by Mark Tufo
Visit us at marktufo.com
and http://zombiefallout.blogspot.com/
and find me on FACEBOOK

Cover Art:
Artist Alex Raspad and designer Shawn T. King

Dedications -

To my wife - there's a reason that word rhymes with life. I'm a better man with you at my side and I thank the fates we met.
To my beta's who selflessly donated hours of their time to help me improve this story, I cannot thank you enough for your time, proof-reading and suggestions.
Joy Buchanan
Vix Kirkpatrick
Kimberly Sansone
To my fans and readers, I cherish each and every one of you. The incredible support I receive from you is the reason I can put books out, and for that I am appreciative.
To the first responders and men and women of the armed services...Heroes, each and every one of you.

Table Of Contents

Prologue
Chapter 1 - Mike Journal Entry One
Chapter 2 - Mike Journal Entry Two
Chapter 3 - Mike Journal Entry Three
Chapter 4 - Tommy and Azile
Chapter 5 - Mike Journal Entry Four
Chapter 6 - Mike Journal Entry Five
Chapter 7 - Xavier and the Zombie - Winter 2010
Chapter 8 - Mike Journal Entry Six
Chapter 9 - Xavier
Chapter 10 - Xavier's Past
Chapter 11 - Mike Journal Entry Seven
Chapter 12 - Harbor's Town
Chapter 13 - Mike Journal Entry Eight
Chapter 14 - Mike Journal Entry Nine
Chapter 15 - Denarth
Chapter 16 - Mike Journal Entry Ten
Chapter 17 - Mike Journal Entry Eleven
Chapter 18 - Mike Journal Entry Twelve
Chapter 19 - Mike Journal Entry Thirteen
Chapter 20 - Azile's Story
Chapter 21 - Mike Journal Entry Fourteen
Epilogue - The Story of Tommy/Tomas
Western Front 1918
Talbot-Sode #1
Talbot-Sode #2

Forward - Hello dear reader, as always thank you for your support. I hope you take a few moments to read this as it will answer a few questions you may have in regards to this story. For those of you that are familiar with my writings and the many alternate realities of Michael Talbot, this is NOT a continuation of Zombie Fallout, HOWEVER, it is on the same timeline (that'll make much more sense once you start reading). For those of you who may not know me and this is your first foray into my works, first off welcome aboard, secondly you will not need to read anything beforehand, this is a standalone book. As you are reading this tome you may be wondering what happened to some of your beloved characters from the aforementioned series. The good news on that front is I will be releasing Zombie Fallout 7 in October of 2013. Again thank you and it is my sincerest hope that you enjoy this book. As always Henry says HI (and wants to know where his cookie is).

PROLOGUE

Fuck zombies, they're not the enemy. Death is.

CHAPTER 1 - Mike Journal Entry One

I sat in the basement of my brother's dilapidated house surrounded by my loved ones. Beams creaked as the accumulated weight of time dragged them down. Dust encased the entire room in a heavy protective coating. Rats had long since vacated the property after they had robbed it of anything worthy of their time.

The large armchair I sat in fully enveloped me in its cold embrace. I fingered the lid on the urn I had sitting in the chair next to me. The name 'Tracy Talbot' carefully etched by my own hand on a small bronze plate in the front.

"I miss you most of all," I said to the indifferent pile of ashes.

I was alive, partly. The most unworthy of them all, and yet I still roamed the earth. Much like Longinus I begged to shed my immortality. When I was a youth, I heard the stories of the Roman soldier who had pierced Jesus' side and was now cursed to roam the earth indefinitely; I always wondered what he was bitching about. He had been given the gift of immortality, what more could he ask for? I received that answer when my last family member perished.

Maybe I could find him; we could hang out together and play Canasta. It's been over a hundred and fifty years since the zombie apocalypse started. Man teetered on the edge of extinction for decades. I'd like to think that, in some small way, I tipped the scales, there were so many heroic deeds done back then to give man a second chance. Were we worthy? My initial cynical guess would be no, but I'm a lonely asshole so who knows.

It had really only been in the last ten years that men, women, and children began to dribble out of their bunkers and hidey-holes. Apparently, we have an inherent need for community. Didn't understand that philosophy when I was a regular man, and it sure doesn't strike a chord now that I was half of one. The year for anyone marking time like me, was 2167. There were no hover cars that had been promised in my youth, no traveling to the stars, no deep-sea cities, none of that science fiction bullshit. The world was mostly gas lamps and some intermittent power when some industrious people began to relearn lost technologies.

It wouldn't be too long before some idiot rediscovered television. I placed my hands over my face as I sobbed. I was thinking of when I had played the Wii with my son; now nearly a hundred years later, he had been reduced to the basic vestiges. What I wouldn't do for an odiferous whiffing of my Henry, my steadfast English Bulldog who had lived far longer than he should have. They were all gone, every last bloody one of them. Each day I sat here longing for just one more moment to share with them. Their laughs. Their cries. Their excitement and merriment. The good, the bad…any of it, all of it. Life is fleeting, even more so to those of us who live forever.

At some point, the night had yielded its darkness over the planet, not my heart though, that stayed as black as pitch. I watched as the shadows of trees traveled along the back of my brother's yard. I heard footfalls approaching. I couldn't even muster enough energy to care, I could only hope it was the local townspeople come to off my head. I didn't know to what abyss I would be relegated, but I was convinced it couldn't be any worse than the one unto which I was now assigned.

"Mr. T, you in there?"

I hadn't moved much since I had pulled the last living relative off of their funeral pyre, and my guest knew that. He came every year or so to bring me some food and, I guess, just see how I was doing. Maybe even partly to adjudicate his guilt, considering it was him that put me in this state. It had, ultimately, been my choice and it did save my family if even only temporarily.

"Where else would I be, Tommy?" I replied.

"There's a whole new world out there, Mr. T. Why don't you come out and we'll travel."

"Did you bring me my food?" I grumbled.

He sidestepped around some new debris. "She's tied up out front like always," he said, looking around. Tommy knelt to pay his respects to those around me before standing again. "This place is going to come down soon." He placed his hand against one of the supports.

"Good, maybe it'll pierce my heart."

"That won't return your soul," he said solemnly.

I stood abruptly, shaking in rage. "My soul? No, that's gone forever. Tommy, you of all people should know that!" He turned away. "All that I ever loved, all that ever mattered to me is gone. And yet, here I am! A derelict of a man...no soul, no purpose, no hope!" I shouted as I sat down heavily.

"I'll see you next year," he said as he walked out.

I did not acknowledge him as he left. I can't even remember the last time I had. Hunger gnawed at my stomach as I watched the light be chased away. I ventured forth from a huge hole in the wall. It was fall, and the night air should have felt cold and crisp upon my exposed arms, but they were as numb as my spirit. I walked to the front; where a large dairy cow was tied to a tree I couldn't recall from previous years. The cow had been chewing on a stack of hay that had been left with it.

It looked up at me and its eyes widened as it watched me approach; it began to back up and pull against the rope that had it tethered in place. It began to moo in full-on panic mode. I never had been one to play with my food as I savagely ripped into its neck with my teeth. I drank heavily and deeply of its rich iron-laced blood. My eyelids drooped down as I savored every moment. The cow, at first, was trumpeting in panic but calmed as I took more and more of its life from it, one liquefied morsel at a time.

    I returned to my throne, sated, and for a moment…almost at peace. I slumbered, my hands over my full, sloshing belly. Could have been a day, maybe a week when I re-awoke. Maybe longer since there was now a good three or four inches of snow on the ground. The house was groaning from its frosty covering. Would I stay once the house came down? Odds were, yes; I was as much a part of the house as any of the fixtures, I was a semi-living haunt of the residence. It would take a talented real estate agent to explain me away to a prospective buyer.

    Oh don't mind him; he hardly ever makes any noise.
    I sneered at my own thought.

    The winter was a particularly bad one; snow must have got to about two feet at one time. The spring was heralded with the happy cries of birds and gophers – none of which would venture forth into my underground lair. Spring rains turned into the muggy heat of summer, legions of mosquitoes patrolled the air looking for their next blood meal. The air began to cool at night and then the days themselves were cool and crisp, it was almost time to eat again.

    Tommy came in. He didn't announce himself. In fact, he didn't say anything to me as he once again paid his respects to his adoptive family and friends. I'll admit I was more than a little pissed. I had my normal practiced rant, and much like a performer, I wanted an audience to witness it.

    As he was leaving I yelled at him. "Where's my food?"

    "Where it always is," he shouted over his shoulder before heading out.

    I arose from my seat when I was sure he was gone. I

rounded the corner and tied up to the tree was something that dropped me to my knees. I pressed my palms into my eyes; I pulled my hands away to notice they were wet. I had not felt human for so long I was unsure I was still able to produce tears. I ran over to the tree and untied the puppy, a small leather collar around his neck with a tag shaped like a bone attached to it, his name clearly marked. 'A. Purpose'.

I hugged the puppy tightly, then I pushed him away. I grabbed him roughly and placed his neck against my teeth. I put him down and hastily urged him away.

"Go away, Purpose! I don't want you!" I shouted at him, stamping my feet. He thought I was playing and would growl and bark trying to bite at them. "NO!" I retreated to my man-made cave. I got back into my seat and threw my head back. Languished cries of remorse and mourning pounded through me. I cried to the Heaven's…I cursed to Hell…and everything in between got an earful. I might have stayed in that state until Tommy showed the next year, but I felt a small tugging at my foot.

I pulled forward and looked down, Purpose was growling at my boot. I stared at him for hours. He stared back for a few minutes, yawned, and immediately fell asleep at my feet. I pulled my legs up so we weren't touching. He cried, and something akin to emotion snapped inside of me. I picked him up and placed him on my lap. He would not find warmth there, though. I shook off the old coverlet and wrapped him in it. He licked my hand once and was almost immediately back asleep.

His belly grumbled like only an empty stomach can, mine followed suit in sympathetic notes. It was then that I realized Tomas had not brought me food. I was starving, and when Purpose woke up, he would be also. I stood up as quietly as I could so as not to disturb the dog. I gently placed him down in my seat and went out in to the woods. Deer, turkeys, moose, and bears had all rebounded nicely with the absence of the apex predator. It would not be difficult to find us sustenance. I did not know it then, but I already loved him.

Tommy had succeeded in what he'd set out to do…he had given me Purpose.

***

I moved out of the house that following day, not far mind you but out. It was too dangerous for Purpose in there, and I didn't want anything to happen to him. I made a small lean-to in the yard and kept a fire going the entire winter. When the spring thaw came I buried each urn and marked them with a small headstone. I said a hollow prayer as I laid each to rest. I didn't find comfort in it, but I hoped that, as they watched over me from above, they would.

Purpose stood next to me solemnly as I did the unenviable task. When I was done he bounded off chasing after a rabbit that had strayed into his territory. Purpose wasn't an English Bulldog, but he was close. As man neared the brink, so did his most trusted and loyal friend, dogs that could not adapt were now gone forever. Only the medium-sized, smarter breeds like Retrievers, Huskies, and Pit Bulls survived and even thrived. Purpose looked something like an Old English Bulldog, with longer legs like an American Bulldog, a square head like a Rottweiler and a semi pushed-in nose; much like my beloved Henry. His markings were as near to Henry as I could remember, his body was fawn colored, with black rings around his eyes and his face was white.

I was standing over Gary's spot in the ground when I heard Purpose barking a warning. I turned quickly. Somebody was coming.

"Come, Purpose," I told him as we strode back into the house.

I heard Tommy stop by the headstones: a few moments later he called out. "Mr. T, you here?"

Purpose bristled at first and then relaxed when I

assumed he recognized the voice.

"Where's the dog?" Tomas asked from outside.

"You mean that morsel you brought me to eat last year? I do hope you upped your game this year, I've been very hungry."

"Does your food always leave droppings?"

"Busted," I said to Purpose who I let go. He immediately bounded out of the basement to greet our guest properly.

"What is he feeding you?" Tommy asked as Purpose bowled him over. After a few minutes of rough housing Tommy stood up. "It's good to see you up and about, Mr. T."

I didn't answer him.

He motioned to the small, marked mounds. "I'm glad you finally put them at peace."

My heart panged as I realized the finality of my act. "I wish I was at peace."

Tommy had seen the hurt on my face and the pain in my words and quickly moved on. "How has Purpose been doing?" he asked.

"Who, that mangy mutt? He eats more than any dog I've ever known. It's difficult to keep him satisfied."

"You look better."

"You didn't bring any food?"

"Pop-Tarts have been extremely hard to come by in this new world of man. My hope is someday that someone finds the recipe and begins to replicate it. There is a baker in New Detroit that bakes an awesome blonde brownie with a caramel center, though."

"I was thinking more along the lines of meat, but now that you mention it, sweets sound pretty good too. I'm curious, though, we've had this routine you and me…for over a century as a matter of fact. I sit morosely in the house and you bring food. What changed?"

"The world changed, and I need you involved in it. So, either you were going to hunt for the puppy I brought, or you were going to eat him and then we were going to have a serious problem."

I didn't ask for clarification. Tommy might be a boy in outward appearance but he was five hundred years my senior and significantly more powerful than me. 'We' had a serious problem really meant that 'I' had a serious problem. I was thankful that Purpose had been too small at the time to get an enjoyable meal out of.

We sat down on a small bench I had in my lean-to. Purpose was busy patrolling his domain and reveling in every moment of it.

"What now, Mr. T?"

"I don't know, Tommy. I guess I always thought the pain of loss would diminish. But, if anything, it's grown over the years. Maybe it's because I will never be able to honor my last words to Tracy as she died in my arms."

"We will be together again," Tommy murmured, remembering back to that snowy winter day.

Tracy had been closing in on ninety, and I loved her as much then as I did when we met. Even more so, I guess, because I knew our time was coming to an end. I always thought that 'Soul Mate' was just a term that lovelorn teenagers gave to the fleeting loves they had in between classes. But that was Tracy – to me, we were connected on so many different levels, that I think she had felt the loss of my soul just as deeply as I had, maybe even more so. To realize there was an afterlife, and that I could not spend it with her, well that was just a pain that at times became too difficult to dwell on.

"Something is different, Tommy. I can tell by the way you're lingering. Normally you can't wait to pay your respects, drop off your food, and be gone. I'm not sure if part of it is from the guilt of my condition, which, by the way, you have no culpability in, I made the choice. Or it's just my shittier-than-thou demeanor, hell; I don't even like being around myself and why Purpose stays is beyond me."

"He sees something there, Mr. T, something you had a long time ago. It's still there…you just have to dig a bit deeper."

"So what gives? Remember I grew up in Boston, I know when I'm being played. Damn, I miss the Red Sox."

"They've started playing a version of baseball. Looks more like hockey with base pads, but they're calling it baseball."

"Full-contact baseball? I love it; maybe I'll have to catch a game someday."

"What if that day were a little sooner than expected?"

"Could you please just tell me what's going on?"

"There's a new threat to man."

I didn't say anything; man had been on the edge and had come through the other side – not unscathed, but they had made it. "And what concern of that is mine?" I finally asked.

"You are still half-human, I would think that would be enough."

"It's not." I answered flatly and a bit too quickly.

"Purpose is a fine dog, and he seems to love you even with all your faults. Treated kindly and with love, he will most likely live fifteen years, maybe a few more. What then, Mr. Talbot? You going to go back and stink up your hovel?"

"You leave him out of this!" I shouted as I stood. Purpose was on the far end of the yard; he looked over at me, his head cocked to the side, wondering why I was so upset. "Do not lecture me, Tommy! I think I love that scraggly, gangly damn dog, and I will not listen to you talk about his eventual decline and death!" I was shaking in rage. "Why would you make me go through this again?" I asked as I sat heavily, my face in my hands as I hid the shame of my outburst.

"I gave you Purpose, to give you a purpose, Mr. T. You can still be a part of something even if you are apart from it."

"That's pretty philosophical."

"I've had a lot of time on my hands," he said in a placating manner.

"Please tell me zombies haven't made a resurgence. I never knew how sweet the smell of fresh air could actually be."

"Worse."

That perked my interest somewhat and I think Tommy knew it.

"Fine, I'm listening…what's worse?"

"Lycanthropes."

"What? Listen, I know I haven't seen a dictionary in years, much less read a book, but what the hell is a lycanthrope?"

"A werewolf…sort of."

"Oh, come on." I stood. Purpose, again, stopped what he was doing to look at me, the crazy part-human. "Werewolves? Really? How about a Frankenstein or two just for fun?"

"No just the werewolves or actually lycan would be the correct term."

"If that's true and not just some ruse of yours to get me out of this yard, then how bad could it be? Last movie I watched there was like one of them and they ate a person or two every full moon."

"That's myth."

"What's myth?"

"The full moon aspect," he answered. "Lycan can change at any time, they just happen to be strongest during the full moon."

"Stop dancing around it and get to the meat of it, please, I'm a busy person."

Tommy looked up at me, his eyebrows upraised as if to say 'Really?'

"I have to get dinner for Purpose and me," I told him in haste.

15

"The zombies killed some Lycan, but not nearly the same sort of percentages that man suffered. It was always man's vast numbers that kept Lycan on the periphery of existence. They didn't dare disturb the sleeping giant. They would take only what they needed to feed. Often times relying on the homeless and destitute to satisfy themselves."

"But…?" I prodded when he paused.

"But the balance has shifted. Lycan have numbers now that can truly end man's reign as king of the hill."

"This can't be serious. This seems entirely too far-fetched, even after what I've been through."

"Oh, it's true. They've gotten bolder as they've begun to realize their superior position."

"Wait…so you're saying they're not attacking yet, but they will? How could you know this?"

"Azile—" he started, but I stopped him.

"Azile, *the* Azile? Are you hearing yourself? This is the worst Grimm Brothers' fairy tale I've ever heard. They would have laughed you out of their office if you brought them this story. Okay, let's get all the pieces straight. We've got you – a vampire. And me – a half-vamp, apparently there's werewolves…and now you've just informed me about a witch that lived a century and a half ago. Oh, and Purpose the wonder dog," I added when the pooch licked my hand.

"Azile sends her regards."

"How is she still alive? And how long have you known?"

"It was her that brought me the information regarding the Lycan. That was a little over four months ago. I was nearly as surprised as you when she showed up at my doorstep."

"You have a house?" I don't know why that sounded so insane. A vampire home owner; would the milkman deliver? Did he get satellite or cable? Right now, a domesticated vamp sounded like the most normal thing this weird afternoon.

"In Florida, more of a mansion, than a house - overlooks the ocean. I find peace there."

"Florida? Plan on retiring soon?" He looked at me crossly. "How did she find you?"

"I'll be honest, Mr. T, she's as much a mystery to me as she is to you. She's obviously a very powerful witch if she can cheat death of its rightful property."

"How hard can it be? You and I do it every day."

He gave me that cross look again, until I shut up.

"She did a locator spell to find me and warn me about the Lycans. She said she had foreseen it."

"Prophecies…wonderful…those are always so much fun. Why can't she see stuff like marshmallows falling from the sky? Stop looking at me that way," I told him. "Okay werewolves, what are we, I mean you, supposed to do about it? You're only one person."

"We'd be three if you joined. Four including Purpose."

"There is no way, Tommy; I will not put Purpose in harm's way. Not another loved one, not ever."

"Lycan hate vampires, they eventually will seek you out and destroy you. One-on-one you may have the advantage, but they hunt in packs."

"It would be mercy from them if they were to end my existence."

"You cannot have forgotten."

"No, I haven't forgotten. I die without my soul; I'll never be able to retrieve it."

"Do you perhaps think your soul is going to come looking for you here?" he asked, spreading his arms wide.

"It could happen," I told him.

"Come with me, Mr. T, it will do you some good."

"I'd love to, but I'm agoraphobic."

"You're afraid of leaving this thing you call a home? There's a whole new world of man starting up. We could help see that they have a fair chance of making it. How many families are out there right now where the father is doing his best to protect his family from the monsters that go bump in the night?"

"You really do know how to hit a man below the belt. I'll go only because I need to see what this new baseball game is all about. But if this is a true quest, don't we need a fifth so we can be like the *Lord of the Rings*."

"I have a surprise for you in that department."

"I'm not big on surprises," I told him.

Last time a friend of mine had thrown a surprise birthday party for me, I had punched him square in the mouth when he had jumped up to announce himself. He had spent the majority of the night making calls to dentists to see if they could fix his tooth; I subsequently got hammered. I was twenty-one, not much phased me back then. He would call me a dick after every desperate attempt to find an emergency dentist. 'I'll toast to that' was my normal response.

"It's got nothing to do with your sister right?"

A pained expression showed briefly. "No, nothing to do with Eliza. She has paid her penance and is at peace."

"There's jail in heaven? You're kidding right?"

"We all must atone for our deeds while we live."

"Well holy fuck! That doesn't sound all that fair. I mean, those of us who live longer lives…well, we've done more, meaning we'll have more to atone for. Oh, this is bad."

"To be fair, Mr. T, you really haven't done anything this past century to be overly concerned about."

"That's a true enough statement, but I did plenty before that. Shit, shit, shit," I said as I began to pace. "Okay, so is there like a balance sheet, one bad deed gets outweighed by a good one? Maybe I could help little old women across the street while I sell them Girl Scout Cookies, that's like a two-fer."

"It doesn't really work like that."

"You a theologian?"

He shook his head.

"I'm going with my model then."

He shrugged his shoulders.

"We should get going," I told him. "I have a shitload of good things I need to get done."

It took me under a minute to pack up what I was taking, and that revolved around some rope dog toys I had made for Purpose. It was, however, another hour as I said goodbye to my family. My head throbbed from my tears as Tommy led me away. One way or the other I knew I wasn't coming back here, not ever. That thought produced such a wide and varying range of emotions; it would do me little justice trying to capture them here in my journal.

Ah, my journal, how I have missed you. Like a true friend, you have waited for me these many long years. I hadn't written much in one in a long while, but that hadn't stopped Tommy from bringing them to me every so often. Now that I come to think of it, where in the hell was he getting them? The pages were new and crisp, not yellowed, dry and crumbly like they should have been. The kid was one giant question mark. I would have to accept this as I did a long line of anomalies that swirled around him.

CHAPTER 2 - Mike Journal Entry Two

"Where to?" I asked him as he had patiently waited for me on what was left of the road that led to Ron's house – now it wasn't much more than a game trail. Growth had pressed up through the hard, compacted ground, and trees had created a canopy overhead. I dragged my hand over the rusted out hulk of something that had meant so much to me once-upon-a-time. Just for luck I put a piece of the red painted flecks that had come loose into my pocket.

Purpose bounded ahead as we walked. I feared he might become extremely dehydrated as he desired to mark everything. At one point, I had even gone up to a tree to check. "There's nothing even coming out, you crazy dog," I told him when there was not a hint of wetness where he had just lifted his leg. He came back to me, smelled again and lifted his leg. I laughed, "Any dryer, pooch, and you'll be shooting powder."

He didn't care and trotted off; tongue lolling about wildly.

We had been walking maybe twenty minutes or so, when Purpose began to bark excitedly. I ran up to see what had him in such a fuss. Two black mares were dancing around, their hooves stomping on the ground as Purpose kept running in quickly, barking, and then dashing out from the giant animals. The two horses were tethered to a small cart.

"This yours?" I asked Tommy as he approached. He nodded. "I wondered if we were walking the entire way."

"No more Jeeps," he said smiling.

"Yeah, I know," I told him as I fingered the small piece of metal in my pocket.

We were bumping our way down the road; Purpose had finally settled down in a small bundle of blankets that appeared suspiciously like a bed. It had taken him a while to get used to being around the horses. But when he realized his barking didn't scare them, he had given up.

"Pretty sure about how this was going to go?" I asked after turning from petting Purpose's head.

"I still had my doubts, but I figured I might as well be prepared."

The silence was welcome; it had become something of a friend to me over the years. I knew it well.

"I thought man would be on other planets by now," Tommy said to me. "When your kind got to the moon I figured it was only a matter of fifty more years. I would have found a way to go."

I don't know that I liked how he distinguished himself from 'my' kind, but that was overshadowed by thinking about Tommy the Star Traveler.

"I read so much science fiction, I swear I could taste some of those other worlds, I wanted to travel so badly," he told me.

"We could still get there."

"I've got a feeling that if it ever happens it will be past my time," he said in an unusual morose tone. The kid was usually the living embodiment of a cheerleader, so it was strange to see him down. "Did Azile say something?" I asked.

"What? No, but even vampires have a shelf life."

"What?"

"Oh, nothing written in stone, but after around a thousand years we kind of hit the wall. Immortality has its limits. The world around us changes so vastly in that time frame that vampires simply cannot adapt, and they seek ways to die. That was partly why Victor turned my sister and treated her so cruelly."

"Suicide by vampire...wow," I told him. "You should be alright then."

"How so?" he asked.

"Shit, man has done a complete reboot. We're almost two hundred years in arrears at this point. Maybe by the time we get our shit together you'll still be around to take that trip."

He smiled and urged the horses on.

"Not buying it?"

"It's a nice thought."

"What am I getting into, Tommy?"

"Maybe exactly what you need," he told me, and that apparently concluded all discussion for the remainder of the night.

As vamps, sleep wasn't absolutely necessary, I suppose I needed it more than Tommy did, and really only because it was such an ingrained human habit that I still even did it. I stayed up most of that night; maybe I cat-napped a couple of times, but I did it while sitting up and with the cart rocking back and forth – no easy feat.

As the sun came up, I could tell we were on what was once some major thoroughfare. "This I-95?" I asked, breaking the easy silence.

"It is. What do you think they do with all our tax dollars? They sure don't use it to fix the roads."

"Funny. Are there governments?"

"Nothing like there used to be. There are regional types of governments. Some are ruled with an iron fist, more like dictatorships. Others are almost lawless like the early Wild West."

"I always fancied myself a cowboy," I told him.

"That means you'd have to ride a horse."

"Okay, so we'll pass on that." I've never been a fan of any animal that's bigger than me. Time and frost heaves had completely ravaged the thoroughfare. Larger trees had still not completely cut through the eleven inches of roadbed. But refrigerator sized chunks of the broken material was pushed up at odd angles everywhere. The carriage was constantly cutting back and forth among the mini monoliths. It got so bad at some points that I was convinced that for every mile the horses walked we had only gone a tenth of that in roadway.

"This gets worse every year," Tommy replied.

"I guess it's a little late in the game at this point, you already told me that where we're going is a surprise, but can you at least tell me how long we are going to enjoy this hard-ass seat?"

"You could always get in the back with Purpose. He doesn't seem to mind."

"And miss all this?" I said, pointing to the trees.

"We'll be in Portland tomorrow."

"Two days for a normally two hour drive? Is that it, is that where we're going?" My heart dropped for a moment when I realized I sounded like my kids when they would ask 'Are we there yet?' Seemed so damn aggravating at the time. The stupid shit we got mad at meant nothing when you get right down to it. There's family, there's love…that's it. The rest is bullshit that we heap on ourselves. 'We' complicate our lives. We've always striven to make the world a harder place than it needed to be. Family and love.

"You alright, Mr. T?"

"Fine, sorry. I'm fine. Must be allergies or something."

"Vampires don't have allergies."

"Then can we get dust in our eyes?"

"We can," he answered.

"Then that's what happened."

"Portland is one of the places that most resembles the Wild West."

"Portland, Maine? Are you kidding me?"

"It's actually called Robert's Land now."

"Do we really need to stop there? I don't really play well with others."

"There is no way around it. Robert's Land is pretty much the last outpost in Maine, not many people live north of it. We just stay low, get a room, some supplies, and leave in the morning."

"Have you met me? I've been tossed from Chuck E. Cheese, and once I'd even had a priest try to punch me out…then, to top it off, he banned me from his church. How does that happen with a religion that preaches forgiveness?"

"Do your best, please."

"I'm not promising anything," I told him as I folded my arms across my chest. "So, about this Robert's Land, talk about an egotistical bastard."

"That's the kind of thing that's going to get us in trouble. The people of Robert's Land love him."

"The bastard is still alive?"

"Mr. T, he saved Portland when it was attacked by the Micmac."

"Indians attacked Portland, Maine? I spent way too much time in my yard. Is it alright to call them that now? Or should we go with something like Pre-Apocalyptic Indigenous Peoples?"

"I really should try to find another way," Tommy replied.

"Are there Indians around now?" I asked, spinning in my seat.

"We've been surrounded since late last night."

"What? And you decide to tell me now?"

"I've made a tentative peace with them. They let me travel through their land."

"In exchange for what?"

"I don't destroy them."

"Really?"

"They know what I am and they leave me alone. They know who you are as well."

I looked at him incredulously.

"Not much happens in the woods that they don't know about."

"Would you really hurt them?"

"If they tried to hurt me, what choice would I be given?"

"Makes sense. So they're really not going to bother us? No arrow to the back or anything?"

"They would have to get too close and I'd be able to tell. Had a brave once that was trying to make a name for himself."

I had opened my mouth. Tommy answered before I could ask.

"I took no pleasure from what I did to him, but it was a clear message of my capabilities. It will not be tried again."

I doubted that seriously, there were stupid young men born every day who thought they were invincible and had something to prove. Back in my day, you just joined the Marine Corps.

I was looking around as casually as I could, which was about as pronounced as a third grader getting ready to lift a box of crayons from his drawing partner. So, not very, if that visual wasn't clear enough. I hadn't spotted one Micmac when Tommy spoke.

"There's something else I need to tell you, Mr. T."

"When are we going to be done with the revelations, Tommy?" I asked as I sat back down, convinced that Tommy was incorrect about us being followed.

"It's about Purpose."

My beating heart skipped a beat, even the half that technically didn't have a heartbeat (yeah… I don't know how that works either, not like there was another half-vamp around that I could ask). "What about him?" I asked, not ashamed at all to let him hear the panic in my voice.

"It's nothing bad, I promise, I just thought you should know."

"It's nothing bad…you promise?"

"I swear," he told me.

"Alright out with it then."

"It's about his name."

"I get it, no need for explanation. He was the purpose I needed to get out of that house."

"That's part of it, Mr. T, but you missed something."

"What? What did I miss? Is there something more philosophical?"

"No. His name was A. Purpose."

"The 'a' is long? I'm not getting it."

"On the card there was an A and then a period."

"Yeah, I guess there was, I must have figured it was just a handwritten typo."

"No, the A is for his first name."

"Purpose has a first name?"

"Augustine."

"What? Augustine Purpose Talbot?" I asked. "Apt?" Purpose stood up barking merrily at me, I turned to pat his head. "Well, I guess he knows. Can I call you Oggie? Short for Augustine, because otherwise that's a mouthful." I asked him, his tail wagged crazily in reply.

"I told you I'd tell him," Tommy said to Purpose, or Oggie.

Purpose barked once in response to him.

"You can talk to animals? Forget it, I don't want to know."

Tommy smiled and was looking forward. "We're getting close. Do you want to start practicing your lines?"

"You should take your show on the road you're so funny. I still don't see any damn Indians." I told him as I whipped my head around as fast as I could trying to catch one of the slower ones off guard.

"They're starting to pull back."

"Is it because I've almost seen one of them?" I asked puffing my chest out.

"Not so much. We're getting closer to Robert's land."

"Nice ego bruising," I told him. We passed the burned out husk of a log cabin. "Raiding party?" I asked, not taking my eyes from it, wondering about the panic the man of the house must have had trying to defend his family from the advancing savages as they tried to kill his kin or take them into their tribe. The fear must have been overwhelming as he did all in his power to keep them safe. I thought I could just make out a swath of blood on the remnants of the door. Most likely the final resting place of John Q. Settler.

"Lightning strike."

"Well, you ruined that story."

Tommy looked over at me with a queer expression. (Hey, it's my journal, they used to use queer and gay all the time in literature from the 19th century and there was no negative connotation associated with it - I figured it was far enough in the future to bring it back, fashion always cycles around. Besides, the likelihood that anyone from the 21st century was around and going to be able to read this was very slim).

It was a mile or so when we came upon another house, although to call it more than a shack was being optimistic. There was a small plume of smoke funneling out of the hole in the chimney. A severe-looking man stopped doing whatever it was that he was doing in his field of rocks (if you had ever lived in New England you'd know what I was talking about) to stand and look at us. Even from this distance, I could see his hand tighten on whatever farming implement he was carrying. An even more severe-looking woman opened the front door (and I would imagine the only door) to watch as we passed. Now I knew why he looked so cross at least, then, from behind the wide skirt of the woman, came the biggest surprise of all, a cherub. That's the best way I could describe him.

Couldn't have been more than five years old, fat cheeks and a plume of golden ringlets encircled his head. He was smiling from ear-to-ear as he peered around his mother. He waved mightily, which I felt compelled to do back. His mother grabbed his hand and ushered him back into the house.

"He'll be important someday," Tommy told me.

"He's important now," I told him, he nodded in response. I was now affixed with a lopsided grin which Oggie felt needed a licking.

It had been a good ten minutes after we passed the house that I could see smoke on the horizon. "Robert's Land?" I asked already knowing the answer.

I was nervous. The world had moved on, life had moved past my existence, yet, here I was. Would they recognize me for the outsider that I was?

"Maybe this isn't such a good idea," I told Tommy. I was squirming in my seat.

"You'll get used to it, there's just a little adjustment period."

"As long as my 'adjustment period' doesn't get my neck on the gallows," I half laughed.

"That would be bad." Tommy answered.

"They have gallows?" I asked rubbing my neck.

The town, for that's what it was, was bustling. They had built a community on the ashes of Portland, and they seemed to be thriving. It was a strange interplay of the old and new, a hardware store owner was using the husks of old televisions to display his wares. Plastic had survived the ages and seemed to be in high demand if the prices were any consideration, but I had no idea what a 'Robert buck' was worth.

"Provincial money? Do they not trade with anyone else?" I asked as the cart moved past the store. We had attracted some attention; most kept to themselves though. In a lawless world, going unnoticed is often advantageous.

"Travel is difficult, and distrust runs deep. Many of the smaller settlements are mostly self-contained."

"Do they have beer?" I asked as our cart was approaching an establishment named Bradley's Tavern. My mouth was watering at the prospect of the golden amber liquid.

"Mead and some rot gut they call whiskey that's more likely to make you go blind."

"No beer then?" I asked longingly as we passed. Oggie was standing up and surveying the entire scene. I had to imagine seeing so many two-leggers was unsettling. He didn't bark, which I was thankful for. Unlike when we were passing through Micmac territory, I now felt that we were being watched and scrutinized.

"We don't like your kind here!" someone shouted. It was difficult to follow the voice as it echoed off some of the buildings.

"I didn't say anything," I pleaded to Tommy. "I get the feeling it would just be better if we passed on through."

"I know you're right, but I need to get things for the horses, and for us, and we'll have to wait until morning. Getting a room at the hotel is the least suspicious thing we can do."

"Camping outside the city and waiting until morning would have been the least suspicious thing," I told him.

"Didn't even think of that." Tommy answered.

"How old are you?"

"Here," Tommy said, handing over a small bag.

I opened it up. "Is this gold?" I asked looking up at him.

"Why don't you shout it? That ought to make us real popular."

"Sorry."

"How old are you?" he asked me.

"Fine…we're even. But why are you giving me this?"

"I'm sure at some point you're not going to listen to me and go try that mead. If you don't pay for it, they'll flog you."

"Flog? What is this Thailand?"

"You've got to be careful with the words you use. There is no Thailand anymore and none of these people have ever heard of it. You start talking about airplanes and satellite TV and they'll start calling you a witch."

"Boston Bruins?"

"No, Mr. T."

"What am I going to talk about? Tumbleweeds?"

"They don't have those either. I'll say it again, we should just get a couple of rooms and you should rest."

On one side, that sounded like the most sage advice I'd ever been presented with; low key meant no trouble. On the other side though, I was curious, how many opportunities did one have to see the rebuilding of civilization?

Tommy gave a stable boy some coins and he led the horses off to be housed and groomed. We walked into a house that Tommy told me, at one time, had been a funeral home and was now the only hotel in Robert's Land. It was not a thriving business as the town did not receive many guests. My guess was its primary revenue was derived when some local citizen wanted to have a roll in the hay with a woman of ill repute. Might be a new world, but men had been paying for sex since Cathy Cavewoman decided she wanted new deer-skin boots. A thick layer of dust covered the cloth that was draped over what I was sure was once the steel table that cadavers were drained of all their internal fluids.

"Ambience is everything," I mumbled as we approached.

"I don't want no trouble," was the first thing out of the concierge's mouth.

"How is this place for amenities?" I asked. "Three star, four stars perhaps?" I asked looking around.

Tommy smacked me in the shoulder. "We just want a couple of rooms for the night."

"Full up," he said as he looked down to a shelf that

I'm sure housed weaponry of some sort.

"Comic-con?" I asked.

The man looked at me with a sneer. "What's wrong with your friend?" the man asked, stooping lower so his hand was within grasping distance of whatever was down there.

"He's got the dumbs," Tommy answered.

The man relaxed somewhat – but not completely. "He don't look like he's got the dumbs."

"Trust me, he's got the dumbs. He ran off into the woods nearly six months ago and his mother paid me a handsome reward to bring him back."

"She would have been better off letting him roam."

"I agree," Tommy stated. "A mother's love..." he let trail off as if that explained everything. And I guess it did. "I'll pay for two night's stay for the night, if anything opens up."

The man did a good show of looking at the nearly full rack of keys behind him. "I think we can muster up one room. It'll cost you two nights for two rooms though. Especially on such short notice."

My blood was boiling and I was about to let loose with a litany of abusive terms that no one on this side of the apocalypse had ever heard. I would have too, had Tommy not gripped my forearm so hard I thought he was going to grind my bones into meal. Oggie could sense my distress and barked once.

"The dog will cost extra."

"Of course," Tommy said, smiling. Tommy handed over the coins and the man handed over a key.

"Out by first light or I'll call the Judge."

"Again...understood. Thank you."

The man had already stopped paying attention to us as he looked greedily at the money in his hand.

"Dick-head," I mumbled, his gaze shot up. I rolled my eyes and twirled my finger next to my temple. "Twas the dumbs!" I shouted.

***

"There's only one bed," I said to Tommy as we walked into our room. "And that thing they're calling a mattress looks like it's been steeped in seminal fluid."

"You know you're impervious to germs now, right?" Tommy asked, putting down his small saddlebag.

"Doesn't mean I like them. Who knows, maybe there's a new vampire super strain out there."

"How has so much time elapsed and you're still the same?"

"It's a talent," I told him.

"I'm going to make sure that what we need will be available. If I leave you here alone, will you be alright?" Tommy asked with concern.

"I'm not a child."

"You are to me."

"Fair enough, I'll be fine."

When Tommy left, I sat in a wooden chair in the corner somewhat secure in the knowledge that there shouldn't be too much microscopic swill swimming around on its surface. Oggie was pacing about; he kept looking at the door. I knew that look; he had to go. It wasn't usually a problem because he would just wander about until he found a decent clearing and let loose. But now, he was confined and the dog really did like to crap in peace and quiet. So much so, that if he even thought I was looking his way, he'd move behind a tree or bush.

"And so it begins," I said as I opened the door and we went down the stairs and out into the burgeoning night.

Purpose seemed a little out of sorts with no soft grass in which to take care of his business. I led him down to the tavern, mistakenly thinking there might be some grass down that way. He dropped his offering in a small alleyway. I wondered if there was a city ordinance that required me to pick that up or not. I figured I hadn't seen anything, so I would go with ignorance of the law. I opened the door to a ramshackle establishment; slightly bummed it wasn't the double swinging door from the movies.

"We don't serve them in here," the bartender said as we walked in.

"It's alright, the dog will vouch for me," I said.

"The dog, we don't allow dogs in here. What are you…stupid?"

"Apparently, but I have money."

"Let me see it first, and then I'll decide if he can stay."

I really should have gotten clarification from Tommy before I flipped the man a gold piece. When his eyes grew to twice their size I knew I had showed too many cards.

"Dog can stay then?" I asked.

He quickly dropped the coin in his pocket. "As long as he doesn't disturb my other customers."

"Yeah, wouldn't want to wake the guy up in the corner."

"What do you want?"

"My friend here will take the finest bowl of water you have and what the hell, I'll try this mead stuff," I told him.

Oggie hopped onto a chair at an old card table and I pulled a chair up next to him. He waited patiently as the man dropped him a bowl then handed me a cloudy mug of what I guess was mead. It looked like oatmeal and smelled as bad. He was heading away.

"No chance you've got a nice pilsner or lager hanging out back there do you? Shit, I'd take a stout right now," I said, lifting the mug up, trying to look through the liquid.

"I don't know where you're from and I don't care. I've never heard of those drinks so don't ask me again," he answered brusquely.

"You don't know what you're missing," I said as I ate through the top layer.

"I like the dog more than I like you," he said when he got back behind the bar.

"Most people would probably agree with you."

He went back to pretending to clean the glasses, but the rag he was using was dirtier than anything he was attempting to clean. I hoped my halfling blood was as strong as Tommy said, or that the mead had some anti-bacterial properties. Although looking at this crap, I bet mushrooms could grow in it.

Maybe it was because I'd gone a hundred and fifty years without a drink, or the mead was particularly strong, but I choked down three of them and I had a decent buzz by the time I pushed back my chair. Well, 'push back' isn't quite right, more like fell over. Hey, it was a cheap piece of plastic lawn furniture. Oggie jumped down nimbly to lick my face as I rolled to get up.

"You should go," the bartender said with a slight hint of nervousness. I saw him look through a window before he said something. My dulled senses were still able to pick up on it.

"You call someone to way lay me? Take my money perhaps?"

He nervously licked his lips.

"I'm telling you right now if you value any of the people out there you should call them off."

"Get out," he said sternly.

"When I'm done with them, I'm coming back here."

"Get out!" he shouted loud enough to wake his only other customer.

"Oggie," I said, getting down to the mutt's level, I grabbed his face. "I hope you don't think any less of me for what I'm about to do." His tail was wagging. "And whatever you do don't get involved."

I had a slight stumble as I headed for the door, even missed the knob the first time I reached for it. I had no sooner stepped onto the wooden plank-way when I heard the door lock behind me.

"That won't help you," I told him as the shades were quickly drawn. "Douchebag," I mumbled. "Bet you never heard that word before either. I'll have a few more for you when I get back." I heard the crack of a bullwhip. I, at first, had mistaken it as a firecracker it was that loud. I turned to see the origin of the sound. A large man with a whip flanked by two good-sized men approached.

"Hello, pardner," I said. "What are the chances you know someone named Durgan? I guessed I'd always hoped all the true assholes would have died with the rest, apparently this was more than I could hope for."

He paused but did not speak. Who knows maybe it was beyond his capability. I think he was a little off put that I wasn't crying for my mama. The whip cracked again, I've got to admit, it was impressive. The other two men fanned out, one had a long knife the other a rake.

"You're kidding right?" I asked. "You brought a rake to a mugging."

"Oh, this ain't no mugging, *pardner*," the man with the whip snarled. "This is a good old-fashioned murder."

"Well, I don't know what jury is going to consider this a murder, it's merely self-defense on my part," I told him.

"What's he talking about Clyde?" the one with the knife asked.

"Shut up and gut him," Clyde told the knife wielder.

"There's no harm yet. I suggest you go back home to your butchering duties," I told the man as he approached. He hesitated, and then kept coming. "Fine, have it your way." I sat down on the small boardwalk, my legs out in front of me on the hard dirt-packed roadway. I patted Oggie's massive head as he sat next to me.

"What are you doing?" the man asked.

"What's your name?" I asked as he halved the distance.

"Lionel."

"What are you two doing? Get a room!" Clyde shouted.

"Lionel, got a wife? Kids maybe?" His head bobbed as I asked the question. "I will kill you if you come closer. Do you believe me?" I asked, looking over at him menacingly.

"I do," he gulped.

"Here's a gold coin." I flipped him one out of the bag. His eyes grew bigger than the barkeeps. "I would imagine that will keep you and your family in whatever passes for food in this time for a long while. Now get the fuck out of here." He looked over once at Clyde and bolted.

"I knew you were yellow!" Clyde shouted to his back.

"All these years and they still use that crappy insult. Funny."

"You going to try and buy my balls too, funny man?" Clyde asked.

"I don't have a small enough coin for that," I told him. "Odds are you're too stupid and greedy to take what I'd offered anyway."

"Why settle when I can have it all."

"Screw this," Rake man said, tossing his rake to the side and following Lionel into the night. The rake must have been worth something to him though because he skulked back quietly and retrieved it before once again heading to parts unknown.

"Not like I needed them anyway, and now I don't have to share," Clyde said as he approached, the whip snapping not more than an inch from the toe of my boot. "Hand over the bag, or the next one takes out your eye, and then I'm going to cut up your dog and eat him for Moon-day dinner."

"Oh, Clyde, why are there always men like you? Why can't we evolve past this? Well, you know what? I'm going to do my part to end your lineage. There will always be assholes, you're proof in the pudding, but you'll never be one again. You crossed the line bringing my dog into this."

His whip was already in motion as I got up. I noted it would have struck my head had I not. I snagged the leather before it had a chance to crack; I was at his side in an instant.

"How'd you do that?" he asked, his mind trying to race and catch up to the events.

"You see, Clyde, if you're going to pick a fight…you really should make sure your opponent isn't a bigger asshole than you are." I gripped his throat in my hand. He fell to his knees as I forced his airway closed, blood began to spill around my fingers as they dug in.

"You there!" an authoritative voice rang out. "Stop what you're doing, I'm Judge Rory."

"Impeccable timing, Judge," I sneered. "Did you wait until the tables were turned before you made yourself known? Maybe you even had a stake in good Clyde's venture here?"

"Unhand him now and you won't swing," he said.

"I walk away or he dies."

"This is an assault, you're going to jail."

"Three men sent by your purveyor of shitty beverages meant to strip me of my money and my life. I am merely teaching the one stupid enough to stay, a lesson," I said Clyde was clawing at my hand trying to find a way to get air into his lungs.

"I know Clyde's an ass. He's married to my sister, but family is family."

"You of all people should know then. Hell, I'm doing you a favor."

"Perhaps, but I can't have a stranger come into my town and cause trouble."

"I walk, Judge, or he dies and then I walk, the choice is yours," I said, gripping even tighter. Blood was beginning to drop to the ground. Oggie growled as the Judge reached for something is his pocket.

He showed Oggie the handkerchief as he wiped his brow. He took a little longer than was necessary to answer. My guess is he knew Clyde had it coming and maybe this was a lesson he wouldn't soon forget.

"You leaving tomorrow?" he asked.

"I am," I told him.

"Coming back?"

"Highly unlikely," I answered truthfully.

"We have a deal then, let him go and you can leave."

I loosened my grip and pushed Clyde backwards into the dirt. I leaned down close. "You ever threaten my dog again; I will rip the throats from everyone and everything you love. Then I'll let Oggie finish off what I started. *Capisce*?"

Pretty sure he didn't know what *understand* meant in Italian, but he understood the context of the words. He was sucking wet breaths through his tortured windpipe. His face turned back from its angry purple into a more savory beet red.

I tipped my head to the Judge and walked off.

"Get your ass up," I heard the Judge say to Clyde. From the sound of it, he may have even kicked him in the ass.

"How long you been watching?" I asked Tommy as I walked down the street.

"Long enough to realize I can't leave you alone," he told me as he fell into step.

"Find what you were looking for?" I asked.

He nodded.

We walked to the hotel. "Mead sucks," I told him as I opened the door.

As Oggie and Tommy got on the bed I opted for the uncomfortable chair. Didn't matter much, I didn't sleep.

The sun had no sooner spilled into the window than we were on the move.

"Thanks for your hospitality," I told the man that had checked us in. I flipped him the finger, he semi-waved back with a look of confusion on his face.

Tommy smiled and softly told me that the gesture hadn't made the leap into the future.

"You're kidding?" I asked astonished.

He shook his head.

"The most universal, beloved way to tell someone to go fuck themselves and no one in this time knows it?" I turned and flipped the man with both middle fingers. He again waved then mimicked my gesture, still shaking his head in confusion. "I might like it here after all," I told Tommy as I clapped his back.

We picked up a fair amount of supplies from the general store-slash-hardware-slash-feed store. I looked up at a wicked looking hand axe; it was polished to a high sheen.

"The steel is from the Ago Age," The owner said, bringing it down to show me. It took a moment to realize that the 'Ago Age' was my age. "The wood was all rotten, so I made that handle myself, put some carvings in it to make it special. I ran my finger along the wolf's head he had engraved.

"How much?" I asked him.

"Pardon, sir, I hadn't meant to sell it. I just wanted to use it as a display piece."

"Seems a shame to have such a wonderful piece, rust and dull without ever being used," I said as I reached for my bag.

"Even so, finding things in this good of condition is becoming exceedingly rare."

I couldn't tell if he was trying to drive up the price or convince me he wasn't selling. "What's it worth?" I asked as I held open my free hand with three gleaming gold coins shining back at him.

"In honesty, my friend, not even one of those," he said, never picking one up.

"I'll give you all three."

He stepped back. "Do you mean to rob and kill me?"

"I'm trying to make a deal."

"Sir, you could almost buy everything in here for that price."

"Listen, odds are I won't live long enough to use all my money. Put it to good use; buy your wife that dress she's been looking at."

"How did you know?"

"Women are women. Deal?" I asked placing the coins on the countertop.

"It's a deal only if you decide that tomorrow when you realize you overspent, that you just merely need to ask for the money back and I will do so."

"I'm a lot of things, some good some bad, but if we strike this deal be secure in the knowledge I will be exceedingly happy and will never come back for the coins." He seemed to feel better when we shook hands. "Incredible craftsmanship," I said as I peered at the carvings heading out the door.

"What took you so long?" Tommy asked from his perch on the cart.

"New toy," I told him as I climbed aboard and handed it to him.

"Wolf," he said, looking at the carving.

"Seemed appropriate don't you think?"

He snapped the reins and the horses started forward. The Judge tipped his hat as we sauntered by. I thought about giving him the finger, too; not because of the man, but rather the badge. What can I say? I have a real issue with authority. But, even though he might not know what the finger meant he would understand the intent. Something about cops, they just knew. Maybe because they always expected the worst out of people; I, instead, nodded slightly at him.

"Here, I got you this," Tommy said, reaching into a bag next to him.

"A black cowboy hat? How friggin' sweet! Did it come with a gun by any chance?" I asked as I donned it. I crooked it to the side. "Do I look like a gangster?"

"You look like a drunkard."

I straightened it out. "Thank you for this," I told him.

"I figured you'd like it."

Oggie was snoring contentedly as we rode out of Robert's Land. All in all, I think it went excessively well. I didn't die, I didn't kill anyone, and I wasn't in jail. Might damn near be a record for me.

"Want to drive?" Tommy asked.

"I don't have my license."

"Just keep it under eight miles per hour and we'll be fine."

"What's the matter?" I asked him.

"I think your friend is following us."

"Once an idiot, always an idiot."

"We'll wait for tonight when he intends to strike. We'll be far enough from the town and then we can drink."

"You mean you. Right?"

"*We* need to," he stressed. "We can live off animals just fine, but you'll be stronger taking human blood."

"I...I don't think I can, Tommy. First off, the idea of placing my lips and teeth on any part of that vermin gives me the chills."

"I wouldn't tell you to do it if it wasn't important. The Lycan are strong and fast, we need to be stronger and faster."

"I'd rather eat ham," I told him, referring to my legendary dislike for the cured meat.

"You haven't gotten over that?" he asked, turning towards me. I shrugged.

"Tommy, why don't we just keep going? He won't be able to keep up when we don't stop for the night."

"You said it yourself last night; we'd be doing the world a favor."

"Yeah, but that was a hot-blooded response, this is so cold and calculated."

"Would it help if I told you that, if he stays alive, he will cause great harm to that small boy we saw coming into town?"

"It would. Would it be true?" I asked.

He didn't respond to the question. "We'll stop here for the night," he said as we pulled into a small clearing. A circle of oaks had been hewn, and a thick plush carpet of moss had taken up residency. Lord knew it was going to be more comfortable than the night's previous chair and cleaner than the mattress.

"I wonder what purpose this was done for?" I asked as I walked around the perimeter.

Tommy was not his jovial self as he, once again, ignored or declined to answer my query.

"I'll take first watch. Clyde is not smart enough to be patient and wait until we're deep asleep. He'll attack as soon as it's dark enough."

I saw hints and bits of Eliza, his evil sister, in Tommy as he spoke of eating this man. Although that wasn't completely fair, Eliza would have said it with a smile, Tommy was all clinical.

"Wow, he's not even that smart," I told Tommy as I saw Clyde running from tree to tree closing in. A cat wearing a cowbell would be less conspicuous. "Tommy, this is worse than taking candy from a baby, at least the baby has a mother to protect it.

"It must be done," Tommy said, leaving our small encampment. I heard a slight commotion about fifty yards off and then Tommy was back, a struggling Clyde in his iron clutches.

"What are you two?" he begged.

"Unfortunately, the last thing you'll ever see," I told him.

Tommy tilted the man's head to the side and began to drink quickly. The man's eyes began to close as if he were in a trance. "Get in here," Tommy said, pulling his fangs from the man. A droplet of blood formed in each hole, then they quickly coagulated.

"I can't, Tommy."

"Suit yourself," he said as he drank his fill. I won't lie, my pulse quickened as I watched him eat. A large part of me wanted to join in the festivities. Granted, the part of me that wanted to feed was in the minority, but it was still a significant portion.

Tommy threw the man over his shoulder and headed over to the cart. I was curious to see what he was doing and I followed. He grabbed a shovel, found an area that wouldn't be too root tangled and dug a hole. It wasn't any shallow grave either, it was a good six feet down. He tenderly laid the body down, filled in the gravesite and even mumbled a small prayer. I'd never seen a lion pray after eating a gazelle. I'll admit I was pretty confused.

"What...what was that all about?" I asked him later as we sat around our small campfire.

"I prayed for his quick return to where his soul was forged and asked forgiveness for those transgressions he had committed during life."

"Do you have that kind of pull...up there?" I asked, wondering if he could do the same for me.

"Doubtful, but it can't hurt to try." And with that statement, we were done.

Oggie had been patrolling the woods and came back with a fat rabbit, he dropped it next to me, I drained it dry and then put it on a small spit. When it was done to his liking I stripped the meager meat from it and let him eat. He rested his head in my lap as I sat there through the night.

I had a hard time getting the image of Tommy killing Clyde out of my mind, and it was with that thought we started our next day. The day was dark and dreary; it looked like a storm was brewing both inside and out.

I don't know how long we were traveling, the rhythmic rocking of the cart had me slightly in a trance, and the day was too dark to follow the progression of the sun. I was yanked from my mind when I saw the black-cloaked figure of a person sitting astride an extremely large black horse up ahead. My heart skipped as I tried to peer through the gloom.

"Eliza?" I asked with a start. I began to arise. She was back! The desire to turn around and haul ass was prevalent.

"Hello, Azile!" Tommy shouted, waving towards her.

She pulled her cloak back; even as I was seeing the woman's face I had a hard time reconciling it. My mind had superimposed Eliza's beautifully stark features atop Azile's softer ones. Not to say that Azile wasn't beautiful, just in a different way from Eliza. Our cart had just pulled up to her, and I was still trying to regain control of my emotions. When I got close, I realized the black of her cloak was actually a deep red made even darker by the muted light of the day.

"Hello, Tomas," Azile said warmly. "Michael." She nodded, smiling at me.

"Hello, Azile," I said.

"I had my doubts whether you'd come or not. Tomas was relatively sure, I wasn't convinced. I'd visited you a few times over the years; you grew more despondent each season."

"I never knew," I told her.

"Purpose!" she said happily as she alit from her horse. The dog that had grown to near pony proportions charged her, tongue lolling, tail wagging. He jumped into her arms. She caught him and twirled him around as if he were still a pup.

"Everybody know my dog before me?" I asked, slightly jealous.

Azile kissed Oggie's muzzle and gently placed him back on the ground. He nudged up against her leg.

"You didn't know because I didn't want you to, Michael." Azile said, referring back to my prior statement. "It was difficult for me to see you so morose."

"Just imagine my discomfort," I told her. "You should have said hello."

"Would it have helped?" she asked, coming towards me.

"No." I let my head drop a little. She placed her hand tenderly on my cheek, much like someone I had loved over a millennia ago used to.

I shied away from the intimate contact.

"I'm sorry," she said, quickly retracting her hand. "It's just so good to see you." She turned towards Tommy. "Did you get everything?"

"It's been difficult…but yes." He removed a blanket from the back of the cart, a gleaming pile of metal shone back.

"Holy shit, is that silver?" I asked, going over towards him. There were trinkets, coins, serving plates, and even some swords. When Tommy nodded, I asked. "This really works on werewolves?"

"It won't kill them outright," Azile said, "but it inflicts more damage than normal steel or lead. Every town we go to I will instruct them to glaze all the tips of their weapons with it."

"We could all retire comfortably with this much treasure," I said, looking at the large box nearly overflowing with the booty.

"I wish that could be the case, but the fates have determined another path for us," Azile said with a faraway stare.

"Who, exactly, are the fates, because I've got a couple of choice words for them."

"Ah, there is more of the Michael I knew," Azile said, smiling at me.

"What makes you think these towns are going to do anything but keep the silver you give them?" I asked.

"You'll have to watch them cover their weapons." She smiled back.

"Wonderful, what now? Do we just find some werewolves and start hacking away?" I asked.

"First, I believe we should find some shelter. Rain and wind may not affect either of you too much, but I can't stand it, and holding it off is beginning to wear on my reserves."

"You have power over weather?" I asked in awe.

"There is a reason your brother's house has not yet crumbled in on itself from crushing snow."

"I just thought I'd been lucky…or unlucky really."

She snorted slightly. "Come. There is an old house up ahead that I used last night. It should be suitable for this evening as well."

The 'old house' was in fairly good condition considering its age. It was a log cabin style kit home; from the outside it appeared to be roughhewn from large logs inside it looked more like a ski chalet.

"Had I known how long I was going to exile myself, I would have chosen a place like this," I said as I looked at the grand staircase. Candles were blazing in nearly every corner making the house much brighter than outside. "Not very safe leaving these on while you were out."

"They were being tended," Azile said.

"Our fifth traveling companion?" I asked Tommy.

I nearly fell over Oggie trying to get out of the house when a scaled animal came strolling out from a side hallway. It walked on four legs, after that, any familiarity to any living animal was gone. It was red and covered in the aforementioned scales. Its head, which was triangular shaped, had small horned protrusions arising from it. Large reptilian eyes blinked at me, its leathery wings seated high on its back flapped once or twice.

"What the fuck is that?" I asked Tommy, using his shoulder to prop myself up.

"Sebastian, what are you doing?" Azile said, approaching what I could only call a mini dragon.

"It's her familiar," Tommy said, dropping his pack onto the ground and striding into the house as if that explained everything.

The thing flickered once, the scales seemed to melt away, replaced with fur. The wings folded and retreated into themselves, and the angular head took on a roundish shape, whiskers poked out.

"A cat? It's a fucking cat? I would have rather had the dragon," I said.

Sebastian hissed at me. "Oh look at you, Mike, making new friends wherever you go," Azile said, spreading her arms to catch the cat as it leaped onto her. You're going to hurt his feelings."

I wanted to tell her I really didn't care about his feelings; his distant relatives had taken the life of my best friend and nearly my own as I had tried to destroy them. We would always be on shaky ground.

"What's with the dragon thing?" I asked, pointing at the Gatekeeper to the Underworld.

"He likes to pretend. Sometimes he's a dragon, sometimes a lion, and whatever else he feels like turning into," she said, stroking his fur. He was purring contentedly whilst also mean-mugging me. If the cat could have somehow stayed in contact with her petting and slashed a claw across my face, I'm pretty convinced he would have.

"Wonderful…a shape-shifting cat. Any chance he could turn into a cheeseburger?" I asked, giving him the same stare back. He didn't seem like he gave a shit. Go figure.

"I think it is time you made peace with cats," Azile said as she absently stroked the cat's back.

"Let's give it a few more centuries and see what that brings us," I told her. "Speaking of which, how is it that you're still with us?" I asked, not realizing how callous my question was until I saw her expression change. "No, no I didn't mean it that way," I backpedaled.

"Same Mike…same womanly charm." Tommy laughed, heading upstairs. Azile shared in his merriment.

"You guys use this place often?" I asked of his familiarity.

"It's one of many way-stations we have across the land," Azile said.

"And with Azile's concealment spells, most stay hidden from prying eyes," Tommy said as he reached the top of the stairway and headed right.

"Most?" I asked.

"There are others with power that can see beyond it, including some of the Lycan."

"Wonderful," I answered her. "Is that going to be a problem here?"

"No, not yet anyway."

"Please don't get me wrong, Azile, I'm more than thrilled to see someone from the past, but how? And you still look so young."

"Would you rather I look like this?" she asked sweeping her hand across her face. She instantly transformed into an old woman. A large hooked nose peeked out from the deep folds of skin that created crevices in her face. A wart the size of a rat's nose was nearly lost in a forest of thick coarse facial hair.

I took in a sharp intake of air.

"Relax." She smiled, her more customary face coming through.

"Which one's real?"

"Touch me." She leaned in towards me.

I tentatively reached out with my hand and touched her face. It was as soft and smooth as any young woman's face should be. I pulled back quickly. "I'm sorry," I told her.

"For what?" She asked smiling, I think she knew why.

"You're nearly half my age."

"Michael Talbot, I am a hundred and seventy-three

years old, there are not many beings that can claim I am half their age."

"You know what I meant," I said with embarrassment.

"How about this?" she asked once again running her hand past her face.

I staggered. "T-Tracy?" I cried. "I-I've almost forgotten what you looked like." I was sobbing now. "Please, no more." I put my arm up and out to block her from view.

"I'm so sorry, Mike. I just thought you might be more comfortable if I looked like her."

Her words were lost as I stumbled out of the house. Fat tears fell from my eyes as my steps faltered. I don't know how far I traveled, but when I looked up I could no longer see the house. I don't know if that was because of Azile's spell or if I had just wandered that far away. I could hear Oggie barking in the distance. Right now I wasn't sure if I even wanted his company.

"Maybe I should just keep going," I said aloud. I caught a glimmer of something bounding through the woods. Oggie had sniffed me out and was even now coming at a full tilt. I could outdistance him and be away from all of them. I stood my ground as he leaped, placing his paws on my chest. He drove me to the ground and licked the salt from my tears.

"Yeah, that was a stupid idea," I told him as I wrestled his head.

Azile was standing at a tree not more than five feet away. She must have been at the head of her craft class. "I'm sorry, Michael. I won't do that again."

I nodded. Oggie grabbed my arm and helped me to my feet.

We walked back to the house. At first it was an uneasy silence and then it became a comfortable quiet. Sounds roughly the same, but what can I say, it's how I felt. Oggie would wander off and come back. He sounded like a bear in some of the thicker underbrush.

"Was Purpose, your idea?" I asked her when we got to the door.

"Tommy's. We had discussed how we could get you to this point. He came up with a dog. I had a different idea."

"What was it?" I asked curiously.

"It's a pity you're as handsome as you are and not the brains to match. Good night, Michael Talbot." She lightly touched my face and went into the house, disappearing down the hallway from which the dragon cat had originally emerged from.

I waited for Oggie to come bounding into the house, I shut the door behind him; it finally dawned on me what in the hell Azile was talking about. "Oh," I said, and then I may have blushed, tough to tell without actually looking in a mirror.

I went upstairs and found a room that seemed to be to my liking. Oggie hopped up on the bed, his tail wagging. I shut the door and joined him. Thoughts of my beloved dominated my night. I hung onto that momentary image Azile had given me. I focused on every detail, trying my best to burn it into the folds of my mind. I'm not ashamed to admit, a good deal of that time was spent with a pillow over my mouth muffling my sobs. I bet at some point during the night my face was probably puffed out enough to look like I had been on the losing end of a prizefight. If that was the case I was going to imagine it was at the fists of Iron Mike Tyson when he was in his prime. If you're going to get your ass handed to you, might as well be from the best.

How pissed off could Chuck Norris really be having lost to possibly the greatest fighter of all time, Bruce Lee? Gotta love me some random thoughts. By the time I got up, Oggie was no longer in the room. I wasn't sure when that had happened since I didn't really remember falling asleep, and last time I checked, he couldn't open doors. Tommy and Azile were sitting at a small table, Azile stood as I approached.

"You get stung by a bee?" she asked as she touched my apparently still puffed up face.

"Allergies," I told her.

Tommy looked over at me.

"Fine, sand in my eye," I told him. I couldn't pull out the standard 'I sat on my keys' without a car.

"Where's Oggie?" I asked.

"He's rounding himself up some breakfast, I would imagine," Azile said. "Speaking of which…Tommy tells me you did not feed."

"I ate," I told her defiantly.

"Not properly," she chastised me. "Make no mistake, Michael, we will soon be at a war we may not win. You are not preparing for this correctly."

"By not eating people? How would that possibly be helping the human race by eating them?"

"It is the sacrifice of the one for the lives of the many," she replied.

"I've always hated that argument, Azile. That *one* you speak so casually of is special to someone. How do I go back and tell that person's mother or wife or children that they gave their lives up in a noble cause?"

"And what of those men you killed in the zombie war, did they not have a special someone somewhere?" she retorted.

"That was different. It was a war." I didn't know if I was winning the argument or burying myself, but considering I was talking to a woman, odds were I was on the short end; you know, the part that's been swirling around in the shit.

"Michael, these people would willingly give themselves to you if they knew the devastation that was going to be wrought on everything and everybody they love. The Lycan are not human and never were. They do not have human emotions, they kill without impunity or value. They will lay waste to a village merely because they can."

"They weren't human? They weren't infected like

zombies or vampires?" I don't know why that was so important to me, but it was.

"Never. The only reason man has become the dominant species on the planet is his relatively quick reproductive cycle. Lycan mate once every five years."

"No wonder they're so pissed off," I said.

Tommy snorted.

"So they have marriage, too?" I asked.

"Michael, this is serious!" Azile fairly demanded.

"Sorry, every five years, that's a long time to keep the pipes backed up," I told her.

"How is it that you're our best chance at victory?" She asked.

"Hey, you said that, not me," I told her. "If I had it my way, me and the Ogster would have stayed up in Maine." He came over and licked my hand when I mentioned his name. I noticed that he had to bow his head to do so. The dog was growing in leaps and bounds.

"Michael, they will destroy all of mankind, eating and enslaving as they go. The Lycan clans are uniting under one leader, and when they decide how they will divide the world up, it will be too late."

"Azile, maybe it's their time. Since the beginning of time some species rule for a while and then yield to another after some cataclysmic event. Humans had a decent run, considering we got too smart for our own good. Too many brains, not enough morality. I don't see the Lycan being any better or any worse."

"Would you have said those same words if *your* family were alive, Michael? Would you not fight for all you and they were worth?"

I wanted to rant at her that she wasn't being fair.

"Don't other men with families deserve the right to raise and protect their families as best they can, men like you?" she continued.

"To be fair," Tommy interjected, "there really aren't

too many men like Mike."

"Thanks…I think," I told him.

"No problem." He smiled at me; I noticed some red jelly gooped around his gums. I didn't ask.

"Would you like to see what you're up against?" she asked.

"Not really," I told her, being honest.

"Tommy, let's gather our things and get ready to travel," she said curtly to him.

"What about me?" I asked.

"What about you?" she asked, turning back around. "You made yourself clear in your intentions."

Had I? I thought. I guess I did; sometimes being argumentative can cause problems. "I promised the Judge in Robert's Land I wouldn't go back through town."

"You've already broken one promise…what's another?" she asked.

"What promise did I break?" I asked Tommy quietly.

"Your bond with mankind," he answered sincerely.

"Did you learn the guilt trip shit from Tracy? Because she was a master of it. Or is it just an inherent thing in the female species?"

"Do not hold me responsible for pointing out your conscience," she told me.

"Dammit all. Fine, Oggie and I will go a little farther with you…but no promises."

"As you will," Azile said as she went back to the house.

"I think she's smitten with you," Tommy said, backhanding my shoulder.

"Smitten? Are you kidding me? Just because it looks like the 1800s doesn't mean we need to talk like it," I told him, as he smiled at me, I heard something rustle in his pocket that sounded suspiciously like a foil packet; again I didn't ask.

I walked next to the wagon. Truth be told, my ass was

53

hurting from the lack of cushioning and shocks. Oggie had no such compunction; he was sitting next to Tommy on the wooden plank bench. Tongue hanging out, he looked as happy as a witch in an apothecary store. I wanted to keep the analogy relative.

"Comfortable up there, you lug?" I stroked his paw. He looked over, a long string of drool dropped on my arm. "Nice," I told him. His tail thumped.

It was a long day, sometimes I got up on the cart, but for the most part I walked, it was nice to stretch my legs and enjoy the day. Dusk was beginning when Azile had us stop. I figured we had another half hour of light. We could have kept going, and I didn't see a particularly good spot to set up shop, but it looked like she was the boss of this little expedition so we stopped.

"You ready?" She asked, as she got down off her horse. She produced a lantern from the back of Tommy's cart and with a one-word incantation we had light.

"Cavemen would have loved you," I told her as we followed her into the woods on the right side of the path.

The sun had just about set when we finally got to where we were going.

"Help me," I heard a weak voice utter.

"Who was that?" I asked looking around.

Azile strode a couple of paces further to a large iron cage, made with columns and cross sections as thick as a man's leg.

"What the fuck you got in there, elephants?" I asked as I approached.

"Please help me, sir," an ancient man asked. He was huddled in the far corner of the cage, shying away from Azile's lantern.

"How did you know he was here?" I asked her.

"I put him there," she replied calmly.

"He's almost as old as I am, Azile. What the hell are you doing?" Then it dawned on me. "Oh…I get it. Old guy, probably has no family no one will miss him. I told you I AM NOT going to sustain from humans!" I was bellowing.

"Oh, he has plenty of family. When he grew too weak to keep up with them, they abandoned him. I found him."

"And then stuck him in a cage? What happened to the Azile I knew?" I asked.

She went to the large lock. "If you can kill him," she said, talking to the old man and then pointing at me, "I will set you free to roam the wilds as you please."

"You speak the words of the Moon, Spirit Woman?" he asked her.

"I do." She nodded.

What happened next is almost beyond description. As she removed the lock, the man began to transform. I don't know if it was a trick of the light, but he seemed to double in size. Silver hair sprouted from every part of him. His mouth elongated, as did his arms, legs, hands, and more importantly, claws. A snarl pulled his lips back to reveal fangs a Saber-toothed tiger would have been proud to display. He stood on two legs but that was now the only thing he had in common with man. Tommy moved away, he grabbed Oggie who was barking wildly. The old man-slash-wolf-thing lunged at me, a backhand from its right hand/paw sent me sprawling, and I found myself sliding on a bed of wet leaves, moss, and broken branches.

"What the fuck?" I asked, trying to shake the cobwebs from my head. The thing was already in the air. I turned to my right and his claw cut a swath in the forest floor. The same leaves I had taken a joy ride on most likely saved my life as the beast slid away from me, giving me time to regroup.

It wasn't long – not by any stretch of the imagination – but at least I was able to get up on my own two feet. I was aware of the penetrating stare Azile was giving me and the look of hope and sadness on Tommy's face; he was fighting savagely trying to keep Oggie out of this fray, I sincerely hoped he succeeded.

I ducked as a massive paw swiped above my head, pain flared from my crown as at least one claw had found purchase, blood began to flow freely from the wound. As it encircled my face. I must have looked savage as I flashed my canines. The Yeti before me didn't give a shit as he plunged in trying to get his snout wrapped around my neck, which wouldn't have so much been a bite as it would have been a beheading. My arms corded as I tried to keep him at bay. His mouth was opening and snapping shut with a loud cracking sound. Drool puddled on my chest as I fought desperately and seemingly on the losing end to keep him away. I felt his hot nose press up against my carotid artery.

"Azile?" Tommy begged.

She did not reply. Her eyes burned fiercely at me, this I could tell as I craned my head trying to pull away. His arms had wrapped around me in a cruel embrace, the power that he used could have crushed a Yugo. Although, to be fair, they're mostly made of tin cans. I was going to lose, of that I was sure; the animal was easily twice my strength and it had a primeval nature I could not match. When the beast/man-animal realized its initial attempts to tear my neck open were being thwarted, he picked me up and savagely threw me to the ground. Everything in me rattled. I was convinced he had realigned my internal organs.

"Azile, this has gone on far enough," Tommy said, taking a step forward.

"Do not break your Moon word," the animal snarled.

Of all the effed up things going on right now, hearing Bigfoot talk was one of the weirdest.

"No, Tommy, this is the destiny Michael has chosen for himself. He wants to die, how many times does he need to tell you that before you believe it? Pity he won't see his family again," she said as she walked away and back towards the roadway.

The animal picked me up by the neck as I weakly

tried to keep this from happening. He redoubled his efforts when he realized his pardon was not going to be recanted. *Use his size to your advantage*, entered into my mind. I'd like to think I thought of it, but I was in too much of a panic. Wanting to die and actually having it thrust into your face are two vastly different things. How was I going to use his size to my advantage? That was like saying use the speed of the bullet heading in your direction to your favor. How does one go about that?

"Tommy, come!" Azile beckoned.

Oggie was howling as Tommy dragged him away. It was that mournful cry more than anything that spurned me on. I was thankful the monster hadn't lifted me off the ground as I hooked my right leg behind his. I was able to push his muzzle far enough away to swing my shoulders and get some thrust as I tripped him up over my leg. We went down, with me landing on his chest. He momentarily 'oomphed' as my weight knocked the wind out of him. My blood was dripping on his face as I wrapped my hands around his neck. I tried to press my hands into his flesh, but it was like trying to puncture wood. He was yelling as I dug in deeper, small welts of blood began to well up around my fingers. This wasn't going to work; he was kicking around and would eventually be able to turn his head enough to chomp right through my forearm.

His left hand shot out and rocked me hard. I began to see stars – and not of the celestial type. My moments on this plane were numbered. I released his neck with both of my hands and pushed up on the bottom of his chin, and with all the speed my condition afforded, I leaned down and ripped out his vulnerable Adam's apple. Even as the animal gurgled and drowned in its own blood, it flung me a good ten feet in the air. I landed hard on my side, breaking a rib against a small rock outcropping.

He stood much faster than I was able to. His right paw went to his neck and then he pulled the claw up to his face to see the thick coating of blood. He raised his mouth and tried to howl, what came out was more of a wet wailing. He fell to his knees as blood began to pool in front of him. He never stopped glaring at me as the collection of liquid grew in size. His gaze never wavering until he fell, face forward, I knew he was dead. Pretty sure Lycans didn't know the word 'quit.' I stayed long after his heart ceased beating his life-fluid onto the soil. Long after the blood soaked into the ground, long after the moon made its journey across the sky, I stood over its body, vaguely wondering if it would revert to the form of the old man. It never did.

The sun was, once again, making its dispassionate race across the sky when I heard the approach of feet or rather paws. Oggie had finally been released and had come to find me. He alternated between whining and growling as he approached. I was still, my back to him. My rib had mostly healed, but I was still in a great deal of pain from the beating I had taken.

"It's alright, Oggie," I managed to get out as I turned. The pain of just that maneuver was almost a little more than I could bear. Oggie came over and sniffed at the dead Lycan, whined once, and then nuzzled his head into my leg where I gladly pet it in spite of the pain it caused me to move.

"What do you want to do, boy?" I asked, getting down on one knee so I could be face-to-face with him. Oggie placed his head on my shoulder and growled softly. "You want to fight? I'm not convinced, pup. I couldn't imagine anything happening to you," I told him.

He pulled back and licked at the blood, in hopes to clean me up, much like a mother will do to a child before they meet company. "Can you help me back up?" I asked him. He stood still as I placed my hand on his shoulder and stood with a grunt. I felt more like the old man in the cage than myself.

And now, how did I deal with the betrayal – because that's what it felt like. Azile had quite literally left me to the wolves and without so much as a warning. I was beyond pissed off, ancient witch or not, I was going to give her a piece of my mind. I would have stomped through the woods but anything more than soft steps hurt. When I came back out onto the path, they were gone. They must have left during the night. Oggie had been tied to a tree with a rope thick enough to tow a truck. It must have taken him this long to chew through it as I picked up the frayed end. My bag of money plus my axe was sitting by the base of the tree. The latter would have been nice to have last night, didn't think I was going to need it surrounded by friends. Lesson learned.

"That's just wonderful," I said as I looked at the path.

Fifty percent of me wanted to go home – if that's what I could even call it. Another fifty percent of me wanted to know what was on the other side of this quest. Then just the minutest part, probably the weight of a fly shit tipped the scales, I wanted to confront Azile with what she had done. With that happy thought, I slowly followed Tommy's wagon wheels westward.

CHAPTER 3 - Mike Journal Entry Three

As the day progressed, I felt better and worse. Better because my numerous injuries were healing and worse because of the toll it was taking on me. I needed to feed and I needed to do it quickly. Oggie picked up on my distress as my steps began to falter and I was zigging and zagging more than I was making forward progress. He went into the woods to find us some food.

I finally found a log with my name on it and sat down hard, nearly missing it completely. I would have lain wherever I had landed. My head was hanging low, my elbows on my knees. It was from this angle I could tell that my clothes had taken a serious beating, a good seamstress with a bolt of cloth wouldn't be able to put them back together.

"Least of your problems, buddy," I said aloud.

"You can say that again," a man said as he approached. He was smiling, his top two teeth had vacated his head years ago, and by the looks of his brown-stained smile, they were the smart ones.

"What can I do you for, friend?" I asked trying to keep my head upturned.

"You can give me everything you've got for starters." He pointed his half-sword at me. Half-sword because the other half had broken off at some point. The jagged, broken edge still looked mean enough to do some damage, though. The eighteen inches of blade which probably couldn't cut butter could still be used as an effective bludgeoning tool.

"Look at me. How much do you think I have?" I asked.

"Well, less now that I've come around I guess."

"Man, I thought my time sucked. This new world is no fucking bargain." I stood slowly gripping a nearby tree for support.

"You don't really look like you're up for a fight," the man said, placing his piece of steel between him and me.

"Maybe not me, but my friend there may have a thing or two to say." Oggie came out of the woods on the other side of the man, he dropped the rabbit he had been carrying, a low, deep grumble formed in his chest and issued forth from his menacing mouth. "Oggie, meet Waylayer. Waylayer, meet Oggie."

"The lady said I could take what I want from you, said you wouldn't be any trouble at all." The man nervously licked his lips.

"The lady said?" I asked. "That's fantastic. I really must have pissed her off. This is twice in less than twenty-four hours she's tried to kill me. We're not even dating," I told the man, as if this would explain her anger at me.

"I could just leave," the man suggested; bullies, pirates, thieves, muggers…all of the lower vermin only strike when odds are in their favor, like the cowards that they are. The chances for a successful outcome had been altered, and now he wanted nothing to do with it.

"Drop your sword thing first," I told him.

"It's all I've got to defend myself. There are a lot of bad people in these woods," he told me.

"I'm sure there are, and now I'm going to need it to defend *my*self. Drop it. The last time Oggie, over there, bit a man…took his whole hamstring with him. It was horrible, guy was screaming for his mommy. I think they took his leg off with a saw, don't really know, we didn't stick around long enough to find out." The steel clattered to the ground.

"I don't want any trouble," he said his hands

upraised.

"Yet you came looking for it. Strange. Get the fuck out of here, I'm done with you."

The guy began to slowly reach down, at first I couldn't figure out why…and then I heard it. Back up was coming; the odds were once again shifting. Vegas was going to get whiplash trying to keep up with this betting scheme.

"Deal's off then, I suppose?" I asked, as he stood back up sword in hand.

"What can I say, I'm one of the bad ones, my word doesn't mean much. Sold my last wife for this sword. I couldn't just leave it behind."

"You are not making a case that men are worthy of saving," I told him.

"Did not know I was an emissary for mankind, my lord," he said mocking me.

He did not approach, but kept his sword leveled in Oggie's direction, I'm sure the way I looked he did not consider me a threat, and for the most part he was right.

"You could still live through this day," I told him.

"Oh, I fully intend to."

"Listen, I've been through a war in the desert, and a zombie invasion. I even lived through dealing with the most evil vampire that has ever roamed the world who was hell bent on my destruction. I survived an alternate reality that involved Night Runners, scary business that was. I've killed all manner of men, some just rednecks others trained military killers and just last night I killed a Lycan. What do you think the odds are that I'm going to be done in by a common highway man?"

Most of what I was saying made absolutely no sense to him, but it was pissing him off for good or bad.

"Common? Fuck you, twat."

"Twat made it and not the middle finger. Weird time…weird time indeed."

"I think you've got the dumbs."

"Been accused of that before. It sure would explain a lot."

"Gregor, you there?" one of the men called out from the woods. They were close.

"Gonna look pretty pathetic, that you, big, strong, strapping Gregor, had to wait for his men as he was held at bay by an unarmed man on his last legs and a puppy. Yeah, they'll sing songs about you for years. You piece of shit." A racking cough came out as I spat those last words; a phlegm clot of blood dangled from my lip and fell to the ground.

The cough probably saved my life as Gregor saw the weakness he needed to make his move. He charged the sword out in front of him. He came without a war cry as he meant to impale me with the blade. I turned, but not enough, he was just fast enough or I was more hampered than I thought. The barbed edge of the blade pierced my side; I involuntarily let out a cry.

"Bet that fucking hurts," he said as he drove it in and through. His face was inches from my own.

"You have no idea," I told him breathlessly.

Oggie bounded over and bit deep. The man's scream was much more high-pitched, and less manly, than my own. As he pulled the sword out, I could feel the pull of it as the blade dragged across my internal organs. The suction caused it to pop wetly as my body released it. His body was turning and he meant to use the short sword on my dog. I used the only weapon available. As he turned, his neck was exposed. I leaned in and tore into him. I ripped twice with my canines and then I let them sink in as I drank. It was easily the most vile and wonderful thing I think I had ever done.

I felt like Popeye finally getting his can of spinach; only this spinach was laced with steroids. The little blood that spilled was from where Oggie had torn into him. I discarded his husk just as the first of his troops came through the woods.

The man froze as he looked at me, my long canines

were exposed, blood masked the lower portion of my face, and maybe he couldn't feel the power radiating off of me, but he sure as hell could feel my murderous intent.

Oggie turned and growled at the new player to our drama. I upturned my face to the heavens with my arms outstretched by my side.

I roared.

I roared with the power that coursed through me. The man tried to turn and run, but I was on him before he knew what hit him. My teeth pierced his main artery; his heart was pumping wildly in its flight reflex, which sent copious amounts of his life-fluid coursing into me. I raised his body over my head when I was done and shattered his bones against the nearest tree. Whoever else had been in the woods that day had seen enough, they left quickly.

I cursed and alternately thanked Azile as I plodded after her. Whether to thank her or end her life I hadn't decided yet.

CHAPTER 4 –Tommy and Azile

"This isn't right, Azile," Tommy said as he tied Oggie up. The dog was whining trying to get back to Mike.

"He needs to know what we're up against," she said indifferently as she tightened up her saddlebags.

"This isn't the way to go about it. He almost died."

"I wouldn't have allowed it. You should know me better than that. We're still talking about Michael Talbot…the man has an uncanny penchant for getting out of trouble."

"He has to because of his even more uncanny knack for getting into it."

Azile laughed. "The gods favor him, we need him, and if this is what it takes to get him motivated, then so be it."

"The gods?" Tommy asked.

"They are more prevalent now than they have been in centuries."

"What gods do the Lycan pray to?" Tommy asked.

"Let's go. We need to be as far away from this place as we can when he emerges. I fear he will be blinded by anger and may not listen to reason."

"I can't imagine why," Tommy replied. "Are you so sure he'll follow?"

"I'm not, but he will feel that some measure of payback is called for."

"Just what I want, a pissed off Talbot gunning for me."

"Relax, it's me he's angry at." Azile smiled.

They had traveled along the small trail for a few hours when they came across a felled tree.

"You there, stop!" a voice called out from the woods. "There is a toll to pass through these woods." A burly, sparse-whiskered man emerged from the woods. A broken sword in his right hand and a flask in the left from which he took a large swig. He wiped his mouth as the amber liquid sluiced down his chin.

"What would that toll be?" Azile asked.

"You're a woman?" the man asked, raising his glassy gaze to Azile's high perch.

Azile removed her hood. "I've been told that, yes."

"You're a looker." The man leered and laughed. "The price was merely your lives…now I think I'll have to raise it."

"If you pull that little shriveled thing you call a cock out of your pants I will cut it off and make you chew it. Slowly I might add," Azile said.

Tommy couldn't contain himself as he snorted between his fingers.

"Something funny, lad?" the man questioned, trying to save face as his men gathered around him.

"I'm good," Tommy said, nearly laughing outright.

"Whaddaya have in the cart?" the man asked, pointing with his blade.

"It is of no concern of yours," Azile told him.

"You see that's where you're wrong, little lady." The man with the blade said. "I am Gregor King of the Wild Woods."

"Seize the horse, Jon," Gregor told one of the men.

"I wouldn't if I were you," Azile told Jon as he approached the reins.

Jon hesitated, her words held conviction.

"Taking orders from our next victim, er one night stand now?" Gregor asked. "You won't be so high and mighty when me and my men are done with you.

"As you wish," Azile said.

Jon grabbed the horses' reins. The large mare swung her head around, catching the man in the temple. The concussive force dropped the man to the ground. The horse stepped up and placed a well-aimed hoof deep into his skull, shattering it much like a person would a cockroach; and with a similar – but louder – sound. Everyone but Gregor backed up.

"Do not leave!" Azile commanded. "You will remove this tree for my companion and me, and then you are free to go."

Gregor was shaken up, but it was still five on two, one being a young man and the other a woman. "It's just a warhorse!" Gregor shouted. "We haven't had pussy that fine in months and I'll not let it go."

"Correction, you've *never* had anything this fine and never will," Azile told them.

"It's always the haughty ones that are the funnest to ride. When they break, it's a wonderful thing to watch."

"Move the tree or I will save you for last," Azile replied.

"Let's get out of here, Gregor. She's a damned witch if I ever saw one."

"The smartest of the lot." Azile turned to Tommy, he nodded.

"You're an idiot. Take her from her horse!" Gregor commanded.

The mare stomped her feet in response.

"I will not," the man told him.

"Why don't you, Gregor?" Azile asked.

He stared at her intently, took another long pull from his buckskin flask. "I am King. Kings do not soil themselves with dirty work."

"Then I suggest, your *majesty*, that you order your men to remove this tree," Azile said, flourishing her words with a bow.

Gregor gazed long and hard at her. When he realized that the opportunity for harm to befall him was too great, he spoke. "Well, since you put it so kindly. Let's go you lecherous lot and move the log for the woman."

Azile paid them no attention as she waited. The men grunted and groaned as they swiveled the large log from the path.

"You are free to go," Gregor said. He swept his arm down the path as if he had allowed it.

"A few hours back you will find a rope tied to a tree. If you see it you've gone too far, a man should be on the path behind us, you can take our toll from him," Azile said as she spurred her horse on.

"Azile!" Tommy said. "He is wounded. We shouldn't have left him in the first place, and now you send more to attack him?"

"He will take what we both know he needs."

"He doesn't like to be manipulated."

"He'll never know we sent them."

"That *you* sent them," Tommy clarified. With that, he followed her.

CHAPTER 5 - Mike Journal Entry Four

"What the hell is that?" I asked Oggie, looking at the figure of what looked like a prone man on the ground, but he didn't look quite right. I approached slowly, looking around for signs of a trap. There was a large tree moved off to the side.

"Oh, friggin' gross," I said, turning away when I got close.

A man whose skull had been crushed was on the ground. Gray matter was spread in a circle outwards from whatever had done this. My first thought was giants, giants with large wooden clubs.

"Not out of the realm of possibilities," I told Oggie. "Let's get out of here." He sniffed around the area and barked in reply. "Yeah, I know they went this way," I told him. "I can almost smell her treachery." Oggie whined.

For two days I tirelessly followed them, only stopping long enough to hoist Oggie up in my arms occasionally so he could sleep. With his paws draped over my shoulders he would snore. I could not remember when I had been so happy in a very long time. Happy to have his companionship, even if that entailed the back of my tattered jacket getting soaked as he drooled while he slept, or snored so loud I could barely keep an ear out for anything that might be sharing the woods with us. He would awaken happy and, with one large swath of his tongue across my face, I would let him down so he could hunt for his breakfast.

I could only believe that Azile and Tomas were not

stopping as well, otherwise I would have caught up to them that first night. She was running, she knew I was behind her and she was afraid! And then I laughed at that thought, I had yet to meet a woman that was afraid of me.

"She's moving at this pace because she has to," I said aloud. I surveyed the woods more carefully this time, trying to determine if what she was so concerned about was out there even now…watching.

Oggie trotted up a few minutes later as I leaned against a tree. "What you got there?" I asked him. He looked down as I approached, and he dropped a squirrel leg. A chicken claw had more meat on it. "Hungry?" I asked him. It's alright, you don't need to find me food anymore, I said as I rubbed his head. He grabbed the leg and headed back off. "Not too much longer," I told him. I wanted to be off soon. Wherever Azile was going in such a rush, I wanted to be there as well.

It was midday, on the third day, when we finally came out of the woods. I had to admit it was something special to finally see the sun not cloaked behind a curtain of leaves. I had found myself once again on an old highway. This was grown over in parts, but it wasn't in nearly as rough a shape as I-95 had been. I was semi-convinced that this was Interstate 80, no real way to tell until I hit a toll booth. The world may have collapsed, but somebody, somewhere, would always be collecting tax.

A hawk circled high overhead. I could see smoke to my left, most likely a settlement of some sort. I watched for a moment as the smoke drifted lazily. A good day's march, and then what? Just grab an old man and have myself a little drink at his expense? Oggie was running around enjoying the wide-open space. I waited until he had wiped himself out. It had become a routine with us. He would come up to me, tongue hanging out, then he'd sit on his butt in front of me and bark. This was my cue, to bend down and pick him up. Half the time now he wasn't even falling asleep he just enjoyed the ride. Who wouldn't? If he could have done the same for me I would have taken him up on it.

Occasionally I would 'stretch' my mind out in an attempt to pick up on the telepathic link me and Tommy shared. It was like I was in a continual dead spot, if I had to place a bet, then good money would be on Azile throwing up some sort of interference. Friggin witches messing shit up since the Medieval times. Should probably make that into a bumper sticker.

***

"He's a few hours behind us," Azile said, looking off into the distance.

Tommy turned as if he'd be able to see him. "Determined," was his response.

Azile smiled.

"Should we let him catch up?" Tommy asked.

"Right now he's so determined because he seeks some measure of revenge against me. We need to give him another reason for this pursuit."

"I don't know if you did some spell on yourself, but my behind is killing," Tommy told her.

"Why don't you sit on all those pastries you keep procuring?" she asked.

"You did not tell me that you are now performing the dark arts, Azile!" Tommy exclaimed.

"Come on. Let's put a little more distance between us, were he to somehow catch us now, I'm not sure I could convince him of my intent."

***

I was getting tired, and I needed a change of clothing. I turned towards the smoke; I could only hope they were more hospitable than the folks I had thus far encountered.

Odds weren't good, but I could hope. The traveling was difficult as I left the roadway; there were no pathways as I struggled through. The village or settlement or whatever it was appeared to be off the beaten path. Made sense; the more difficult to get to it, the less likely someone would bother. I don't know why I didn't reason this out further, it also meant they didn't want visitors. Mental block on my part most likely, lord knows I'm prone to them. It took most of the day before I began to smell the scent of the living. Roasting meat, sweat, work, and wood fire – they had it all going.

I was not prepared for what I saw as I came out upon a man-made clearing. It was a walled town; large wooden walls were erected and held together with rope so thick I don't think Oggie could have chewed through it in a week. The tops were shaved into foreboding looking spikes and every fifty or so feet was a manned turret.

I now knew what had caused the immense clearing. Every available tree of significant size had been plundered to erect that fort. I was standing there at the edge wondering if I should advance or retreat. But the smell of roasting turkey was all the impetus Oggie needed as he began to trot towards the fortification. And to be honest, it smelled delicious to me as well. I still had what most would consider a vast amount of money, and I would gladly share for a bird or two.

"You there!" one of the men in the turret to my left shouted.

"Me?" I asked, looking around.

"State your business."

"A hot meal, followed by a hot bath, maybe a deep-tissue massage for me and my traveling companion. That would be for starters."

"You see these walls?" the man asked. I noticed movement in the turret to my right.

"He looks like a brigand," the man on the right shouted. "I could shoot him."

"With what?" I asked trying to peer into the shadows

of his enclosure. The tip of a sharp looking arrow shone brightly in the sun as he moved it forward.

It was a crossbow; I could just make out the perpendicular arms of the bow.

"That'd be a hell of a shot," I told him. "Been shot with a crossbow once, it was not an experience I would like to re-live."

"Then you'd better get moving," he replied.

"I've got money, I'm just looking for some food and new clothes."

"Did the poor bastards you slaughtered on the road give you your money and your wardrobe malfunctions?"

I initially thought he was referring to Gregor, and I was wondering how he could possibly know. And then my quick-witted mind figured out that he was more likely to believe I was with Gregor or his ilk.

"I came across this money honestly. I can assure you it's mine," I told him, although I really didn't know how Tommy had come by it, but he had given it to me.

"Nobody wants your money here," the man on the left said.

"I was attacked three days ago. I defended myself and came out victorious. I do not mean to set up residency in your fair city, I just mean to eat, get some presentable clothes, maybe sleep one good night on something that does not smell of pine and old leaves, and then I will go. Gladly spending my money while I'm here."

"Do not move," the man on the right said.

"Can I sit?"

"Easier target, sure go ahead."

Oggie was running circles around me trying to get me going towards the wooden wall. "I'm trying, puppy," I told him.

He finally succumbed to weariness, yawned once, and laid his head in my lap.

"Hello, sir, my name is Chancellor Saltinda. My men

have informed me that you wish to seek sanctuary for the night." A voice called down from the turret I was looking at.

I stood up before answering. "If that's what you call eating and getting a decent night's rest…then yes, I am requesting sanctuary."

"Where are you from?" he asked.

"Maine," I told him without even thinking.

"The Old Lands?" he queried.

"Shit," I said softly. "Sorry, Chancellor, I have spent the fair amount of my life away from people. I lived North of Robert's Land."

"Impossible, that is Micmac territory."

"We had an understanding."

"And what was it?"

"I never knew they were there and they apparently left me alone."

"Your story has holes."

"It would appear that way. Sir, I was traveling with two companions, when I was attacked and we were separated. (Mostly true). I saw your smoke and I have sought help at your gates."

"We don't generally receive guests."

"I gathered that. I'm not asking for anything, I have money."

"Robert's Land money is not good here."

"Really? You don't take gold?" I asked, jangling my bag for him to hear.

He paused. Who doesn't when they hear that much wealth clattering around?

"Theodore, it's one man and a dog. What harm can befall our city if we let him in?" I heard a woman question the Chancellor.

"Do you have weapons?" he asked.

I turned completely around.

"I could shoot him, sir. We could take his money," the man on the right suggested.

"You will do no such thing," the woman shouted out. "We would be no better than the brigands we so desperately despise and defend against."

"And yet, my dear, here is a man incredibly far from his home with a king's ransom…if we are to believe that what he holds is indeed gold."

"You know what?" I asked. "I'm done here. I keep questioning why I'd want to help people and every time I get a little closer to wanting to, I meet more and more reasons not to."

"He seems to have the—" the chancellor began.

"The dumbs, yeah, I have the dumbs, you idiot. When the storm comes, I hope that flimsy wall holds," I said hotly.

"Are you threatening me and our town?" he questioned angrily.

"Oh come on! You can't be so daft as to think thieves and muggers are the worst thing out there can you?"

A crossbow bolt landed about a foot away from me. "Don't you dare speak ill of the chancellor again," the man said.

I reached down and plucked it from the ground. I shifted it around in my hand and tossed it back at him with more force than it had arrived. The bolt quivered in a log next to his head. "If you plan on shooting at me I suggest next time you kill me," I told him.

"My gods. Did you see that?" the woman exclaimed "What storm do you speak of?"

"The Lycan," I said solemnly.

I noticed movement; it appeared all of them were doing some sort of rote prayer or gesture, most likely to ward off evil.

"We have heard things," a new female voice added.

"Lana, stop. He is merely playing on our fears," the chancellor said to his wife, daughter, or knowing men of power, mistress.

"Does this look like I'm playing?" I asked pulling

back the remnants of my shirt. Four angry puckered slashes stared back at them.

"He's marked!" one of them cried.

"He's a werewolf!"

"Maybe, maybe not. When did these wounds happen?" the chancellor asked.

"Two days ago. What difference does that make?"

"All the difference. Werewolves can only turn into form on the full moon, Lycan can turn whenever they like."

"They're not the same thing?" I asked confused.

"A werewolf is an infected human, the Lycan is their master."

"I had no idea. Figured one furry beast was the same as the other." Oggie barked at me. "Well, of course I'm not talking about you."

"How do you feel?" the man asked.

"Hungry, somewhat tired, got a little road rash going on in my lower regions. Some blisters on my feet, I could probably take a shit if prompted."

"There's a lady here!" the chancellor shouted.

"You asked. I'm merely trying to be honest."

"I meant, how you feel in regards to your injuries."

"I feel fine."

"It was not even close to a full moon two nights ago. If what you say is true and you were attacked by a Lycan, you are now infected."

I paled at those words. Infected meant germs.

"Unless."

"Unless what?" I asked, grasping for straws.

"You killed it or it dies before the full moon."

"What?" Sometimes this world made me feel like I truly had the dumbs.

"It is widely believed that the host Lycan that inflicts the damage must remain alive until the first full moon for the change to take place in those it has infected."

"Okay...wait. So you're saying if the beast that did

this to me is dead, then I'm fine?"

The man shrugged, "That's common folklore."

"Sir, he probably is a Lycan, I should just shoot him and be done with it. If he's not a Lycan, chances are he's a werewolf. Either way, he needs to die."

"I defeated the thing that attacked me."

"Isn't that what a Lycan would say?" one of the wall walkers said.

"If I was indeed a Lycan, that twelve-foot wall you have would not be a problem. The beast I fought was at least eight feet tall. I imagine he could have just reached up and pulled you down from your lofty little perch," I told him.

The man stepped back a pace.

"Listen, this has been informative, and I've got plenty to think on, but I need to catch up to the rest of my party. I'd like to thank you for your hospitality, but I guess that won't be the case. Do yourselves a favor though. Build higher walls." I turned to leave.

"Wait! Wait!" I heard from behind the gate. I turned as one of the women from the wall came running out.

"Lana! What are you doing! Stop immediately."

She came running out to me; long, red hair trailing behind her. She was younger than I had originally thought – probably why she came out the gate – she hadn't lived long enough to truly distrust people. She'd learn.

"I didn't want you to think all the people of Denarth were rude." She handed me a sack sitting atop a small pile of clothes that looked like they'd been made from burlap.

Yeah, that was going to help the old road rash, I thought sourly.

"I brought you some bread and cheese," she added.

I opened the bag. It smelled heavenly; the bread had just come out of the oven. I was taking in the smell when the wind kicked up, her soft hair floating up into the breeze. The delicate curve of her neck quickened my pulse. I could feel the beat of her blood as it slid by just underneath her skin. I recovered as her hair fell back into place.

"Thank you for this," I told her, wanting to leave her company as quickly as possible.

"Did you truly fight a Lycan?" she asked, eyes large.

"I did."

"And you won?"

"I did."

"How?"

I looked at her for a moment. I thought about telling her, but there were already enough monsters in the world. Why did she need to know about another one? "Grace of the gods, I suppose," I told her instead. "Listen, if what my friends have told me is true, then Lycan are coming. You need to convince the chancellor that what you have isn't adequate to stop them. They are planning a war."

"I will try. Father can be stubborn. Thank you," she said as she gripped my hand. She pulled back quickly from the contact. I looked down to her hand, and with that, I left.

***

"Dammit, Michael," Azile said with the same far away stare.

"What's the matter?" Tommy asked, pulling up alongside.

"That man! He's like trying to catch falling leaves in the winter."

Tommy sat back not sure how to respond. "Azile, there are no leaves in the winter."

"Exactly," she said, exasperated. "He went off the pathway."

"Should we go get him?" Tommy asked.

"No, for whatever reason he left, it must be important. We will continue on."

***

I walked away from the fortress happy to have some food. I alternated eating bread and cheese, always giving Oggie a piece of whatever I was having. Normally he liked to roam around, but he was hanging pretty close since we started eating. I found a small copse of trees and removed my destroyed clothes. I enjoyed the feel of the sun on my skin and actually took a moment to lie down. I had to admit, there was something extremely primitive and inviting about being this close to nature. I let my eyes close. Oggie was sniffing around the bag.

"We'll eat more in a minute," I told him groggily.

I heard him go bounding off. I think Oggie took the *minute* part literally I heard him come traipsing back much quicker than I had anticipated, or I had fallen asleep and more time had elapsed than I thought. I sat up when I realized those weren't the sounds of paws on grass, but rather, shoed feet.

Nothing makes you feel more vulnerable than nudity, and besides some clinging twigs and leaves, I was as naked as one could get. I was staring at the clothes Lana had given me; I reached out and snagged them. My hand nearly rebelled at the feel of the scratchy Rayon-Burlap hybrid. I think I would have put my shredded clothes back on if I hadn't shed them back at the opening to the copse. There was no way I was getting into a fight with my talliwacker flapping about. I had just pulled the rough material over my head when I heard her.

"Sir," Lana called out.

"You're kidding right?" I said softly, ducking down and putting my arms through the torturous sleeves as quickly as I could. "I'd rather wear rusty armor," I said as I pulled the pants up. My socks were a lost cause and I had discarded them with the rest of my previous clothing. The boots could use a thorough rinsing, but they were in great shape. I put them on, foregoing tying them for the moment.

"What are you doing here?" I stood up. She had gotten a lot closer than I had expected and gasped in surprise when she saw me.

"I told my father. He did not believe me that a war is coming. My father said that you were just trying to scare us because we would not let you in."

"So how did coming to find me seem like a good idea? You have no idea who I am. I could very easily be the monster your father believes that I am. Or worse," I added, bending over to tie my boots. The wind had kicked up exposing that damned delicious looking neck again.

"This a test, God?" I grumbled.

"Excuse me?" Lana asked, thinking I was talking to her.

"Nothing." I told her, thankful her hair had dropped back down. "Go home, I appreciate what you've done for me, but there's nothing except danger out here."

"Where are you from...really?" she asked, completely blowing off my warning.

"I love teenagers, such a uniquely obstinate being."

"Your clothes, I couldn't tell from the wall, but I knew they were different. And then when I saw your boots, I knew you weren't from Maine and you have an accent I've never heard before. It's so exotic."

"You've never heard a Bostonian accent before?" I asked.

"Where? Are you from across the ocean? Father told me that people used to travel over the waterways covering vast distances."

"I'm from..." I let it trail off, Massachusetts would mean as much to her as Boston would.

"And more importantly," she pressed on, "What are you?"

"What?"

"I touched your hand...you are no man."

"You have no idea what I am or where I'm from, and

you come out alone and unarmed. And they say I have the dumbs."

She looked slightly crestfallen. If she had lived during my times, though, she probably would have been a cheerleader with how quickly she rebounded.

"You are no Lycan like my father believes."

"How do you know that?" I asked in between whistles for Oggie.

I wanted him to come back quickly so we could leave before her father sent out a brigade of men to hunt us down. And truth be told, being alone with a teenage girl scared the shit out of me. Not because I felt like I would commit any impropriety, but rather because like I've pointed out in other journals; the female teenager may be the most foreign creature on this planet. That includes zombies, vampires and now even Lycans and werewolves. They were an emotional bundle of drama, and I dreaded being around the ticking time bombs.

"You are not Lycan because they nearly burn to the touch. That is why I grasped your hand. I had to know."

"Have you ever heard the phrase, curiosity killed the cat?"

"Many times," she replied.

"Apparently that didn't resonate with you, I'm thinking."

"What is your name?" she asked, completely ignoring me in a perfect teenage fashion.

"Fine, I'm Michael Talbot."

She let that roll around in her head for a moment before she spoke. "Again, sir, you are no Lycan, and I do not believe you to be any ordinary man. You are cold to the touch, but do not show any signs of hypothermia. My original question stands."

"Listen, Lana, go home. Do whatever it is teenagers do during this time."

"Teenager?"

"A person of teen years. You know fifteen, sixteen, etcetera."

"Middling, you mean?"

"Sure, take your middling ass and go home. Your father is going to want my head now, and I'm very attached to its present location."

"I am nearly an adult. I will do as I please!" she informed me in no uncertain terms.

"Great really, but go rebel somewhere else."

"Why are you avoiding my questions?"

"You will not like the answers."

"I know more than you think I do."

"Most teen...middlings do."

"I can sense something in you. Are you attracted to me?"

"Listen, Lana, you really don't want to be around me. I don't know what you sense or why you feel the need to be here. I may be attracted to you, but not in any way that is flattering."

She looked at me crossly, my words confusing her.

I laughed, before realizing my folly. "Where is that damned mutt?" I asked impatiently wanting to extract myself from this socially awkward situation.

"You're laughing at me? Is something about me funny to you?" She was truly angry now.

Poked a bear, wonderful. "Lana, I am many years your senior and have been in a time vastly different from this one. I find humor wherever I can get it. Go home, find someone you love to be with. Enjoy him while you can. Love hard, life is fleeting."

"Why is there so much sadness around you?" she asked, stepping in closer.

Oggie finally trundled up. He was all wags and kisses to our new guest.

"Great of you to finally show up. We're leaving, pooch," I told him as I grabbed my meager supplies. I walked out of the copse and back towards the roadway. Lana did not immediately follow. But she would. How did I know that? Because what middling isn't defiant?

"Don't make me carry you back!" I shouted into the woods behind me where she trailed by a couple of dozen yards.

"You cannot see me!" she shouted in reply.

"I'm no woodsman, but a bear in heat would make less noise than you."

"I want to see the world. I have only been out of Denarth once, and I was still within sight of her walls."

"The world sucks, Lana. There's all manner of unsavory things out here. "Even right here." I mumbled that part. "Your father was wise to keep you inside."

"A life half lived is not worth living," she said as she approached.

"Why are you so desperate to cut both of our existences short?"

"My father will understand," she said, coming abreast of me.

"No, he won't. I was a father once."

"Once?"

"Last chance, Lana, I have to catch up to my *friends*. (For lack of a better term.) Where I go I do not foresee a rosy ending. I have done things in this life I must atone for, and I have a fate to fulfill. And apparently it starts with these clothes. Are they used as some sort of punishment?" I asked, pulling the shirt away from my chest where it was abrading my many wounds.

"I have a salve I can put on those." she said, realizing my discomfort.

"NO!" I said much too quickly.

"I think I frighten you, Michael Talbot." She laughed.

"You have no idea."

"What happened to your children?" she prodded.

"Time," was my solemn answer.

"Surely you are not old enough to have outlived them."

I stopped and turned to look at her. "You are a smart one, aren't you? Fine, this may be the only chance I have to be rid of you." My pupils dilated as I opened my mouth, long canines pulled down pointedly, my heart raced as I felt the beat of her heart. The delivery of so much blood quickened my pulse in return.

"What are you?" she cried, pulling back.

"I am the worst of what this world has to offer," I told her truthfully as I wrestled to regain control of my emotions. Oggie stood and watched purposefully. I wondered what he would do if I attacked the girl. He had seemed to grow fond of her, and I can't imagine he would stand idly by as I devoured her. "I am a vampire, Lana."

She raised her hand to her mouth. "Impossible. You are lying! This is some sort of trick to make me leave," she said, but she was still backing up and looked like she would bolt at any moment. "That is why you are so cold?" she asked, stopping.

I nodded.

"Your family…all of your family has passed?"

I nodded again, tears threatening to fall. "Most of my friends as well."

"You poor man." She came closer, placing her hand against my cheek.

"I am no man." I told her in a whisper; though I had meant to say it with force. "Lana, I am constantly in a whirlwind of destruction, and those around me usually pay for my transgressions. Go be happy, live your life out. Forget the world outside, it is not a place for those with kind hearts."

"How can you say Lycans threaten our very existence and yet you wish me to sit by while they come for us? Will our walls hold?"

"No."

"I must do what I can then to prevent that."

"Yes, by going back and convincing your father his defenses are inadequate. That is the best thing you can do."

"You would have me go back by myself, with all the hidden dangers lurking about?"

"It's not that far."

"What if I got lost? My death would be on your conscience."

"Advanced degree in manipulation I take it?"

"It's getting dark. I don't think I'd make it back in time…being a silly little girl and all."

"Let's go." I said, grabbing her arm, she tried to pull away. "We're going back to your home."

"I'll tell father we kissed, Denarth laws dictate marriage."

"What?" I asked, almost flinging her arm away as if it were on fire. "Now you're lying."

"Am I? What would you do then?"

"Run for the friggin' hills, I suppose."

"I do not wish to marry you Michael, but I will threaten you with Denarth laws."

"So you would do something you do not wish to do just to spite the both of us? How is it that teens do not learn from those that went before them? Marriage would be horrible; you'd be talking about new hip-hop bands and shoes you wanted to buy. You'd probably want to go out dancing every night. Folks would tell you how nice it is you caring for your grandfather."

She laughed. "I don't know what hip hop bands are, but I do like shoes."

"Go figure. Let's go." I'll take my chances with Denarth law.

"Do you hear that?"

"No, do you have bat ears?"

"Horses," she said, ducking down.

I didn't hear them, but I heard the braying of dogs. "Hounds. We're being tracked. This your dad's doing?"

"Yours is the first dog I've seen in five years. A trader came to our gates once, had this old gnarled thing that lay in the back of his cart most of the time. I, at first, thought it was stuffed, it moved so little."

"See, Lana, this is the kind of shit I'm talking about. I'm walking around minding my own business eating bread and cheese and I guarantee you these people are chasing me – now us – and want to do us harm."

"We'd better get moving then."

She was right, but we were going to have to move away from the area I had wanted to travel towards. For now I was stuck with Lana.

"Any idea who this is?" I asked her as we ducked behind some bushes. I was trying to get my bearings so we could get back to the general direction I needed to be going.

"I don't," she said, her eyes wide. I figured with fright, but I would later learn it was excitement. I'd forgotten how adept at lying middlings were.

We had been moving at a good clip, and, at times, the dogs' barking sounded far distanced at other times it approached. The problem was, I could go a lot longer than Oggie, and Lana looked like she was already beginning to flag; youth or not, she had led a relatively sheltered life. Oggie was looking over at me from time to time, I think wondering when I was going to pick him up. In theory I could pick both of them up. I don't know how much I'd be able to see at that point, or how comfortable a ride it would be for either of them. And with the thought of fresh blood being that closely pressed to me also had its own distaste.

"I'm exhausted," Lana said, nearly stumbling.

"Having fun yet?" I asked with a sneer. "Told you it was a barrel of laughs out here." The sun had set; the moon, which was at a little over three-quarters, shone brightly. "Whoever is chasing us is determined," I said to her as we took a quick respite.

Oggie quickly laid down, his eyes shutting. His ears

would swivel when he heard barking, but he couldn't be bothered enough to look up.

The next round of dog barks was within a football field away; we were sunk. I could not carry two and outdistance a hound. Then we scored a mild victory. I heard men talking – only wisps as the wind would allow – but the retrieval of the dogs was clear enough, they were bedding down for the night. We could take a few more minutes to recover and then we would start out again. Oggie I would carry. Lana would have to make do. Maybe the harshness would send her back.

That tactic didn't work out so well either, she was out. When I went to wake her, nothing short of dropping her in an ice cold bath was going to work. That and I felt somewhat guilty for the predicament she found herself in.

"I don't even have a soul! Why the fuck do I need to be hampered down with morality?" I said as I shifted Oggie's wriggling body around. I had each of them draped over a shoulder like sacks of potatoes. I walked throughout the night, not caring what sort of trail I was leaving. There wasn't a damn thing I could do about it anyway.

"Where…where am I?" Lana asked.

I put her down and my back cracked in response. Oggie wasn't quite ready to face the day. "You friggin' lug," I told him as I also set him down. I stretched and was rewarded with multiple pops and squeaks as I tried to realign myself.

"Are they still after us?" Lana asked, looking around. "None of this is familiar."

"We're about twenty miles from your city."

"Tw-twenty miles? How is that possible?"

"We traveled throughout the night. And we're going to have to keep traveling. Dogs and horses are going to be a lot faster than we are. They'll make up most of this ground before dusk."

Lana absently scratched behind Oggie's ears.

"I should have known," I told her.

"Known what?"

"That you were lying. How would someone who'd never been exposed to dogs know to scratch behind the ears?"

"It just seems—"

"Stop, just stop. My bullshit meter is pegged."

"Meter?"

"The dogs are your dad's?"

"The finest hunting dogs. They're used to round up meat for the winter."

"You tricked me. I carried you for miles to keep you from danger, and instead I brought you into it. This is no fucking game!" I raged at her. "I'm not some knight come to rescue you from your castle like in a fairy tale."

"A lot of people die in those fairy tales," she said. "I knew what I was getting into."

"But I didn't. I don't have the time or the inclination to babysit you."

"I'm nearly an adult, I can do everything you can."

"You can carry me and Oggie? That would be fantastic. Walking without socks sucks."

She continued on without waiting for me.

"Stop! This has gone on long enough," I told her. "We will wait here for your father, I figure he'll be here around noon or so." I sat down.

She turned to look at me. "Have you ever heard of the Right of Affiance?"

"No." I broke a small piece of cheese off for Oggie and myself.

"If my father catches us he will use it."

"What lies are you spewing now?" I asked, trying to get comfortable – a rock under my ass making that nearly impossible.

"If a couple lies together for the night the Right of Affiance is invoked."

"Invoked? Sounds like something Azile would do. What are you getting at?"

"He will make us wed," she said, a whimsical smile on her lips.

"Wed? Why?" I stood up quickly. "Wait…lie the night? We did no such thing!" I said hotly.

"My honor is at stake. He may detest you, but he will not allow his only daughter's virtue to be sullied." She was still smiling.

"This is another trick," I told her, although I wasn't so sure.

"Do you want to hang around and find out if I'm telling the truth?"

"What if I just tie you to a tree?" I asked. "Dad 'rescues' you." I said with air quotes, her face took on one of confusion. I'm going with she'd never seen the gesture before. "And then I can be on my merry little way."

"He will keep hunting for you, Michael Talbot. We are betrothed now."

"I am not marrying you, Lana."

"Then we'd better get moving," she said, walking down the roadway.

"Son of a bitch," I said, following her.

We had walked for about a mile before I asked her a question. "This isn't another ploy?"

She smiled and kept going. Women have been beguiling men since the dawn of man, why should she be any different. Now it was imperative we caught up with the others, maybe Azile could fix this and *then* I'd exact my revenge on her.

When the wind shifted the right way, we could just make out the dogs barking. They had regained our scent, although I'm positive they'd never lost it. We hadn't done anything to throw them off of us. Speed was going to be our only weapon. I had no real clue as to where Azile and Tommy had gone, there were tracks on the roadway, but they were far from the only travelers that used it. If they left the road at any pathway, I'd never know. How far would the chancellor chase his daughter? To the ends of the world would be my answer.

"If I knew how much this food and clothing was going to cost I would have stayed naked and hungry," I told her.

She blushed.

"Sorry, wrong visual. I would have kept my old clothes. Here…take some cheese. We've got to find water soon or we're all going to be in trouble soon."

"You're not a very prepared traveler."

"I've run into a bit of a rough patch on this trip."

"How far ahead are the friends that abandoned you?" she asked later that afternoon. I noticed that her steps were beginning to falter. She was exhausted, hungry, and most likely on the verge of dehydration.

The braying was getting louder. The dogs had an inkling of how close they were getting.

"Plan B it is," I told her as I snatched her up into my arms. She gasped in surprise. "Oggie…water," I said. We hadn't yet established that he knew my words exactly, and I was unsure as to how he would react. For all I know he heard. 'Oggie, blah-blah.'

Anything not immediately followed by the word 'treat' was generally ignored by him. He looked at me and the parcel I had strewn across my shoulder. He looked to the direction the dogs were barking, and then he immediately headed off the road. The traveling was extremely difficult, more than once we had to backtrack due to the underbrush becoming so dense. Lana periodically would protest her position, but it was weakly done. We both needed to replenish, but her even more so.

"I'm sorry, Michael," she whispered in my ear as we moved. "I should not have done what I did. It was impetuous."

"Wow…humility, took you long enough. How about a little honesty? The Rights of Affiance?"

"Is no lie."

"Son of a bitch," I said, pressing through a dense area of mulberry bushes. I momentarily lost sight of Oggie, I wasn't overly worried we would lose him; Lana and I were about as stealthy as a drunken rhino.

When he returned, he was sopped from head to toe.

"You are the best dog ever!" I told him, giving him a large chunk of cheese. "Henry," I said softly, pivoting my head upwards, "that doesn't include you, you were my fourth kid."

"Henry?" Lana asked, but she would not hear a reply even if I gave one; she had either passed out or fallen asleep. The only two types of people I'd seen sleep in the weirdest, most awkward ways were teenagers and military personnel. Either one could fall asleep at the drop of a hat with either rock music blaring or artillery shells raining down in the distance.

We pressed on and the denseness finally gave way to a fairly good-sized stream. It had to be about ten feet across, maybe two feet deep in the middle. What I wouldn't have done for a canoe.

"Well, I guess we'll see how good these dogs are trained." I stepped into the icy coldness of the fast flowing water. I could hear horses now, they were panting heavily The dogs were going berserk. They were at the roadway. I don't think we had much more than a tenth of a mile on them at this point. But they were going to have a hell of a time getting the horses through this mess.

"Bring back my daughter!" bellowed forth from the chancellor.

I wanted to tell him I hadn't taken her, but he wouldn't see it that way. Odds were, he'd stick a spear in my gut and then ask.

"How the hell do I get in these situations?" I asked as

I wallowed along in the stream. Oggie liked splashing in the water, but he wasn't nearly as big a fan of staying in it. He kept going onto the banks shaking off and then coming back in.

"Father?" Lana asked, raising her head.

I moved towards the shore and put her down. "Get some water."

She didn't need to be told twice, she was scooping up handfuls. I shuddered thinking what manner of animals had used the stream as their personal rest stop. Old habits die hard. Right now dehydration was a much bigger enemy than Giardia. I also drank deeply; I was only somewhat appeased that nothing short of nuclear waste was going to affect me. Didn't matter, drinking other animals' feces and urine is not something I generally want on my menu.

"Lana, this doesn't feel right. Seems more like a kidnapping."

"I put you in this situation," she said, letting her head dip a little. Water dropped from her chin.

"Can't you go back and explain?"

"I don't want to go back," she pleaded.

"I get it…I do. I joined the Marines to see the world. Well, hold on, that's a lie, I joined because it was that or jail. But I get it, there's a big world out there and you want to see it, but coming with me this way is not how to accomplish it."

The dogs were barking in the distance, the brush had slowed them down.

"See how they like being in the thorns for a while," I said.

We rested for a few more minutes, sating our thirst.

"It's too late now," she told me. "He will not be able to bring me back without us being married. He'll have the Trinity with him."

"The Trinity?"

"The man that will perform the nuptials."

"Talk about a pitchfork wedding."

"What?"

"Old saying."

"My father is a public figure; he cannot have the scandal of an unmarried daughter that has spent the night with a man."

"We did not spend the night!"

"Yes, we did. It does not matter in the least that nothing happened."

"Camping trips must be a blast. Have a bunch of weddings during the summer months I take it?" I asked sarcastically. "Wait...what if you stay here and you tell him I was killed?"

"Killed?"

"Yeah, giant salmon or something took me out. Maybe a knife wielding clown."

"Clown?"

"Can you tell him I got killed and you're just wandering around now?"

"They will still marry us."

"So? Then you can get a divorce and move on with your life."

"Widowed women can never marry again."

"What? Who the hell makes these rules up? What if you were widowed and then stayed the night with a man?"

She blushed.

"You know what I mean...like we did."

"Death for both."

"You guys are worse than the Muslims."

"Muslims?"

"Religious fundamentalists. Always took things to the extreme at the expense of all others...and themselves, I suppose. That makes about as much sense as non-alcoholic beer, WHICH by the way I would drink if this damn age would just make some. We can't keep running forever and he won't stop, Lana."

"I know."

"We're done. We'll wait here for him. I'll explain…even give him a demonstration. I'm sure he doesn't want his daughter married to a vampire."

"Soul stealer."

"Sounds much more menacing."

"The old books say vampire, but we call your kind soul stealers. Usually just a story to scare the children. None of us believed you existed."

"Yeah, sometimes I feel that way."

The sun was beginning its journey down. I don't know if the pace had slowed them up, or if they were as tired as we were, but they had seemingly stopped as well. The dogs were quiet, as were the men. The sun appeared to be handing the day over to the moon in a tag as they passed each other up. Something should have clicked in my head – but it hadn't – the woods had gone silent. If not for Oggie's nervousness, I would have been caught with my thumb firmly entrenched in my asshole.

My first assumption was that the pursuers had realized how close we were, and instead of having a loud barking pursuit, they had gone for stealth mode. I was partly right. I made sure Lana was more than a few arm lengths away so no one would think anything more than what was going on, was going on.

Lana had her hands in her face, I guess trying to figure out how she was going to face the music on this one. Hopefully the truth would set us free – only MLK knew. I was standing by a tree. Oggie came up next to me, bristling, a growl on the edge of his pulled back lips. Out of my peripheral vision I caught movement off to my right. A good ninety degrees from where I was expecting the chancellor and his men to come from.

"Did they encircle us?" I asked softly. The hair on Oggie's back was raised so stiff he looked more like a porcupine hybrid. "We'll be fine." I caught more movement. Too fast and too big to be human. "Shit. Lana, get up!" I said quickly, motioning with my hand for her to come close.

"How close are they?" she asked, thinking I was referring to her father.

"Shhh." I told her. "Werewolves."

Her eyes looked like saucers, her breath quickened, and her wonderfully beautiful pulse raced. *Wrong thought!* I admonished.

She produced a wicked looking dagger from under her sleeve. I was impressed.

"Know how to use it?"

She nodded curtly.

"Would you have used that on me?" I had to ask.

"If I had to."

"Fair enough."

I'd been in enough scrapes in my life to wonder at the complexity of an event. For seemingly long moments nothing happened. The air was still, the breeze not even blowing for fear of missing something. I'd seen it in Iraq, Afghanistan, Little Turtle, Carol's Farmstead, Camp Custer, and a dozen other places. Nothing, nothing, nothing, EVERYTHING!

"Unhand my daughter!" the chancellor said, springing from the woods with sword in hand. A few men on each side flanked him. I hoped they were enough. The dogs unfortunately were nowhere in sight.

The chancellor's sword had not even the time to finish its sway and settle its point at me when the first of his men screamed out in alarm and pain. Blood splashed across the chancellor's left side as the man on his flank farthest from him was torn open. By the time they turned, the threat had passed.

"What kind of sorcery is this?" the chancellor asked me as if I were responsible for it.

"Get over here!" I shouted at him. "Werewolves!"

I don't think he believed me, but I was unarmed and his daughter was next to me; that was all the incentive he needed.

"Lana, are you alright?" he asked, rushing over. I noted he made sure to keep the blade leveled on my midsection. Honestly, couldn't say I blamed him.

"Oh, father, I'm so sorry to have put you through this." She cried on his arm.

Of the six men that had come with the chancellor five were now in a loose circle around us swords drawn, looking outwards.

"Where are the dogs?" I asked.

"I had them brought back to the roadway once we caught sight of you two," Lana's father told me.

As if on cue they began their barking.

"How many men are with them?"

"Three men, five dogs." Then the cries and terrified screams of man and animal alike assailed our ears.

The men around us looked like they wanted to flee. Well, I guess so did I, but unless you could outrace the moon, that would mean certain death. There were growls and the shouting of men pitched in battle. We could hear the horses as they whinnied in alarm; the earth shook a little as they must have been rearing up and slamming down.

"Warhorses. They won't run, they've been trained to attack," the chancellor said.

The sound of swords singing as they sought targets was captured in the silence that enshrouded us. One by one, the horses, dogs, and men began to go silent – and not in the pre-victorious war-chant type of way.

I broke the small ranks and headed out.

"Where are you going, coward?" the chancellor asked me.

"Kind of harsh aren't you?" I asked back as I bent over and picked up the sword from the man that had fallen first.

"Are you going to marry my daughter now that you sullied her?" he asked as I came back.

"First off, I did not sully her. The only time I touched

her was to put her over my shoulder while she slept. And maybe right now isn't the best time to talk about this. If we make it through the night, we'll talk more."

"Movement," the man to my far right side said.

"Do not break this circle," I told them. "We are going to have to rely on each other to protect our backs."

The chancellor had a look on his face like 'Who died and made you boss?' but he held his tongue, because the likelihood that we were all going to die was pretty high, and at that point, who gave a shit who was in charge. The movement traced around our circle to the point where I could see it. The moon was bright enough for little else in the dense woods. I could get a sense of height and speed – neither of which I liked. Then a beast darted from behind a tree and was making great strides towards me. I'd like to think he came at me first because he figured me for the biggest threat, but most likely it was because of the inexperienced way in which I held my sword.

Small saplings unfortunate enough to be in between me and Bigfoot Junior found themselves quickly trampled underfoot. What I had at first figured for a scouting attack was actually a coordinated full on assault. Werewolves were charging from all sides, I did not have the luxury of time to turn and look. The cries of alarm and the cutting of air as swords moved back and forth was all I needed to hear.

The beast coming at me was huge, but more in the large – I mean large – human realm. Certainly not nearly the size of the monster I had squared off against a couple of nights ago. I still wouldn't want to face this thing in a darkened alley – or a lit up one, but you get the point. It was scary as hell and had a murderous intent, but it was not the same creature Azile had paired me against.

A large paw swiped down towards my head. I instinctually moved my hand to deflect the blow. My sword pierced the werewolf's hand. He howled in rage as he brought his other arm up. His teeth snapped violently as he pressed the attack. I ripped my sword free, severing two of its fingers. A strange dog-like whine whistled through its nose. His uninjured arm crashed against my side, rocketing me into a tree. I was partly grateful that I had the tree to stop my momentum as I was hurtled away…and pained as I collided with the immoveable wooden object.

    I was fairly convinced my left shoulder was dislocated, aggravating an old injury that had never been properly treated. I grunted as I rammed my shoulder into the tree, the audible pop let me know I had reengaged the mechanism. I ducked as the werewolf swiped at my head. Two swaths of bark were sheared away; leaving bloody streaks where my head had been. Had I not made my new friend a permanent lefty, he would have ripped off the top of my head.

    Somewhere distant I heard a man scream, I was so far removed from everything as my world was reduced to my opponent and myself. That was all that mattered, my survival, his death. Steel slashed as I had the audacity to press the attack. There was a moment (most likely in my imagination) where the werewolf couldn't believe my nerve. He pressed on and I caught him high on the chest, slicing a wound that would have stopped a man. As he moved past it, my sword sliced into his biceps, the muscle curling as I cleaved it. Now I had his attention. His rage howling drowned out everything around me. He rushed past my sword, making it no more effective than a bullet-less rifle.

    I didn't have the room to back up; our circle had been compressed to a dot. We were fighting for our existence on an insignificant parcel of land the size of a kitchen table. I didn't yet know who lived and who had fallen, that would have to wait. When I could back up, that would mean I was on my own. The werewolf was inches from my face, his muzzle dripping saliva all over my hand as I fought to hold him at bay. His left arm had fallen to its side, almost useless, and he could not get a grip on my arm with his now disfigured right.

My shoulder screamed as I caught him under the jaw line. I could feel his windpipe begin to close as I clamped shut. His feet began to rise up as I simultaneously cut his air supply off and lifted him into the air. I thrust him back far enough that I could pierce his chest with the sword. I shoved it through his chest plate and then wrenched the steel upwards. Cutting through his being, the left side of him began to slough off. I quickly pulled my sword all the way up, and with a determined slice, I chopped his head off. I kicked his body away before he had the chance to fall.

I screamed – it was my war cry. I had defeated an enemy in battle and my blood was boiling. I became a tempest as I moved to my side. The chancellor had suffered a wound defending his daughter. She had blood on her, but I didn't think it was her own. The werewolf looked to me as I got between it and its prey.

"Dead now, motherfucker," I told it. Its head cocked to the side much like Oggie's would. It rang my bell as a hand caught the side of my head. "Worth it," I said as I drove my sword home.

I was hilt deep before I pulled away. His jaw was still snapping but it had lost some of its vigor. It was bringing its arms back up to defend itself when Oggie circled behind and chewed at its Achilles tendon. The beast fell to its knees; to say I was concerned about where his large cavernous, teethed mouth was in proximity to my well-being was a vast understatement. I hadn't used my equipment in its intended manner in millennia, but that didn't mean I didn't want it exactly where it was supposed to be. I danced back, raised my sword and drove it straight through the animal's mouth as if in protest for what he threatened. He fell over with a louder thud than I should have been able to hear.

I was in a full on rage. I was hyper-aware, not a sound or a move could escape my attention. A bat swooped past capturing a large moth as I pivoted. Blood slammed through me as I sought out another. I could feel individual heartbeats even as they rivaled the pace of a humming bird.

Three of the chancellor's men had fallen. Lana and her father were keeping one of the werewolves at bay. I pinioned my head, sweat came off in sheets, individual droplets hurtled out into space. I could hear them as they splashed down onto the leaves below. The two remaining men were fighting off the other werewolf and seemed to be winning. I turned back to the chancellor and Lana; and once again stepped in front of him, nearly catching a sword for my troubles.

Oggie was barking at the beast, trying to distract it. It was working; he or she, I don't know and I wasn't going to stop and ask, kept stealing glances behind to see how close the dog was. When it looked like it was going to turn and attack its distant cousin, I pounced.

"Hurt?" I asked it as I pierced its side.

It howled in rage and agony. Oggie kept spinning as the werewolf did, making sure he was always at its back. When it realized it was losing the battle, it rushed me – I guess hoping to off one of us so it could focus on the other. Before I could bring the sword to bear, he crashed into me, sending me hurtling towards the ground. I knew this was going to suck, I'd had enough two hundred-plus pounders knock me into the turf when I played football. Air wasn't so much expelled from my lungs as it was compelled to leave. My vision blackened as large spots drifted across my visage.

As I struggled against my opponent, I wondered why he wasn't delivering killing blows. That was when I saw Lana removing her short sword from the side of the werewolf's head. She had stuck it through its temple hard enough that it had exited the far side. Her father helped roll him off of me. Oggie jumped in to lick my face.

"I'm fine, pup," I told him, standing quickly.

As I got my feet back under me, Lana helped me the rest of the way up. Her Dad turned to help the other two men.

It was three on one and it was still close and about the time Lana and I turned our attention his way we heard a loud piercing whistle. The werewolf's head swiveled to the sound; I could tell he was about to bound off. I ran my sword through him before he had a chance. He turned back towards me but it was too late. The two men were taking out their fear and aggression – and a fair measure of revenge – on him. Repeatedly cutting him with their swords.

I pulled back to let them finish. Not more than thirty yards was a figure watching us. It stood a couple of feet taller than the werewolves, broader at the shoulders as well. That look was pure malevolent intelligence.

"You are marked," It growled.

"Get in fucking line!" I yelled at it. "Or better yet, bring your mangy ass over here and we'll settle this now!"

It roared; there's no other descriptor I can use that will better describe what it did. Howl just sounds so weak to define the sound that came out. It gave one more long searching look, maybe to decide if it had a chance or, more likely, to burn my image into its memory…and then it was gone. Almost faster than I could track it with my eye.

Plumes of breath issued up from our hard fought victory, all of our chests were heaving as our bodies came down from their battle highs. The breathing was heavy and sounded like a sex operator's wet dream. I was the first to speak.

"They're gone." I was finally able to catch a full breath after the werewolf had taken it from me. My shoulder throbbed, as did my head. I had a fair amount of gashes, bruises and bloody spots, but I was far from the worst of those of us that still lived. "Are you hurt?" I asked spinning to Lana. She shook her head.

"Dad?" she asked.

He had a wicked looking cut on the side of his face, but other than that, he looked fine. We turned our attention to the other two men. The skinnier of the two was helping his stout friend slowly to the ground.

"Delano's got a broken arm," he said, resting him against a tree.

"He's got more than that," I said, getting down next to the man. "What's your name?" I asked the man.

"Pieter."

"Pieter, go grab that man's scabbard and break it in two. We'll use that as a splint, and grab his belt as well. We'll use that to secure it." I was looking at the gash on Delano's right thigh. Splint or no, he was going to die from blood loss long before he needed to worry about a broken arm.

"Got it," Pieter said.

Lana got down next to me; she ripped Delano's pants wider. She produced a small leather pouch with a needle, thread, and a jar of some sort of apothecary medicine.

"What the hell else you carrying?" I asked. Hoping that maybe somewhere on her she housed a beer.

"Lana's always been one to be prepared," her father said proudly. "I should check on the other men and the horses. My poor dogs."

"There'll be time enough to bury them," I told him as I grabbed the scabbard parts from Pieter. "This is going to hurt," I told Delano.

"Wait, wait," Lana said, giving a small bottle to Delano. "Drink it all, tastes really bad, but in a few minutes you won't care."

"Got any more of that?" I asked, wondering what it was she had just given him.

"Just give it a few minutes. You'll know when it has started to work and then you can set his arm," Lana said to me.

"What are you?" the chancellor asked me.

"What?" I asked back, I had been intent on Delano's condition and with watching Lana clean out the wound.

"I saw you lift that werewolf off its feet," the

chancellor said.

"Adrenaline," I told him. He was shaking his head. "Trick of the light?" He was still shaking his head. "He was very skinny. You're still shaking your head. I gave you three valid excuses, you can use one or a combination of any of them."

"The drug is starting to take effect," Lana told me.

"Will he turn into a werewolf?" I asked, looking at the wound she was now sewing up.

That got everyone's attention. Pieter had re-drawn his weapon after having put it back in its sheath.

"These were werewolves, only Lycan can infect people," she said, pulling another suture tight.

"How can you tell?" I asked.

She pointed over to the body of a young woman.

"What the fuck?" I asked, falling back.

Oggie was sniffing at her body.

"They always go back to their original form when they die according to the legends." She cut the thread. "You want me to splint his arm?" she asked, trying to regain my attention.

I pulled my gaze from the raven-haired beauty that had died at the point of my sword. It would have been much easier if she were a he, maybe a little older and covered in lesions. Or, better yet, had retained the lethal form of the animal that had tried to kill us all.

"Dammit." I pulled away from a woman that wasn't much older than my own daughter when we had started fighting zombies. "You set it, I'll splint it," I told her.

Delano groaned a little as we worked but, for the most part, he was off in La-La Land – a place I wished to visit.

When we were finished, I looked at the rest of the fallen werewolves, all of them had reverted back to their human forms. The oldest male was ruddy, his hands calloused.

"That's Yolen Penderast," the chancellor said aloud. "That's his wife, Hilda and their two kids Zeta and Poolin. They work the west fields; used to live in the city and decided that they wanted more space. We hadn't heard from them in a few weeks and had sent out a couple of teams looking for them, with no luck. Now we know," he said sadly, the weight of his office pressing on his shoulders. He had lost a family of charges on his watch, and it was not sitting well with him.

"What is going on?" I asked, standing after Delano's arm was fixed in a crude splint. "You guys saw the other one, right?"

Lana nodded. "Lycan. It was almost like he had these werewolves out on a hunt."

"Scouts or a training mission," I said, but it could have easily been a question.

"This is preposterous," Lana's dad said.

"I agree," I told him. "Preposterous that there are werewolves and Lycan."

"These were good people." He looked at the fallen family before him.

"This is my fault." Lana stood, wiping the hair from her face or possibly a tear. "If I hadn't run off, these people would all still be alive."

I saw a different spin on the events; I was wondering which way the Chancellor was going to see it. His face was twisted in anguish.

"You may have just saved your entire village," I told her.

Lana's confused expression matched her father's as they both looked at me.

"You told me he didn't believe you," I directed to Lana. "You have to accept what's right in front of you now," I said to him.

"A war? Hardly," he said, I guess not wanting to realize the truth and who could blame him.

"This is just the beginning. If what my friends say is true, the Lycan are amassing an army. Who knows how many other people have been turned and are even now roaming these woods or country, getting lessons on how to be a destructive force."

Pieter didn't look so good as he listened to the conversation.

"Your walls will not hold them back, sir," I said to the chancellor. "Listen, I get all funny about tooting my own horn, but if I wasn't here, you'd all be dead."

"If you weren't here none of us would be!" he shouted at me. That was partially true.

"Father, I left of my own free will. I want to see the world beyond our walls, the merchants talk of great cities and wonders beyond imagination."

"Silly girl, it is the merchants' job to make up stories so that their wares seem more exotic. They have nothing but time to weave these tales, and each retelling is more fantastic than the next."

"Post-Apocalyptic advertising," I pondered.

"What?" Lana's father asked.

"The loss of your men, horses, and dogs is regrettable I agree, but if that is what it takes for you to realize the danger to the rest of your community, then their lives were not lost in vain. Someday you can erect a monument for their courage."

"We must get back to the village; I will need to talk to the elders about this."

"I'm not going back, father," Lana said.

"Of course you are," the chancellor and I said at the same time.

"After we talk to the council, we will prepare a feast for your wedding." The Chancellor was looking at me.

"Me? I'm not going back, and I'm certainly not getting married."

The chancellor looked like he was about to blow a

gasket. "You take my daughter's honor and then dismiss her? You cad!"

Lana gasped as her father drew his sword. "Father, no!"

"Cad?" I asked.

"It is the highest form of insult," Lana replied. "He is challenging you to a duel."

"Sir, I took nothing from your daughter, certainly not her honor. She is a bright, beautiful, capable woman, and someday she will make some man extremely happy, but that is not me."

"Our laws dictate that any man and woman that lie the night must be wed!" he said hotly.

I started laughing, I couldn't help it. Maybe I was a cad. "Then we have absolutely no problem," I told him.

"What?" he asked, still holding up his sword.

"For I am no man." I flashed my canines. I moved in before he could register the movement. I removed the sword from his hand and was back in my original spot before he could even track it.

Pieter dropped to his knees and prayed to whatever god he thought would listen.

I stretched the truth a wee bit but only because I didn't want the Chancellor to find a loophole in his Puritan values. "I'm no man, I'm a vampire." I told him.

He stood his ground but his face drained of color.

"You again doubt your own eyes?" I asked him. "If I was a man we'd all be dog chow right now." He didn't get the reference or his brain was still struggling to keep up with the events.

"I will kill you," he stated.

I closed the gap until I was inches from his face. I nearly hissed at him. "I saved the lives of your daughter, you, and two of your men, and this is how you wish to repay me. I should drive this sword through your stalwart heart right now and drink my fill!" The force of my words pushed him back.

Lana slid between the two of us. "NO!" she said, trying to push me away – about as effectual as a child pushing on a stone wall.

I eyed him for a few more moments. My thoughts ran from anger to hunger. I tossed his sword to the side. "And Azile wonders why I have no desire to save the species. Man is the most traitorous, treacherous animal that has ever walked the planet. Maybe it's time someone else ran the show." I grabbed my stuff and began to walk off.

"Michael, I'm coming with you!" Lana shouted.

Again the chancellor and I said the same thing in unison. "NO!" Neither of us got our way. Apparently as long as women are alive they will always be the same.

"Father, go home, get the people ready. Do whatever it takes to keep them safe. I will send word when I can."

"How can I keep them safe if I can't even do the same for you? I will constantly be worried for you."

"Why? I walk with the Shade. What could possibly do me harm?"

"Those who walk with a Shade are usually obscured from the light, my little dove," he said, grabbing her head and pulling it close. "You always had too much of your mother in you." He kissed her forehead. "Michael!" he shouted.

"Oh, for the love of God." I mumbled turning.

"My daughter wishes to travel with you."

"I get that," I told him.

"She is more precious to me than the air I breathe."

"I get that, too," I told him, toning down my apathy.

"What are your intentions?"

"With Lana, or do you mean overall?"

"We'll start with Lana."

"Honestly, I wish she'd stay with you." Lana looked crushed. "Where I'm going and what I'm getting into, I wouldn't want anyone I cared for to follow. Lana," I said, turning my gaze, "you've done what you set out to do. Your father now has the proof he needs to defend his city. There is nothing more you can do with me except die."

She put her hand to her chest, the color which had been coming back to the chancellor's face now begin to flow back out like low tide.

"I can help," she said weakly.

"You can help by not getting in the way," I told her as I turned and walked away. Oggie nudged her leg once and followed. She was weeping as her hand trailed along the dog's back.

"Yeah, I'll miss her company, too," I told Oggie. "But this is for the best." The dog turned once, whined and continued along.

CHAPTER 6 - Mike Journal Entry Five

We slept for a bit after the fight, before starting out again. It was morning when we got back to the roadway. I was ravenous. I hadn't even thought to grab what was left of the bread and cheese, although I had taken a sword with me. Not sure how the steel was going to taste.

"Oggie, you ready for a break?"

I sat down. The sun felt good on my skin, but it did little to warm me. I looked up, as a hawk lazily drifted overhead. It was hunting, something I needed to do soon. A nice stag would do Oggie and me some good. Instead, we got to walking again; we were back in catch-up mode. I had no idea how far ahead Azile and Tommy were now or even of their exact pathway. And still I walked. As dusk began to set in I grabbed a flagging, grateful Oggie and plopped him over my shoulder. The pooch was sleeping before I went ten feet. I felt sorry for the pace I was inflicting on him, even if he wasn't complaining.

Time seemed to be running out. The flame of anger I had been carrying for Azile was beginning to peter out, and then there was the Lycan attack. That was merely a foreshadowing of events to come. The Lycan may be slow to reproduce, but they could produce an army relatively easy. Once a month the world could be a living hell, and once man was prostrate, the Lycan could stroll in and claim what they'd sent others to fight for.

And then came the kicker...did I care? I was fairly convinced I could strike a bargain with the Lycan, they leave me alone and I'd do the same. "Yeah, then I'd have to look at the self-righteous face of Tommy when he finally tracked my ass down."

Son of a bitch if I was going to be guilt-tripped into a war. I'm sure there were people like Lana, good decent people, but for every one of her there would be ten assholes. I had come no closer to an answer and still I lumbered on. The sun had set and was once again peeking up when Oggie stirred, I knew the dog had to eat; his energy level was a quarter of its normal self.

I placed him a few feet off the roadway under a bush, concealing him from the sun and prying eyes. "You stay here, my friend. I'll be back with a feast for the both of us."

I was out looking for game a lot longer than I wanted. The woods were almost devoid of wildlife, either it had been cleared or they were driven out by fear. Both scenarios reeked of werewolves – which made sense if they had been patrolling about the previous night. I saw two squirrels way off, a garter snake up close, which I was not going to eat, and bugs, lots and lots of bugs but nothing that was going to feed the Ogster and me. I was defeated as I began to find my way back to his hiding spot.

"Oggie?" I asked as I came back and he was nowhere to be found. Panic ensued, I felt like a parent in a packed department store who takes their eye off their child for a moment only to discover when they turn back around the child is missing. I couldn't even think straight as I tramped about looking for any signs of him.

"Oggie!" I yelled. *Did he follow me into the woods?* I thought. No, I would have heard him. "Purpose!" I yelled, walking towards the roadway. I saw hoof prints in the mud, the soft shoulder revealing Oggie's disappearance. I saw his paw prints, the shoe tracks of someone, and lots of horse tracks.

Someone had grabbed Oggie! Red blinded my vision. "I'll fucking tear them limb from limb!" I said as I started to run.

I had not gone more than three or four miles when I saw them. The murderous thieves would soon find themselves in a hell they could not fathom. The closer I got, the less sense the scene made. Oggie was on the ground jumping around, as was a person. Two horses were on the opposite side of the roadway pulling up clumps of grass.

Oggie started barking, his tail waving crazily as he took notice of me. Red began to peel back to reveal what was going on.

"Lana?" I asked as I approached.

"Surprise!" she said, trying to gauge my reaction.

"What the fuck is the meaning of this? You think taking my dog is a fucking joke? I should tear you apart for that. He is ALL I have, and I will destroy all that mean him harm!"

I had backed her up against a tree. "I meant him no harm, Michael. I followed your trail along the road. When the tracks stopped, Oggie came out, and he looked in desperate need of water and food – both of which I gave him in abundance. I thought perhaps you had gone to hunt, and I took Oggie a couple of miles up the roadway to see if we could find you. We were just about to turn around."

Oggie jumped up and placed his paws on my thigh as if to say 'Here I am, I'm fine.'

I would have wept with relief and joy if I could see past the cloud of anger. I grabbed Oggie, hugged him tight, and began to walk off.

"I brought you a horse," she said to my retreating back. I kept walking; though I had slowed.

"I brought food," she added. I slowed more but kept going.

"There's a place for Oggie to ride on the horse."

"Dammit, woman, I'm trying to leave you."

"Venison."

"Damn you," I told her as I turned back.

"I can travel with you?" she asked.

"Any beer?"

"Beer?"

"I'll think about it," I told her.

Oggie and Lana played as I took my fill. I did not know how hungry I was until I had started eating.

"How, Lana?" I asked when I finally finished. "How did you convince your father to let you go and with horses and supplies?"

"Denarth sent more riders out. They heard commotion all night around the city and were concerned with my father still out there. When they found us, I told him that I could do more for our city out here then back home."

"He agreed to that?"

"I wore him down." She smiled.

"That I understand." I frowned.

"Besides, he will need all his energy to convince the council, not watch me."

"Will they be convinced?"

"Not at first, even with three men relating the tale, one of them being the chancellor. They won't want to believe. But when they drop the body of one of the torn up hounds on the council table, they won't be able to deny it any longer."

"There's a visual I would not like to witness."

"I grabbed two horses and enough supplies for a week and came after you."

"I thank you for feeding us. I wish you weren't coming, but it doesn't look like I'm going to be able to get rid of you just yet. Let's get moving." I placed Oggie up in a over-sized basket that was seated behind a leather saddle on a large black mare.

"Her name is Shadow," Lana told me.

The horse looked scared as I approached, and who could blame her. I'm sure she knew me for the predator that I was. "Let's have an understanding, Shadow," I said as I stroked her neck. "You don't toss me and my dog and I won't eat you – fair enough?" The horse's head bowed quickly, as if in understanding, I don't know. More likely she was trying to get away from my touch. Either way, I think I got my point across.

Oggie seemed to love being king of the world in his specially designed dog transport. My innate fear of anything bigger than me was in high gear.

"Thank you," I finally managed after some distance punctuated with silence.

"You're welcome," she answered. "Are you planning on turning off?"

"Why?"

"Your friends did." She pointed towards an old off-ramp.

"How do you know?" I asked, looking for any signs that would lead me to believe that.

The wheel on your friends cart has a nick on the outside track and it leaves a telltale imprint." She got off her horse and pointed it out. I got down with her as well and couldn't see anything other than an old wagon wheel rut.

"If you say so," I told her as I climbed astride my horse. "Alright, Tonto, how far ahead are they?"

"Ten…twelve hours at the most," she replied without missing a beat. "Tonto?"

"Famous Indian guide. They've slowed up; they're trying to let me catch up. How do they know where I am or if I'm following? Must be witchcraft," I added.

"Your friend is a witch?"

"One of them most definitely is, has it on her identification card and everything. Azile probably has her master's degree is spell brewing. Who knows what power Tommy has?"

"She could have spies everywhere."

That I didn't like. This was almost as bad as the 21st century and a video camera on every corner. "The hawk," I said. Thinking back, it was hunting alright, but a different quarry. I looked up, and although nothing was there, I flipped it the finger anyway, knowing full well Azile knew the intended meaning of the gesture.

"Is that a signal of some sort?" Lana asked, shielding her eyes from the sun.

"Of sorts," I told her as we followed the tracks. "She'll understand if she's watching."

One more night of traveling through and we'd be on their heels. I had the anger and stamina to do it. Not sure about Lana, although she had youth. How many times as a kid had I pulled an all-nighter? However, those were generally chemically induced.

"You okay?" I asked Lana. The further we got from her home, the more nervous she seemed to get.

"I'm fine."

"I've been around enough women in my life, Lana, to know 'I'm fine' means anything but. Homesick?"

"There is one I miss above others. I sent a note back with my father, though."

"Oh, that ought to fix everything," I said sarcastically. "It's not too late."

Although, it really was. I wouldn't feel right sending her back on her own, not this far out. And I was too close to want to turn back. That stupid invention called time that man marked was beginning to press heavily on me. Bigger things were already in motion, no matter whether I was involved or not. What overall part I had in it, I had no clue. More than likely I was a piece of flotsam hurtling down a raging river, no more likely to turn the flow than a submerged rock. At least the rock might cause a ripple or a momentary break of white water but no more. The piece of debris I felt like, was just being swept downstream, powerless against the flow.

"I won't go back," she said defiantly.

"I'm not your father, not that it would matter. You wouldn't listen anyway. I'm not telling you to go back, I was wondering if you wanted to."

"I'm fine," she repeated.

This is going to be a blast, I thought. Silence ensued for miles as we rode on. It was strange seeing the world as it now was. A few years back, when the world of man still existed, I used to watch a show called *After Man* or something along those lines. It talked about how all of our greatest structures would fail and Mother Nature would reassert herself. I enjoyed the computer simulations they featured, it made for interesting thought. In a sick way, it was fascinating to watch how the planet would heal from our scourge. The vast majority of creatures were harmonious with the world around them; they lived and died in the world provided to them they did not try to alter it to fit their needs as humans did.

We traveled through an industrial park, the corroded, rusted-out shells of warehouses lining the roadway. It was mostly the skeletal remains that stayed. The roofs and the walls were mostly gone or covered in aggressive ivy. Steel studs stuck up like the bones of an ancient, long dead animal.

"That would be hilarious if one of those were a Twinkie factory. I'd have to see if the myths surrounding them were true," I said, looking over to my right. Grass nearly chest high swayed in a small breeze.

"Twinkie?"

"Huh?" I asked, coming out of my trance. "Small sponge cake, entirely too sweet for my liking, but it was rumored they could last for a hundred years."

"Sounds delicious," Lana said.

"Yeah, not really." I pushed my horse on.

"They need to rest soon," she said, referring to the beasts.

"How long do they need?" I asked, having no clue.

"About three hours if they get a good place to lie down."

"I thought horses didn't lie down."

"Not generally, but if they can find a comfortable enough place, they will, and they'll be better for it."

I guided my mount over towards the grass. Oggie jumped into my arms once I was down, his feet in motion before I set him on the ground.

I helped Lana down and then removed my saddle once I saw her begin to do it for her horse. The two steeds began to eat, not having to travel too far to do so. Lana stretched, I did the same.

"Rest," I told her. "I'm just going to walk around. All these ghosts of the past have me curious."

I pushed through the small field and towards one of the structures that still had its west wall. I had great hopes it might be a munitions or arms factory. Hey, it's my journal I can suspend as much belief as I want. It was mattresses, rat-chewed mattresses. "What are the chances Colt set up shop next to Sealy?" I asked, moving on.

None to be specific. The warehouse floor had long ago been replaced by a carpet of dirt and grass. Whatever had been here must have been perishable, because it was empty. I smiled wanly and bent down to pick up what had caught my eye. It was a Dunkin Donuts plastic cup, someone had been enjoying an Iced Coffee when the world died. *At least they went out awake*, I thought as I turned it over a couple of times and then discarded it.

That thing would still be there even when I was ground to dust. Vampires weren't immortal; plastic was. When future civilizations come to unearth ancient artifacts, what would they think of us when they found condoms and potato chip bags?

"Fat fuckers, I suppose. Oh, Talbot, they get worse with age," I said, berating myself for my bad joke.

It was Oggie's barking and the horses neighing that got me quickly moving, then I heard Lana.

"What do you want?" she asked. I could hear the tremor in her voice from here.

What I saw when I came out of the tall grass stopped me in my tracks. "It can't be."

Oggie was barking and jumping around the figure that haltingly lurched at him.

"Purpose, come here now!" I said with enough force that he knew disobedience would be frowned upon. The zombie wavered between following the dog and going for Lana.

"Does it have the plague!" she yelled as she came towards me.

"Yeah, he's got the plague alright. What the hell is it doing out here. They're all supposed to be gone."

"What is that?" she wailed.

"Zombie."

"That's a zombie?"

"That's a zombie," I reiterated, studying the creature as it approached.

"How is that possible? The vaccine, the great eradication, we've always been told that none existed. That none could exist."

"A holdover from another time. There will always be some creature that escapes the net."

I wasn't even sure what was holding this thing up; any clothes it had ever donned were long gone. It really wasn't much more than skin-wrapped bones. It was difficult to even imagine what color she had been, all of its pigmentation had turned a uniform color of gray. Its hair and teeth were gone, a snail on a mission would make better time. I mean, not really, but it was going to be difficult for this thing to catch anything living. However, it was still not a good sign; the odds that this was THE very last zombie were not good.

*In this one creature was the potential for another outbreak and with swords as the only weapon...*I left the thought unanswered. Lana turned away as I took its head off. The torque of the blade barely slowed as I sliced through its pencil-thin neck.

"Are we safe here?" she asked, looking around.

"Mostly...I think. Stay on the road, I'll stay here and keep a watch out. I want to travel through the night so the more rested you all are, the better," I told her. I don't know how 'safe' she felt, but the horses had already calmed down and were once again eating as if nothing had happened. Oggie sniffed once around the body and he'd had enough. I knew how bad those things smelled, and his nose was worlds better than mine. "It'll be alright, I promise."

She grabbed her saddle and put it out square in the middle of the trail; she used it as a backrest as she leaned up against it. I had the unenviable task of hurling the zombie into the weeds. It was difficult gaining purchase on it as its skin sloughed off in my hands.

"This is fucking gross," I muttered. The head I kicked and rolled to its final, final resting spot. I found a small puddle created by a deep wheel well and washed the grime off of me as best I could. I looked longingly at the warehouses; wishing one of them was a Lysol factory.

"That adds a new wrinkle. One more thing to keep an eye out for."

True to my word, I stayed close to Lana, not too close, though; the pull of her was beginning to wear on me. I was hungry, and traditional food still held value in my diet, but the blood she thought so little of was sometimes all I could think about. I let her and the horses rest close to four hours if my reckoning was right. Oggie stayed somewhat close after our little encounter, but he still had a lot of energy to expend hunting.

My small fire and the roasting of two rabbits is what got Lana stirring.

"That smells delicious," she said, rubbing her eyes.

"It's just about done." I told her. Oggie was foaming at the mouth waiting for his portion.

"How bad were they?" Lana asked, referring to our

earlier guest. "I've read about them, but the people that were writing about them had never seen them. They were relating stories that had been handed down to them."

"It was a nightmare from which we could not wake," I told her as I stared into the flame. "They were everywhere, fast ones, slow ones, smart ones, and fat ones and they all had one thing in mind. It was a relentless pursuit of the hunted. They were never sated, no matter how much they ate."

She shuddered in the dying sunlight.

"At the height of their reign, they must have outnumbered us a thousand to one or more. Never did the math; the only ones that mattered to me were around me. The only reason we won was because we became so scarce."

"That's not a great tactic," she said as she got closer to the fire.

"Not so much, and it wasn't by design, that's for sure. But the less readily available their food source, the more likely they were to go into a stasis or hibernation. It wasn't uncommon to find great hordes of them numbering in the hundreds maybe thousands just asleep or whatever it was they were doing. We burned them, we burned them all. Well...except for that one." I pointed with a stick to the approximate place I had disposed of our holdout, finally taking my gaze from the flame.

"I'm sorry," she said.

"For what?"

"For all you've been through."

I stood. "Eat before it burns." I strode away, grabbed my saddle, and did my best to undo what I had done when I had taken the thing off.

Oggie was growling playfully as Lana stripped meat off the small animals. The smell was alluring, but my stomach had turned. After a few minutes Lana came over and adjusted some straps.

"Not bad," she told me.

Another five and we were back on the road. Twilight faded to dusk, dusk faded to night and still we rode on. The industrial section gave way to a neighborhood, although, without knowing what to look for, you'd never know it. There were few remnants left. A few shingles, an occasional piece of a toy that may have been unearthed by playful raccoons; occasionally there was a hint of a car or some broken glass. Another hundred years and a traveler would never know anyone had inhabited this place. Maybe that was for the best. I'd always thought mankind was an aberration upon the world, a genetic abnormality that should have died in prehistoric times. We weren't equipped to deal like other animals were. No long teeth, no claws, no heavy fur for the elements. The best that we could muster was huddling in deep dark caves that other bigger animals had vacated.

Fire was the tilting point. One hairless monkey was just bright enough to figure its importance. One lightning strike had spelled a near disaster for the entire world, at least up until the point we got so smart we figured out how to get rid of ourselves *en masse*. If nothing else, we were resilient. How many years would it take until we were, once again, in a position to make our extermination final? Again, it was time to question why I was bothering with what I was doing. Killing Lycan would not let me recover my soul, and I didn't have enough love for man to care, at least what was on the outside of them, the delicious stuff flowing inside was another matter.

"Michael, I can't see anything," Lana said nervously. The moon was currently alternating between shining brightly and hiding completely. Thick, heavy clouds raced past, sometimes blotting out our illumination for many moments. The horses liked this less than Lana. "The horses could get hurt," she added when I didn't say anything in reply. For as little as I cared about man, I cared less for the horses, and if they fell I would drink them dry then cook their flesh.

No horses, however, meant slower traveling.

"Dammit." I got down. I grabbed Lana's lead and began to walk the horses, I couldn't see perfectly, but I was the best suited.

Lana didn't say another word that night, I think a higher echelon of self-preservation had kicked in somewhere within her. I'd almost be able to justify what I did to her if I couldn't see her face when I twisted her neck to the side. I kept my head down, looking for any unsure footing and just marched.

It was a hundred and seventy years earlier in my head – summer break, freshman year. Paul, my best friend who had suffered an end that should befall no one, had come down to my house; he lived about a half hour away. His girlfriend had to work, and I think mine was off on vacation with her parents or busy screaming at babies and taking their candy (she was a mean one, never figured out why I hadn't seen that, oh yeah, now I know, it was difficult to see anything past her large mammaries – sue me, I'm a guy – I eventually got it right). However it happened, it was just my best friend and I. My dad had split for the weekend and my mother had actually moved out of the house for some reason or other, I think the word "infidelity" came up a few times, but I was too wrapped up in my own drama to pay them much heed. Either way, I had the house to myself; well…and Paul…and a lot of beer. I liked the company they both afforded. Again, I'm a guy, sue me. We were three beers in when he pulled out a small baggie.

"Wanna know what I've got in here?" he asked, shaking the bag my way.

"I don't know…do I?" I asked him, enjoying my beer. "Well, it sure as shit isn't weed." I looked at the flat baggie.

"Cid."

"What? You have acid?"

"Wanna take it?" he asked, no more concerned than if he asked if I wanted potato chips.

"Sure," I answered, no more concerned than if he had offered me said potato chips.

It was about twenty minutes on the dot when we began to feel the effects, although I'd be lying if I knew exactly. One isn't necessarily concerned with the mere frivolity of time during a trip. All I knew was that the next time I went to refresh my beer, it was something akin to a quest of near mythical proportions respite with orcs, trolls and one furry beast of a dog named Dusty. Before we knew it, it was dark out and our minds were in shards.

"The hill?" I asked.

We both knew what that meant; I was asking him if he wanted to take the two-mile trek to our old childhood playground. Rumored to be an ancient Indian burial ground, Indian Hill as it was called among the local teenagers was more of a party hot spot. At least until the cops had found a way to get their cruisers onto the expansive parcel of land. The parties had died and moved on. But nostalgia has a powerful siren call to it. Odds were there'd be nothing more up there than the ghosts of parties past and maybe a pissed off Shaman or two.

The night was charcoal black, illuminated only by a sliver of moon no larger than a cat iris. There were a couple of spots that required crossing man-made impediments, but in the middish 80s – 1980s that is – Walpole was still a sleepy town, only on the cusp of becoming a burgeoning yuppie-ville. Once the enemy roadways were traversed came the woods. Trees swayed without movement, a secret language was spoken among them as their leaves rustled in the breeze. The snap of twigs and the crunch of leaves as we moved was amplified and echoed within the cavernous chambers of our minds.

More than once we had to call out to each other due to the darkness; one could almost imagine that they had been lost in the vacuum of internal space. We were walking like zombies, now that I think about it, hands outstretched; not in search of meaty treats, but rather to keep our faces from making contact with oak. I'm not sure how we navigated so successfully without taking an eye out or at least getting a bloody nose. My guess is that the trees moved out of the way. But, like I said, that's just a guess on my part.

I can't be sure how long it took us to get up The Hill; it had become something of a Homer-esque epic by this time, interspersed with bouts of uncontrollable laughter, followed by beer toasting for our latest accomplishment. When we finally did come to the end of our quest – the Great Oak that dominated the open field – we sat and enjoyed each other's company, talking about all manner of profound ideas. I would imagine we solved world hunger, found a way to incur World Peace, and may have turned the theory of relativity into a working model. Of course, if anyone had recorded it, I'm sure it was mostly a couple of guys cooked off their rockers talking about women, sports, and beer and intermingled with tears of laughter.

I tried to hold onto that bygone time as long as I could while I walked through the night. Oggie was snoring loudly in his basket and I hadn't heard from Lana in quite some time. I kept expecting to hear a thud when she fell out of her saddle. I had been looking down at my feet and barely recognized that they were getting brighter. Well, I mean not just them (they weren't on fire) but rather, this region of the world was receiving sunlight again. Birds were chirping and a fine layer of dew was soaking through my boots as I walked.

"Have we been traveling the entire night?" Lana asked.

I looked back at her. "Were you sleeping?"
She nodded.
"How the hell did you stay in your saddle?"
She shrugged. "Can we stop for a moment?"
"I'd like to keep going. They can't be that far ahead of us."

"Okay, let me restate. I need to stop and so do the horses."

"Right," I said, remembering that she was completely human.

Oggie jumped into my arms and headed off in search of grub. The stop turned into a half hour layover as Lana and I ate dried beef…or lamb I think she said. Oggie came back, dejected he hadn't caught anything. I was all too happy to share my portion of the dried lamb, never did like the stuff, but he had no problem with chowing it down.

"Your friends' tracks are fresh," Lana said, scouting the ground out ahead of us. "What are your intentions?"

I had been absently sliding my finger along my sword. "I don't know," I told her honestly.

"We should be able to catch them by noon. Let the horses eat a little more and we can go."

I nodded to her; I deferred when it came to the beasts.

"Do you find me attractive?" She leveled her gaze on me. "I want an honest opinion from a man that is not trying to woo me."

"I find you to be extremely young."

"That is not what I asked."

"And yet, that was my answer," I told her. "Are we about ready to go?" I stood, not at all comfortable in which direction the conversation was going.

She didn't press it as we got the horses into a slow trot. The encompassing woods finally gave way to an opening that looked over an expansive greenway; we were roughly a hundred feet up on a bluff, a trail traversed down the side of the hill and across. In the middle of the field below us was our quarry. Tommy turned and waved the moment we broke into the opening. They were a mile from us and about a half mile from a settlement. My concern was they would get lost in that village. Unfounded perhaps, but I was sick of the chase. It was time for a payout. I spurred my horse on, well, at least as much as someone can without spurs on.

Lana got her horse going. "You should be careful!" she yelled as we made our way down the incline.

"Probably." Oggie had placed a paw on each of my shoulders and was watching intently as we chased down Azile and Tommy. His tongue was lolling back like we were riding in my old Jeep and he was sticking his head out the window. "Having a good time?" I asked him.

He rewarded me with a slobbering kiss up the right side of my face, which was now rapidly cooling as wind rushed by. I had many moments of fear as I pushed my horse faster when we hit level ground; I was being bounced around like I was riding a trampoline.

"Graceful!" Lana yelled as she pulled up alongside.

I smiled weakly at her.

"Get lower and lean forward!" she shouted while demonstrating.

I did as she showed; it was marginally better – from trampoline to the equivalent of four-wheeling without any shocks. How Oggie was staying so steadfast was beyond me. The distance was closing and it was going to be close as to whether I killed them outside or within city limits. I vaguely wondered if the laws would be any different based on locale.

"Just fucking stop!" I shouted at them when I was within distance. "I know you know I'm behind you. The game is over!"

Azile turned her horse around and waited. She lowered her hood and smiled. "The game had just begun, Michael," she said as I pulled up alongside her. "Ah, I see you picked up a plaything along the way. And you called me too young?" she asked haughtily.

"Groupie," I told Azile.

She raised an eyebrow.

"Long story, and it's not like that. She's like every other woman I've ever known. Once they make up their mind about something, nothing I say is going to dissuade them.

And that has nothing to do with this, Azile. You betrayed me, you left me to die."

"By the hands of Alexandr? Hardly. That ancient Lycan was so old his clan had sent him on his *Mojid*, or his final pilgrimage. He was preparing to die when I ensnared him."

"You're telling me that that Lycan was on its final legs? He nearly killed me."

"Yet, here you are." She smiled.

"This a fucking joke to you, Azile? I've been attacked four times since this little adventure has started. Well, I guess three…you can't really count the zombie."

"You saw a zombie?" she asked, looking concerned for the first time.

"Azile!"

"I heard you, Michael. I sprung Alexandr on you so you could get a sense of what we're dealing with…what *people* are dealing with!"

"And then you take off? What kind of bullshit is that?"

"Hey, Mr. T," Tommy said, grabbing Oggie and playing with him.

"A little heads-up from you would have been nice as well!" I directed some vitriol at him.

"I didn't know what she was going to do, and then she told me you'd be alright," he said sheepishly, grabbing a stick so he and Oggie could play fetch and he could be away from the turmoil.

"Lover's spat?" came another voice.

I was still astride my horse and damn near eye level with an Amazonian Goddess. Her chocolate-brown skin was nearly iridescent in the high sun. It took me a moment to notice she was flanked by a couple of other people nearly as impressive as she was, and they were all armed, with rifles.

"What the..." I started.

"You should let me handle this. My name is Azile

Ashon."

"Why has the Red Witch deemed us worthy of a visit?" the goddess asked.

"Red Witch? Is that because of your cloak?" I asked.

"It has to do with the blood she spills," the stranger intoned, I didn't notice any reverence or fear in her response.

"So apparently they know you as well," I said.

Azile looked at me crossly. "We have come on official business," she said, speaking to the woman. "I, along with Tomas, have come to—"

"You wish to bring a vampire among us!" the woman shouted. The two men behind her tightened the grips on their weapons.

Tommy turned to look as if to say 'Who me'?

"What business does this man have with you? If the grip on the hilt of his sword means anything I would say he wished to kill you," the goddess said, referring to me. "A word to the wise, stranger, when one encounters the Red Witch and wants her dead, he should swing first and talk later."

"Your advice is warranted," I said loosening the death-grip on my hilt.

"I will not allow you entry into our city, Red Witch," the goddess told her.

"Bailey, of the house Tynes, you would deny my entry on my sojourn?"

I nearly swooned at the words.

"I would," Bailey responded.

"I have brought Michael Talbot," Azile said as she reached over and steadied me on my mount.

Bailey said nothing for many moments. "What sort of trick is this, Azile?" Bailey questioned menacingly.

"None at all, I can assure you."

"Michael Talbot is myth, a story spun by my Great-great-grandfather. A champion created to be worshipped in dark times. Nothing more…nothing less."

"Yet you name your town after this figment?" Azile asked.

My head snapped up to the wooden sign suspended in the air by two cross beams, it was massive. 'Talboton' - "Nice ring." I said.

I got off my horse and approached the post on the left. One of the men watched but did not bar my way.

I shielded my eyes and looked up. I turned and came back to Bailey. "You are Lawrence Tynes' relative?" I asked, a mote maybe making its way into my eye causing a tear.

She gasped. "No one knows that name! It is a familial secret, he wanted it that way and we have respected his wishes. How, demon?" Bailey asked with vehemence. She looked at Azile.

"I did not know," Azile told her.

"BT was my best friend. I knew as much about the man as any man can know about another." My eyes were full on glossy now.

Bailey turned to look, or more correctly look down. She towered over me. "It cannot be?"

"Oh, it can be," I told her. "I miss him so much."

"It is truly you." She knelt; the two men with her did as well.

"Bailey Tynes," I said as I touched the side of her face. "Can I call you BT for old-time sakes?"

"No!" she said as she arose.

"Fair enough."

"I thought you would be bigger," Bailey said.

Azile snorted.

"Legends often are," I told her. "What are the chances you have beer?"

"What of them?" she asked, referring to Lana and the rest.

"The young lass is my charge, Oggie here," I said, petting my dog's head as he came over, "and the horses, would all love a place to get cleaned up and get some food."

"The rest?"

"I'll deal with them tomorrow." Bailey and I headed into my town; the two armed men remained behind.

"We don't have time for this, Michael!" Azile shouted.

"Probably should have thought of that before you left me with Alexandr the rabid Lycan."

"Lycan?" Bailey stiffened.

"It's okay, my lady, he killed him," Lana informed Bailey.

"You? You killed a Lycan?" Bailey asked.

"You sound surprised," I said to her.

"Your exploits – if they are even half-truths – talk about great victories, but I feel as if I could beat you in a wrestling match."

"I think I would greatly enjoy wrestling with you. Wait...that sounded a little off."

"To be fair, the Lycan was on his *Mojid*," Azile added.

Bailey snorted, "You killed a dying Lycan? How very lion-hearted."

"You're ruining this for me, Azile. Bailey, I do believe he left a little too early on his final quest. I think this was just a practice run for him. That was the toughest old bastard I'd ever come across, except for maybe Jed...but that was eons ago."

"There is not the time to exact your revenge, Michael. You needed to be brought up to speed as quickly as possible, and I could think of no other way," Azile entreated.

"Then why run afterwards?" I asked.

"So I could be sure you would follow and that I could lead you to her." Azile pointed to Bailey. "I knew you didn't want in this fight, I could think of no better way than to bring you to a relation of BT's."

"This whole thing has been a manipulation, Azile. I fucking hate being manipulated."

"See, I told you," Tommy said.

"Did it work?" she asked.

I looked over to Bailey. "I will do all in my power, Bailey Tynes, to ensure your safety and the safety of this township."

Bailey nodded.

"Let the witch in," I said, turning back around.

Azile had got down off her horse and caught up to my side. Bailey had gone ahead to make preparations for our arrival.

"Is it weird I find BT's great-great-granddaughter extremely attractive?" I asked her.

"Yes, yes it is."

"I wanted to kill you, Azile." I told her.

"I thought you might."

"You set me up, and then you sent those men knowing that I'd blood them."

"Another necessary evil," she told me.

"How many more of those are there?" I asked.

"How do you think I got my name?"

CHAPTER 7 – Xavier and the zombies - Winter 2010

The Lycan had moved further south than any of them could remember to do their hunting. The herds of man had dwindled, and it was becoming increasingly difficult in the frozen, hostile tundra to eke out an existence. The lights of the Great Lycan shimmered in the sky as the trio of Lycan led by Xavier entered into the outskirts of Nome. There was a nervous excitement among them as they slunk into this stronghold of man.

"Do you smell that?" Xavier asked the pair. Slate and Long-Tooth both nodded.

"It is the stench of dead men," Slate said excitedly, the gnawing pit of hunger in his stomach not allowing him to think properly.

"We have not yet done anything to cause this smell," Xavier said.

"A rival clan perhaps?" Long-Tooth asked.

Xavier grumbled. It had been his idea to raid the city, and if someone had beaten him to it, they would pay dearly.

"There are so many of them." Slate sniffed the air. "We could eat for the entire cycle. Surely, they will not miss them."

"We will take enough to eat and no more," Xavier said. "These humans are weak and very attached to each other. It is said the women cannot even make waste alone without someone holding their hand."

"How are there so many of them if they are so weak?" Slate asked.

"They breed like field mice is why," Xavier replied. They all dashed into the shadows of a nearby alley as they heard the firing of the hated rifles.

"It must be another clan," Long-Tooth stated.

"And they have been discovered apparently," Xavier snorted. "Fools. We need to eat."

A dog barked off to their right, another joined in the chorus. More dogs barked as lights began to go on throughout the city. More rifle fire. The trio looked around wildly, shadows were rapidly retreating.

"It is like an angry beehive," Slate said, looking for an avenue of escape.

"Humans come," Long-Tooth said as he peered around a corner.

"How many?" Xavier asked.

"More than we can eat."

Xavier looked to the rear, as a column of humans approached. "We have been found."

Slate began to mutter words to the Moon Gods.

"Fool, we are not dead yet. There is no need to ask for a spot just yet," Xavier said.

"Why do they not shoot at us?" Long-Tooth asked.

"Might as well ask me why they rule the world, neither thing makes sense," Xavier told him.

"Dead," Slate said.

"We are not!" Xavier roared.

"No...them," Slate replied. "They are but shadows in this world."

"Impossible," Long-Tooth said as they began to be pushed in from all sides.

"Up," Xavier ordered as they jumped and scrabbled onto a shingled rooftop. They sat and looked down at the throng, all of whose eyes looked up at them.

"Dead," Long-Tooth reiterated.

Slate wanted nothing to do with them and traveled up and onto the peak of the small building. A lone shot rang out;

it had caught Slate high in the shoulder and he had lost his footing, rolling down and past the wide-eyed stares of Xavier and Long-Tooth. His claw shot out just as he fell over the precipice. He landed on top of the humans that had converged in the alleyway.

Xavier and Long-Tooth were leaning over watching, both looking for either the rifles or the sharpened steel the humans used as Slate stood. His left arm hung awkwardly from the wound, his right however functioned perfectly as he cut great swaths in the advancing horde. No matter how much damage he inflicted, they kept coming.

"What madness is this?" Long-Tooth asked. "This is not how the hairless ones react."

"They are trying to bite him," Xavier observed. Lycan do not possess empathy, they are not inclined to help one of their own in a time of need. If he survived they would celebrate his return; if he did not, there would be no mourning or remorse.

"The smell is almost more than I can bear," Long-Tooth said as buckets of black, brackish bile spilled on the ground. Slate was panting heavily from the pain and the exertion of keeping the crowd off of him. Cries would periodically ring out as one of the humans would sneak through his defenses and sample his taste.

"This is madness," Xavier said. "They are trying to eat him." He had never been so distressed in his entire life. "The ram does not chase down and eat the lion, this is madness!" He repeated.

Slate tore through midsections, disemboweling all that came within his span. Throats were sliced open. Faces were halved, and still they pressed. He was finally able to leap high enough to grab the lip of the roof. His claw dug grooves into the roof shingles in his attempt to pull himself free. Xavier and Long-Tooth watched with detached stares, neither moving to grab and help him up. Not that he'd ask for their aid anyway; it just wasn't the Lycan way.

Slate's face peered over the lip of the building before he was dragged back into the fray. The sounds of multiple mouths tearing and rending his flesh dominated, even above that of the firearms being used in different parts of the city. Xavier kept his belly low to the roof as he approached the peak, Long-Tooth following. They were both looking over onto the main thoroughfare, hordes much like the one behind them were approaching, although these men were armed with all sorts of weapons, some more effective than others.

"The humans attack each other. It must be a war. This bodes well for our kind," Long-Tooth said.

The wars of man were well known to the Lycan; in fact, these were among the times that Lycan thrived. With the confusion of men rushing into battle in desperate attempts to kill each other, whole squads could be descended upon and removed without the humans becoming suspicious.

"It is a war," Xavier said, "but it is unlike any war we have ever seen before. Have you ever seen the hairless ones fight without weapons? They always pride themselves on their death dealing machines. Yet these ones fight with nothing more than their hands and mouths. It is more honorable…but certainly not their way."

"Does this not make it easier for us? Humans without weapons, they might as well just walk into our bellies. Our young…our clan…will never starve again," Long-Tooth said happily.

"Wait here," Xavier said, going back towards the alley. The man-beasts had finished off Slate and were beginning to wander away. Xavier leaned down and wrapped his large paw around the head of one of the lingering people. He lifted it up and onto the roof as if it weighed no more than a cardboard cut-out of a human.

Xavier dragged the thing up almost to the top. Long-Tooth was watching with curiosity.

"Why does it not cry out?" Long-Tooth asked. "They are always crying out for one thing or another, like squeaky little rats."

The zombie's mouth opened and closed repeatedly, trying to seek purchase on the meaty flesh of Xavier's paw that was tantalizingly close. Its hands were trying to grip the ribbons of muscle in Xavier's arm.

"Hold its arms," Xavier said.

Long-Tooth moved from his perch and pinned the man's arms down, sitting on his legs as he did so.

With his free hand, Xavier dragged a claw across the throat of the zombie.

"That smell!" Long-Tooth exclaimed, turning his head to the side. The wound went nearly to the spine and still the thing thrust about.

"It is dead and yet it isn't." Xavier moved in closer to peer into the monster's eyes, the zombie biting quicker as Xavier's snout came close.

"Let us just eat him and be done with this distasteful thing," Long-Tooth said, his nose wrinkled up.

"I think you are letting your hunger get the best of you. This one is diseased somehow."

"Human diseases are no concern of ours," Long-Tooth said. And he was right, not that he knew it, but the two animals were so different from each other as to not share enough similarities for any known sickness to cross from human to Lycan although the same could not be said for the werewolf virus that transferred entirely too easily.

"Rip his groin off,"

"Gladly," Long-Tooth replied, always loving the tender snippet of meat and the high keening cries that it produced from his victims.

"With your paw," Xavier clarified when Long-Tooth dipped his head down low.

Long-Tooth dragged his claw down the side of the man's leg, shredding his fake furs and digging deeply into his thigh. With one pull, he was able to rip the clothes free.

"Would have been hardly more than a snack," Long-

Tooth said sadly as he grabbed the man's reproductive organs and tore them free.

"Nothing…" Xavier said, "like he doesn't even care."

"Xavier, I just wish to eat this one and be done with it. Somehow, his stench is making me lose my appetite."

"I've watched you eat, that would be some feat," Xavier said in a rare display of humor. Long-Tooth was salivating and looked like he was going to eat regardless of what Xavier said. "I do not think they are safe to eat." Xavier looked down at the man who was still trying to bite at him. "They smell of the infected."

"I will gladly deal with an upset stomach over this cloying pain I am getting from starving," Long-Tooth said.

"I do not think it wise."

"I would listen to your judgment if I cared," Long-Tooth said, dropping his maw into the man's middle, ripping free his belly and its contents. Xavier noticed bits of human fingers spilling out from inside the burst sac.

The smell was infinitely worse as blood poured down the roof, and yet the man still moved.

"I am done with this. I am finding a way to leave this madness." Xavier stood up. The man immediately bent at the waist and bit a piece of Long-Tooth's ear off.

Long-Tooth laughed. "Now I will have a story to tell on Moonday! How the human ate the Lycan!" And with that, he continued his foray into the man's midsection this time keeping a paw on the man's forehead to keep him pinned to the roof.

"This isn't right," Xavier said. Long-Tooth had created a cavern in the man and still he tried to bite at the paw that held him in place. Xavier peeked back over the edge. The men with the rifles had pulled back and the biters were in pursuit. "Are you coming?" Xavier asked, looking back over his shoulder.

Long-Tooth wasn't moving; ribbons of spittle hung from his mouth. "This meat tastes bad," he said breathlessly.

Xavier crawled back down and ripped the human from Long-Tooth's grasp. He had expected a protest, and was mildly surprised when he received none. He stood and tossed the thing from the roof. They heard it smack against the concrete below.

"Let's go," Xavier said. "There is no one below on the other side. Long-Tooth?" Xavier asked as his hunting partner breaths began to become labored.

"Go, I'll follow," Long-Tooth replied, bracing his body with his arms, his head hanging low, his forehead nearly touching the roof.

"Fool," Xavier spat as he once again went to the top of the roof and over. He jumped down silently; biters began to walk towards him.

Long-Tooth's vision began to dim as veins of white viscous material formed over his iris before congealing into a milky mass he could not see through. "Xavier?" he asked. He rolled off the roof, nearly landing on top of the biter Xavier had tossed. He was dead before he came to rest.

Xavier bounded off, Nome was engulfed in flames. Shots still rang out, he was thankful that none of them were directed his way. The ensuing weeks were extremely unkind to the Lycan. Humans were in an exponential decline. Lycankind as a species was starving, and when the biters finally found their lairs, the Lycan considered it a boon. They descended upon the infected people with a vengeance. More would die from eating tainted meat than the season of the great deprivation.

Word had spread quickly of the human disease, but the devastation had been wrought. Lycan and human were now locked in an unknown alliance for the survival of their respective species. It was during these dark days that Xavier had experimented with using werewolves for his own devices, never out in the open, though; he would have been shunned from his community.

He had lost fifty pounds of mass since the biters had

come, and it had been difficult to not devour the small pack of humans he had found hiding in a remote cabin in the place the humans called the Yukon. He had eaten the male to stave off the worst of it; the female he had meant to turn, but as his canines sunk into her arm, he had lost control and ripped the appendage free. When he realized she would not make it until the following night and the full moon, he finished what he had started. Her whelps had cried in protest as he did so, but they were weak as all humans were. The girl had just started her blood, the boy had not yet matured…and never would.

With his hunger held at bay, he bit them both on the fleshy parts of their arms. Almost tenderly, he was afraid that, if he sunk in too deep, they would soon follow their mother down his gullet. The weather outside was harsh even for a Lycan; the wind howled and snow was driving as he forced the younglings to walk towards the nearest human settlement. He didn't understand how humans could thrive up here. The two he was shepherding hadn't gone more than a mile and already their feet were red and bleeding. The girl had cried about not having shoes, and at the time he had not understand the squeaks of the food.

"We will never make it at this pace," he said to them in his guttural voice. The children had shrunk back as he did so. As distasteful as it was he scooped them up in his arms and loped towards a settlement.

He reached the outskirts of the small city the following day. He could see the columns of smoke from the human fires, and he saw many biters milling about in the streets. He found a large snowdrift and deposited the children into it. He kept his head up and over so that he could keep an eye out for any approaching danger. The sun shone brightly but lacked any warmth, he barely noticed, his fur insulating him against the worst of it.

He turned back to the children when he realized he could no longer see his shadow. The boy was blue and unmoving. The girl had shattered a few of her teeth from shivering so hard. Xavier had grabbed the boy and stripped the meager meat from him. He eyed the girl as he ate, wondering if she would make it until the moon's rising. He almost hoped she wouldn't – it seemed a shame to waste the morsel. Her eyes were glassing over as the sun faded into the horizon. The chattering had mostly stopped and a small smile began to spread her lips. Xavier thought she may be going mad, he'd seen it happen before. The humans did not do well with watching members of their packs destroyed. It made his job easier when they gave up; less squirming around as he ate.

    A cold wind whipped past as the moon began its journey. The top of it cresting over a distant mount. The girl had stilled moments earlier, Xavier had once again been tempted to finish her while warm blood still flowed through her and the infection hadn't taken root. Her hands and feet had turned a shade of black he knew to be frostbite. He leaned in close as a fine down of fur began to sprout along her cheekbones. Her bones cracked as the Lycan virus within her began to force the change. Her mouth elongated into the hideous facsimile of her creator. Her useless human ears sprouted tufts of hair on the ends and began to pull out as if someone had grabbed the tips and pulled violently. A silent scream was plastered in the throat of the girl as her feet snapped and reformed into the oversized paws. Her spine curved like only a severe case of scoliosis could cause.

    "Abomination," Xavier said as he watched the transformation. He'd heard about werewolves and had thought they sounded disgusting just by the description. To watch it happen in front of him had taken on a whole new meaning. The shape tried so hard to take on the form of the greater species but was so hampered by the genetic differences between the two as to create the distorted thing in front of him. He knew it was too late to eat her but thought that perhaps his experiment had gone far enough and that he should just end it.

The minimum of clothes she had on tore from her body as she gained size and mass. Her eyes took on a yellow hue. She looked at Xavier, a wild power in her eyes. Xavier roughly grabbed the beast and threw her over the snow mound. He watched as she eyed the town ahead. She howled weakly and bounded off.

"Fetch," Xavier said as he stayed low and approached slowly.

The girl ran for a pack of the biters even as they saw her and began to converge. The werewolf seemed confused. Messages in her Lycan-infused brain told her she was the predator and all below her should cower. She fought savagely and bit deeply as more and more of the biters attacked. Xavier didn't watch too long, but he did take note of how many biters she had felled and how many more she had distracted. He was free to roam the small city in search of a viable food source.

He would remember next time to bring more werewolves when he found himself almost riddled with bullets. He had taken care of one threat but not the other. In the end, he had sacrificed one meal and taken down six. Even bringing back two to his pack. The tainted humans had nearly cost his kind their existence, and he would forever harbor a deep-seated hatred against them. He already had disdain as they were nothing more than cattle with teeth, but that had turned into a seething, red mass of anger and resentment; one which would propel him in his quest to control the united clans and finally drag man down from its lofty perch as top dog.

He had another lesson he had learned from man: herding. Hunting was exhausting and dangerous. How much easier would life be if they had to do nothing more than pull one from a cell? Feeding them was laborious but they needed very little in comparison. A few rats and some wild onions and the vermin could survive almost indefinitely. At least until feeding time.

CHAPTER 8 - Mike Journal Entry Six

BT was a man I loved, an incredible friend, confidante and ally. A person who I would have given my life for if he had merely asked. I mean I would have questioned him on it, but if he had a valid reason, I would have done it. The last few chaotic years we had fought, the zombies had exhausted us all and strengthened an already steel-encased bond. When he had come to me at the end asking my blessing to leave and see if he could start a life anew, what could I say? I couldn't deny him that. What future did I hold for him?

I had missed him intensely for years, mourning his leaving as if it had been a passing, because, in those days, it was. He had taken a radio with him and we had talked often those first few months. He said he had finally settled – somewhere at the edge of Pennsylvania, I believe. Said he had found someone and they were going to start over, their own Garden of Eden. We had laughed. I don't know if he ran out of batteries or life just got too busy, but our communication stopped. I had momentarily entertained visiting him after the love of my life had passed and then it had sourly dawned on me that he would have as well; or even worse, he would have been so diminished from the ravages of time as to be unrecognizable. I would not replace the image of him I held dear with the shell of an old man who might not even remember me. I never thought about his relatives; it was tough to care about people I had thus far never encountered.

And now his status had been moved from that of mere mortal to god…maybe demi-god. I don't need to piss any other deities off. I lifted my glass of amber pilsner to my mouth and drank deeply.

"They say he started to experiment with brewing when he couldn't find any more," Bailey told me as I showed her how to clink our mugs together.

She looked at me questioningly. "It is a custom of celebration," I told her.

"By the bumping of cups?"

"Well you're supposed to say 'cheers' as well."

"He has many other strange customs," Azile said, sipping on a goblet of wine.

"My great-great-grandfather devoted entire chapters to those customs," Bailey said. "He called them the *Idiosyncrasies of Michael Talbot.* They were so humorous I thought them to be completely fabricated."

I downed a big swig. "Wonderful, he's giving me shit a hundred years in the grave. God I miss him," I said, swigging the rest of the pale ale down.

The rest of the night, at least for me, was spent in a foggy daze remembering past events, forgetting present grievances and some talk of future planning. I left that to the adults as I kept checking to make sure they weren't going to run out of ale any time soon.

I tell you, there are some perks to having vampire blood coursing through your system, when the sun streamed through the small window the following day, I should have been half blinded, head pounding, and stomach swimming in acidic stew. I sat up entirely too quickly and half expected to swoon. My feet hit the floor and I stood with not so much as a hiccup.

"All the benefit of getting a drink on with none of the nasty hangover," I said, stretching. It was out of the corner of my eye I got my first inkling something might be wrong. The blankets which I had been under were still harboring a form.

As inebriated as I was last night it could damn near be anyone, Lana, Azile, Bailey, shit maybe even Tommy. I laughed a little at that part. But what had I done, more importantly…who?

Oggie rolled over, and my heart rejoiced. I had not done anything foolhardy. I wasn't even sure I knew how to anymore.

"Hey, you big lug," I said, wrestling his head. He rolled back over; apparently he'd had a little too much celebration himself.

I opened my door to realize I was in some sort of hotel. A man was seated in a chair right outside my door.

"Sir!" he said, standing quickly.

"Relax. Are you there for my safety or yours?" I asked.

"Sir?"

"I was just wondering why I had a guard."

"I'm no guard, Bailey Tynes told me to stay out here until you woke up and then I was supposed to get anything you might need. And when Bailey Tynes tells you to do something it is not wise to not do so."

"That's a lot of words," I told him, "but I would have to agree with the gist of what you're saying. Anything?"

"Yes, sir."

I thought about BT's brew for a few moments. "Can you make sure my dog is let out when he awakes?"

"Certainly."

"Thank you," I told him, and then I walked down the stairs and outside into the center of a bustling community.

I walked down the boardwalk enjoying the feel of the sun on my face, careful to make sure I stayed away from people so I wouldn't have to interact. I got a few sidelong glances at first, and then it became more pronounced. Folks were beginning to stare…and then I heard the whispers.

Were they talking about me? I thought. *Did they know me for the monster I was?*

I was half a heartbeat away from retreating back to my bed with my furry friend when I caught sight of Azile heading my way.

"It's about time you got up," she told me, like it was high noon.

"Cut me some slack, I got hammered last night. And it can't be more than eight in the morning."

"Seven-thirty, and you do know as a half-vamp, alcohol has very little effect on you, don't you?"

"Well I do now, don't I? Got anything else you want to ruin for me? Like maybe Santa isn't real."

"How can so many things hinge on you? Come on, we've got to talk to the city council."

"How come folks are looking at me?" I asked as she led me away.

"Word has got out."

"Wonderful."

"It could help our cause."

"Oh, I doubt that, but you live in whatever fantasy you want. Who am I to take that away from you?"

"Who is Lana to you?" she asked directly, stopping our forward progress to do so.

"She's a pain in the ass, is what she is. Tried to shake her twice. Had no idea Davy Crockett had been reborn, girl could track an ant on ice."

"Your evasiveness gives me pause to consider."

"You pause all you want," I told her as I started moving again. I smiled though, it'd been a long time since I'd had someone of the female persuasion interested.

She led us back into the saloon; I liked the idea of that, Azile's words be damned, I had been crocked the night before. But having woke without any ill effects, it had given me that damn pause to reconsider her words.

"Multi-functional place," I said as we walked in. I noticed that two tables had been joined together. There were nine people sitting there, Bailey included. Five women and four men, although it was quite possible on further inspection one of the females was a man, as her facial features were entirely too dour to get a read. Well…that and the significant amount of facial hair she had.

Bailey stood and spoke. "This committee has been called to hear concerns that Azile the Red Witch has in regards to the Lycan of the West."

There was some murmuring amongst them. Most of it looked like grumbling.

"I have a business to run, of what concerns are the Lycan to us, Red Witch?" Dour-Faced asked. "We have always known of their existence, they leave us alone as we do them. We should leave it at that."

"Normally, Chairperson Gount, I would agree with you. Choosing to fight the Lycan is never a healthy endeavor. But the time is rapidly approaching where they are going to force the issue."

Chair-thingy Gount flapped her hand at Azile as if to say 'whatever.'

"We have heard your concerns before about the Lycan assembling armies. And yet, not one person east of the Mississippi has ever seen one. Your case to cause hysteria and panic among the population is not well received here," she continued.

"Michael?" Azile nudged.

"What?" I asked.

"Tell them who you are."

"Don't they know?"

"Ah yes, the so-called Michael Talbot, how convenient that you were able to unearth a myth to further your cause," the chair-thingy said. "How old does that make you, sir? A couple of hundred years old?" There was some snickering among the assembled.

"I'm heading home," I told Azile, turning to leave.

"You will do no such thing, Michael Talbot," Bailey said. "You will stand there and convince these people who you are and why we need to help."

"Bailey, your relationship to our Town Forefather is how you won your seat on this council, but I fear that your youth is impeding your judgment. Michael Talbot – IF he was truly a person and not a character in your forefather's memoirs – would have passed years ago. And I have read all of the manuscripts. Michael Talbot would have been bigger.

"I get that a lot," I said as an aside to Azile.

"Michael?" Bailey asked.

"Dammit, Bailey, if you were anyone else except who you are, my dog and I would now be heading home. Alright folks of this esteemed council (dripping in sarcasm, that was) how could I conceivably convince you that BT was indeed my best friend." More scoffing on their part. "We traded off saving each other's lives so many times I can't even be sure who did it more, I mean most likely it was me but I'm not positive."

"Michael," Azile chided.

"Sorry. We fought side by side in a world that had gone mad. We had no idea if we would live to see the next day, if humanity would live to see the next day. But knowing that man had my back made everything just a little better. If he were here now he would not back down from this challenge."

"Our most revered founding father was indeed a man of action and bravery, of that there is no doubt. And perhaps if he was as long-lived as you, he would surely side with you." More snickering. "Or throw you out for the impostor that you are."

"No mention of the vampire thing?" I asked Azile quietly.

"Not in the books he wrote, only his private notes. He didn't want any persecution to find you or Tommy."

"I guess this does seem slightly strange then. A man claiming to be somewhere in the hundred and ninety-year-old range, dressed in burlap, asking you to fight a war with a creature that isn't even threatening you, hell, one I didn't even know about a week ago. Well, I guess to get to point B we'll need to get past point A. I sped around the table and grabbed Chair-Thingy's head, tilting its neck back. I still wasn't a hundred percent sure on sex, had some cleavage, but I'd known a few guys in my time that could have rocked a bra.

The Chair Leader did gasp as I grabbed him/her, but quickly recovered. "Parlor tricks" she (yeah, most likely, but not definitively) said as she stared at Azile.

"These as well?" I asked exposing my feeders.

The color drained from her face, as she struggled to get away from me. "The Red Witch and a demon are in our midst!" she screamed finally, and was able to scamper back as I released my grip. She pressed herself against the wall behind her.

"I'm no demon," I told her. "I carry demons, those of my lost friends and loved ones, which I can never reunite with. That pain is almost too much to bear," I told her, walking back to my original spot so she would be able to somewhat relax.

"Why should we believe anything you two have to say?" another asked, an older gentleman off to the side.

"You don't really," I said, "but in regards to the Lycan, Azile tells the truth."

I think he was about to scoff again until I lifted my shirt, pink welts where the Lycan had clawed me gleamed back at them. His color drained much like the woman's had.

"I received these three nights ago in a fight with a Lycan no more than fifty miles from here. Two nights ago, a small party I was with was attacked by four werewolves being shepherded by a Lycan."

"It is my belief that the Lycan are turning humans to bolster their army. It is well known that Lycan care little for their infected kin. Most times that a human survives to become a werewolf was that the Lycan was somehow stopped from finishing its feast. But that doesn't seem to be the case anymore," Azile said.

"You knew?" I asked her, she nodded. "A heads-up would have been nice."

"If you hadn't stopped to pick your girlfriend up, I would have. I thought we were going to be together sooner, before the full moon."

"She's not my girlfriend."

"That's preposterous," the chairwoman said as she sat back down, I was happy to note she was absently rubbing her neck.

"It is true that Lycan suffered to some degree much like man had with the zombies. They were as big a contributor to man's ultimate victory as anyone during that time. Albeit for differing reasons," Azile explained. "Without us, they stood to lose their main staple. When man was in abundance Lycan were content to stick to the fringes and eat without having too much notice taken of them. Well, that has changed. A new leader has risen among their ranks. Fueled with brutality, he has savagely placed himself on top. He has a hatred for mankind that seems to have no bounds.

"He has determined that he will not allow man to overpopulate the planet and flood it with their poisons that come from an industrialized civilization. He sees a chance to accomplish that. And he is preparing diligently for it."

"Lycan have no stomach for war, they are cowards that hide in human form and slink in the night, preying on the young and the infirm," another gentleman chimed in.

Cowards? I thought, touching my chest. The one I fought seemed anything but.

"They are not cowards, Councilman Merrings," Azile retorted. "It is true they do not usually wish direct confrontation, but that has more to do with survival of their species. Their reproductive cycle is excruciatingly slow compared to ours. An untimely fatality affects them much more than it does the human race."

"So that's why they're using werewolves," I said more to myself.

"Perhaps we should be afraid once a month for more than just our women's cycles," one of the men said. There was a riotous amount of laughter, even the women joined in. Not Azile, Tommy, Bailey, or myself though. I knew better, a man never made fun of a woman's period, at least not anywhere she could hear it.

"Yes, next full moon, when a thousand werewolves descend on your sleepy little hamlet, I would imagine you all should be afraid. Then everyone can bleed alike…women, men, and children," Azile said. That shut them up pretty quick. "When the sun comes up, the unlucky few that are still alive will be picked clean by the werewolves' masters. Let's go, Michael."

"Really? Can I get a beer first?" I asked. She had already stridden through the door. "Dammit," I said as I followed.

"Fools!" she spat as we walked down the roadway, more like a power walk she was going so fast.

"Hard to help those that don't want to help themselves," I said to her.

"Agreed," she replied. Though I didn't know if she was talking about the Talboton residents or myself.

"Hold up!" Bailey said, running to catch up. I wasn't sure if Azile was going to or not. "Red…Azile, please stop," Bailey said with her hand upraised. "I am sorry for the ignorance the council has displayed, they are afraid and this is how it's manifesting."

"How many souls do you have here?" Azile asked.

"Nearly twenty-five hundred the last time we counted," Bailey replied.

"They will be wiped clean within the next few months, Bailey, of this I am certain."

"We have rifles," she replied defiantly.

"I was going to ask you about that." I interjected.

"How many rounds, Bailey?" Azile asked.

Bailey's head dipped.

"We have not progressed to the point where we can manufacture new rounds," Bailey said sadly.

"So you're using reloads which are good for three or four shots before the casing fails. You have held off rogues and renegades with your weapons, which is great. But any sort of battle, and you will quickly find yourself in hand-to-hand combat with a far superior enemy."

"Why are we, alone, put at the fore of this fight?" Bailey asked.

"I am making the rounds, and it has been an uphill climb, certainly, I have not been able to get it through more than a few thick skulls that isolationism can be a favorable tactic when you want others to do your battles. In this case, it won't matter; the Lycan will bring the battle everywhere. Individual towns will never stand a chance It will only be under a united front that we will be able to succeed." Azile told her.

"This is worse than zombies," I said.

"Quite," Azile replied.

CHAPTER 9 - Xavier

The Lycan had, for as long as any of them could remember, taken up residency in the wilds of the Yukon. Sometimes venturing as far south as upper Washington when winters were particularly difficult and food stores had suffered. When the zombies had come, the Lycan had approached them as they would any enemy, savagely and without mercy. And then more had come in numbers so vast that the only strategy afforded to the apex predator was to run. The command had come late and the Lycan had suffered grievous wounds to their clans. Fully sixty percent of their kind had fallen in those first few years before they learned that they could not fight the far superior hoards head on.

They used man as more than a meal, turning swaths of them into an uneasy ally. Werewolves had done as much to turn the tide of zombies as any man-driven army had. When the dust had settled and the zombie scourge had been purged from the lands. The Lycan found themselves with nearly unsustainable numbers and a deep hunger that their remote corner of the world could not quench. With great reservation they ventured further south than they had since mankind had crossed the ice bridge in great quantity. Mankind had been pushed further to the brink and the Lycan had to travel far and wide to feed. It wasn't food that completely drove them; they also had to reign in their wayward children. Werewolves were untrained savages that killed for the enjoyment of it and, if left unregulated, would quickly destroy any vestiges of man.

Some of the Lycan had fought savagely against their own kind to let that happen. Man had been its own plague against the Lycan, and some saw a better world without them. Others argued that man was the reason Lycan were so powerful and without them they would be reduced to shepherds guarding flocks of sheep and cows from wolves. A fracture that the animal could not survive began to form until one came forward and ruthlessly cut off the heads of the opposition – the rest had fallen in line.

"Xavier, our scouts are back." Ashe, the second-in-command, said to his leader who was sitting in an old office chair looking out over the land.

Ashe did not like the fact that they were so high up in what the humans once called a skyscraper. Lycan were not meant to be up this high. The wind howled around them, the glass had been blown out ages ago. The smell of bird scat dominated the area. Xavier was inches from the precipice, his back to Ashe.

"This will all be ours," he said, standing and turning. Ashe was tall for a Lycan, but still Xavier dwarfed him not only in height but also in breadth; it had been no wonder that he was now the Storm King. "How did the training go?" Xavier asked.

"Mostly well."

Xavier's eyebrow arched.

"We lost a couple of werewolves to a village to the east. One was lost, fell down an old well and was impaled. Lost a group to a small band of humans, perhaps."

Xavier was waving the losses off they were inconsequential to him.

"Normally I would agree, but scout leader Smoke said one of the humans was different."

"How so?" Xavier asked.

"Faster than he should have been."

"Interesting, is Smoke up here?"

Ashe turned and walked a few paces, opening up a

door that seemed to be holding on merely by force of habit.

Smoke, the Ranger, came in, even more visibly upset with the height than Ashe was.

"What excuse for failure do you have?" Xavier asked.

Smoke growled.

"Careful or I'm going to see if your arms move fast enough for flight," Xavier said.

A look of consternation passed over Smoke's features. His desire to live won out over any sort of vengeance for the slight. "The werewolves were performing as necessary. We had killed and destroyed three of the men and their mounts we then tracked another six deeper into the woods. The werewolves attacked, killing one of the men. But one that was with them killed two almost in an instant, and then assisted in killing the third."

"Did you fight?" Xavier asked.

"No."

"So you watched as your pack was destroyed and did nothing?"

Smoke shifted uneasily from foot to foot. "My orders were to train the werewolves, not fight by their diseased sides."

"Did you feed from their kills?" Xavier asked. Smoke's head bowed. "I thought as much. They were good enough to eat with but not fight with?"

"Sir, one of the men was an Old Worlder," Smoke replied, licking his maw.

Xavier moved quickly. He grabbed the smaller scout around the neck and lifted him off the ground with one powerful arm. He turned and moved towards the open window.

"DO NOT SPEAK TO ME OF OLD WORLDERS!" he raged. Smoke's feet were dangling over a two hundred foot drop. "Ashe, what do you know of Old Worlders?" Xavier asked as he clamped harder on Smoke's throat.

"They were vampires, my lord," Ashe stated.

"And?" Xavier asked.

"And in the time of Flining (flining was the process of vampires proving their prowess) they would perform their rite of passage by hunting and killing Lycan," Ashe added.

"We came to this new land, Smoke, to be rid of the bloodless ones!" Xavier screamed as he shook Smoke around like a rag doll. "They hunted us into the deepest depths of the world that they could until we were a huddled petrified mass of fur hidden in caves. It was our ancestors that found a way to hide us in plain sight disguised as the humans. We were wolves hiding in sheep's clothing, not because we wanted to but because we had to. The bloodless ones hunted us for sport and because we were a threat to them. Competition amidst the top of the food chain is not tolerated well. Instead of fighting, we slunk off, much like you, Smoke." Smoke never cried out as he hurtled through space, his body cracking open as he violently collided with the earth.

Xavier turned back around as if nothing had happened. "Where was he patrolling?"

"East…by the human dwelling Denarth." Ashe replied.

"Do you believe him?" Xavier asked, sitting back down.

"He was one of our top Rangers. I have no reason to doubt his words."

"An Old Worlder joining in the fight with humans…this could get interesting," Xavier said. "We will be able to exact some measure of revenge on two enemies."

Ashe wasn't as confident. Like all other Lycan he had been brought up with a dark fear of the bloodless ones. "Will they have marshaled an army?" Ashe asked, swallowing back his fear.

Xavier laughed. "Relax, Ashe, vampires despise their own kind almost as much as they do us. They would never unite."

We could say the same about us and werewolves, but

yet here we are, Ashe thought but he did not put it to voice.

"We may have to push our attack," Xavier said to Ashe. "That idiot Smoke may have given our plans away. Ashe, send up a human, I'm starving."

"Right away," Ashe said, bowing and heading out.

A few moments later he returned pushing a small child onto the floor.

"I ask for a feast…you throw me a scarecrow."

The girl was a huddled mass on the floor. Dirt covered her from head to toe. She was shivering from the cold.

"How have these hairless monkeys survived?" Xavier asked, stepping closer to the girl. "Rise, child."

The girl looked wildly about and did as she was told. "Yes." She held her chin high, but her quivering thighs and knees showed her true feelings.

"I'm sorry, my lord, we are running low on stock," Ashe said.

"Then get some more!" Xavier replied.

"Where are you from, girl?" Xavier asked, placing his large paw under her chin. He turned her face from side to side. "You could have cleaned her up before you brought her to me."

"Harbor's Town, my lord," the girl said trying her best not to cry.

"A lot of people there in Harbor's Town?"

"Yes," she replied meekly.

"How many?" he asked, squeezing her jaw until she squealed in pain.

"I…I don't know, my lord. I don't know my numbers."

"Ashe?" Xavier asked.

"Five hundred."

"Wonderful, that will be our test. Next moon we will descend upon Harbor's Town and start our war against mankind in earnest. Now leave us, I do not like to eat in front of others."

Ashe bowed and left. The cries of a girl where quickly replaced by the rending of meat as Ashe walked down the corridor. They weren't ready, not now and possibly not ever. The werewolves would do their bidding up to a point, but they were wild beasts more likely to cause trouble than eradicate it. Ashe was not alone in his disgust about tainting a diminishing food supply, add to that they would have to go out on multiple hunts to kill any werewolves that got away and it just didn't make any sense.

Letting the humans repopulate was the wiser course of action and then the entire clan could cull them at their leisure. They were not overlords, they weren't rulers and conquerors; they were predators that dragged down their prey and ate the steaming pile where it lay. To destroy man was to destroy themselves. He had doubted that Xavier would someday see the error of his ways. He could only hope he would fall in battle before he did any lasting damage.

CHAPTER 10 – Xavier's Past

Xavier's story isn't unique, not the beginning anyway. Lycan, by nature, are not a nurturing race; more than one mating has resulted in bloodshed and occasionally death. Litters are born on blue moons, the second full moon of a calendar month. The rarity of the event and a savage birth are what keep Lycan population low; only one can survive no matter the number born, and sometimes not even the one if he or she suffers grievous enough wounds in the battle. Sometimes siblings will ally if only to defeat a bigger brother or sister. Then, when the common enemy is defeated, they would turn on each other. What results are either the biggest Lycan or the most cunning; and in Xavier's case…both.

It was June 1990, the night Xavier and his littermates were born. His exhausted mother crawled out of the cave and into a nearby stream to wash the stink of birth off of her. The scent could instill fierce fighting if it lingered. Many would begin to remember their birth nights and violence could erupt within the encampment. The odor of it was pervasive in the small confines of the cave. Xavier was the first to open his eyes, the pheromone triggering something primal and instinctual in him. His sister lying closest to him was the first to go as he fell over more than lunged. His placenta-covered jaws ripped into her abdomen as she squealed in pain.

The sound alerted the remaining three. Two of his brothers were able to quickly identify their biggest threat. With nothing more than a weak telepathic signal, they formed a blood bond. Xavier, realizing he was outnumbered, sought out the runt, promising to protect him if he would stand at his side. Lunos knew the lie for what it was; as the runt, he stood very little chance of emerging from the cave. He promised his allegiance only so Xavier would turn his fierce gaze away from him. When his brothers attacked, he pulled himself out of the cave much like his mother had. By the time he reached the mouth, he was standing on shaky legs trying to put as much distance between himself and the cries of pain and demise behind him as possible.

    He knew he couldn't stay. Just because he had emerged from the cave alive didn't mean he would stay that way. Xavier would either hunt him down, or a full-grown would toss him back into the mix – or more likely - kill him on the spot for his cowardice. Lunos' mother snapped at him as he stumbled by; she was too exhausted to pull herself from the water to terminate his existence. Without the pack, his chances of survival were about as good as they were in the cavern.

    When Xavier emerged from the cave, he was covered in the gore and viscera of his dissected and digested kin. He had a glistening wound on his face and leg that would fester for a week, almost completing the job his brothers had started. There was no welcome for him as he emerged – no congratulations, no celebration – just the looks of the pack as they recognized one of their own.

    Xavier picked up the scent of Lunos who had slunk away, and he would have followed if not for the fever that was already running through him and sapping his strength. He lay there for three days; a driving rain had sprung up the second night, making him shiver so hard he had nearly bitten his tongue off. It was the fourth night that he was finally able to stand, and by then, Lunos' scent had been wiped clean. He thought about those days a lot over the years. It was a failure and a discontentment that he had never truly gotten over. His mother had remained quiet about the escape of one of her children, partly to protect Xavier who might be shunned from his pack, but more so for herself for whelping a traitor to their ways.

Xavier grew strong quickly; the scar on his face had been a ceaseless source of teasing by some of the older Lycan – but by his tenth year, no one mentioned it again. He had been lurking on the outskirts of the clan as they ate their latest kill waiting his turn to find some leftovers or coughed up morsel to eat when Triblos and Herrin from the previous Blue Moon's litters located him. They detested the disfigured Xavier.

"It's still alive," Triblos hissed as he came in front of Xavier.

Herrin slid behind the younger pup. "Not for long, though. I can see his ribs," he said as he nipped at Xavier's hindquarters, catching the younger male on the hamstring.

Xavier did not yelp; he would not give them the satisfaction. The two older Lycan were slowly starving him to death, not allowing him to enter into the feeding circle even after the alphas and the rest of the pack got to eat. Not to suck marrow from an undigested bone, or even to eat the hair, the part that no one wanted (but when you were starving none of that mattered).

Xavier turned quickly, showing his canines to Herrin who jumped back. Triblos bounded in and pushed Xavier over, sending him sprawling in the dirt. Herrin pounced, his front paws landing on Xavier's chest, forcing the air from his lungs. Xavier's eyes were rolling into the back of his head as he struggled to stay conscious. To pass out would be disaster, Lycan detested weakness and would finish him off – it was hardwired into them. Those that could not provide for the pack were not worthy to live in it. That and the two that harassed him were low enough on the food chain that they were only a scrap or two above starving themselves. They would tear him apart and devour him before his heart would know enough to quit beating.

Triblos came closer…waiting…expectant, great swaths of drool dripping from his mouth as he watched Xavier's eyes fluttering. "Pounce on him again," Triblos said excitedly.

Herrin raised up high. Xavier pulled in ragged breathes of air, he sat up quickly his jaw coming into contact with the underside of Triblos neck. He latched on, Triblos yelped in rage and pain, standing quickly. Xavier bit down deeper, he was holding on with a vise-like grip. He draped his front paws over Triblos shoulders as the much bigger opponent tried to push him away. Herrin watched in horror, too shocked to react. Triblos eyes grew wide as Xavier cut off his air supply, closing the windpipe to a quarter of its normal diameter. Blood began to flow from around Xavier's mouth as he punctured through the tough hide. He shook his head back and forth violently. Shock was beginning to set in as Triblos' struggles became less furtive.

Triblos fell over on to his back, with Xavier still clutching his throat. Xavier almost lost his balance as he pulled a piece of Triblos' neck away. The bigger Lycan sucked in a wet breath, and Xavier dove back in taking a bigger bite this time. He held on as Triblos bucked wildly about fighting for elusive air. When the animal finally died, Xavier began to burrow through his comparatively soft belly and to the nutrient-rich internal organs for which he was starving. Herrin moved in to share in the kill.

Xavier turned and displayed his crimson-coated teeth. "Mine, unless you want to join him," he snarled. Herrin bounded off. From that point on, Xavier jumped forward in the pecking order. It was still the less desirable scraps he feasted on, but no longer did the pangs of hunger dominate his entire being. It was a year after he had taken out Triblos that Xavier had been able to get Herrin into an advantageous spot. Herrin still outweighed Xavier by at least fifty pounds but he now wanted nothing to do with the more aggressive youth.

It was a moon-less night, and Herrin had gone to the stream in an attempt to catch some fish. This was considered below a Lycan's station, but hunger possesses its own power. Xavier had followed Herrin, always keeping the wind to his front so as not to give himself away. Xavier crept to the shore and hid under the brush as he watched Herrin wade into the water. Herrin looked about, when he was confident no one was looking, he started studying the water for signs of watery travelers.

Xavier hated him more for this, even when he was crippled with the void in his stomach he would not come to the stream for anything other than release. Herrin pounced, the second time coming up with a small fish, which he ate greedily. Xavier knew Herrin had been doing this for a while, his movements were too practiced and his success rate too great. Xavier crawled out from his cover, darkness, and the angle that he approached, keeping him concealed. Herrin kept constantly looking around for any signs that he was being watched. Xavier began to lope on the shore of the stream gaining speed, when he was certain he had enough momentum, he leapt. Herrin looked up, aware that something was not right. He noticed the smaller Lycan in flight towards him and turned to avoid the collision. Xavier was flying past when he snapped down, grabbing hold of Herrin's left ear. He ripped the large appendage clean off as he landed on the other side of the stream. Cries of pain mewled forth from Herrin's mouth as he turned to face the threat.

"You should have just killed me," Xavier said as he paced the side of the stream.

"I should have killed the bitch that littered you." Herrin said, puffing his chest out in an attempt to gain size and intimidate the younger, smaller Lycan.

"What do you think the tribe will say when I tell them that you are fishing?" Xavier asked menacingly.

Herrin growled. "I will finish what Triblos should have," Herrin said as he launched himself at Xavier. "I will feast on your bones tonight!"

Xavier ducked back under the brush, confident that Herrin would not be able to follow as quickly. He had almost misjudged Herrin's desire to hide his secret. The larger animal came away with a significant tuft of fur from Xavier's hindquarters, prompting him to redouble his efforts. Herrin was snapping branches as he chased after his darting prey.

"You'd better taste better than you look," Herrin said from behind him.

Xavier was running out of traversable real estate. The thickets were doing what they do, thickening, Herrin had fallen back a few paces but was now quickly gaining as Xavier was slowing down. Xavier could feel the hot breath of Herrin on his rear quarters. He was waiting for the needle-sharp pierce of pain as he was about to be bitten. He had turned his head slightly to see how close Herrin had come, and when he turned back around, he almost impaled himself on the branch of an oak tree. He pushed off to the right, his shoulder taking the brunt as he slammed into the trunk of the tree. A loud yelp came from Herrin who had not been quick enough to realize the danger.

Herrin had also pushed off to his right, but the branch caught him underneath his left front paw and punctured deep between his third and fourth rib. A barb at the end of the branch was scraping against the lining of his left lung as he panted in pain, each breath sending the sharp wood, just a little deeper, like rubbing a pin along the outside of a balloon. When his lung finally collapsed, he sagged on the supportive branch.

"I hate you," Herrin said with his final words.

"There is no hate in Lycan only fear and death, and tonight you will suffer both," Xavier said as he tore into Herrin.

Five years later he was allowed on the hunts a full ten years before most. Even in his youth he was nearly the size of the elders and almost as smart. The winters where the pack lived were severe; it was not uncommon for temperatures to reach forty below, but no one groused. First off, because it wasn't in their nature; and secondly, they didn't know another way. That was the way it had always been.

Two separate events would shape Xavier. He was in his twentieth season, leading a hunting expedition; something that was normally reserved for someone much older. There was a village fifty miles to the south, normally the hunters would wait until a group of men separated from the larger village, going out on their own hunts, usually for seals and fish. At some point, man would separate from the group and the Lycan would take him down. If they were lucky, they may be able to get two without getting discovered.

For three days, Xavier and his pack lurked around the shadows of the community waiting for someone to depart. By the fourth night, he became too impatient to wait any longer; he warily walked onto the snow-lined streets.

"This is not how it is done, Xavier," Guerros, his second-in-command, said.

"Should we wait another Moon Day while our clan starves, Guerros? I don't like hiding from these inferior creatures. We are their masters, not the other way around."

"Man is dangerous," Guerros said.

Xavier pinned him up against a structure. "I AM DANGEROUS!" he commanded.

Guerros deferred. Xavier's mouth began to water as he smelled the sizzling of rending fat in one of the wooden huts. He smashed the door open with his head, an Inuit boy of about seven stared back at him, dropping his fried blubber onto the floor. Xavier tore him in two with one bite. The boy's mother came out from behind her counter, filet knife in hand. She had not been expecting to see an animal nearly thrice her size. Xavier grunted as he charged, the blade striking off the top of his shoulder. He crushed her spine as he pushed her into a wooden post.

Guerros was next in, and any issue he had with this

type of hunt were lost as soon as the blood lust struck his nose. He tore through the house and found a girl of middling years hiding under her bed. She screamed as he slammed the structure out of the way. That was quickly cut short as he bit through her skull. The small band grabbed their kills and raced home. The feast had been of near mythical proportions as, two other hunting parties had also succeeded; the clan would eat well.

Yutu the Claw, came home to a community in mourning. He was the leader of his village; it was his house that Xavier and his hunting party had sacked. He had cried even as he prepared to follow after the savage animals that had done this. Almost all of the men that were of age joined him for the hunt. Xavier had made great time getting home, but the weather was not on his side, with no wind or fresh snow to cover his tracks, he gave the hunters a perfect trail to follow. With dreaded determination Yutu urged the dog sled teams on.

When the Inuit's began to notice more tracks than the four sets they had been ruthlessly pursuing, they knew they were getting close. They put up the sleds, tied the dogs down and advanced slowly on foot. Within an hour they heard the noises of a great many guttural beasts. They swung to the left to ensure their scents would not be picked up. They crawled up a small incline that overlooked the encampment. None of them had been prepared to witness what they saw. They had believed they were chasing large timber wolves. A blind man at night would have a difficult time not knowing the two animals were different. Human carcasses littered the ground and clothes were strewn about. Heated conversations and arguments erupted over various morsels of meat.

Xavier looked up when he heard the first of many metallic sounds. Men were priming their weapons, not that he knew the sound at that time, it just sounded foreign and dangerous. He saw the wisps of smoke a split second before he heard the loud percussion of bullets being expended. And still he did not know the danger; at least until he saw the head of the elder next to him mushroom out as it absorbed a bullet. The exit wound splashed onto the side of his face as Zugrut fell to the ground in an awkward, splayed out position. His pack was bounding around, unsure of what to do next. Xavier knew where the threat was coming from and was attempting to circle around when a bullet caught him in the hindquarters. He had never before in his life felt the extreme pain like that which was coursing up his side. It tore at him every time he moved, but to stay motionless meant death. He headed towards the stream. The loud sounds that hurt his ears continued on for many more minutes.

  He could not move, so he let the water clean and numb the wound. When he was finally able to venture out, the men and their weapons were gone. Fully two-thirds of his clan had been destroyed; the rest scattered as they ran to save themselves. Xavier sniffed at the wounds the weapons caused, the smell of burnt flesh sticking in his nose as he did so. He looked up towards the small ridge and limped towards it. He sniffed around when one scent in particular caught his attention. It was a familiar scent, smelling much like the boy he had eaten. He had brought this death upon his people. For the first time in his life he howled in pain, not an external, but rather an internal one that could not be assuaged.

  Hunters were fair game when they went out into the wilds. The unspoken rule Xavier had broken was attacking a family at home, and his clan had paid dearly for his transgression. It took Xavier a full week to heal from the leaden bullet. When he was ready, he followed the diminishing scent of The Destroyer. For two weeks he prowled around the edges of the human habitation waiting for a chance. He watched as the people had their strange custom of burying their dead; which he found amusing since most of the dead were in and out of his belly by this time.

  It was the fifteenth night when people finally stopped showing up at the hunter's house. Xavier hated what he was to do now – and as of yet had never done it. His body lanced with pain as he forced it into change. His entire body began to shrink, feet, hands, snout, everything.

"At least that has stayed the same," he said with a snarl as he looked down. It was long moments before he felt he could move; and even then he looked to have the drunken gait of a sailor on shore leave.

"I feel weak," he mumbled. He had observed enough of the human customs to do what needed to be done to gain entry. He knocked heavily on the door, rattling it within its frame.

"Come in," A voice drifted out.

Xavier pushed against the door. It moved slightly, but did not budge.

"It's unlocked."

Xavier growled, his hand came in contact with the doorknob. He fumbled with it until it turned and the door swung open.

The hunter's eyes grew wide for a moment in surprise then returned to their saddened state. "I had heard rumors of shape-shifters. I always thought it was tales to tease the children." A smile creased the hunter's face. "I was wondering when you would come. Next time you may want to consider bringing clothes with you. Not too many people, even the hardy Inuit walk around in the snow without clothes."

Xavier looked down at his body, where he was used to seeing dense fur he saw only a light sprinkling of hair.

"And your ears, they are much too large to be considered human." Yutu said, tipping a bottle of something into a glass. The smell of it was very astringent to Xavier's nose. "Care for a drink?" he asked, showing Xavier the bottle.

Xavier spoke the human words, something he had been taught in his younger years. At first it sounded like he was dragging them through weed-choked mud. Finally he lost his throat clapping tones and moved to more of the soft lilt of human speech. "Are you not afraid of me?" Xavier asked.

"Petrified," the man replied. "But I am also ready to be reunited with my family."

Xavier thought the human was crazy. How did he plan on doing that? "After I eat you, should I shit in the same place I deposited your son? Is this the reunification that you speak?"

Yutu's eyes narrowed in anger. "I figured a savage animal such as you would not understand a higher power. But then again, why would you? You have no soul…there will be no ascension for you. When death finds you that will be the end. Blackness." He slammed down the drink he had poured for himself and quickly refilled the glass. "You sure?" he asked again, showing the bottle.

Xavier took a step closer.

"Hold on," Yutu said. He pulled a large rifle up from under the table. "I want you to know that I could have killed you at any time since you walked in that door…even sooner. I've smelled your funk for more than a week. Out there slinking around like a common coyote."

Xavier snarled.

"I didn't kill your entire clan because I had hoped for this meeting. If I had the courage to kill myself, I'd kill you first. Come here and do what you intended, my family awaits," Yutu said as he once again quickly drank his whiskey. He leaned back and closed his eyes.

Xavier was turning back into his true form as he approached. His less-than-Lycan teeth ripped into Yutu's neck. He did not eat the man in the off chance that by somehow eating him he would allow the man to reunite with his kin.

"I am no coyote," he said as he pushed the man over. Blood ran freely from the hole in Yutu's neck.

A smile formed on Yutu's lips. "Epnic? Braytura? It

is good to see you again."

    Xavier looked about wildly for intruders. "There is no one here," he said to the hunter, but the man would not be saying anything again, not in this lifetime. Xavier walked out the door and ran into the night.

    When he returned, what remained of his clan had come back to the killing grounds. Most wandered around, without a leader they were unsure of what to do next. With so many lost at once, the ordering within the pack had been lost, Xavier came in and quickly placed himself amid the top of the tribe despite being too young. The others followed because it helped to restore order into their worlds.

    Some of the elders that still lived protested mildly, but they were in no position physically to vie for the role. Xavier decided that eating the boy had been the best thing he'd ever done, the loss of his mother in the subsequent revenge hunt meant nothing to him. There were not families in the pack, only individuals with three common goals: eat, survive, and procreate.

CHAPTER 11 - Mike Journal Entry Seven

We were on the road again. Bailey joined us, she was sent as an emissary of Talboton or, more likely, a spy to report back what she discovered. I did not harbor any secret notion that Talboton was going to willingly join in any fight. And honestly I didn't blame them; as of yet, nothing had happened except stories from strangers they did not believe no matter who they were. Lana seemed overly morose with the addition to our party. Oh, she got along fabulously with Oggie and Tommy, but Azile and Bailey were threats to her.

Oh, I love women in all their flaws and foibles. I'd learned long ago that women aren't in competition with men; they are in competition with each other. Constantly sizing each other up for battle, but not with swords, knives, and guns....no, nothing that crude, they use something much more dangerous: their looks and their biting wit.

"I've heard the Red Witch devours her mates," Lana said to me as we were riding along.

I laughed. "I don't doubt that at all," I told her.

"Then I shrink their heads and stick them in this saddle bag," Azile said from twenty yards up. Not sure how she had heard, but I laughed again.

We traveled the next three weeks from town to town; with pretty much the same result we had suffered in Talboton, scorn and derision. We were sitting just outside the city limits of Harbor's Town – a name which made absolutely no sense considering they weren't anywhere near a body of water. Tommy and I were sitting in the back of the

wagon watching Oggie run around in the grass.
"Gonna have to check for ticks tonight," I said.
"Why won't these people listen, Mr. T?" Tommy asked.
"Because it's easier not to. Who wants to think the end of the world is around the corner. If you had come to me a week earlier before the zombies showed I would have called you crazy and shut the door." I paused. "No...that's a lie. I probably would have invited you in and at least listened to your entire story." I paused again. "Shit, who am I kidding? I probably would have quit work and started prepping the house that night. Okay *most* people don't want to think about doomsday scenarios."
"What now, Michael?" Bailey asked, as she approached.
I looked over towards her. She was framed in a midday sun. "God, you remind me of him, and you're beautiful. You're really messing with my head, you know that? He would kill me if he knew I was looking at you like this."
"You're not really my type," she said.
"Too pale? Vamps aren't really known for lying out in the sun. I could try and find some spray on tan."
Bailey smiled.
"Is it an age thing? I mean...because what's a hundred and something years among friends? It's all subjective. It's how you feel, and honestly I don't feel a day over eighty-six, ninety-two tops."
"You haven't answered my question." She continued to smile.
"I don't know really. I'm not even sure why I'm out here. It's Azile's game as far as I can tell."
"He loved you," Bailey said.
"And I him," I told her, my head sagging a little.
"I've read all his writings at least a dozen times. Said you were crazier than a rabid bat, but always found a way

out…no matter how bad the odds."

"Not always unscathed," I said, pointing to where Tommy had bit me and then lifting my shirt to show her where I had gotten shot and where the Lycan had raked his claws against me. "And the same cannot always be said for those that choose to stand with me."

"Do you believe the Lycan are amassing for a war?"

"Azile believes it…that's good enough for me. I just haven't completely decided on my role."

"That does not sound like the man BT wrote about," Bailey said.

"That man died on a rooftop," I said.

Now Tommy's head sagged.

"I have no soul, Bailey. Do you know what that does to a moral compass? It's like having a fan on a pinwheel – thing spins around crazily," I told her. Bailey had a look of confusion on her face. "Fan or pinwheel?" I asked, realizing she probably didn't know either one of the words.

"Both." She replied.

I laughed.

"But I get the idea without any further clarification," she said. "Know what I think?"

I nodded my head in response.

"I think you made up your mind the moment you left your home." And with that, she pulled her horse away.

I watched her leave. Lana was up next.

"We should have gone fishing," I said to Tommy.

"Want one?" he asked, pulling a gummy fish out of his pocket.

"I'm good."

"What do you see in her?" Lana asked.

"Besides being a bronzed goddess, what else do I need to see?" I asked, egging the girl on. It wasn't often I could claim a position of superiority with a woman and I was going to relish it for at least a little while.

Lana snorted and walked away.

"Why?" Tommy asked.

"Why not?"

"You have been alive too long to have learned nothing," he said as he hopped down from the cart.

"Don't choke on that candy," I told him.

I hopped off as well, figuring I'd go down by the small stream and see if I could catch some dinner while we waited for Azile. We had traded in the previous town for a small net, some hooks, and a thin line that looked like it would snap if anything bigger than a sunfish snagged the hook.

Oggie's head stuck up as he heard me walking off. He came bounding over. "Want to go take a nap with me?" I asked. Of course he did, as he stayed next to me.

I found a decent pole – looked like hickory from the feel of it – tied the line and hook and tossed it into the water. Without bait, the only way I was going to catch something was if it got impaled on my hook. I dug a small hole, jammed the pole into it and braced it with a couple of rocks. I wasn't quite sure why I had gone so far with the illusion of fishing, but I was already 'in' so I might as well make the most of it.

I leaned up against a tree; I think the same one that had yielded my fishing prop. Oggie's head immediately rested on my chest. I draped an arm around his neck and pretended to slumber almost as much as I pretended to fish.

I 'lived' in the past; today meant nothing to me, tomorrow even less. I was constantly reliving things that had happened. My brain, which should have been so much oatmeal by now, had been honed into almost a hard drive of information from which I could retrieve data within an instant and with as much clarity as the day it happened. Another 'benefit' of the vampire half of me. No wonder Eliza was such an evil bitch, she never had the luxury of forgetting all the bad that had happened to her. I, however, was weighed down with all the good. I could not forget the love and touch of my wife, the laugh and twinkle of my daughter's eyes. The growth into manhood of my sons. Henry the air-fouling wonder Bully. They were as real to me now as they had ever been. Like a ghost, I could walk in my memories with them. Always seeing but never touching. I knew this to be one of Dante's circles of Hell. And not just any circle…but the most torturous of them all. To constantly see your loved ones and never be able to touch them or interact. To never be able to have their memories diminish, yup, pretty much hell.

"How long you going to stand there looking at me?" I asked, never raising my head or opening my eyes.

"I sometimes forget how enhanced your senses are," Azile said as she strode across the small stream. I felt Oggie stir, but he did not awake. "Fishing I see?"

I shrugged.

"I cannot get these people to listen to me, Michael." She pulled up some bark and sat next to me. Due to the curve in the trunk, she was facing away slightly at an angle. "I fear by the time they figure out what is going on…it will be too late."

"You've warned them, Azile. You can't force them to fight."

"I could," she said absently.

"Like zombies?" I asked, then dropped it. "You've warned them. And if I know anything, they will at least prepare. They may not believe you or want to believe you, but they will still want to protect their own even if the threat is minute. They will post more guards, they will make more weapons, and they'll fix or improve any holes in their defense.

"That won't be enough. Xavier will lay waste to everything."

"Why do Lycan have names? That makes no sense."

"I see the way the girl looks at you."

This time I opened my eyes. "That's an abrupt change of subject. Are you talking about Lana or Bailey?"

"Both. Lana has fallen for you. Bailey eyes you

suspiciously…she does not truly believe who you say you are or your intentions."

"Well, she's the smarter of the two then."

"And what of Lana?" Azile asked.

"Seriously, Azile?"

"Then you won't mind this," she said as she moved in, kissing me tenderly on the lips. I almost pulled back – the betrayal to Tracy almost too much to bear. It was that contact, the basic human connection that kept me there. Although, on further reflection, I was a half-vamp and she was a witch. How much humanity was involved?

Oggie had since gotten up and positioned himself so that his head was near to my own. Our kiss was broken when Oggie decided he wanted to join in. The magic was broken the moment that large swath of tongue rode up my chin, across my lips and the side of my face.

Azile laughed merrily as I pulled away. Her face lit up as she did so, it was a side of her I had never seen. If I hadn't known any better, I might have assumed she had an enchantment spell working. I felt something for her. The cynical side of me thought this was just a ploy on her part to keep me committed to her cause. The other part didn't give a shit. If that look in her eyes wasn't genuine, then she was an Oscar-worthy actress and I would do all in my power to find one of the now useless statuettes to give to her.

"Does this mean I have to buy you chocolates for Valentine's Day?" I asked.

She smiled and tenderly touched my face before getting up and walking back towards our impromptu encampment.

"I feel so used," I told Oggie as I grabbed his face. He went for lick number two and I was able to pull back before he could make contact; he then sneezed abruptly. That, I could not escape as spittle peppered my face. I dipped my head into the stream and exhilarated at the feel of the cold water as it stung against my flesh.

I stayed down there a while longer, trying to wrap my head around what had just happened and what I actually felt about it. When I decided I couldn't come to a conclusive answer, I grabbed my line that not surprisingly had nothing on it and headed back up.

Azile was as aloof as ever, which, considering the dynamic of our merry little band, was probably for the better. I think Lana was pretty good with her knife, and I'd just as soon not have her try and open me up.

"Where to now, Azile?" Tommy asked.

"One more town, Wheatonville, and then back to Talboton before the full moon."

I almost wanted to tell her 'why bother.' Until it happened, it hadn't...and that's how these towns would see it. Also, I was quickly learning that the Red Witch was not widely loved. I was going to have to get that story, soon.

The trip to Wheatonville was fairly uneventful. Azile never once approached me and Lana wouldn't stop. Bailey laughed at every one of the girl's fumbling, inexperienced attempts.

"You sure do have a way with women, Michael," Bailey said, flashing a wide smile.

"BT pretty much said those exact same words. He may have had one or more colorful phrases in there, and he certainly didn't call me Michael, but other than that, pretty much the exact same," I said as we both watched Lana stomp away, which was impressive considering she was on horseback. The girl really wanted nothing to do with me. I think it was that she didn't want Bailey or Azile to win whatever game she thought we were all playing.

"My great-great-grandfather wrote a lot about you and your family and the events that had happened up to and into founding our town...but he spoke very little of himself."

"Would you like to know?" I asked.

She nodded.

"He was a large man." Bailey nodded. "No, I don't

think you're getting the full picture. He was huge and not in a cutesy hippo kind of way but in a charging Rhino sort of way. Man scared the hell out of me for the first few weeks I'd known him; thought he was going to pull my head off like a spoiled child pulls a doll's head off." Bailey nodded in understanding. "I take it that still happens?"

"Mostly things younger brothers do to sisters, but, yes, it happens."

"So you can imagine how I felt."

Bailey laughed.

"And he was no gentle giant. The man had no problem whatsoever using his genetic freak-dom to scare or intimidate people into doing what he wanted to do. Did he write that in his journals?"

"Not quite that eloquently," Bailey answered.

"On top of that, Bailey, I thanked God every night that, that man was on my side. Once we got over our pissing contest—"

"Pissing contest?" she asked.

"Yeah, kind of a non-life threatening way of determining who's in charge."

"And what was the outcome of this 'pissing' contest?"

"Oh, I think BT let me win. I'm not entirely sure why, but the man had more confidence in what I could do than I did."

"He said that you could get out of trouble with no more than a candle and a prayer."

"Did he also tell you about my penchant for getting into trouble?" I asked.

"Yes, he did not leave that out."

"That man sacrificed everything to stay by my side. I know he had family he was never sure made it through."

"He considered you family after he lost his wife."

"He was married? He always gave me so much crap about it, I figured he was a lifelong bachelor."

"She died on that first night."

"Oh my God, that explains a lot of his surliness. I always thought it was because his shoes were too small and they pinched his feet."

Bailey looked up strangely at me.

"Sorry…random thought," I told her. "The longer you hang around me the more sense they'll begin to make. I loved that man," I said with a faraway look. "I considered him family – as much a brother as Gary or Ron." A pang chased through my heart thinking about Gambo singing a Survivor song or Ron giving me crap for finding his secret stash of firearms.

"He wrote that leaving you was singularly the most difficult thing he had ever done, but he could not watch as your affliction ravaged your soul. He said day by day it was taking a little more of you."

It wasn't so much the vampirism that was undermining me it was the slow degradation of those around me. I knew with crystal clarity what was going to happen, and I was powerless to stop it. It is difficult to watch a grandchild be born and know without a shadow of doubt in your heart that you will outlive it. I didn't know how to respond. I was thinking back to that day. I wished him well even as anger bubbled in me that he was leaving.

I was saved from further reflection as Azile called out. "Watchers!" She brought her horse back around to be with Tommy, who was directly ahead of Bailey and me. Lana had stayed directly ahead of the cart when she realized her advancements weren't making any headway.

"What the hell is a Watcher?" I asked, bringing my horse up. "Sounded like a different word for scout. Azile was pointing off somewhere to the left on the horizon. Tommy was straining to see what she saw.

"I'm sorry, Azile, I don't see it," he was telling her.

I thought I might have caught a ripple in the air – much like one would see heat rising from a roadway during the summer months – but there was significant chance that was exactly what I had seen.

"There were a dozen of them heading roughly towards Wheatonville or perhaps Harbor's Town," Azile said, a look of deep concern was etched on her face.

"What the hell is a Watcher?" I asked. Lana and Bailey both seemed to be doing prayers, different in words but with the same context. Tommy was still struggling to see the unseen. Oggie, bless his heart, was asleep in the back of the cart.

"Watchers will usually gather before a great calamity. They play no part in it that I have been able to discover but, rather, are impartial observers"

"Sounds like news reporters," I told her.

"The only difference is they show up *before* something happens."

"That is different." I said. "How big a calamity?"

"Many believe the Watchers are death's tabulators. The more there are, the more death will be dealt," Tommy said.

"Must have been a lot of OT during the zomb-apoc," I answered callously. "Should we warn the towns?" I asked, trying to cover up my earlier words.

"The fools won't listen," Azile said. "They will just believe that I have ratcheted up my rhetoric."

"Should we stand with a town?" Tommy asked.

"Which one?" Azile asked. "They are heading in a direction that could be any of half a dozen, and just because they are going this way doesn't mean there aren't more heading towards Talboton or a dozen other locations."

"I must get home!" Bailey said, tightening her grip on her reins.

"The full moon is less than a week away, does this have anything to do with that?" I asked.

"I cannot be certain, but it would appear that way. The Watchers generally arrive a few days before an event.

They seem to thrive on the buildup, and then the subsequent destruction and carnage."

"Fuck...they *are* reporters," I said. "Maybe worse because they know and do nothing...but not by much. Is it possible to stop a Watcher?"

"Can one stop the rain?" Bailey asked.

"You can get out from under it," I responded.

"Bailey's right, we need to get back to Talboton," Azile said.

I turned to look one more time where the Watchers had been. I wouldn't swear it on a stack of Bibles, but I was fairly certain one had stopped and was looking in our direction. Chills had raced up and down my spine. Whatever I was seeing was entirely too far away to get any refinement from; it was like looking at smoke in gale-force winds and trying to pick out a discernible shape.

"Can't it ever just be pissed off chipmunks or something like that?" I said as I turned my horse around.

We spotted nothing amiss when we got back to Bailey's home. There were two days before the full moon and everything looked, as it should in a thriving, healthy community. We weren't exactly welcomed back with open arms. Bailey had spent the majority of the day in with the elders giving her account of what had happened the last few weeks. I figured by the time she got to the Watchers we would hastily be escorted from the city gates.

Bailey came back a few hours later. "They said you could stay through the full moon and then must leave."

"Convenient," I said sarcastically. "They make sure we're here just in case and then, once the 'all clear' is sounded, we have to get out of Dodge."

"Would you rather be out there, or in here if something happens?" Azile asked.

"You should probably remember who you're asking that question of. The answer would have been the same even when I somewhat liked people," I said.

"When was that?" Tommy asked.

"See? *That's* comedy. Let's go in, and the only reason I'm staying is because they have beer."

I don't care what any of them said, the beer was still affecting me. Maybe it was just a remembered response, but I thoroughly enjoyed the numbness it afforded me. Word of what we had sighted had spread through the town like wildfire, and there was an expectancy that hung in the air. Part hope, part despair. Not many folks were going to sleep tonight. Me? I was going to be at the bar.

That thought lasted until Azile found me that afternoon. "You coming?" she asked.

"I'd rather not," I told her in all honesty.

She kept looking at me.

"Fine." I quickly downed my beer. Noon had long passed, shadows were growing longer. A coolness hung in the air that belied the date. If I wanted to wax poetic, I might have gone with "the cold finger of death was present" but that seemed a little much. Azile and I climbed up into a small turret, crowding in with two archers. It was normally a one-man job, but the council felt it wise to double up on at least this night.

"If one of you starts farting I'm tossing you out." I told the two guards, neither seemed overly amused with my light-hearted threat. Then I began to wonder how I'd feel if the threat of mass-extinction was hanging over my head. I really had the social grace of an ox. The only plus side to this whole evening was how close I got to be to Azile; she smelled like an earthy blend of sage and lemongrass.

CHAPTER 12 - Harbor's Town

The werewolves were kept on short leashes as their Lycan masters led them through the woods – the smell of the humans nearly driving the untamed hoard into a frenzy. Muzzles dripped with long spools of spittle. Large, yellow curved teeth glinted in the burgeoning moonlight. Choke collars were pawed at as werewolves did their best to howl through the constricting devices. Fires were burning all along the human wall-way. The smell of the smoke incited instinctual responses in Lycan and werewolf alike. For the Lycan it was fear, for the werewolf it was the pang for what was familiar and now lost.

"Wait," Xavier said as he walked among the werewolves.

He loathed that he had to use them, that his race was not yet strong enough to destroy the humans grated on him. To use mankind against itself was a brilliant leap on his part, but he longed to be in the midst of the fight and not watching from the sidelines. He wanted to be there when man fell; not need to have the information relayed back to him. The werewolves cowered when he was in their presence, their tails tucked deeply between their legs, more than a few groveling in their fear urine, some whining uncontrollably. It was not lost on him that he was sending cowards to kill cowards.

Then he remembered back to Yutu. That man had not been a coward. In fact, he welcomed his journey into the underworld and the great passing. To be a great leader he would have to remember not to underestimate his enemy – something he had not grasped quite yet. He waited a little while longer until the moon in all its intensity and cruel beauty was overhead.

"Leave the collars on and release them," he instructed his handlers.

Three hundred werewolves raced across the fields that led into the small city. Stalks and crops folded under the assault as they were ground into the dirt. Farm animals were the first to warn of the danger as the silent enemy bounded towards them. Sheep bleated and ran as the herds were torn apart.

"Stupid werewolves," Xavier hissed as the alarm was being raised. "They could have been over the walls before anyone knew it. Now there will be a battle. More of them will die."

"Does it matter, my Lord?" One of the handlers asked. "It is still man killing man."

Xavier spun. "You, of all Lycan, should know the resources that went into capturing this many of the hairless ones. Housing them, feeding them, training them. Once this attack is over, the humans will be alerted to what we are attempting to do and it will be twice as difficult to round them up in numbers. If this doesn't go well, more of us will die."

Yelling could be heard from the village. Questioning words quickly became cries of warning.

Torches began to blaze. The twang of arrows being loosed was quickly being replaced by the sound of steel being drawn as the werewolves drew close. The cries of men were intermingled with the stunted grunting of the werewolves on the prowl.

The moon was making its final descent when the screams began to tail off and diminish into the wind that pulled them away. By the time the Lycan strode in, the village had been destroyed; some structures still stood but would not make it through a winter untended. Bodies and parts of bodies littered the small street that led down the center of town. Werewolves were in the process of turning back into their more familiar form. Some were languishing in guilt and horror at the travesties they had performed mere moments ago.

The werewolves would remember their actions through a haze of confusion and feral feelings. Some, if given the chance, would find ways to make sure they could never again perform these atrocities. Werewolves and humans, alike, who had been injured in the fight, were disposed of with impartial justice by the Lycan. The werewolves who had survived were rounded back up and leashed. Nearly a hundred had died in the attack. The residents of Harbor's Town had suffered far worse. What remained of the settlement was huddled in the town center, in a small, steeple-capped structure that served as the religious and governmental headquarters such as it was. There was a minor skirmish as the Lycan broke through the doors, two old men with pitchforks tried to keep them at bay.

The fight was over before Xavier strode over. Women, children, and the infirm were pushed into the far corner as four Lycan closed in.

"Take the women and anyone of middling years or greater, throw them in the cages with the other infected," Xavier said, his guttural language not understood by the congregation.

"The rest?" one of the herders asked.

"Is it not feeding time?" Xavier asked as he strode out.

It was midday when the Lycan left a smoldering Harbor's Town. The crying as mothers mourned for their lost children was compounded upon by the cries of the ones that harbored the guilt for bringing this calamity upon them.

CHAPTER 13 - Mike Journal Entry Eight

I was down from the small enclosure almost at the same time the moon crested below the tree line.

"Time to pack," I said to Azile as I helped her down the ladder.

"Just because nothing happened here, does not mean something did not happen," Azile said, seemingly angry that she had been proven wrong from the events.

She was not really seeing the bigger picture that, if she had been right, many people would have died last night. Could be part of the reason she was named the Red Witch, but I sure wasn't going to say anything.

Bailey met us as she came down from one of the other towers. She looked exhausted. "Do not leave until I talk with the council. They will convene within the next few hours."

I didn't personally see the necessity in waiting, the sooner we were out of here the sooner I could go back to wherever I was going back to. The world now had Lycan, Werewolves, and whatever Watchers were, I should have stayed in Maine. Right now, that sounded like the best idea. The Micmac sounded like right good neighbors at this point.

The council did convene before noon, but whatever they were talking about was now running into the dinner hours.

"They wish to talk to you," Bailey said, coming to get us.

I was lying on my bed pretending to rest. Azile kept

staring out the window, perhaps looking for a sign. Maybe the Watchers, a one-eyed Raven, maybe even a black cat, I didn't know.

"Then we can go?" I asked.

A haggard looking Bailey looked back at me.

***

"We received a rider," the lead councilwoman said.

My blood chilled, I had only been kidding when I said Azile was looking for a sign…and now here it was. She had said the words so gravely, I knew whatever she said next would not be welcome news.

"Harbor's Town has been attacked," she added.

"How many casualties?" Azile asked.

"All of them." The councilwoman was almost crying.

I was a little slow on the uptake, any casualty would be considered a death and would be thrown in there with 'all of them.' Unless, she was referring to how many had died. I wanted clarification.

"How many lived?" I asked.

"Not more than a handful, they fled to Wheatonville where the rider was dispatched from," she said burying her face in her hands.

"How is that possible? We were just there," I said to Azile. "Has to be fifty miles. He must have pushed that horse hard."

"We now know where the Watchers were headed."

"Hope they had a great show," I said, more than a little pissed off.

"It was exactly as you had said it would be…hundreds of werewolves handled by their Lycan masters. They took the survivors and killed the children. Slaughtered and ate them in the church."

Azile turned away.

"What must we do?" the councilwoman asked. "They

would have decimated our city had they attacked here last night instead of Harbor's Town."

"What you should have been doing the first time I came before you!" Azile spat. "Do you think I roam the countryside crying wolf because I seek attention? I should have forced you into action. That will be something I will have to live with. You and this council, on the other hand, will have to live with your own inaction. I will be back before the third full moon. If I am not, I have been lost. Either way, you must improve your defenses, train your people, and seek out other cities to build an army the likes of which this new world has never seen.

"It's always war," I said as we hit the road once again. "That is the nature of man. If not the Lycan threat, one town would feel another was using some of their resources…whether it was land or water. Or perhaps gold will be rediscovered in one of these mountains and there will be a dispute. Man knows no other way, Azile. Why are you in such a rush to preserve that?"

"I still have my soul, Michael," she said, turning towards me.

"Well, that was just a low blow," Bailey said to me. Azile kept riding.

"I know, right?" I said back.

"I do not see why I must go back home," Lana entreated for at least the twentieth time.

I, for one, would be happy to drop her ass off. I felt like a letch every time she looked at me.

"We have been through this, Lana," Azile said, trying to soothe Lana's ruffled feathers. "You must convince your father to join with humanity."

"The riders have been sent. What more can I add?" she pleaded.

"You are his daughter, your word carries weight. You will have firsthand knowledge."

"I have no such thing," Lana replied.

"You will," Azile told her.

"We're going to Harbor's Town?" I asked Bailey, overhearing Azile's words.

"It would appear that way. I believe she wishes to convince more than just the girl."

"How much of BT do you have in you?" I asked, looking her up and down.

As we rode, I passed a pouting Lana who would not even look my way. That was actually an improvement. I caught up to Azile's lead.

"Why?" I asked.

"That's a very broad question, Mr. Talbot. Are you asking why I kissed you?" she asked with a smile.

"Are you trying to get me knifed in the back?" I looked back, making sure Lana didn't hear.

"We are shielded. She has not heard."

"How powerful are you?"

"We will see. I believe my biggest tests are yet to come."

***

Birds circled the town in great concentric circles. The stench was one with which I was all too familiar. Smoke drifted up from a dozen different areas. Huge swaths of blood blanketed entire walls of structures that still stood. Bodies were strewn about in all manner of pose, with no sanctity for the dignity of the essence the shell once housed. Men were eviscerated, some still clinging to their hemorrhaging innards. Throats were ripped out; bodies were torn in half as if they had been frayed ropes in a tug of war that had finally given out. Some held ineffectual farm implements as weapons; most were unarmed.

"This was a wholesale slaughter," I said, stepping over a headless boy.

"They did not even feed," Tommy said.

"This was a statement," Azile added.

Lana had gotten sick when she encountered her first casualty; he had been split from his groin to his chin, splayed open like the world's most grisly pop-up book, his broken bow still clutched in his hands, the arrow still notched but never loosed. Bailey was faring better, this was not a sight for the faint of heart.

The men had not put up much of a defense; some had been smashed against the ground, their broken bodies now being picked over by legions of carnivorous birds. I could not fault them for doing what was in their nature, but if I'd had a flamethrower I would have made them pay for the right.

What I thought could not get worse, did, as we approached the town meeting hall. What was left of the city population had pulled back to this central location for their final stand. Bodies had fallen over bodies in this hopeless stand. They still writhed as birds fought for juicy spoils. It was then I noticed the naked bodies that none of the birds seemed interested in.

"Werewolves?" I asked, walking over to the fallen form of a small female. A pitchfork had been stuck clean through her neck.

"Other animals will not touch them due to their infection," Azile said, moving towards the hall.

Oggie steered clear of the werewolves and whined whenever we passed a human. If I had my way, I'd be back at Talboton doing my best to erase this vision from my mind, although I don't think they had enough on tap to do that.

"Have we not seen enough?" I asked Azile as I heard Lana retching behind us. Bailey and Tommy were comforting her. She kept walking, and I kept following.

The doors to the hall/church were shattered, the right one completely torn from its hinges. What awaited us inside made outside look like a walk in the park, albeit a bloody walk in the park. I could only hope the women had been shepherded out before the werewolves had done what they had. I will not go into description of the atrocities I saw there, to do so would help to further etch them into my mind, and these images needed no further help. Suffice it to say, it was among some of the cruelest imagery I had thus far encountered in my life – and I'd been through a fair amount.

"The Lycan did this," Azile said, bending down to look at something.

"Directly?" I asked. "Not the werewolves?"

"It seems they waited until the city was won and then they came in for this final deed." Azile stood back up.

"They *are* cowards. I guess that's good to know." I was seething.

Azile said a few words, and a small light emanated from her hand. She tilted her hand and let it slide to the floor. "We should leave," she said.

That was a no-brainer considering the hostility of the place we were in, but if she thought that matchstick of a flame was dangerous, I didn't understand her point. That was of course until I watched veins of flame lick out from the original tiny spark. Everything it touched caught instantly.

"Neat trick," I said as I headed for the door.

Tommy was crying as we watched the building burn.

The zombies did what they did because they knew no other way. They didn't kill for the enjoyment of it; they killed for nourishment. Sure, it was an unrelenting hunger they tried to sate; but it was quite literally the nature of the beast. And that's what I believed had happened here. A creature with cognitive thought had wrought this damage. The Lycan had killed as a display of their power; they were drunk with it.

"You still think the world would be a better place with them running the show?" Azile asked.

I'd seen enough. Man was a seriously flawed animal that would continually strive to find ways to kill other men in new and unusual fashions. However, I was past the point of being able to sit on the sidelines while this new threat came forward. There was no mercy in the Lycan's actions. They would crush everything under the heel (or paw I suppose) of their war machine.

We left Harbor's Town in a somber mood. Even Lana did not have the compunction to argue about her return home. Maybe the thought of being wrapped up in her father's arms right now actually sounded pretty good. If I could have pulled it off, I would have enjoyed it my damn self.

When we got to Denarth we were ushered from meeting to meeting. Her father thanked me profusely for bringing his daughter home unscathed. I wasn't so sure about that, physically she was fine, but she'd never be the same after what she'd seen. I didn't pay much more than half my attention to any one thing people were saying. In my best of times I had a tendency to drift off, and now my thoughts kept being pulled back to that infant child that had been thrown so violently and with so much force he had been impaled on the chandelier that hung from the church's vaulted ceiling. Was it a lucky toss or had the Lycan been trying for just that. Like a trick basketball shot?

Azile got what she was looking for – a promise to help. Lana didn't see us out as we left. Can't say I blame her. If she was smart, she'd try to forget she'd ever met me…met any of us.

"Where to?" I asked. I was downtrodden.

"We go to see Xavier," Azile said.

The gears in my mind took a minute to fit the cogs together. Bailey beat me.

"The Lycan king? You wish to bring us to the Lycan king? Has he not bloodied the soil enough?" Bailey spat out.

"We will see him under the banner of the crescent moon," Azile said.

"And that means *what* exactly?" I asked.

"That means he will have to listen to us without attacking. He will be honor-bound."

"How much honor do you believe a baby killer has?"

I asked incredulously.

"Lycan care not for people. We are a dangerous food source to them and nothing more," Azile said.

"Then I guess my original question still stands. Why will he honor anything when it has to do with us?" I asked.

"He may not care about us, but he will care what the other clans think. He is trying to unite them under one cause, and if he goes against their laws he will appear weak."

"This sounds like a bad idea," Bailey said. "You bring him the Red Witch and two of the Old Ones…it will be a prize too big to forfeit."

"What she said," I said, pointing towards Bailey. "Except for the old part."

"I meant no disrespect," she added to me. "Well…maybe a little."

"Whoa! For a second there you almost lost the ancestral relationship, but you brought it roaring back home," I told her. "I agree though, Azile, you yourself have said he is bringing them under his rule by intimidation and cruelty. Why would he care if he forced them to accept this newest twist?"

"His rule is not absolute. He cannot do as he pleases. As long as he forwards their common cause he will sit upon his forged throne. Once he breaks all ties to their traditions, they will abandon him."

"Are you confident of that?" Bailey asked.

"More or less," Azile said.

"More or less? Are you friggin' kidding?" I asked incredulously. "I am not bringing my dog into that kind of situation, Azile."

"You can leave him with Tommy. He is our back-up plan," Azile said. Tommy was smiling.

"So that's how sure you are of this working. You've already thought out a contingency plan? And what is it if I can be so bold?" I said. I was near to shouting.

"It would be best if you didn't know the particulars.

The plan is not because I fear what Xavier will do, but rather what you will." She pointed at me.

My mouth opened, thoughts were flying about my head, but I couldn't put any of them to voice.

"Is this where BT would have told you to close your mouth, you're attracting flies?" Bailey asked.

"Yeah, something like that. You'll need to work on your timing though," I told her. "Everyone needs a smart ass. And they say I'm the insane one."

***

We had been on the road three days, always heading north. The pace seemed unsettlingly slow considering the urgency that the world had taken on. More than once I tried to urge Azile on a little faster. She was having none of it. The fourth night I got my answer why.

Azile brought our small band of travelers to a halt. A man of indeterminate age was laid across the roadway up ahead.

"Shouldn't we go check on him?" Bailey asked.

"He's naked," I said aloud.

"Probably robbed of all his belongings," Bailey said.

"Or…" I stated.

"Or he's a Lycan," Bailey finished.

I heard some noise off to our right. It was quiet, but I saw Tommy react, so I figured I wasn't imagining it. Azile looked off to our left. It was a trap – a Lycan trap. Now I figured I was among some of the best company I could be in just this event, but I would have felt a whole lot better maybe inside a tank. I wondered if my brother had one of those hidden in his doomsday locker.

The man in the road stood, his transformation happened so fast it was difficult to remember he had at one point looked human. Other Lycan began to materialize out of the woods around us…had to have been a half dozen at least.

We were on the precipice of an attack. It was so thick you could taste it, and to be honest, it was bitter as hell. Oggie was bristling; Bailey had her rifle at the ready. *Game on*, I thought, then Azile spoke.

"I call for a Covenant of the Crescent Moon," she said loudly with not a hint of panic in her voice. I'll be honest, I was scared, and I think so was everyone else in our troop.

The original Lycan seemed to sag for a moment and was rethinking his plan.

"Come, come," Azile said, "have the Lycan forgot the old ways?"

The Lycan growled. "We have not forgotten our laws, Witch. You will have your convening…and then I will tear you open."

My original estimate had been low. We were surrounded by at least ten of the beasts. They had a very disturbing scent; "savage death" would be an accurate descriptor. Maybe I could market it to serial killers.

Our pace picked up from turtle-slow to healthy trot. When we cleared the woods, I realized the reason for Azile's malingering pace. A pale sliver of moon hung over the top of the trees. A crescent moon.

"What are you getting us into, Azile?" I asked, coming abreast of her.

"It is what I am trying to get us out of," she replied, answering nothing.

"You know about this?" I asked Tommy. He shook his head and shrugged his shoulders.

"No talking," our *guide* said.

"Are we not guests of this meeting?" I asked.

He didn't respond.

"Then I'll damn well talk when I want to," I told him.

He turned and came at me. I gripped the hilt of my sword. He stopped; he was in range with his unnaturally long arms. Even with a sword drawn, I would be lucky to give him a shave. He began to sniff the air around him. I saw maybe the slightest enlargement of his eyes and then no more as he turned back. It could have been wishful thinking on my part – his whole fear thing, I mean – I could only hope it was. I was never one to rest on luck. Okay, that last part reeks with sarcasm.

"That's what I thought," I told his back. "Chicken shit."

His shoulders hunched, Azile's head dipped a bit. "Are you trying to get us all killed?" she hissed.

"No. I figured you already covered those bases. If I'm going out…it's with a bang," I told her. (Why? Why? Why? What is my problem? There are times in my life, where I just see red and actions and or words will come out without any sort of filter. Many times I have been able to undo this particular idiosyncrasy with a well-placed 'sorry' or pride-swallowing apology, but I had a feeling our host wasn't going to listen.)

"Take this." Azile pushed something into my hand. I was repulsed and compelled at the same time. I could smell the blood through the leather boundaries of the canteen she handed me. "Drink it all. You're going to need it before the night is through."

I was ashamed of myself even as I uncorked the lid. I saw more than one of the Lycan swivel their heads. They must have also caught wind. I felt like a meth-head that hated himself for what he did…and then I drank heavily.

Night was in full force by the time we were told to stop. The horses were sweating and panting hard but the Lycan looked as refreshed as if they had just awoken from a nap. We were deep in the heart of an old city, which one it was I had no clue. I hadn't seen any signs to give me a clue. The skyscraper we were in front of looked on the verge of collapse. The ground around the building was sheathed in six inches of broken glass. It sparkled like a field of diamonds under the light of the stars.

Our ten hosts quickly swelled into the fifty-plus range as more and more Lycan came to see the spectacle. What I wouldn't have done for a rifle like Bailey's. She had hers cradled in her lap, I wondered if she'd let me borrow it. I saw movement in the lobby of the building. Originally I thought it was a trick of the light as by far the largest Lycan I'd ever had the displeasure of seeing, strode through the front doors of the building, having to stoop down as he did so.

"Fuck, I bet his name is Durgan," I said. Tommy snorted when he heard me.

"The Red Witch seeks amnesty and calls forth the Covenant of the Crescent Moon," our guide announced to the big brute that stood almost head and shoulders over a monster I thought was already preternaturally huge.

"You are foolhardy to come here," the leader said. "We are at war with your kind."

"Xavier Villalobos, the slaughtering of a town of innocents hardly constitutes war," Azile rang out.

"Careful, witch," he growled. "if you wish to live."

"How easily you would brush aside the covenants that have guided your kind for the ages," she said defiantly.

"You are here and I am listening. Say what you wish so that we can end this distasteful meeting."

"I am asking you, Xavier, to veer from this path you have chosen. We have all seen too much death and destruction. No good can come from this."

"No good?" Xavier roared. "A world devoid of mankind would be the best of all worlds. What have you ever brought except death through over-population, deforestation, pollution, diseases, hatred, plague, and war? Those are your terms; we have lived in harmony with nature since the birth of Great Mother. Your kind has lived in direct contrast, always trying to bring nature to her knees, to make her your servant. You have brought both of us to the brink of extinction time and time again. I will not sit back any longer and allow it to happen. We have been given a chance to wipe the stain of you clean."

"You are using the tainted ones to do your dirty work," she said with vehemence. "This is something you have only done in great need, not to wage war."

"I am fighting fire with fire. Your kind unleashed your zombies."

"That was a plague that affected all," Azile offered.

"Brought on again by man," he said.

"What does the Council of Thirteen say about your actions?" Azile asked.

"There is no more council. I am my own ministry." He beat his chest.

"He even sounds like Durgan," I whispered.

"I came here hoping we could avert this disaster," Azile said.

"The only disaster will be among your own kind," he said triumphantly.

"I think you underestimate the humans and their allies."

"Allies?" Xavier questioned.

"The Old Ones do not take kindly to their food supply being slaughtered."

"The Old Ones? You talk as if they still exist," Xavier said, trying to quiet the murmur that had arisen among his people.

"My name is Tomas of the Old World, I have come as an emissary for my people." He arose from his seat on the cart.

"You did know we were coming here. You could have given me a heads-up," I told him.

The Lycan began to talk animatedly among themselves. Lycan and Vampire had been at war since the dawn of time if the old testaments were to be believed. Top of the food chain predators always sought ways to diminish their competition.

"You lie!" Xavier shouted. "Humans would no sooner

ally with the Old Ones than they would the cows they eat."

"You have forced their hand, Xavier, self-proclaimed king of the Lycan. Extinction is a powerful motivator for both. Perhaps your kind will not suffer from the loss of the symbiotic relationship you share with man, but the Old Ones do not wish to put it to the test."

"One Old One will not turn the tides, Witch."

"We are legion," Tomas said forcibly.

"Legion?" I mouthed. Bailey pushed my shoulder when she saw me question him.

"Fool, do you not know a bluff when you see one," she said in my ear.

"Almost knocked me off my friggin' horse," I said, rubbing my shoulder.

"BT was right about you," she said, not elaborating.

Xavier paused before laughing. "You come seeking a peace you know I will not grant and then lie in hopes that I will run scared into the caves we have inhabited for generations untold. I AM DONE HIDING! The world will be ours. You are free to leave. If you are still here when the Crescent has dropped I will consider you gifts to be spread among my people." With that, Xavier turned to go back into the building.

"My Lord, the man on the horse insulted me," our guide said to Xavier's back, pointing at me.

"Ah...it appears that we will yet have fun tonight. I thought this was just going to be a boring war of words. We have an affair of honor to settle."

"We are under the banner of the crescent moon," Azile elicited.

"You who seem so versed in our ways must also know that an insult must be bathed in blood before it can be laid to rest."

"Fucking Talbot," Azile muttered.

"I get that a lot," I told Bailey.

"You are a fool. No one willingly fights a Lycan," she

replied.

"I will fight in his stead," Azile shouted.

"A double dishonor!" Xavier intoned. "You would have a woman be your champion?" he asked me.

"No." I got off my horse. "I meant everything I said to the flea bag. If he wants to try and get a piece of me...let him," I said, standing my ground. Had to have been the damn infusion of new blood.

Xavier sampled the air. "You are not human?" It seemed to be more of a question.

I shrugged my shoulders. "Debatable, I suppose." I was all bravado on the outside, and maybe some of that was the blood I had coursing through me, but on the inside I was a wriggling mass of seizure-prone worms. "Rules?" I asked, holding up my sword.

"Only that you must die." Xavier said.

"Can I see that manual? It seems mighty biased," I told him as I withdrew my sword. "Should have grabbed Bailey's gun." I brought a fist to my forehead. "Wait, wait," I said to the stretching and snarling form of my opponent. "I write these journals, and I'd like to know the name of the beast's head I'm about to sever and have rolling on the ground."

"I am Timbre!" he shouted as he came at me.

I barely had enough time to bring my sword up; the steel fell from my hands from the contact. I had drawn first blood, but I was pretty sure the scrape on his knuckle wasn't going to slow him down too much.

"You lost your toy, dead man," he said.

"Wait, don't you have a journal you'd like to remember my name in?" I asked.

"Do you also name your dinner?" he asked, coming at me again.

Good point, I thought.

It was tough to fathom a creature so large having so much agility and speed. I twisted to the side as he lunged at me, and still he was able to spin and rake a paw against my midsection. He hadn't broke skin, but the Salvation Army wouldn't take this jacket in. My side ached, a little harder and he would have cracked ribs. Already the thing was on the move back towards me. Like some futuristic Parkour, he ran a few feet up the side of a building and had redirected himself back towards me. If he hadn't been trying to kill me I would have marveled at his athleticism.

The only thing I had going for me was how much bigger he was than me. I know, one wouldn't necessarily think of that as an advantage. Instead of dodging, I rolled this time. The air he pushed over my back was cold and rippled with death. I had a purpose as I snagged my sword, comforting in its weight.

"Finish him!" Xavier shouted at Timbre. Like the beast needed any incentive. I don't even think he heard his king over the snarling and the snapping of his jaws. Hell, the sound of his drool splashing on the ground would have been enough to drown out a jet.

He was coming back at me. I had gotten up off the ground and was in a half-crouch, my sword out in front of me. It was a game of chicken as I held my ground. What happened next is difficult to explain as it happened so fast and I was nearly knocked unconscious. Timber slammed one of his large arms into my blade, which unfortunately turned to the side as he did so. The sharp steel sought purchase and was only moderately rewarded. Although, in retrospect, it was probably for the best that the sword turned in my hands as the flat side slammed into my forehead. Blood which I had been containing fairly well thus far, poured from the wound. The blade broke in two as I spiraled to the ground. My teeth rattled from the concussion. Now I know some people *say* that, to use as an effect. I am saying my teeth literally rattled. The pain was excruciating as it spread around my entire skull.

I had a death-grip on the twelve inches remaining, but

I think that had more to do with not being able to remember how to open my hands than anything else. I was swimming in a fog, blood poured into my eyes making vision nearly impossible; that would have been a problem if my eyes weren't rolling towards the back of my skull.

"Get up!" Fired across my brain.

"Is it time?" I asked.

"Talbot, get your ass up!"

"Tracy? Is that really you?" I asked. A lithe form came out of the murky mistiness in my mind. She was initially shadow and smoke before form began to define her. "It is you." I was sobbing on my knees before her. "I've missed you so much," I told her, reaching my hand out to touch her.

"I've missed you as well, my love. You cannot die here," she told me.

"It would be so easy."

"We're waiting for you."

"We?" I asked. Now I had tears to contend with. Even if I could get my eyes to stop turning like a slot machine wheel, they'd be blurred out.

Light as a feather, her hand stroked the side of my cheek. "Get up, my love. Fight this fight, get your soul and rejoin me. I will wait for you forever."

"You were always my favorite wife," I told her (it had been an inside joke between us).

"Timbre comes," she said as she slipped back, her form losing definition and finally dissipating into white smoke.

Not sure how much time had elapsed. Timbre was indeed bearing down on me. I must have looked the captivating prize. Me, on my knees, head bowed, sword half pointed into the ground. A berry ripe for the picking if there ever was one. I could hear Oggie barking wildly, Tommy had a death-grip on him. Words were buzzing through my head. I think they were Tommy's, he was also urging me to arise.

There might have also been an incantation going on from Azile. All of a sudden, my head was becoming increasingly crowded. And, still, the hairy bastard kept coming.

He was now down on all fours loping towards me, I fell back as his muzzle snapped closed where my head had just been. A string of drool caught from the top of my forehead to my neckline. He was still running over the top of me as I was falling back. I brought up the hilt of my sword. I could feel the shiver in my arm as the jagged edge of my broken blade caught him above his pelvic region. The blade at first tugged and pulled in my hands as his forward momentum brought his nether regions in contact with the steel shards.

High yelps of pain pierced the night as the blade pulled against his Lycan-hood. I pitied him at that point; that was no way for anyone to go out of the world – but still, better him than me. He slid to a grinding halt ten feet from where I had lain. I stood groggily to my feet. The entire Lycan crowd, which a moment earlier had been going crazy, was now silent, as crickets began to dominate the night's symphony. Timbre was on his side; his front paws exactly where you would expect them to be. Blood spread around him, his eyes wide with rage and fear.

He kept moving his mouth as I drew near, maybe to ask me to spare him his life or perhaps he thought I'd stumble into his jaws and allow him to win. In reality he was asking me to kill him.

"Talbot two, Lycan zero!" I shouted as I drove the sword into his midsection, twisting it around until it went deep enough to crack into his spine. I gave Xavier the finger and headed off to Tommy's cart. In retrospect it was probably a very good thing indeed that Xavier had no clue what the finger meant or I would have been involved in my second insult-inspired battle of the night.

I had barely the energy to pull myself onto the back of the cart. My head was ringing like I had the bells of Notre

Dame slamming around in there. I was pretty sure Timbre had busted a rib, and no matter how hard I tried, my eyes seemed to want to close.

"This is not possible!" Xavier shouted.

"Sooooo.... I take it this means the peace accord is over?" I asked Bailey.

"You really don't know when to shut up do you? I thought BT was expounding for the purposes of his journal," she whispered to me.

"You guys figure this out. I think I'm going to take a nap," I told her before laying my head down on the hay bed. Oggie stood a protective watch as the world drifted away, I was unconscious in moments, and no matter how hard I searched…I could not find Tracy.

CHAPTER 14 - Mike Journal Entry Nine

It was light out when I awoke. I had dull pains throughout my body. Nothing like the blistering pain I had from whatever night I had fallen asleep. I was looking up, Oggie was by my side sleeping contentedly, and the sun was nearly overhead. I checked my teeth with my tongue they all seemed to be there. I would be using Sensodyne for a month until they felt better. My rib had set; in three or four days I'd be able to breathe without a hitch.

"No Lycan?" I asked, sitting up.

"Oh, I'm sure there's a couple following us," Tommy said from his seat. "How are you feeling?"

"To be honest, I feel like I lost the fight. They let us go?" I sat up

"A small display of power from Azile and their code to honor the crescent moon, and sure, they let us go."

"Why not attack now? Seems like we'd be easy pickings." My head felt like I had been at an all-nighter and I didn't even have the benefit of drinking some good ale. I stepped over the seat and sat next to Tommy. The slight swaying of the cart was not doing me any favors.

"Same reason. It's seen as cowardice to attack an envoy."

"But slaughtering an unarmed village with women and children isn't?"

"They are not human. They view the world differently than we do," he replied.

"It is good to see you up," Bailey said as she trotted

up.

"I didn't know you cared," I told her.

"It would have been bad if you died on my watch," she told me flatly.

I smiled wanly at her.

"Where's Azile?" I asked, looking around and noticing that she was nowhere in the vicinity.

"She's scouting the way up ahead. I think she's setting up some surprises in case our travel companions get a little frisky."

"Frisky? Hardly seems like the appropriate word," I said to him. "Thank you for your encouragement," I told him, remembering his words of urgency.

"You would have done the same for me."

"I've got a feeling I wouldn't have had to. Seems I have an affinity for getting the shit kicked out of me."

"I had been meaning to ask what that smell was," Bailey quipped from behind us.

"God, if her voice was deeper. I could almost imagine she was BT," I said. "That's what everyone needs…comments from the peanut gallery."

She looked at me sternly, I would imagine not knowing what 'peanut gallery' meant and if I had just insulted her or not. Timbre had nothing on her; the last thing I would want to do is make her mad at me.

"You may have been friends with a distant relation," Bailey said. "But we have yet to set our friendship."

"I'll keep that in mind."

"You would be wise to do so." She let her horse fall back.

"You could get kicked out of a convent," Tommy told me.

"She started it." I told him.

"You keep telling yourself that."

"Aren't you on my side?" I asked.

"Not if she's on the other," he smiled.

"Nice, I'll remember that."

"Good to see you up," Azile said, coming quietly up on my side.

"How the hell did you do that?" I asked.

"How are you feeling?" she asked, getting close enough to place her hand on my chest.

"If you press too hard I'll probably fold in on myself." Although I have to admit the touch from her felt electric.

"Drink this." She handed me another leather pouch, as she took her hand from my chest; apparently satisfied with what she had detected. If I had my way she could keep her hand there, it was comforting somehow.

"Blood?" I asked queasily. That sounded about as good as shots of whiskey with a world-class hangover.

"Yapatas root and mulberry."

"Sounds horrible."

"It'll make you feel better," she said as I took the pouch reluctantly.

The whiskey would have been better. Bitter was such an inadequate descriptor; it was like calling Godzilla a pissed off iguana.

"What's the matter, couldn't find any elk piss to make this taste worse?" I asked her gagging.

"Drink it all."

"Are you poisoning me because I messed up the covenant thingy?" I asked her, choking down some more of the vile brew.

"On the contrary, you may have bought us some time. Timbre was one of Xavier's greatest warriors and his death will affect his confidence. He will not strike now until he is assured of victory."

"Not sure if that sounds better or worse," I said as I muscled down the rest of the contaminated contagion.

CHAPTER 15 - Denarth

"Father, I saw what they did with my own eyes," Lana said to her father.

"I am not saying I disbelieve you, Lana. I'm saying that women have a flair for the dramatic." He regretted it even as the words came out. It wasn't that he was attempting to be mean or belittle his daughter; it was truly his sincere hope that she had indeed embellished the grisly reports.

"Is that what you believe, father?" she asked. "That I merely thought up young boys and girls torn into pieces? Perhaps in affairs of the heart I have often thought of my knight in shining armor, but this? Do you honestly even believe that I would have the capacity to think of such atrocities? Not one person remained, not *one*. Have you even sent anyone to look? Talboton received riders requesting help when the attack began, you must have as well."

He had received them, and as quickly as he could, he had burned the message and sent the riders away. He had convinced himself it was for the best.

"What would you have us do, Lana? Assemble an army? We don't have one. You yourself know that most of our citizens are farmers. We have some wall guards and that's about it. We will have to hope that towns more equipped like Talboton can protect us."

"What makes you think they're going to go out of their way to do that? You certainly aren't going out of yours. I do not think there is a single town that will be able to stand against them, father. We may not be next, but we will be eventually. And when they come, no one will be spared…including myself. Or perhaps it's yourself you're more concerned with," she added intuitively.

"Do not let this Michael Talbot cloud your judgment! He is far from the white knight you have sought."

"Is that what you think this is about? Your poor lovelorn daughter can't see straight. Perhaps you're right, father, perhaps after seeing a true man, my mind has been clouded," she said before she stormed out.

The chancellor waited a few moments before calling in the captain of his guards.

"Sir?" the captain said.

"My daughter Lana, I want her under surveillance at all times. She is not allowed to leave the city. I would imagine she will give it a go this evening."

"And what should I tell her?"

"I don't care if you throw her in her room and lock the door. You don't need to tell her anything as far as I'm concerned. The world is far too unsafe for someone to be walking about it alone…especially my daughter."

The captain bowed before leaving.

Lana was already packing a bag when she heard boot steps coming down the hallway. She opened her door and quickly glanced out. Two guards were heading her way.

"Dammit." She closed her door.

CHAPTER 16 - Mike Journal Entry Ten

"We are being followed," Azile said as she stood in her stirrups.

"I thought we'd already established that?" I asked, turning towards Tommy.

"Xavier's warriors have already turned back," she replied.

"How do you know that?" I asked.

"I didn't give them much of an option."

"Always with the half statements. Doesn't anyone like elaboration in this age?" I asked.

"Shh," she said.

I heard nothing except the distant ruffle of feathers from birds being disturbed.

"Let's just wait until nightfall, I'm sure our stealthy guest will attempt to make themselves known in the most deadly way possible," I said cynically.

"If I ever have children," Bailey said, "please stop me if I desire to have you tell them a nighttime tale."

"They'll be bigger than me anyway. They can tell me stories of comfort," I said.

When we finally stopped for the night, it was a welcome respite. Each of us had been lost in our own thoughts. Not more than a handful of words had been spoken the remainder of the day, which was strange, because we had stayed in very near proximity to each other, not yet knowing what was out there or what its intentions were. Although, if I've learned anything in my existence, anything following generally does not have the followees best interests at heart.

"Zombies?" I asked, once I got the fire started.

"Doubtful, stealth isn't their normal forte," Tommy said. "Plus, the stink would have given them away by now."

"Who would have thought they'd be preferable to whatever is out there." I threw another small log on the fire trying to offset the chill I felt.

"Did you truly believe going to the Lycan king and petitioning for peace would work?" Bailey asked Azile.

Azile was quiet for a moment. "No I did not. It was all I could think to do. I felt I had a better chance with that than I did with convincing man to fight. The towns will fight when pressed, but each individual hamlet will not be able to stand up to his assault."

"I should have stayed in Maine," I said – not for the first time – and if I lived longer, not for the last. Azile didn't even have the gumption to berate me for that statement. I knew she had to be feeling a little down. "Although, I guess if I had, I would have never met my new best friend." I reached over and hugged Bailey's shoulder.

She pulled away. "That hasn't been established quite yet."

"Oh, it's only a matter of time. I'm entirely too charming to be denied for long."

"We'll see about that."

Azile stood up abruptly. I reached for a sword I no longer possessed. "I have got to find a weapon with a little longer range than a hand-axe."

"Come forth," Azile said sternly.

"Me?" I asked

Azile whipped her head back at me.

"Fine, fine…come forth," I said.

Oggie whined low, I stroked his back. I caught a flash of something darker than the woods moving quickly by on my right.

"Azile?" I asked.

"I do not know," she said.

Bailey had her weapon at the ready. Tommy was looking in the complete opposite direction from which I was.

"I do, however, think it's safe to say that they are all around us," she did finally answer.

"Maine sounds better and better all the time."

"Be quiet, I cannot get a fix on them," Bailey admonished.

"The fire, Michael," Azile said.

I quickly overturned the pot we had been heating water in. "There goes my bath," I said as the fire sizzled. Darkness quickly enshrouded all of us. A few of the hardier cinders kept going, but for the most part, the night was black as ink. An arrow whizzed by and struck the side of Tommy's cart.

"I fucking hate arrows," I jeered.

A ball of light shot forth from Azile's hands – much like a flare. The entire surrounding woods were enlightened in a bluish-green wavy haze as the ball hung a good hundred or so feet above us.

"What the fuck?" I asked as I saw twenty or so figures around our periphery. The shadows danced as small breezes caught the flare. Some had the heads of wolves, the others bears. It looked like the island of Dr. Moreau out there. "Are there things you guys haven't told me about yet? I mean I'd understand, because I just flat out would have refused to come."

"Tribal hunters," Tommy said, pulling the arrow from his cart.

"Indians?" I asked. "I thought you had an understanding."

"That was the Micmac. I do not know who these people are," he said with some concern.

"I swear to God, if I get shot with an arrow, I'm going to be extremely pissed off!" I shouted.

As if on cue, another arrow was loosed. This time I

saw in which direction and, more importantly, who loosed it.

"Fine, we'll play your game." I easily sidestepped the projectile. I moved with a speed and grace that my miscondition afforded. I wrapped one hand around the warrior's throat; with my other I knocked the bow to the side.

I'll give him this, he wasn't going out without a fight. He reached down to his side towards a nasty looking knife.

"You grab that thing and I'll crush your throat," I told him.

As his hand kept moving slowly towards it, I tightened my grip. "Do you not understand English?"

"I understand your words fine," a distinctively feminine voice croaked out. I removed her headdress fashioned from a fox's head.

"I'm not the forgiving type," I told her as I effortlessly lifted her off the ground. Her feet kicked a bit as she struggled for air. I heard the ululation of a war cry, and then all was still. With my free hand I plucked her knife from its sheath. "A fucking Ka-Bar? Are you kidding me? I'll consider this a spoil of war," I told her as I pulled the sheath free from her leg, breaking the leather twining as I did so.

"Are we done here?" I asked her rapidly stilling form. "Oh, right…I should probably put you down." It was then that I noticed I had a good five or six people around me and they looked relatively hostile.

The woman rubbed her throat, once her feet were firmly back on the ground.

"Let's everyone back away," Bailey said forcibly behind me. She had her rifle trained on some of them.

The woman who I had suspended like a piñata barked in some savage language. The men around us relaxed somewhat, but I had yet to see any of them put their weapons down.

"What are you?" the woman asked.

"No need to be rude, and considering I am the victor in this little battle, it is me that gets to ask the first questions."

"Victor?" she asked. "Look around Old One."

"I'm getting a little sick of that moniker," I told her. It was then I noticed there was another much larger ring of warrior's around us. "Not thrilled I'm in the middle of a Mexican stand-off."

"Why are you here?" the woman asked.

"Spa day," I told her.

"My knife." She held her hand out towards me.

"You won't try to stick me with it?" I asked.

She didn't answer. I didn't take that as a particularly good sign. I handed her the knife hilt first, she held her hand out until I handed her sheath back.

Azile joined in the mix. "Chieftress Inuktuk, it is truly an honor to finally meet you." Azile bowed slightly.

"As well as you, Azile of the Red Order," the Chieftress said. "What brings you on to our lands? You reek of Lycan."

"That would be me," I said, sticking my hand in the air.

"We met with their leader in an attempt to forego a war," Azile told her.

"And he allowed you to live?" she questioned.

"Even the wild ones have laws they must obey," Azile said.

"Come, we will feast," Inuktuk offered.

"Really? Are you shitting me? You just tried to kill us," I said.

"If the Chieftress had wanted you dead, you would be," one of the braves said in a smooshed language kind of way. It was broken English to say the least, but that was the general idea behind his words, and he looked pretty irked that that wasn't what happened.

I pointed at my eyes and then at him in the traditional 'I'll be watching you' gesture. He had no clue what it meant, and I've got to admit I was somewhat amused watching him mimic it.

"You give him the finger, Michael, and I'm going to tell him what it means. So help me. We're going to need their help before all this is over," she told me as we were following the Indians back to their camp. Wait...do I still have to say Native Americans?

It was a strange settlement they led us to; large canvas and fur structures dominated a small plain, some were free-standing with supports made from heavy timbers, others were attached to existing structures that had not yet succumbed to nature. To say it was Indian would be like saying casinos belonged on their land. There were less implements being used here than in the other towns I'd seen along the way. Those towns seemed in a rush to try and get back to where we had once been. I don't know what the rush was; the 'good old days' were anything but.

These people seemed to want to stay in sort of a homeostasis with the world around them. Take only what they needed to survive. That's a hard way to make your path through life, but it's honest. There was some agriculture, couldn't really tell in the night, but it was easy to tell from the planted straight lines that this was not wild caused.

We were 'guests' in the same way mental patients were 'wards of the state'. We were completely surrounded, knives might not been out and bows may not have been drawn, but hands hovered by hilts, and each warrior had an arrow in one hand and their bow in the other ready to nock in a moment. Now, I know there are other dangers in the night that might necessitate this, but it still isn't a comforting feeling when you're the stranger in the strange land.

We were led into the biggest tent structure in the village, had to have been forty feet across, the wall to our right was cinder block and appeared to be the foundation of some old factory, old graffiti still ingrained on the surface. 'Spence' might not have made it through the zombie apocalypse, but his name lived on. I raised my fist in his honor. In the center of the structure was a large fire that looked extremely inviting. And then the strangest thing I'd seen all night – and remember, this included seeing people wearing animal heads in the woods, was over to my left.

There was an old roll top desk almost completely encased in dripped wax, and more being added to it every second as at least a dozen candles blazed. Two guards stood a vigilant post over something I just could not explain, a blue visor protected under a Lucite container. The familiar golden arches logo were neatly embroidered on the front of the visor.

"What the fuck?" I asked so softly I don't think I even said it aloud. It was then I noticed that, had I been paying more attention, I would have seen that almost all of the headwear the warriors were wearing, had the logo either burned, stitched, or etched in. This time I couldn't help myself.

"Want some fries with that?" I asked as I approached the shrine, for that's what it was.

Azile intercepted my course, grabbing my arm and steering me back to the fire. The tent was rapidly filling with the inhabitants of the village.

"You see that?" I asked her.

"I have. You had best think twice, no make that three times, before you say anything condescending."

"Me?" I asked incredulously.

"It obviously means something of great significance to them."

"Me too," I told her indignantly. "What I wouldn't do for a Quarter Pounder with cheese."

"Michael," she admonished me.

"These people don't strike me as Native Americans," I said in her ear. "Shit, I'm darker than most of them, and I'm of European descent. Plus, I don't go out much."

"I will give you an incurable case of diarrhea if you don't shut up."

I stopped short. "Wait…can you really do that? I don't want to know. Although, if I wake up with a gurgling stomach I will always make sure I am upwind of you."

"Stop."

Oggie and Tommy were sitting on a large plank bench by the fire, Bailey was nervously pacing behind them. We all had to give up our weapons before entering the sacred tent and she was not dealing with it very well. Azile possessed a strength I did not think a woman of her stature could as she pretty much placed me in a spot next to Tommy.

"Witchcraft?" I asked her. I had to have some excuse to how easily she manhandled me.

"Whatever it takes to shut you up." She sat next to me. She grabbed my hand, but I think it was more so that she could squeeze the living shit out of my digits if I started to say anything that might get us into trouble. I felt like we were in a zoo as seemingly the entire population walked by us; more than one would reach out and touch Bailey. I couldn't blame them, if any among us looked like the gods of old, it was her. Bailey was statuesque, beautiful, dark, and deadly. She seemed none too happy to be the object of so much attention.

"If one more person tries to touch my hair, I will break their fingers," she growled.

That seemed to endear the throng to her more.

"See! She can say some stuff and they're not throwing stones at her," I said, trying to further my case. Somehow, Azile made my pointer finger and pinkie touch. "Fine!" I blurted out.

Bailey stepped over the bench and nestled herself between Tommy and me; it seemed the crowd was in no great rush to get by our sides, and that she was marginally safer under our wings.

"Having fun?" I asked her.

She rolled her eyes.

People began to settle down. Rough, woven blankets

were set down as they began to sit. The murmurs quickly diminished and then, somehow, the fire went from this blazing inferno to something you'd expect to see in a responsible Boy Scout's camp, although I'd never been to a Boy Scout's camp, having had a problem with authority even back then. Well, to be honest, I never had the opportunity to join; I had been tossed from the Cub Scouts and banned from future events. It was a mess, just some political bullshit.

"Magic?" I asked Azile, pointing towards the flame.

"It is not magic, it is more a harnessing of the earth's energy."

"So, magic then?" I winced as she squeezed my fingers.

"In the beginning," Inuktuk spoke as she entered the structure, "the world of man was poisoned with the curse of 'The Death'. This was his transgression for questioning the might of the one true leader. Man fought back, finding ways to extend lives unnaturally…even approaching the point of immortality."

"Not all it's cracked up to be," I said so softly that even Azile with her bat ears couldn't pick it up. Tommy looked over though and smiled sadly. He knew.

"The Creator watched as His wayward children played with a fire they could not control." On cue the fire blazed up for a brief second, the crowd 'oohed' and 'aahed.' I noticed as Azile swiveled her head around; probably looking for the special-effects supervisor. "He became angry, His children had turned their back on Him, and like any good father, he needed to teach them a lesson. The dead were brought back to drag man down from their lofty perch."

Inuktuk's words were mesmerizing to the gathering. Women clutched children, men hugged their women. Eyes were wide with fright.

I wanted to shout what kind of God would do that, but that seemed wholly unacceptable. Man had been his own downfall; he needed little help from outside sources to destroy himself.

"The dead destroyed life, cleansing it away like the pestilence that it was."

"This is rich," I said, barely holding on to my rising anger. The cleansing away she so casually talked about were my family and friends. "What do you know about the cleansing?" I shouted. I think Azile broke one of my fingers as I stood.

The crowd had completely hushed as they all looked to me, I had interrupted something important, a ceremony they'd probably been having for years.

"I knew those people that were 'cleansed' as you so eloquently put it. They weren't vying for God's positions. They didn't want immortality…they wanted to live and to love. They worked hard to provide for their families, they were normal people who put too much trust in a government that did not have their best interests at heart. So, don't you stand there all high and mighty talking about how they were struck down by a vengeful God. You weren't there. It was people listening to misguided leaders that got us in this world of shit! They spoke lies and the populace believed it, maybe because they didn't think they'd be lied to," I said, pointing at Inuktuk

"Michael, we are guests here," Azile said from my side. "Who are we to question their beliefs?" She tried to pull me down and minimize the damage.

I was shaking with rage. "Beliefs mired in ignorance," I said.

Inuktuk clamped her lips. I could tell she was not used to having her authority questioned. Her eyes bore into me. Bailey stood up as a few armed guards began to move in from the periphery.

She waved them away. "It is not often that we can talk about The Purge with someone who was actually in attendance."

Had I not been so focused on my rage I would not

have missed her reference of 'often'. She did not say 'We have never had the opportunity to talk about The Purge with someone who was actually in attendance.'

"Well, then isn't it your lucky day," I told her.

"May I continue?" Inuktuk asked. "This is more a story of our origins than of your struggle to survive."

"Yeah, let's get this over with," I told her.

Azile sat, rubbing her hand across her face. I followed suit and sat. It was many long minutes before Bailey felt comfortable enough to join us.

"What is it about Tynes' that always feel the need to protect your ass?" Bailey said softly in my ear.

"I must be winning you over," I told her. I was slightly uncomfortable as I realized we were still being watched intently.

"I'm listening," I told Inuktuk.

"When the world seemed at its darkest, one man arose," Inuktuk said, and as a practiced chorus, the crowd chanted, "Samir, Samir, Samir."

"Samir?" I asked. "Fuck that sounds familiar," I said, hardly above a whisper. I saw Azile's lips moving, I think she was prepping an incantation that would keep me wrapped head to toe in heavy cloth if I so much as made a move to scratch my nose.

"The Great French architect," Inuktuk continued, "came forth from the Wild West and, with his Golden Arches, lit the way for a new people."

The chorus started again. "Landians, Landians, Landians." They were swaying to their words.

"What do they put in the water around here, I could go for a glass."

"Talbot, shut the fuck up," Bailey said.

"Ah…there's the Tynes blood line ringing forth," I said to her.

The pieces started falling into place and it started with a pickle. Samir worked at McDonald's. The great French architect was more of a Fry Tech than an architect. I'd had an encounter with him many long years ago. It was a bad day at that point in my life, but nothing in comparison to the ones that were merely right around the corner. Was it all just some elaborate cosmic joke that he would survive the zom-apoc to create this community? I'd like to say yes, but I don't put much stock in coincidence.

    Samir, a hard working immigrant from India, had destroyed my McDonald's order that had quickly spiraled out of control and into a pickle tossing fiasco. You'll have to find one of my zombie journals for a clearer explanation.

    Inuktuk continued. "He knew to keep his people safe he would have to distance himself as much as possible from man's modern ways. Away from the sky flyers, away from the spider web of information called 'the net.' Away from the poisons that were routinely injected into our bodies."

    He got that part right.

    "He began to live off the land like our great ancestors did, taking only what we needed, leaving the rest. We became one with the land, thus naming ourselves Landians."

    The chorus started up again, the whole Landians thing. Maybe with a little mescaline this could be palatable, just needed a drum circle and we'd be all set. She droned on for most of the night. I had zoned out a while back. I know myself well enough that if I had stayed tuned in I would have taken offense to something and voiced my opinion no matter the consequences. Somehow, being drawn and quartered didn't fit well into my future plans.

CHAPTER 17 - Mike Journal Entry Eleven

"Where you been?" Azile asked.

"Huh?" was my informed response.

"Haven't heard so much as a peep out of you, and I know I'm not powerful enough to keep you quiet for that extent of time," she said, a look between a smile and concern on her face. I've got to admit, it was somewhat alluring.

"Different time," I told her, trying to shake the cobwebs of old thoughts from my mind. The crowd around the fire had thinned considerably. The major players were still in play.

"My name is Amy," the woman I only knew as Inuktuk explained when she discovered we were the only ones remaining. "Amy McNea, as a matter of fact. I took the name Inuktuk after I became their leader. Read it in an old book, most of it was falling apart in my hands, not sure if the person was male, female, good or bad. Could have been a dog for all I know," she said with a smile. "But it sounded powerful, like a name that should be leading the last of the free peoples"

I agreed silently with her, there were names that inspired people to follow: Stonewall Jackson, Hannibal, Caesar, MacArthur, Jesus. How far would Fred have gotten? *Fred the Mighty!* I thought. It brought a smile to my face. What can I say? I'm easily distracted.

"We have kept an eye on the Lycan as they have moved further east. Their numbers remain relatively low," she said. "Certainly not enough to threaten man."

"Normally I would agree with you, Inu—"

"Amy, please. Inuktuk is such a mouthful, and it's nice to hear my given name from time to time."

"Amy," Azile corrected. "Something has shifted in the mindset of the Lycan. No longer are they content to stay in their corner of the world. Their new leader has decided that he does not want to lurk in the shadows. He wants for power, for absolute power…and is turning man against his own kind."

"Looks like you'll get your 'cleansing' after all," I said bitterly.

I think Amy wanted to pull her black knife out and ram it down my throat. Funny how pissed off people get when you talk about the destruction of the folks they love.

"Really, Michael that is the best diplomacy you can muster?" Azile asked.

"I'm the muscle," I told her, getting up and walking away from the proceedings. I swear I could feel her gaze boring into the back of my head.

Want some company? Tommy asked telepathically.

I was thankful for the request but told him 'no'. *Keep an eye on Oggie*, I told him I was going for a walk.

I walked out of the large tent structure. The village had settled down for the night. It, however, was far from unaware. Sentries hidden in shadows and camouflaged to match their surroundings were everywhere. I wondered who could possibly be resting with so many of them watching for danger. I just wanted out, out of the village and out of the predicament I had found myself in. I was pissed at everyone.

If Azile had just left me alone, I was fairly confident I could have ridden the whole damn war out untroubled. What the hell does a Lycan want with an Old One? Now I had given them reason to hunt me down. I wanted to rip this settlement from its moorings. I could destroy dozens of them before they would even know what hit them, before even Azile could manage a defense.

At that point, she'd be forced to either put me down like a rabid dog or let me go on my own. I could sense the beat of a heart from a man more than twenty feet away. His eyes shone dully in the night as he watched me come towards him, his pulse quickening as he gripped his weapon tighter. I heard as his wet palm squeaked on the wood of the spear. I was a predator and I had found my prey.

"Time to die," I said as I walked directly towards him.

I had made up my mind. I would drain him dry, leave his empty shell where it was, grab Oggie, and be gone. They'd find the body come daylight. I'd be long gone and free from this burden I did not wish to bear. The spear was coming up, my intentions damn near telegraphing my movements. A gazelle knows the difference between a resting and stalking lion and so did this unfortunate blood sack. A glint of light caught the sharp obsidian point of the spear, but unless I impaled myself on it, the spear was going to be fairly useless. My prey seemed frozen; fear dominated every feature on him, and yet he did not move. I grabbed the haft of the spear and snapped it in two, the thick wood making a resoundingly loud noise in the still night. I reached out and grabbed his neck, tilting his head to the side, I moved in, jets of saliva running from my mouth as I sought to puncture his neck.

Unwise, Old One, came through my head as my fangs scraped off the top few layers of my victim's skin.

I tossed the man to the side.

"You know, I'm really sick of that name!" I shouted. "And does somewhere on my head say 'Always open?'"

Come to the river, the strange voice said once again in my head.

"Yeah, this seems like a great fucking idea," I said as I traipsed out of the village and into the woods. Pitch black had nothing on what was going on out here. Clouds parted just enough to allow the slimmest of light to shimmer down on a figure huddled at the side of the streambed.

"Lycan," I said, looking at the form. Not so much by appearance, but by smell. Whoever it was had donned human skin.

"Would you rather I took this form?" the beast said, changing seemingly from one step to the other.

"That's close enough." I put my hand up, looking around me for any of his brethren.

"I am alone. I am always alone, Old One," the Lycan said, taking another approaching step.

"Listen, you guys aren't the easiest thing to kill in the world, but I'm ready for round three." I told him.

"I'm sure you are. My name is Lunos." He stopped his forward progress.

"Great, you want a dog bone or something?"

He snarled but made no further move.

"I am Xavier's brother," he said almost triumphantly.

"Fine. I'll give you two bones, why don't you run home. Or are you here to deliver some portent message? About how he's going to skin me alive, or maybe eviscerate me, or maybe just a plain old eating? What is it? You interrupted my feeding and I'm growing impatient. I wonder what your tough hide would taste like."

He roared, nearby birds flew from their resting post. I heard all manner of small animals scurrying away. I braced for his charge. It never came.

"That ought to bring the natives coming," I told him.

"You are a fool for an Old One."

"I never made it to the academy, there was a problem with my student loans…couldn't secure any government money, too much red tape."

"I watched as you killed Timbre," Lunos said.

"I'm sorry, did you lose money on a bet or something? Is that what this is about? I'm sure your brother will cover your losses."

"My brother would kill me on sight," Lunos said.

"Intriguing…go on, I'll listen for now."

"Lycan are born in litters much like our distant relatives the wolf, but only one can survive. It is our birth instinct to kill our siblings. It is an evolutionary safeguard to keep our numbers low so that the pack would not starve."

"Or bring attention to their existence," I said. "Yet, if what you say is true, then how are you here?"

"As a newborn pup I realized I could not defeat Xavier even with the help of my siblings who would form an alliance until the greater threat was destroyed."

"What a wonderful welcome to life," I said. "A battle royale among family members, that shit is usually saved until many years later when a parent dies and all the little bastards fight over some useless possessions."

"I snuck out of the den while they were killing each other."

"Where was your bitch?" I asked, half meaning it as an insult veiled in an honest question.

"Her job was done with our birth."

"I really thought mankind was the most screwed up species on the planet, except for maybe the praying mantis that rips the head off her lover when she's done. That's some pretty sick shit."

"Do you wish to discuss the mating habits of an insect, Old One?"

"Listen, asshole, if you're that psychotic's brother, then that means you're not a whole lot younger than I am."

"It is not a term of derogation." Lunos said. "More like a term of respect. An honoring of the way the world used to be."

"That was no great shakes…the world I mean."

"I have never known a time that was worthy of being alive."

"Why are you here, Lunos? Apparently not to fight. The Lycan I have met are more of the 'kill first' variety."

"I have kept an eye on my kind as only an outsider

can. I have watched as my brother took control of the clans and is now uniting them for a war. He has even gone so far as to forbid the gleaning."

"Gleaning?"

"The destruction of litter-mates."

"Oh. Makes sense, increases his numbers, gotta figure that has rubbed a few of his kind the wrong way, though."

"There are many things he does now that goes against our very being."

"Is the domination and elimination of man among them?"

"It is, but that is not at the top of his list of transgressions. Making the tainted ones and using them for his devices is. We are a proud species and he degrades us by having subservient beings do his bidding."

"Werewolves," I said more to myself for clarification.

"There is a reason your history has so few of them. They are creatures that should never exist. Man is not worthy to have Lycan blood flow through their veins."

"Looks like we agree in principle to what you're saying, maybe not the exact words I would use."

"He has entire old world prisons stuffed full of them and each moon he creates more. He is getting to a tipping point where your kind will not survive."

"Lunos, you're talking a lot without really giving me any new information. Have you come to throw your lot in with our side?"

"Never!" he said, full of pride.

"Well, that was pretty definitive. I'm not sure why we are having this clandestine meeting then."

"Xavier threatens more than just man. His ambition will also bring an end to the Lycan."

"Talk about killing two birds with one stone. And why should I care? Seems to me that, that would solve all of my particular problems."

"You talk as if your heart is stone, but your actions

prove otherwise. I saw you kiss the Red Witch."

"You saw that?"

"I've watched your interactions with Bailey and even the dog Oggie. You were a man once…have you already forgotten?"

"Last thing I need is a lesson in semantics from a flea-infested Lycan."

He growled again, this one lower and somehow more menacing. I think I had finally provoked him enough for an attack. He looked over my shoulder the way I had come.

"My time here grows short. I will not defy my kind, but whatever internal battle you are fighting, you need to lay to rest. You must stop my brother at all costs. He will kill all those you say you care nothing for and not once will he have any doubts or regrets about his actions. Those are human detriments…not Lycan."

"Seems you're walking a mighty fine line, Lunos. You give me just enough to be concerned, but nothing I can really use. Where will he be attacking next?"

Lunos looked long and hard at me. "It will not be the place you call Talboton, other than that I don't know."

"Cagey," I told him. He looked over my shoulder once again; this time bounding off after looking at me for another second.

Azile and about a dozen warriors were at my back in a moment.

Azile looked around. "You alright? We heard a Lycan war cry."

"Oh, that's what that was," I told her, looking to the spot Lunos had just vacated. "We need to talk." I grabbed her arm and headed back up into the encampment.

I huddled in our small tent with our group and I related everything Lunos had said to me. Bailey's head was shaking from side to side the entire time.

"It's a trap," she said before my last word stopped pushing airwaves.

"Trap?" I asked. "How? We haven't done anything."

"But you will...or Azile. She'll want us to send guns and people to shoot them, to other villages. And when we are at our weakest, he will strike exactly where he said he wasn't," she clarified.

"He seemed pretty sincere in his words, but I'd be lying if I said I understood all Lycan gestures. The most I've ever seen were grimaces as they tried to kill me. What of it, Azile, are Lycan deceptive?"

"By their very nature," she said, her gaze off in the distance, which was impressive considering we were in a tent no bigger than six feet across. "He said he was a litter-mate of Xavier?"

"That's what he said."

"Was there any family resemblance?"

"You're kidding, right? They all look the same. That'd be like me being able to tell if two squirrels were related."

"There's ways to tell if you know what to look for," she said, almost castigating me.

"I'll make sure to take a Lycan profiling class when we get to our next town," I told her. Tommy thought long and hard about letting out a laugh. Azile's glare shut that down.

"I've never heard of Lycan surviving the Gleaning, some have crawled out of their dens only to be tossed back in until completion," Azile said.

"Welcome to life, now go kill something," I quipped. Bailey nodded.

"I do not know what circumstances would have arisen that the mouth of the cavern wasn't guarded. Lycan litters are important if only for their rarity. It is hard to believe that this Lunos could have survived on his own," Azile said.

"You said Lunos told you that their mothers are done with them when they are born. Does that mean they are not even weaned on milk?" Tommy asked.

"You don't know?" I asked him.

"We don't mingle much," he told me seriously.

I shrugged my shoulders, seemed a valid enough point.

"From what I understand, the survivor is given a liver from a fresh kill as its first meal," Azile said.

"Oh shit, so it just gets worse after the Gleaning?" I asked.

"It is hard to believe this story," Azile said. "But the lie would be too magnificent. If Xavier sent him to put doubt in us...then he succeeded."

"Now what?" I asked.

"We must make haste to Talboton to elicit help for the nearby cities."

"You are asking a great deal," Bailey said.

"How long do you believe it will be before he sets his sights on your community?" Azile asked.

"It could be as soon as the next moon, Azile," Bailey answered coolly. "And then there would be nothing that stood in his way."

"I wish you had kept him longer so that I could have spoken to him," Azile said.

"My bad, I forgot to bring my six-inch-thick barred cage with me."

"What were you doing?" she asked.

As if in response we heard a large group heading our way.

"Shit, I had completely forgotten." I lowered my head.

"Forgotten what?" Azile asked with concern.

"Old One!" came the authoritative voice of Chieftress Inuktuk – definitely not Amy McNea this time.

"Fudge."

"What did you do?" Azile asked.

"I had gone out for a snack," I told her.

"Fool!" she spat. "We need these people!"

"I didn't get the chance, Lunos interrupted me."

"I will not say it again, Old One!" Inuktuk shouted.

"I'm coming."

Azile put her hand on my chest. "You will let me do the talking. They will cut your head off after your first comment," she seethed. I opened my mouth, Azile put her finger to it. "Just shut up, Mike, please."

"Maybe just this one time," I told her.

Azile went out the flap first, with me at her heels. The group surrounding us stiffened. Fuck, I had that effect on people.

"He must answer for his crimes." Inuktuk pointed at me.

"Crimes?" Azile asked.

"He destroyed a weapon and attacked one of my guards. Both offenses punishable by death," she said.

I thought it funny that they valued their weapons as highly as they did their lives. Made sense in this hostile world; without a weapon, your life was forfeit anyway.

"These are grievous crimes," Azile stated. "And I do understand the need for justice to be served."

"Not seeing where your defense is going here," I said softly.

"But…" she started.

"Oh here it is," I said.

"…there are many things Michael must accomplish before he can be tried for these crimes. I call for the Law of Forfeiture," Azile said.

Inuktuk's features narrowed. "He is not one of us. How do I know that he will come to serve out his sentence?" she asked.

"I will stand in his place if he does not," Azile said. The people around us ranged in emotion from gasps to hostility to amazement.

I had no idea what she was saying, but it sure didn't give me any warm fuzzies. The crowd dispersed almost as quickly as they had assembled.

"Any chance you could fill me in on what just happened?" I asked her.

"I plead guilty for your crimes and you will have to atone for them when you have fulfilled your obligations," she said evenly.

"Are you out of your fucking mind?" I asked her. "I broke a stick and barely touched the man. Sure I had meant to drain him dry, but I didn't. I'm not swinging for that."

"Then I will," she said, turning back towards the tent.

I followed her as I wasn't quite done. "You know, I'm getting really sick of these weird customs and laws these people have. I was quite capable of getting out of this jam myself without having to forfeit my life to do so."

"What would you have done, Michael?" she asked heatedly. "Fight and kill your way out? Because that's what it would have taken. Are you worth so much that you'd feel justified in killing five, ten…maybe a dozen of them to garner your escape? Is that what you're saying?"

"Well, when you put it that way," I said, backing up a measure from her vehemence. "I'm still not sure the punishment fits the crime, Azile. Maybe the intent of my crime, but not what actually happened."

"These are different times, Michael. Men were hung for stealing a horse once. During our time, you could steal a fleet of cars and get off on five years of probation. If any good has come from this, I have now bound you to our cause."

"That's one way to look at it I suppose. I could still walk away from this," I told her.

"You could, but then I would stay here."

"Damn you, Azile," I told her as I left the tent. I thought for sure there'd be a small posse of armed men waiting for me and following my every move. Apparently, Azile's oath was good enough for them. "Well, fuck, if I'm to die, I should have killed him, would have made it somewhat worth it."

I stayed right outside the tent almost the entire night. I didn't trust myself enough to go wandering off, and I knew Lunos was still out there. In the mood I was in, I figured I'd push him just enough until we got into one hell of a scrape. That seemed a much more fitting exit from the world than the one Azile had brokered for me. It was the low chanting that got me moving. A tent off to the corner seemed to be the source of the noise.

This one, instead of being the typical canvas-like material, appeared to be made from animal hide – though it was difficult to tell in the night. Paintings covered the entire structure; there were many differing colored hands of varying sizes, a few crosses. I may have seen a Jewish Star and I believe the symbol that was used in Muslim religions.

"Holy man," I said outside the flap. My words drifted off in a breeze.

"I was wondering when you would come," a voice said from within.

It seemed too soft to be meant for me, but I didn't see anyone else standing out here, so I pulled the flap back. I could barely make out the figure seated in the middle. A thick bank of smoke separated us. I think if I tried hard enough, I could have drifted in on it.

"Diviner's sage?" I asked, taking a sniff.

Paul and I had raced down to the local head shop the day we discovered there was such a thing as Salvia Divinorum or Diviner's Sage used by Native Americans for centuries to produce visions. More like drug-induced hallucinations; but who was I to deny someone a good trip? We had experimented a few times with it before the Lord Overseers or the US Government deemed it a Class something narcotic and banned it. Just what I need…another mom. We'd had fun smoking it, more laughs than visions. *I miss you, Paul*, I thought.

"What is lost can be found," the figure said. I was

wondering if I had another mind intruder.

"Where were you when I lost my passport?" I asked. "Spent close to forty hours of my time looking for that thing. Blamed the moving crew that brought our new kitchen table. Know what, though? I found the stupid thing in my suit jacket pocket a couple of years later, probably should have sent Perry's Furniture an apology. Too late now, I suppose."

The man said nothing to my words – in fact, completely ignored them. So much so, I wondered if we had been married in a former existence.

"A man bereft of his soul is no longer a man," he said.

"You take all night to come up with that line, holy man?"

"My name is Feather Hand."

I took another step in, and the flap closed behind me. The smoke was beginning to affect me, I felt a slight pressure around my eyes while it swirled around my head. The figure huddled down by the heavily smoking flame was ancient. He looked like he could have been as old as me, but time had not been as kind.

"Sit," he said, not motioning and I didn't see anything even remotely resembling a recliner.

I thought about just parking my ass where I was, but instead moved to the far side of the small stone fire pit. I found a particularly comfortable flat stone to sit on. Being sarcastic here, this felt a lot like the one I had become intimate with during a close encounter in a cave with John the Tripper. There's a man that would have definitely appreciated this.

My thoughts drifted all over the place; places I'd seen, worlds I'd known, and then others I had not. Images of Red Rocks, respite with large crocodile-like aliens, a young death suffered at the hands of an inexperienced driver, Tracy, Jandyln, BT, Dee; names I knew, and some I didn't flitted across my synapses.

"You have many paths," the man said. "Some traveled, some not," he added, never looking over at me.

"What are you doing to me?" I asked in a panic. I watched as I battled men, as I battled aliens, as I battled demons. And finally, I danced with death. In every case, there was no escape.

"These are lives you have lived…or will live."

"Please," I pleaded as I watched countless ones that I loved – some I had no remembrance of – die. Some gruesome deaths, others after living long, fruitful existences; but always the end was the same.

The man finally moved. He swept his hand over the fire and the images were erased as neatly as if he had wiped a chalkboard with a sponge. I was breathing heavy from the exertion of the thoughts.

"Why are you showing me this?" I asked.

"I have done nothing, what you see is already within you."

"You said what is lost can be found again. What are you referring to?" I asked with hope. I knew what I wanted the answer to be; it was the key to everything. I would gladly leave this plane of existence if I had it back.

"It will reveal itself when the time is right. You have foregone the most special of gifts…that which differentiates us from all the beasts of the world. It cannot be so easily won back."

"A test? More fucking tests? Have I not done enough? Have I not suffered enough?" A little more whining and I'd be bleating like a goat. "Is it not enough? It never is, is it? There's always one more wall to scale, enemy to kill, child to save. That's the hell of it. Within a fingers' width, but always out of reach."

"You must be strong, Michael Talbot." He finally looked up from whatever realm he had been journeying in.

"I've lost my way," I told him.

"We all do. You still must go on until the end. The

final fight you will win. The paths intermingle, Michael. You must find a crossing point."

I understood why, in each of those other realms, I was whole; I was a man undivided. Now the hard part was, how does someone find something when they have no idea what it looks like or did not even have a clue where to look.

The sun was coming up. I was leaning against my own tent, completely unsure as to how I got there or if I had even left. I stood up and looked over to where I swore I had talked to the Shaman; there was nothing there except a small circle of stones that had not seen flame in years. No tent, and certainly no old man, just a clearing and an old pit.

"Life's not fucked up enough?" I asked the heavens, "You have to throw this curveball?"

There was no fanfare as we left in the morning. The man I had almost chowed on was the only one that saw us off. He was holding the broken parts of his spear in his hands. I don't think that he was happy I had prolonged my fate. I gave him the finger. Maybe he knew what it meant as he tossed the pieces to the ground, turned and walked away.

"Lunos follows," Azile said, although she didn't look in any particular direction as an affirmation of her words.

"Probably to report back to his king to let him know we've been tricked by his words," Bailey said sourly.

"That is a possibility." Azile said, "But, the lie doesn't ring true."

I wrestled with the words trying to make sense of them. I made sure Oggie stayed close, he wasn't thrilled that I wouldn't let him go roaming around, but if Lycans killed humans without impunity, I had to figure dogs weren't off limits.

"What do we do if they don't believe us?" Tommy asked Azile. "We aren't even sure."

"We have less than three weeks to convince them," she said sternly.

Again, and not for the first or last time, letting the

Lycans wipe man from the planet solved all my problems. I owed them nothing. I had played my part the last time we were threatened. I had paid the price over and over, and what had it got me but another date with an executioner? Plus, I had created a mortal enemy with what I had previously thought was a mythical creature. I was dour and sour all wrapped in one neat little package. My head was splitting, and it was either a Diviner's Sage hangover or a major embolism that I was suffering. My encounter last night seemed entirely too vivid to be made up.

"Are my eyes red?" I asked Tommy.

"Glowing like coals," he said.

"One or both?"

"Both why?"

"Just trying to figure out what is going on."

"You crying, Talbot?" Bailey asked.

"Just happy to see you," I told her.

Azile came up beside me. "You reek of Salvia. That plant is not indigenous to these parts. Where did you get a hold of some?"

"I don't even think I could tell you," I told her honestly.

"Try."

"I went into the Holy Man's tent."

"The Landians don't have a Holy Man anymore, he left on a pilgrimage over twenty years ago and has not come back."

"You asked me to tell you what happened and I am, have you ever known me to lie?"

She thought for a moment. "Well, yes, actually I have, but I don't think that this time you are."

"He showed me things," I stated. "Nothing that will help our present situation, though," I added when I realized she was looking at me.

I could still feel Azile scrutinizing me, but she said no more on the matter.

It took a couple of days to get back to my namesake town, but the time drifted in a haze for me. I was haunted by memories I had no remembrance of ever making. Drababan the giant Genogerian being among them. We were friends once, I could only ponder on how something like that could even happen. All I knew was that I'd be thrilled if we could hook up again, he looked like he could eat werewolves for lunch.

CHAPTER 18 - Mike Journal Entry Twelve

Talboton went a lot like I expected it would. The council really didn't want to hear anything about what we speculated, and was even less impressed with what we were asking for. And how could I blame them? We were asking them to diminish their guard to help communities that they had little to no ties with.

It was Bailey that fought tooth and nail for them to see our point. In the end we got something, but it was like lighting a fire to stop a flood; basically it wasn't going to do shit. Talboton agreed to send ten men to four different communities with five hundred rounds. And that wasn't each…that was total. Each man or woman would have fifty rounds – less than two full magazines. They had bows and swords as well, but by that point, we might as well start throwing rocks. Then there came the question of would the other villages accept our aid. Ten armed people could actually control an entire population. They might not be so inclined as to let us in even if it was for their safety.

Getting man to get over his innate distrust of strangers was not going to be easy. And then there was also the problem if Xavier decided to do an 'end around' on us. There were only so many frontier places we could assist; if he went further east, he would find places ripe for the picking where Lycan and werewolves were only tales talked about by traveling merchants. Without firsthand experience, those towns would never prepare until it was too late.

Unbeknownst to me, Azile had arranged a plan with

the Landians to track any movements of humans. The Lycan would have to bring their war machine into place before the moon turned full. Humans on foot were slow, noisy, and always left tell-tale signs of their passing; especially an assemblage of that many. We'd know soon enough if Xavier was trying to press further east.

CHAPTER 19 - Mike Journal Entry Thirteen

Ten men and women of Talboton marched out to Denarth. I made sure I was not among them. The last thing I wanted was Lana hanging from my arm. I was to find out that the council had initially refused the 'assistance' but yielded after Lana wore her father down. I'd known that feeling once. Daughters could be relentless; Nicole, on more than one occasion, had worn me down to a nub to get whatever she had wanted. Then I'd always had the pleasure of dealing with my wife after she'd found out that I had once again caved to the wishes of my diminutive daughter.

The only time I'd ever held firm was when she'd wanted a mixed-sex sleepover for her seventeenth birthday. I'd let her have it now if I could only hold her in my arms for just a moment. I stopped what I was doing. Nope…that was a lie, I still wouldn't do it.

Wheatonville had been more responsive to the offer of aid. They had firsthand accounts of the slaughtering going on around them being as they were the closest community to the now destroyed and defunct Harbor's Town, a place in which they had done a fair amount of trading over the years.

Ft. Lufkin, which was really nothing more than some rolling hills and a small barricade, flat out refused any help and became hostile, which worked in our favor as the refused gunmen came to Harbor's Town and bolstered our beleaguered defenses. Azile had decided this was where we would set up shop. The farthest settlement to the south that anyone knew about, New Georgia also turned down the help, those soldiers unfortunately returned to Talboton.

    I watched the moon every night with apprehension; we were in a state of war, and how strange it was to realize we were tied to a schedule. I've been in hostile situations and truly never knew when the next bullet, bomb, missile, or diseased mouth was going to strike. I don't know if this was worse or better. Sure, there were the pros of being able to prepare; but, man, the apprehension…that's the shit that wears you down. Every time you think of the upcoming fight, a heavy squirt of adrenaline cascades through your body, everything in its wake starts tingling, and then when your body catches up and realizes nothing is happening. You suffer a serious crash. This was the cycle, and I could see it taking its toll on these people who were essentially farmers and merchants. They had yet to fight for what they loved.

    That's not entirely true, fighting for one's existence is a challenging job. Battling the elements, bugs attacking crops, the hunt for game, these are human endeavors to survive. But they had not yet had to fight a savage enemy that wanted only one thing: the destruction of their foe.

    I'd seen battle-hardened Marines break on occasion, and besides me, those were on short supply. War sucks. There's no glory in having your innards spill onto the ground, no dignity in having your head caved in. No songs of triumph as you're hewn in half. The residents of Wheatonville would fight because they had to. What was the alternative? I just wish we had a little more than rakes, shovels, sharp pointy sticks, and small hammers. The werewolves were stupid, they only knew one direction, and possessed zero tactical sense, but they were merciless and strong. We'd inflict damage. I, however, had my doubts that Wheatonville would survive the coming onslaught. Tommy and Bailey were in charge of teaching the people some rudimentary fighting skills. Azile had locked herself away doing lord knows what, and me? Well, I was busy fretting heavily.

I repeatedly walked around the small city, looking at the myriad of weak spots and possible points of attack. Without a twenty-foot high stone or steel wall, there was just not going to be any way to stop the invaders. A moat filled with alligators would be welcome. We had mid-sized logs we had chopped down, and sharpened the ends, stuck in the ground at a forty-five degree angle, and then propped up with a stout brace. So now as long as the werewolves ran into them we'd be all set. The best we could hope for was to create a couple of easy access points, ways in which to direct the flow of traffic, so to speak. I don't know if werewolves adhere to the ways of water, flowing in the easiest route, but we could try.

I had a feeling that they weren't going to line up all nice and pretty and wait patiently to get inside. The seven-foot high stonewall which seemed fairly daunting to me was most likely nothing more than a speed bump to a loping werewolf.

"What is your concern?" Bailey asked as she came up beside me. I was underneath one of the logs looking up.

"Not sure if these are going to do a damn thing," I told her.

"These are formidable defenses." She slapped the side of the tree.

"Yeah, we'll probably cause a few stubbed toes for sure," I told her. "Maybe rip off a claw or two…but they'll hurdle these easy enough."

"What do you suggest?"

"We let them."

She looked at me questioningly.

"They have to land somewhere," I told her. She looked at me a moment longer. The dawn of recognition lit up in her eyes.

"I'll get a crew on it now," she replied.

I walked away. I had yet to walk around enough times to create a groove. It was, however, only a matter of time.

It was three days before the full moon when we received word from the Landians. A large contingent of humans had been spotted on the farthest western point of the lands they roamed. The Lycan party would never have been spotted if the three Landian men hadn't been out on a hunting party. The large mountain lion they had been tracking had been responsible for the loss of seven of their goats, and they had been single-mindedly determined to keep that number at the max. That was, of course, until the chained line of humans began to make their way past. The men, a father and his two sons, had hid behind a grove of trees as the column passed.

***

"Had to have been a couple of hundred," Redd, the father, had told Inuktuk when he had raced back to their summer encampment. The mountain lion had been completely forgotten.

"Are they heading east towards Talboton?" Inuktuk asked.

The man shook his head. "They were heading due south, I think doing their best to stay hidden as long as possible."

"It has to be Ft. Lufkin," Inuktuk said.

"Will we help them?" Redd asked.

"No, there is nothing to be gained there but the death of our people."

"If the fort falls…"

"I know what it means, Redd. All that will stand between us and the Lycan is Talboton. This is not an easy decision, but I will not smash Landians against the rocks of futility. Ft. Lufkin was lost before it ever started. Get word to them of the impending invasion and invite them back here."

"We do not have the resources," he told her.

"I'd rather go to bed hungry than with the loss of

those people on my mind. Go now, I need to get word to the Red Witch.

***

"Ft. Lufkin appears to be the Xavier's next target," Azile said to me. I had been summoned to her residence. I hadn't seen her in close to two weeks and those were her first words to me.

Good to see you, too, I thought. Well, two people can play that game. "When are we leaving?"

"I do not believe that to be their primary target," she said a faraway look in her eyes. "The men that saw them said there were only about a hundred or so humans."

"Diversion?" I asked. "But why, what could he possibly fear from us? We're not on the move."

"Not a diversion…impatience." Azile said finally taking notice of me as if she just realized I was there, which was funny considering she had sent for me.

"Xavier's pants getting a little antsy?" I asked. "Big bad wolf wants the world and he wants it now," I said in my best baby pouty voice.

"I wish this were a laughing matter."

"As do I." I replied. "I make fun because I'm scared and pissed all at the same time. We still on high alert?" I asked.

"I have not heard anything from the Landians or my own scouts to indicate that the Lycan are moving further east. No, Xavier will strike here and Ft. Lufkin in three days, believing that both of these will fall as easily as Harbor's Town. With each coming moon, he will move further east until he has destroyed everything."

"Why not the West? I was never a fan of California."

"Maybe you should ask him," she said, smiling.

I realized I had missed that smile. "I'm sure we can have a spot of tea before we try to kill each other. It's the civilized thing to do. Do you think he'll do the raised pinkie?" I asked, mimicking someone of more culture than myself. Didn't really have to look that hard, even in this severe day and age I found myself in.

She was looking at me with curiosity. I really didn't like being under that much scrutiny, especially from a woman, the longer one looked at me, the more likely she would be to find something wrong. I knew a way around this. I'm not going to pretend to say I know women; even as long as I've been alive, they are still a complete and utter mystery, but that isn't to say I haven't discovered some weapons of my own against their beguiling nature. So listen up if you're a man and you have discovered this journal – if you're a woman, God help us all.

Okay, the best way to deflect attention off yourself is to get a woman talking. Sounds stupid, right? Watch this…

"Azile, what happened to you after?" I was referring to one of our last battles against the zombies. She had slipped out into the night. I had never known why. She never told anyone. I had chalked her up as another loss in a sea of them. That was of course until Tommy let me in on his little secret. "I spent close to a week looking for you. Never did so much as find a sign. I was half convinced you had learned how to fly."

"Wouldn't that be something," she said wistfully.

"So you can't?" I asked. She shook her head. "Because, really, that would be pretty cool. There have been so many flying male superheroes that always take their girlfriends for a spin up in the clouds…I just think for once it would be nice to have it the other way around. You know, like maybe I could strap a saddle to your back and we could go check out the sites."

"A saddle?" she asked with an arched eyebrow.

"If I'm going to fly, I'd like to do it in style. You know…maybe even have a cup holder or two so I could put my beer in it. You really wouldn't want to hold me in your arms would you? That seems like it would be a little awkward."

"I'd probably just drop you…and not because I wasn't strong enough."

"Point taken."

"I had to leave."

"I saw the change in you after, you could have come to any of us for help," I told her.

"How many of you were versed in the effects of witchcraft on the spirit?" she asked sadly.

"I read the Cliff Notes."

She had to grab at her stomach as she involuntarily laughed. When she recomposed herself, she spoke. "I'd always had a proclivity for witchcraft. I guess I hadn't known what it was when I was a kid. I'd make matches light without striking them on anything."

"That's called a lighter," I told her, she smiled.

"You do remember you asked me, right?"

"Sorry, it's a bit more difficult to shut off than one might imagine."

"How about now?"

"I'm good," I told her.

"I used to do small stuff – the match for one. I had an ability with animals. Nothing miraculous, I didn't bring them back from the dead. But injuries they suffered tended to heal quicker if I touched them. Back when I was a girl, I wasn't truly sure…maybe I just wanted to be special…to be different, distinct, you know?"

"What teenager doesn't want to?" I asked, I always thought the song the Beatles sang about 'Ain't nothing you can do that hasn't been done' (I'm paraphrasing because I haven't actually heard music in a century and a half – that one still stung) was actually pretty sad. What kind of world would we be living in if there was never going to be anything unique.

She nodded. "Little things, like I said. Sometimes it

was just knowing when we were going out to eat, or maybe when the phone was going to ring. When I was old enough and I knew what it meant, I tried to figure out the winning lottery numbers."

"Any luck?" I asked curiously.

"When you found me in that truck was I wearing a tiara?"

Now it was my turn to laugh. "No…no tiara."

"There's some sort of protective realm in regards to personal gain and witchcraft at least on this side of the dividing line."

"Dividing line?"

"Good, bad, white, black, whatever term makes sense to you."

"Gotcha."

"It was taking its toll on me, though. The usage, I mean, like I was dipping into a well with a very finite supply. Everything I did seemed to strip a little more of me away."

"That sounds terrifying," I told her honestly.

She did pause for a second to see if I was being sincere. "Leaving all of you was among one of the hardest things I'd ever done. By the time I got up the nerve to do so, I was already beginning to feel like a ghost…no substance whatsoever."

I wanted to give her comfort, yet I had no words of solace. I'd had no idea she had been going through that. To be fair, I was wrestling my own demons and we were still in the midst of a war, tough to stop and ask people how they're doing. Besides, we were all suffering in multiple ways – outwards and inwards if that makes any sense.

"I can't imagine how you thought leaving would be a good idea. You left a lot of people wondering and worried."

"I'm so sorry I never got to say my good-byes." She bowed her head.

"Me too." But I was sorry because I *had* to my say good-byes.

CHAPTER 20 – Azile's Story

Nearing the end of the zombie invasion

It was raining the night Azile walked away from the Talbot clan and the safety they afforded.

"What are you doing?" BT asked. He had drawn the short straw that night and pulled the first shift for guard duty. Winter was coming, he could see his breath as he spoke and the rain had a hardness to it that alluded to a near freezing condition.

"My shift is next so I thought I'd start early," Azile replied.

BT looked at her. "Do I look like I just figured out how to put big boy pants on? It's freezing out here. And I swear Talbot cheated when we pulled cards out of the deck."

"If I remember correctly, he pulled a five. You were the one who pulled the two." She realized she had just given herself away.

"That's right…you had a jack. What are you doing out here, Azile?"

"Would you believe me if I told you I traded?"

"No," he told her flatly.

"Then you're going to hate this more."

"What?"

Azile muttered a few words. BT saw a small flash, and for long moments, he found himself unable to move. Azile had walked past him and down the ladder. She took one long look back at the house before she ran off into the night.

"What the fuck are you doing?" Mike asked, coming outside a few moments later to a stock still BT.

It seemed to be the spoken word that broke the spell.

"Shit," BT said. "Azile."

"What about her?" Mike asked.

"Put a spell on me and left."

"You're kidding, right?" Mike asked.

"Yeah, Mike, I let ice crystals grow on my eyebrows and eyelids as some funtastical joke for when you came out."

"Well I appreciate the effort, but it's not really that funny," Mike told him.

"The girl split, Mike."

"Why? Makes no sense. We're relatively safe here and we've seen less and less zombies."

"No clue. Should we go after her?" BT asked.

"How big a head start does she have on us?" Mike asked.

"Not entirely sure, but I think I lost about fifteen minutes."

"What would have happened if I hadn't come out?" Mike asked.

BT shrugged his shoulders. "It was like I was sleeping."

"I could have had the world's largest Fudgsicle if you froze," Mike said with a distant look.

"Politically correct to the end, aren't you?"

"Well, I doubt you'd taste as good as that sounds. It's really just an 'in theory' thing," Mike added with air-quotes.

"I'll shove them fucking air quotes..."

"Hey, man, try to remember I just saved your ass. How about a little show of appreciation? I think that puts me up by two."

"Are you kidding me? You don't get a point just for coming on duty."

"Mull it over," Mike told him. "I'm getting a flashlight." Henry walked outside as soon as Mike opened the patio door. "I wish you were a bloodhound." Mike grabbed the dog's massive head, gently shaking it from side to side as he pet him.

BT, with no small amount of effort and pain, got down to be on level with the dog. "Good to see you, Henry." Henry's stub of a tail wagged as he gave the big man a slobbering kiss. "Want me to come with you?" BT asked, grabbing the handrail to pull himself back up.

Mike looked him over. "Naw, man, I can tell the cold is getting to your leg, get whoever has the shift after mine up. I think it's Mad Jack. Tell him what's going on and make sure the crazy bastard doesn't shoot us when we come back. In fact, give him his Airsoft gun I'd feel much better for it."

"Why'd she leave, Mike?" BT asked before he walked back into the house.

"I don't know, man, but I hope to be able to ask her." Mike secured his gloves. "See you in a bit."

"Don't get into any messes without me. Good luck." BT said. And with those words, Mike left, getting swallowed up in the darkness.

Mike kept the flashlight off. Azile had left on her own accord, which meant she didn't want to be found, and if he had the light on she would move away from it.

"What are you doing, Azile?" Mike had asked so softly and intimately, she thought he had been talking to her.

It was almost over before it had begun. She had been a heartbeat away from responding, thinking he had spotted her. When he moved to her left, she realized he had been talking to himself. She waited until he was far enough away before she moved. This time she would remember just how fast he was. She had barely been able to duck and cover before he was upon her.

"This is for the best," she told his retreating back softly.

Mike went back to the house at first light empty-handed and empty-hearted.

"Nothing?" Tracy asked with concern.
"Not a trace," Mike told her.
"What now?" BT asked.
"Well, I'd like to take a couple of people to go out and look for her."

For over a week, Mike, Justin, Travis – all of them at various points – walked out looking for something. Ever further westward with no luck. It was an impossibility he would ever chance upon her, Azile had headed east towards the ocean. She had walked south down the coast almost to New York before she found what she was looking for; a ship heading away from the devastation. It was rumored that England had come through the zombie apocalypse relatively unscathed due to its isolation.

Nothing could have been further form the truth. London had burned to the ground. The lack of firearms in the country had proved their downfall. Years later, militias would come with the express purpose of flushing out the zombie stasis hiding spots, burning what little remained. Of the forty people on the ship, only Azile and a man named Grant Perry had disembarked in a town near Liverpool. He had family in Manchester and had been trying desperately to get back home since the beginning.

"Wiltshire?" he asked again when they set foot on dry land. "That's clear across the country. Come with me to Manchester."

She politely declined; and not for the first time. Azile was convinced Grant had wanted her company more to bolster his courage than for her protection. She had no real reason why she felt a pull to a place she'd never been, but the name had screamed into her head as she lay in bed at Ron's house.

"You know this isn't really the best time for tourists," he told her, referring to her telling him she needed to go to Stonehenge.

"Good luck, Grant." She shook his hand.

She had never seen him again. She had checked on the address he had given her, but that was more than fifteen years later, and if he had ever found his way back there, he had not left a forwarding address. The decomposed bodies in the foyer did not, however, leave much doubt he had not found what he was looking for.

It was four nights later when Azile had found herself in the middle of the famed structure. She felt like she had finally found what she was searching for.

"I'm here," she said with no small measure of excitement.

Three people dressed in long, flowing brown robes appeared almost as if summoned. "We've been waiting for you," the tallest of the trio told her.

He pulled back the oversized hood he had been wearing. He had a scar that started from below his right eye, curved down the side of his neck, and was then lost in the collar of his garment. He was severe looking, but his words and countenance were anything but.

"My name is Triplos, this is Cerin (the woman nodded), and my silent friend over there is Lanner. We are the order of Druids."

"Home," Azile said.

"Come," he said, taking her hand.

Her tutelage was difficult and painful, but she had unlocked many secrets during her time with them. When she felt she surpassed her teachers is when she finally struck out for home. She had foreseen the winds of war and the ultimate outcome if something was not done. Xavier's lust was without bounds; he knew of the lands beyond the ocean, and when he was done on one shore he would keep moving, striving to create the largest and most ruthless reign the world had ever seen.

CHAPTER 21 - Mike Journal Entry Fourteen

"Stonehenge? I'd always wanted to see that," I told her.

"Perhaps you will someday," she said sadly.

"You really believe that?" I asked.

The dip of her head let me know the truth behind her words.

"Well, like you said, you're not all-knowing, otherwise you'd have that tiara." I tried to alleviate the mood.

She smiled. "This is true. I'm not sure we'll make it through this next moon."

"Think I have enough time to get to Talboton and back?" I asked. "For the beer."

"We make it through the next few days; I'll show you how to brew the nasty stuff."

"Nasty? And wait...you've been holding out on me? At least I have an incentive."

"Holding on to your head not enough?" she asked wryly.

"Unfortunately, no." I told her, being honest. "I wish I had left Oggie in Talboton...or even with Lana. I don't know how I'm going to keep him out of the mix."

"I'm sure the price Lana would have charged to watch him might be too steep," she laughed.

"You're probably right. I wonder how my girlfriend is faring?"

"Girlfriend?" Bailey asked approaching.

"Yeah...you and me," I told her.

"I like my men...bigger." She eyed me up and down.

"Ouch, my ego is going to pretend I didn't hear that."

"The preparations are made," she said, changing the subject. She was much too serious, although BT had been at the beginning as well. If we were to luck out and have more time together, then I'd eventually wear her down. "Now we wait."

I knew that waiting was always the worst, giving men and women the time to let their imaginations run wild was the worst possible idea. They'd break before it started.

"Come morning." I told her, "I want you to double the amount of drills with the populace. You can blame it on me. They'll hate me for the next few days but thank me for it after."

"If there is an after," she echoed my thoughts.

True to my word – and then some – Bailey had the locals out and sweating before the birds of morning could even clear their throats. I got more than one glare as I walked past that day. The smell of smelting silver dominated the village. Townsfolk would periodically line up to give a silver lining to their weapons. Maybe we were all going to die but we were going to do it in style. All manner of weapon received a coating, from the lowly rake to the mighty sword. I even made sure that the bowmen dipped their arrow tips. Besides putting a shine to my sword and axe there was another plus I gained from the whole damn thing and that was from Tommy. I hadn't known his skill with a sword until he approached me.

"Hey, Mr. T, can we talk?" he asked.

"Sure," I told him as I 'swooshed' my sword through the air. I think I even made a swooshing sound-effect…well, just for effect, I suppose.

"It's about your sword."

I stopped moving around. "Pretty sweet, huh? You want me to teach you some moves, I'm damn near a ninja."

"I've seen ninjas, Mr. T." He paused.

I stopped to look at him. I got it. "I'm no ninja is what you're saying?"

He nodded solemnly. "I can teach you some things, though."

I swallowed my bruised pride and we worked all that day and deep into the night. Far past lunch, then dinner, past the call of the crows as they rested for the night. Even the crickets had begun to tire by the time we called a break. I'm sure the clang of our metal kept more than one citizen awake, but if I could keep learning, chances were, I'd keep those same people alive or at least have a better chance of it.

There was a chance I was slightly faster than the boy, though he could have been sandbagging on me; but as for strength, I think he could hammer me into the ground. By the end, we were at full speed. He caught me a couple of times with the flat of his sword, and where he did, my skin sprang up in ugly welts and blotted blood. Although I took small victories in putting a couple of slices in the tunic he was wearing. He would show surprise when I did so, and then try to smash my weapon in two with his parries. I don't think I'd ever seen the boy truly angry before; funny how I can bring that out in folks.

I was breathing heavy, hunched over and leaning on my sword, as sweat sloshed off of me in fat droplets.

"Not quite a ninja…but impressive nonetheless," Azile said.

"Thanks to Tommy…and has everyone seen friggin' ninjas except for me?" I asked. It didn't come out quite that smoothly. I was too busy trying to breathe in between words. I'm not going to lie, I was happy Tommy seemed to be in the same state as myself, although he was actually laying on the ground in your standard 'snow angel' pose. He was looking up at the heavens, his chest heaving.

"Gimme…sword," he finally managed.

I didn't move. Not because I didn't want to, but rather, I was unsure if my legs would betray me before I got there. My hard-fought stalemate would look bad if I fell over now.

"Sharpen," he said as he rolled over and got to his knees.

The ground looked pretty pleasing, but unless I wanted to sleep under the stars, I knew I couldn't go down to embrace it.

"Azile, we should talk," I told her.

"About?" she asked suspiciously.

"Just get over here." Thankfully she did as I asked. "Okay, I'm going to shuffle over to Tommy. When I give my sword to him, I will have basically lost the only thing keeping me up."

"Oh? I am to become your cane then?"

"Shh, don't let him hear you," I begged.

"Men and their little boy pride," Azile said. She gave me a hard time, but was smiling as she did so.

Tommy had finally pushed the upper half of his body from the ground and was now on his knees. He grabbed my sword, thankful that he now had two props.

"Sharpen them my ass," I told him as I leaned heavily against Azile. "I see what you're doing."

"As I see you," he replied. "We will resume on the morrow."

On the morrow, I thought. I like the sound of it, it reminded me of knights. Knights…ninjas…either were pretty cool in my book.

"On the morrow it is. Lead on," I told Azile. I was dragging my feet like I was drunk and had forgotten the necessary motor skill commands to make them work properly. With some difficulty, we found the way to my living quarters. It had housed three other men, but they very much disliked the idea of sleeping with a half-vamp. How 18th century of them. Vampire-ists.

Azile laid me down in my bed – which was basically a raised platform with a layer of feather covered with a heavy quilt.

"Would you like me to stay?" Azile asked.

I had not a clue what she was talking about, but she must have taken my silence for acquiescence. She grabbed the front of her robe and swept it over her shoulders.

"Oh, I get it now," I said softly. Oggie grunted when I gently pushed him off the side. A body I thought incapable of anything beyond sustaining life at the moment began to respond as I looked upon her. I was thankful for the enhanced vision.

I had not lain with anyone since Tracy, and to be honest, I wasn't entirely sure what to do as she got into the bed with me.

"Be gentle," I told her, as she first placed her finger over my lips and then replaced that with her lips.

When I awoke the next morning (okay afternoon) Azile had already awoken and left – if she had ever even slept. I wasn't entirely convinced that the whole thing hadn't been some elaborate dream…or even a spell. No matter which of the three options it ended up being, it was still something special. Even if nothing much past a PG-13 rating happened. Okay, maybe an R rating was necessitated, I think a breast was involved but it was dark. Then, in the blink of an eye or the beat of a heart, the warmth of the remembrance became wracked with a guilt so deep I didn't think I could speak. My beloved Tracy, what would she think? Would she hold this transgression against me if I could ever find my way back to her? It would all be for naught if I somehow won my soul back and she turned her back on me when I approached. I wouldn't be able to take that. It was with that morose feeling I finally got out of bed.

My body ached both physically and spiritually. Extra healing powers or not, I had pushed myself to the brink of exhaustion. I felt slightly better when I saw Tommy; he didn't seem to be faring much better than me as he was shuffling past Bailey doing some basic fighting with the locals. When he did catch me staring, he made sure to put a little extra pep in his step. I found that humorous, I didn't even have the energy to pretend I had the energy.

Bailey looked up at the sun, over at me, then shook her head. I gave her the finger, and I'm being honest when I say that was an exertion. Azile was nowhere to be seen. I think that was for the best. I had a lot of feelings to wade through, and that had never been my strong suit. Feelings weren't for the weak…they were for the strong that could examine them. It is much, much easier to be a creature of action not reflection. I cared for Azile. The question was how much.

I was leaning against a wall actually looking for the next place to park my ass when Tommy approached. I could only hope to God he didn't want to go onto round two. I think I'd just let him stick me through the gut and be done with it.

"We need to feed," he said with no precursor.

I was about to tell him I could go for a bacon cheeseburger when the realization of what he was saying settled in. "Fuck no," was my initial response, even though I knew we had to. "Should we walk down the center of the town shouting, 'Bring out your near dead! Bring out your near dead!'? I'm sure someone will toss out a grandfather or two."

"We cannot fight in this state, and even if we weren't this tired, we would need to be at peak performance for what comes next."

"That's why you did it," I accused.

He feigned ignorance.

"You wore the living shit out of me for fifteen hours so that I would be just like this."

"We need to feed, Mike. If we are to have any chance tomorrow night, we need to be as strong as possible."

"Is Azile in on this with you?" I asked angrily, spinning on him.

This time it was clear to see he had no clue what I was talking about.

"It is who we are Michael…like it or not."

"Not, would be my response." The thing of it was…I knew the validity of his words. Odds were already fairly slim of us surviving, and me feeling like I couldn't punch my way out of a rice-paper house right now only magnified that feeling.

"So now what?" I asked, letting my head sag both because it was hard to hold it up and also because I was coming around to what he had to say.

"We hunt tonight. We cannot feed among these people. They already fear us."

"With good reason."

Tommy shrugged and walked away. Okay, more like limp-shuffled away. I had decided where I was leaning was as good a place to sit as any. I sat with my ass on the dirt and my back against an ancient rock wall. Then I laughed, hard enough that those nearest me stopped what they were doing to look. I was thinking the only way we were going to be able to feed was if we stumbled across a Walmart and some Spandex-wearing old woman was sitting in her little motorized cart and it had finally run out of juice; other than that, I was unsure as to how we were going to catch anything. Anything that moved at least, and it was the insanity of what I had to do that had hysterical tears running out of my eyes.

I didn't move much that day as I let the sounds of children playing and adults working at playing war wash over me. Oggie sniffed around me a few times, but for the most part, he was enjoying the kids. The sun felt great, I wished I had been a plant and able to gain all the sustenance I could out of its rays. The rest did me some good, and I was actually able to stand without assistance as I felt the shadow of Tommy blot out the setting sun.

"You ready?" he asked.

"I never even liked to hunt when I owned rifles," I

told him.

"You did, though. After the zombies."

"I had to, we had to eat."

He raised his eyebrows, in a 'See what I'm talking about' gesture. "We have to eat now."

"Clever, I've yet to stumble upon a deer that begged me not to, though."

"It would if it could."

"That's really not helping."

"I'm just trying to show you the similarity."

"You should be going the other way. Make the human more animal-like, not the animal more human-like."

"My bad."

"Not something you expect to hear from a five hundred-year-old vampire."

"I'm pretty hip."

"What if we come across small kids?" I asked as we headed into the woods.

"The likelihood we'll run into kids is remote."

"Like Hansel and Gretel maybe. I don't want to be a monster immortalized in a children's fairy tale for all ages."

"I think we'll be alright. Any kids we stumble across out here will be more than a match for us."

"You're kidding right?" I asked.

"Mostly."

"Where are we going?" I asked as we pushed through the dense brush.

"There are nomadic people all along the old US-Canadian border."

"Just trying to survive," I said with chagrin.

"Much like we are."

"Yeah, but we're the ones doling out the death."

"Michael, these people out here would do the same to us. They are a self-sufficient lot, that's for sure, but they will prey on anything and anybody that gets within their grasp."

"That supposed to make me feel better?"

"It is what it is. Men as well as vampires are predators, at least they are not so helpless as the deer you fell with your rifle."

"You keep bringing that up. Are you gonna make me feel bad about that, too?"

"No, I'm just trying to make a point," he said with an edge of anger. "I'm about to do something I'm not sure if you will appreciate or not."

He never even gave me an opportunity to respond as he raised his right hand up to the side of my head, he placed the flat of his palm against my temple. And like a switch, literally, he shut off my humanity. My id, my ego, my super ego, rational thoughts just gone, vanished. I became the animal I was. No feelings of guilt, pain, remorse, I was a basic being. Hungry, and on a hunt. My fangs shot down, my blood quickened with the thought of food. I was aware of Tommy, but not as a friend, he was in my pack, and he was there to make our chances of success more likely. Although, at the time, it was merely pictures in my head, eat or not eat. With him...eat, without him...not eat.

My senses dominated, I could smell individual leaves – don't ask, I can't explain that one. My eyes were primed; looking simultaneously for prey and for any threats. My ears twitched with the slightest movements. If ants had been my target, they would have been screwed as I could even hear them scrabble across the hard earth. Time meant nothing as we passed quietly through the woods. Ever-looking, ever-listening.

The moon was on the far side of being done for the night. Embers burned dully in the campfire as we approached. I did not see male, female, old, young – I saw food. The being guarding the fire scarcely had time to raise his weapon as my hunting partner descended upon him. I lusted to feed with him, but the hunt was far from over as a cry of alarm issued from another being. I ripped its throat out, not thrilling in the triumph, I was merely content that I was feeding.

An arrow tore at the shoulder of my jacket. I spun. My eyes narrowed as I took in the being holding the weapon. I dropped the food I had been holding, the being with the weapon turned and fled and I was upon it before it could leave the small clearing it had bedded down in for the night.

We both drank our fill and then, when we were full, we gorged. It was the way of the animal; feast or famine, and I was saving up for the leaner times. The bodies were husks when we finished. I tossed mine to the side like I would an old dinner plate. It meant nothing more to me than that. The sun was making its presence known as I followed Tommy away from the feeding grounds. He led us to a small stream. We stepped in and I drank greedily, the ice-cold water a nice respite from the hot blood as it was washed down the metallic taste of the iron-rich food.

I was aware – but not wary – as my hunting partner approached me. I watched as his hand went to the side of my head. I fell to my knees as everything I was flooded back into me.

"Don't think too much about it," Tommy said.

I could barely hear him over the rush of thoughts in my head. It was like a great wall had been erected between the man and the animal, and when it was torn down, it was difficult assimilating the two distinct halves into one cohesive unit.

It's impossible to put to words how I felt at that point. When I had been operating as a pure predator I don't know that I've ever experienced life in a more unpolluted form. I truly believe that was the way life was meant to be lived. Not racked with guilt, self-doubt, psychoses, neuroses, and any other fucking oses. It really did come down to eat or starve, live or die. That was life. Water flowed around my outstretched arms as they held me firmly rooted in place to the small river-bed. I plunged my head into the near ice water, but even that couldn't break the fog that clouded me.

"What happened?" I finally asked.

"You know what happened," Tommy said, being less than forthcoming. "You wouldn't have done it. And the stakes are too high. I did what I had to do."

"I've said those words before." I stared at my flowing, distorted reflection in the water. "Rarely is it good."

"I'm sorry, Mike."

On one level…I was pissed. Sure, who wants to be manipulated that damn easily? On the other…HOLY FUCKING SHIT what an experience! I would, on some level, grieve for those that we had killed the previous evening – that was the man-side, the animal-side was…what? Not thrilled, not any real human emotion really. Fulfilled? We had survived. And really not even that. Life just *was*, and death was just as much a part of that. There was no baggage tied to it.

My body thrummed as we headed back into Wheatonville. I could feel every ripple of muscle, every hair as it was stirred by my movement. I was definitely switched on high. It was the morning of the war moon. Most of the town's inhabitants looked like they wanted to be anywhere but here. Some had talked with ardor about sending their kids to another town for sanctuary. There really wasn't a point. It was a good chance Xavier was going to strike here, but it wasn't like he had given us his playbook. There were at least a half-dozen places he could strike. Sending the children off was just as likely to endanger them as keeping them here.

What I'll remember the most about that day is there was no laughing; no kids running around screaming and playing. No jokes made or played. I was in a strange place, and everyone around me was in dreadful expectation. I was in an exuberant anticipation. If this thing didn't happen, there might be hell to pay. Tommy and I had sparred some in the late afternoon to try and burn off some jitters, but I was having a difficult time 'play' fighting, and he thought it best if we stopped before I got hurt.

Bailey was setting up her gunmen at the choke point to the city, creating an effective crossfire. Unfortunately, they didn't have enough bullets to keep up a sustained rate of fire. They were surrounded by at least ten men on either side, some had swords, most had deadly-looking farm implements. Who knew tending the earth produced so many dangerous looking items; it was no wonder farmers seemed always able to survive against all odds. Lords knew they'd be tested this evening.

I didn't see Azile until the sun was nearly down. "And so it begins," she said to me.

She was wearing a long flowing red dress, one I had yet to see. She looked magnificent and fierce. Her head was hooded and her eyes half closed as if she was summoning more power from whichever well she dipped into. Bailey was on my right and Tommy immediately behind me, the sounds of him sharpening his sword about the only thing making noise. We were in between the day birds retreating for the night and the myriad of night creatures producing their symphony.

It was in those final few moments I knew that Xavier had set his sights on us. War produces its own climate. A low pressure system to be sure.

"How much time do we have until the moon rises?" I asked no one in particular.

"Fifty-two minutes," Azile replied.

"Tommy?" I asked.

"Mike?" He asked back.

"This is less than savory, and those people are innocents, at least for the next fifty-one minutes and change."

"What are you saying?" Bailey asked.

"I'm saying we bring the fight to them for a little while. We could inflict some serious damage to these people before they change into werewolves," I said it and I almost couldn't believe I had. It was true, they were innocents dragged kicking and screaming into a war they wanted nothing to do with. As soon as they changed, though, all bets were off. They would kill us all without blinking, and maybe those that survived until the morning would feel sorrow, but by then it would be entirely too late. Add in that they would be once again used in some other place to destroy yet another populace.

Tommy stood, he knew the implications.

"You just want to go butchering those people?" Bailey asked.

"No, Bailey, I don't…I really fucking don't." I could have gone into a further explanation, but she knew as well as I did what was going on.

"What about the Lycan?" Azile asked. "Surely they're not going to let you waltz on in and kill their charges."

"What they don't know can kill them," I said. I tried my best to hide the savage smile that was tugging at the corners of my mouth.

"I'm in," Tommy said.

"I cannot leave," Azile said. "I have spells running and I cannot break the circle."

"Damn you, Talbot," Bailey said, checking her pockets for her magazine. She quickly fixed her rifle with a bayonet. "I'm in."

"You are more and more like BT," I told her. "Although I never really wanted to kiss him. Wait…that's a lie…there was this one time."

"You would have had a much easier time kissing him," she said hotly.

"Probably." I stepped back, hoping far enough away from her reach with the pointy end of her weapon before I finished speaking. "But you're staying here."

"I go where I will."

"You need to stay with your men, Bailey. Tommy and I can move faster and quieter," I told her; anger was threatening to break out of her like a disturbed rattler den.

Azile reached up and placed her hand on Bailey's shoulder. "He's right."

I didn't wait for a response or for them to work it out. More than likely, Bailey would shoot me in the foot and then ask 'Who's quicker now?' Add to that we were rapidly running out of time. I'd wished I'd thought of the damn fool idea earlier. But then again... no I didn't.

"You want...?" Tommy began to ask, reaching up to my temple.

"No, I at least owe it to them to be cognizant of their passing."

We moved quickly off to the left where the tree line was less than twenty yards away. I didn't get the sense we had been seen; then again, I probably wouldn't know until a razor-tipped claw took a swing at me. We hadn't gone more than a couple of hundred yards into the woods when I picked up the scent. I looked over to Tommy. He nodded morosely. He knew, too, they were just up ahead.

We approached slowly, making sure that we were downwind. We might have heightened senses, but the advantage of smelling stuff clearly went to the Lycan. People littered the ground, they seemed to all be tied together, with hands bound behind their backs, and a heavy rope tied on a leg from one to the other like a chain gang. The rope would hold the humans, but I had no doubt it would shred like twine when they turned. My stomach roiled; this would be worse than shooting at fish in a barrel. They were defenseless and couldn't even run away. Gorge was ever threatening. I was busy concentrating on keeping it down when Tommy pressed me flat to the ground.

A group of Lycan was on the far side of us talking amongst themselves – their captives a human shield between us. I watched as one stood and looked around. He seemed to sense something, but I've got to imagine with that many people around, it was making it extremely difficult for him to differentiate other scents. The five of them broke up, four of them moving away. Most likely to where their people were staged.

"Any chance if we kill him, these people will be spared?" I asked.

"There's no way to know if he turned them all or if they've already seen their first moon."

"Damn rules," I mumbled. "He's coming," I intoned softly.

He was wary; he knew something was going on out there. He stalked around the side of his people who tried to push out of his way as quickly as possible. Those that did not he kicked at savagely, snapping more than a few ribs.

"You mangy humans aren't worthy of Lycan blood!" he roared when his foot got tangled up in one of the ropes. He stomped down mercilessly, pushing the man into the dirt. By the time he was through, what was left of the man was nearly level with the surrounding ground. Viscera, gore, brains, blood, bile, and bone coated all those who were unfortunate enough to be next to the unlucky soul.

He was coming around towards us, his attention still on the people. I pushed up off the ground, a boy maybe twelve years old saw me as I did so; he gasped as his eyes got wide. The noise attracted the Lycan.

"No noise!" the handler said loudly.

I sprang, maybe I had a twig underfoot, maybe it was the whip of a branch that had caught as I went by – something got his attention. I was in midflight when he turned, his eyes widened much like the boy's had. My sword caught him mid-throat, he was strangling on his blood. Well…that and the steel that was cutting through his air pipe. And still the beast was outstretching his arms trying to get at me. When he realized I was out of reach, he started to drive the sword further into himself pulling me in with it.

Tommy was right behind me widening the gap I had started. The Lycan sagged to his knees with two swords in its throat. His eyes began to close and I placed the heel of my boot against its face, pushing him away. He fell heavily onto his side.

"Fuck," I muttered. Looking at the faces around me, some were completely downtrodden others were hopefully.

"Are you going to get us out of here, mister?" the boy who had almost given me away asked.

"He can't," a toothless old man next to him said.

"Just cut the ropes," another said. "We'll leave!"

"I've lost my taste for this," I told Tommy. "The Lycan was worth it, not the rest."

"Taste or not, Mike, any little bit we can do here makes it worthwhile. Each one of these people has the potential to kill five before the night is through."

Tommy raised his sword, the toothless man stuck his neck out, as the rest shirked away, scrambling to leave this latest horror.

"I welcome it," the man said. "The changing is among the most painful things I have ever endured and I am a man long past my prime or usefulness."

"I will make it swift, old man," Tommy said.

I turned as the blade whistled through the air. I might not have seen it, but it was impossible to not hear his head roll away. The lost souls here were terrified, but did nothing. They seemed to realize their fate, or their spirit had been beaten out of them with the time they had spent among the Lycan. In all honesty, we were doing them a favor; unfortunately the truth of the matter sucked to high heaven.

"Wait," I told Tommy before he could strike again.

"The moon is almost upon us," he said.

I was vaguely aware his chest was heaving, not from the exertion, but of the blood spilled. It was like a man dying of thirst in an ocean, water everywhere and not a drop could we touch. I wasn't entirely sure what would happen if we drank from this well, but I could smell the taint of it from where I stood.

"We wait. Some of these people were surely this

Lycan's victims. If even one of them can run away from this, then it will have been worth it. We strike as they begin their change."

"That puts us in exponentially more danger," he told me needlessly. Might as well have told me that eating a Half-Pounder with cheese and bacon everyday would make me fat, I got it.

In a strange turn of events, we had become these captives' keepers, and ultimately we were going to be a harsher warden. Night was descending quicker than I cared for in the dark of the woods. I couldn't see the moon as it was hidden from our view, but its hypnotic pull began to work on those around us. Adults and children alike began to sprout whiskers, ears began to elongate, clothes tore, screams ripped through the woods as the people were put through torturous transformations. Tommy and my swords sang as we chopped through the sea of what was once humanity. The bodies were twisted into painful contortions as the virus worked its way through their systems.

"Going to be in trouble soon, Mike," Tommy said, wet with sweat.

I had just pulled my sword out of the midsection of woman – she howled more than screamed. Her snout snapped at me. I was moving faster, slicing and slashing, body parts fell like a diseased rain. I noticed a few people who were huddling close to the ground seemingly unaffected by the moon. I was trying to fight my way to them, they were surrounded by werewolves who were in various states of transition. It was also becoming increasingly difficult to kill them as they moved through their metamorphosis. I knew I wasn't going to be quick enough. Heavy rope was beginning to tear, cries of anguish rapidly changing to growls of aggression, and still I moved quickly, my sword blurring into and through those around me. Tommy was lost in a sea of fur and gristle.

I wasn't going to make it.

"We've got to go!" Tommy shouted. One of the first times I'd truly heard him sound alarmed.

"I know."

I struggled to get out. It was kids – it's always kids. They were huddled together looking to each other to protect against what was coming.

"Ahhhh!" I yelled as I felt a claw rake against my back.

I turned and swung, the force bringing my blade nearly halfway into the beast behind. I pulled the sword back, intestines spilling to the ground. I caught an elbow to the head, nearly rocking me to the ground. Now it wasn't so much about would I be able to get to the kids to save them, but would I be able to fight my way out to safety.

"I'm sorry," I said hollowly as I turned.

Tommy was moving closer.

"Mr. T!"

"Yup!" I answered. Not really sure what else I could say. I did my best not to look when I heard the high-pitched screams of the lost. "Damn you, Xavier."

Tommy grabbed my shoulder and was almost rewarded with the business end of my weapon. He was dragging me behind him, and I was still cutting and trying to make sure we could get out of there.

"Run!" Tommy yelled as we broke free. I needed no further prompting.

"Coming in hot!" I yelled to those waiting in the town. I was running like the hounds of hell were chasing us, which was pretty much a truism.

"Fools!" Bailey yelled as her rifle began to shout its protests.

I could hear thuds of animals falling behind me. If I stumbled, they would have be on me. I thought darkly of the old zombie adage, 'I didn't need to be the fastest to get away, just faster than the other guy'. Unfortunately right now Tommy had two steps on me. It was hard reconciling how a kid of his size could be so damn fast. We were through the first balustrades; Bailey's men had taken to arms giving us more of a cushion.

"Have fun?" Azile asked as I got to her.

"A lot of words," I said breathlessly, "that I could use…fun ain't one of them."

Azile's face was flushed, I watched her as a trembling went through her body. She raised her arms over her head. Light flooded her hands; a fire that produced no heat enveloped them. With a heavy exhalation she thrust the cold flame forward. The yelps of the werewolves could be heard as the flame hit the ground and spread, sending up a yellow-red wall of wildfire nearly ten feet tall. Unlike Azile, those that were caught in it began to burn. The animals ran wildly looking for a way to extinguish the conflagration.

"That's handy," I said, catching my breath. I could feel the intense heat even from this distance.

"It won't last," she said with great pains.

"Game on." I tried my best to get put a brave face on.

The ones that had been chasing us were merely one of the many cells of werewolves; we had decimated that group, but there were plenty more to take up the fight. Futility seemed like a pretty good word. The four gunslingers had to pull back and were repositioning from the heat. A lot of the townsfolk had that look in their eye that had me doubting if they would stand their ground. However, there weren't too many choices – stand and die, run and die. One just made you more tired when you went to meet your maker.

"They're coming!" someone off to our right shrieked.

My son Justin would have been so proud. We had affectionately called him Captain Obvious for always ringing out what was right in front of you. How I wished I could good-naturedly call it to his face. The witch-fire began to flag, much like a propane tank on its last legs and always just as you put the steak on the grill. The many-legged, furry blur loping towards us was in a frenzy, all snarling mouths, and long teeth flashing wickedly. Claws upraised, they raced across the small clearing. So intent were they on their prey that they paid no heed to the logs planted into the ground. The first wave slammed into them, with more than a few impaling themselves all the way through.

Their bays of frustration broke the still of the night. The moon was hanging swollen and pregnant, shining brilliantly upon the horizon as the war for Wheatonville had begun. Werewolves began to hurdle over their fallen brethren and into our second surprise. I had instructed Bailey to dig a trench about ten feet wide around the entire fencing structure we had erected. It wasn't deep – just enough to drive wooden spikes into, pointy part up. Werewolves leaped or scrambled up and over our first line of defense only to find their feet impaled.

Three or four townsfolk would run in and deliver deadly blows before the monsters could extradite themselves. Cries on both sides rang out as werewolves fought savagely even stuck to the ground as they were. One swipe from those thickly muscled arms was enough to decapitate a full-grown man. Bailey's men held onto their bullets as long as they could before sending the precious projectiles downrange, it would be mere moments before they joined us in the sword brigade. It was starting to look like the world's largest and deadliest steeplechase as werewolves propelled themselves over first the logs and then their dead and dying kind stuck on the impalers. The first ones over the stone wall and into the town seemed almost lost at first as they were trying to acquire targets.

None were close just yet, but that was only a matter of time. Azile's arms shot out to my own. I turned to look and noticed that she seemed exhausted to the point where she had done so to keep from falling over.

"You alright?" I asked, only sparing a glance, anything more than that was not wise at the moment.

"Fine, fine," she told me.

I begged to differ. "Want me to get you to somewhere safe?"

"If you know of some place, let me know." She smiled wanly.

"The fire, she needs to recover," Tommy said, filling in the blanks.

And then, we were in the thick of it. I don't know if we looked tastier than the rest, or if the werewolves had particular instructions. Maybe we looked like the biggest threat and they wanted to be rid of us. Five of them were heading our way. Tommy and I silently separated slightly lest we inadvertently catch steel from each other.

"What I wouldn't do for my AR," I said as I dug in, hunched down to make a smaller target, keeping the edge of my blade outward. This wasn't the all-out assault we were used to seeing; they were approaching cautiously, almost tentatively. They knew something, this seemed like containment, keeping us bottled up while the rest laid waste. "Fuck that!" I yelled as I ran at them. Typical Talbot, act first think later. One against five was going to get me killed no matter my prowess. Two against five was about even as Tommy caught up.

"I'd almost forgotten how you go about your business," he said wryly.

"Damn fool!" Bailey shouted coming alongside.

"She knows," I told him, and then I slashed out, severing a hand right above the wrist.

I spun and was able to put my sword up in time as a heavy arm sent me sprawling. The beast pounced thinking I was down. I drove the sword through its chest, and once again found myself on the ground, this time pinned under roughly two hundred and fifty pounds of something that smelled strangely like wet dog. The thing flicked off of me as Tommy grabbed it by the scruff and tossed it away. Bailey had drilled one in the forehead and now it was three on three. It just kept getting stranger as the three remaining began to back up, Tommy advanced.

And then it struck me, if I took longer than a blink to think shit through I would have figured out what was going on. It was a diversion, and Azile was the target. No matter how lofty I thought of myself, I was just hired muscle as was Tommy and Bailey. Azile was the prize – if she went down, everything would fall apart. It really is a chore being this damn stupid. No sooner had I pulled myself free from the werewolf and I was up and sprinting back towards the way we had come. Tommy hacked at one that was determined to follow and stop me. Bailey couldn't get off a clean shot and was using her bayonet to hold the other two off.

Three I hadn't seen before had circled around and were approaching Azile from the back, she seemed completely unaware. Her eyes half-closed, hands held up about to her waist, palms facing heavenwards. It was possible she was saying something, but I was running entirely too fast to make out such a small detail. The shockwave caught me mid-flight. I had launched when I realized I was going to come up short in my intercept course. One moment I was leaping headlong towards Azile with the express intent of knocking her over, the next, a wall of wind forced me off course. It was like a bomb had gone off and I was caught in the concussive wave. I was really getting sick of being knocked off my feet.

The werewolves who had been closer seemed to be suffering more. They were stirring – but not quickly – blood leaking from their ears. When I realized I could hear nothing, not cries nor screams, or the clang of metal, I figured my eardrums had been punctured as well. I did not have the time to reach up and touch the sticky fluid I knew would be coming down the side of my face. I wasn't entirely sure what was keeping Azile standing. She was swaying like wheat in a gale. The maneuver had bought me some time, it looked as if one of the werewolves would never move again, I wondered if she had fried his brain. Then I wondered if I had been close enough that she had done that to me, although with all the illegal substances I had used over the years, it would be doubtful if anyone would notice a difference.

I had no idea if she had planned it this way, but she collapsed just as a mighty paw swept over where her head had been. It would be cool to think she pulled off a ninja move like that, but she hit the ground hard and didn't look like she was going to get up for a while. My sword caught the werewolf between the third and fourth finger and sliced through its hand and halfway up its forearm. It was a gruesome injury, half of its forearm sloughed off. It wrenched back pulling my sword with it. I was without my weapon and hadn't felt quite so naked since that one time I had almost been caught with my girlfriend back when we were both sixteen and her father had come home from work early. The couch had seemed like a perfectly acceptable place to have a heavy petting session. Hell, at sixteen, where doesn't seem like a good place?

***

The werewolf was swinging his arm back and forth trying to dislodge the steel imbedded in him. Blood was spraying in great arcs as he did so. A kid, who I guess was trying to make a name for himself, came to my rescue. He had a pitchfork, a fucking pitchfork! It was like the Polish riding into battle on horseback against a German Panzer division. The kid saved my ass, but I'm sure in no fashion he had ever figured on.

The werewolf sheered half his face off. The young man's left eye rolled upwards even as that half of his face fell away. I'd seen some inherently disgusting things in my long life, and at this very moment, that had the dubious award of being the worst. A deli meat slicer couldn't have done it with any more precision. Facial muscles rippled wetly and glowed dully in the moonlight; damaged just enough that he couldn't pull that side of himself into a scream. It looked like a doctor's diorama, and that's what I was going to go with no matter what my nightmares said to the contrary.

His weapon of choice was flung from his hands and to my feet…which I gladly picked up. The handle was slick with blood, and as far as I was concerned it was werewolf blood and not facial. Again, I'm entitled to dilute my horrors as best I see fit. I rolled and jammed at least three of the tines through the soft skin under the lupine's chin, driving its muzzle to a closed position. The handle shuddered as I went further and then through the roof of its mouth and into its brain where the beast finally stilled.

The boy had fallen next to me, his one undamaged eye looking up, pleading with me for help or to help him end his misery. Neither thing could I do for him now as I yanked the pitchfork free. My sword was tantalizingly close; unfortunately, the next werewolf was even closer. I only had enough time to hold the handle up in a defensive posture, which it summarily bit in half.

"Not cool," I said as I backed away.

His teeth were snapping faster than those stupid little chattering gag teeth we all thought were so cool when we were seven. Now, well…not so much. From the way I had pivoted, I could see that Tommy and Bailey were not going to be able to help anytime soon, and I saw no more wannabe heroes heading my way. I hurled the broken wooden half at the werewolf. He, she…it…shrugged it off. I had about a foot of handle attached to the end of my pitchfork. It was about as unwieldy a weapon as I'd ever held, and yet it was all that separated me from certain death.

The only thing I had going for me was that they were fairly predictable – forward it would come. But now it had the reach, if this was a prizefight, advantage went over to him. A claw raked across my chest, ripping through my heavy jacket, my burlap shirt, and across my chest, leaving a trail of blood and fire-lanced pain. I winced and stepped back before he could open the wound further. This was not going according to plan, although that's a huge assumption. I mean the part about me having a plan to begin with.

I knew what I had to do, but just because you know you *have* to get a root canal doesn't mean you *want* to. I had to take one for the team; I let my guard down just enough that the werewolf's next swipe caught me flush on the top part of my arm. I'm not sure how it didn't break, but I didn't have too much time to think about it as my feet lifted from the ground. For two shining seconds I was Superman as I flew through the air. I sure as shit didn't get as high as a tall building, though. I landed close to my sword and THAT was actually what I was hoping for. I may have lost a millisecond or two marveling that it had actually worked as I reached out and snagged it.

The werewolf was on me before I stopped rolling. This time, though, I had a weapon in each hand. With my right sword-clad hand I returned the favor to his mid-section; although I think I paid him back with some interest as I saw the thick muscle walls peel back. The slice was nearly a foot across and an inch or so deep. Might as well have shot him with a bb gun for all the 'give-a-shit' he gave.

"Well, if that didn't get your attention…this will." I jumped, driving the tines of the pitchfork into its open mouth. He tried to howl, but when your uvula is pinned in the back of your throat it can be somewhat of a bitch. I slit his throat to save him the trouble. As he dropped down, I grabbed my pitchfork and pulled it out. It was a crappy weapon for the most part, but I liked the comfort it afforded me. As much as I wanted to celebrate my small triumph, I did not have that luxury. I turned towards Azile. She was still lying on the ground in her crumpled form. A massive werewolf stood over her swiping furiously.

It looked to me, like he had horrible depth perception, because he was few inches short of his mark. He snarled when he saw me coming, but that did not deter him from his single-minded mission in the least. Fine with me. I pulled my arm all the way back before I swung. My blade bit deeply into his neck. I severed head from body as neatly as one can do something so grisly. His body fell forward, sliding down whatever barrier Azile had between herself and the outside world, blood smeared the clear cocoon.

"Azile?" I asked softly. She was unmoving.

I dropped the pitchfork. I wasn't sure if I'd be able to get around the shield, but apparently it was not designed to stop vamps. I grabbed her around the waist and, as gently as I could, saddled her over my shoulder. She seemed so light, like maybe she had drained herself of substance. I didn't know if that was possible. But I knew as much about witchcraft as I did about women in general, so not so much.

I stood up. I did not like what I was seeing; werewolves were pouring in and people were pulling back. I couldn't remember the last time I'd heard a shot, but now that I looked on the scene, I wasn't hearing much of anything. I ran back to the final rally place, the Church of Bob – I'm not going to even go into that at this point. Let's just call it the last sanctuary for the old and the young. There were men nervously patrolling the building that wasn't much more than a log cabin. The walls were stout enough, but nothing short of a foot of concrete was going to stop the werewolves.

"Get her inside!" I needlessly yelled into the ear of the man closest to me. He heard me just fine. "She dies you die!" I shouted again. He blanched. I truly hadn't meant it as a threat; I was merely implying that the only way they could get through to her was over his dead body. Whatever worked I supposed. If we didn't stop the werewolves, nobody was going to be around to defend anything.

He nodded vigorously. "Ye-ye-yes, sir."

"Where are the archers?" I asked, trying my best not to shout in his face. I saw how little I was succeeding by the amount of spittle I shot at him. He pointed towards my left.

The archers were basically old men not capable of wielding anything heavier, although the bows at a seventy-five-pound draw, were no joke. It had been decided to use them as a last means of defense. I determined on the spot that, by that time, it would be too late.

"Let's go!" I told them, motioning with my arm. There were eleven or so. "The arrows!" I said after more than a few left their baskets of projectiles behind. "You have got to be kidding me."

The fight was waging all around us as I headed for the city gates. "Alright, we're going to do this like the British," I told them. They stared at me, probably wondering if the blood leaking from my ears was mixed with my brain matter.

"Six in front, here!" I pointed with my sword. "Five right behind them. When the front bowmen shoot, you will get down and nock an arrow. While you're doing that, the back row will fire. We will keep doing that until you're out of arrows or dead. Do you understand?"

"I'm hard of hearing," one of the older men shouted back, "not stupid! Let me take Dellard's place. He'll never be able to squat and stand."

"Fine, fine hurry up."

Werewolves were attracted to a group this size. Maybe we wouldn't be the tastiest morsels out there, but there were enough of us to make it worthwhile. A group of them were heading our way, knocking each other over in an attempt to get to the feast first.

"Fire!" I said needlessly as the front line loosed their first volley. Yelps of pain erupted from the throng coming our way. It was funny that, of all the things and noises going on, the one thing I heard distinctly were the pops and creaks of old knees doing things they were unaccustomed to as the men knelt.

"Fire!" I told the second group. Werewolves skidded to a halt with arrows protruding from their bodies.

A couple of men stayed on the ground and fired from there. I was surprised at the strength they exhibited to do that. One of them was laughing as if this were the funniest thing in the world. Or the craziest, I figured.

"Fire at will!" I shouted, not that they were listening anyway, they had figured the rhythm of it out easy enough. Shoot or die, pretty basic.

"Don't shoot me!" I begged as I moved off to the side and slightly in front.

"Don't get in the way," one of them replied.

"Comforting," I replied as I hacked at a werewolf coming. He had one arrow driven straight through his cheek and another lodged deep in his calf. It would not take a third to drop him as I struck his upper thigh, my arms shivering as the steel collided with femur. We were on the main thoroughfare, the buildings keeping our flanks relatively protected. The werewolves only had one avenue of approach, and I was going to use that to our maximum advantage.

The people who had been scrambling to get back to the Church of Bob now rallied to our position. I saw one of Bailey's men torn in two as he ran towards us. His legs traveled another five feet before they realized they had nothing steering the ship. Thankfully, the upper half landed out of sight. I had yet to see Tommy or Bailey, but leaving this present location was not a possibility. We were keeping them at bay but barely.

"Are there more arrows?" I asked, taking note that we were starting to scrape the bottom of the barrel in that regard.

My laughing man began anew with riotous, raucous abandon.

"Don't shoot me," I said nearly a fraction of a second too late as I moved in front of the firing line.

"Don't get in the damn way," one of the crotchety bastards repeated to me.

I started ripping arrows out of bodies and tossing them back towards where I had come. I think the main crotchety bastard understood what I was doing.

"Cover him!" he yelled.

I would have been safer on my own. As arrows whistled past me, I think I could have counted individual feathers if I stopped long enough to look. I turned to toss three arrows behind me, Laughing Man had tears rolling down his face he was enjoying himself so much. It was then I noted he was pointing in my general direction, and I was pretty sure his eyes weren't even open.

"This sucks," I said, moving to the side.

The arrow nicked my nose and thumped into the groin of a werewolf that had set its sights on me. The brute was in a great deal of pain as he stood up. I yanked the projectile free and slammed it into his midsection a few times for good measure. He fell over and was trampled by those coming up behind him. We were creating a decent-sized wall of dead, but these weren't zombies, the impediment wasn't going to stop them or even slow them in the slightest. The only thing they had in common with my former foe was that they cared as little about their fallen as the former. Which meant not at all. At least these fuckers screamed when they were coming at you. The eerie silence of a zombie attack was unsettling, although it wasn't like this was worlds better.

We'd set up a sort of stalemate. However, once those arrows were gone, we were going to have to do a tactical withdrawal. I grabbed about a dozen men and women that looked the best suited for what I was proposing. Laughing Man was at the point where he was dry firing his bow.

"Get him out of here! All of you," I said, referring to the bowmen, "go…get back to the church!"

"We've still got a few arrows."

"We'll need them later. Go while you can, we'll watch your back. Where is the damned fire?" I asked of no one in particular.

We had filled in our shallow pit with pitch, the idea being that we would light it on fire and force the werewolves into the teeth of our defense. The damn thing should have been lit a friggin' long time ago…had to figure that the person who was in charge of that ship's had sailed.

We needed that fire. That was going to be the only thing that kept us from being completely surrounded; although that ship was getting ready to leave port as well. *Stupid ships.* I was hacking and slashing, trying to give the people behind me some sort of chance at regrouping. Werewolves were flooding the street. Some even taking to the rooftops and leaping from one to the next. I could see Bailey and Tommy off to my right. Both looked bloody and impossibly far away. I used the only tool available – my mind, and some might say that was severely lacking.

"*The fire, Tommy.*"

He didn't actually reply back, but I could sense his chagrin. He and Bailey turned and were out of sight. We were screwed. I knew it, and the werewolves knew it. Well…probably not, they don't really give a shit. We were going to cause them many casualties, not that their overlords were going to care. As far as the Lycan were concerned, we were two scourges wiping each other from the planet. Hadn't seen one of those bastards yet. And why would they unnecessarily expose themselves? The werewolves were their drones and the Lycan were fighting remotely.

I didn't realize it at first, but I had become completely cut off from the retreat. The only direction the werewolves weren't coming from was below. My sword became a blur; to stop its momentum was death. If I lodged this thing in a spinal cord I wouldn't have enough time to remove it and keep them away. I think the only thing I had going for me was that I wasn't the primary target, but rather, an impediment to that goal. Even as some stopped to end my existence, others streamed past. In fairness, they probably couldn't see me. And now that I thought of it, that was to become my strategy.

I went for maximum viscera as I struck at the soft

bellies of the beasts, ropes of intestines flooding to the ground. Half-digested human remains spilled out with it as stomachs were sliced in two. I went down to one knee just as the werewolf I had devitalized fell over on top of me. As disgusting as this is to write, living it was magnitudes of revolting worse. Timing was crucial as I let his weight push me into the mass of detritus. I was embalmed in everything you can imagine would come from the insides of a cannibalistic werewolf. I may have added my own vomit to the mix, but that would have easily been the best thing in that human stew.

    I was under two feet of fuck-fest. My nose was the only thing not submerged, occasionally the air would be pumped from my lungs as a werewolf or two bounded off the pile. Funny how I once thought zombies smelled bad. The only thing that may have kept my fragile mind from snapping was the smell of burning pitch. Tommy and Bailey had succeeded, the fires were lit. We had filled the entire shallow pit, and now that it burned, we had finally stopped their egress from the sides of the town. It had been long moments since I'd felt the tremble of the ground from footfalls. I sloughed off the brute on me. I looked like a B-movie prop gone completely over the top. I was coated from head to toe, I thought about stripping and doing the 'naked savage' thing, but time was of the essence, and it was slightly chilly out, there'd be some shrinkage. Yes, even in a fight to the death I was concerned for what people might think about my helmeted buddy.

    I wanted to go running through the gates and give the Lycans a little taste of their own medicine, but the real fight was now behind me and getting further away the longer I debated. I waited for a moment, hoping that Bailey and Tommy would come back around. I stayed as long as I dared and then ran to get back to the Church of Bob. The darkest part of the night had long since passed, but we were still a couple of hours from the moon finally taking a bow. Seemed the fat bitch wasn't quite ready to yield her place on the stage yet. And the hundred or so werewolves that remained were going to make the most of their time left on earth.

I wanted to ask them to stop jumping around so I could get an accurate count, but they were worse than first graders mainlining on Halloween candy. I came across the infirm werewolves first. The one I came upon had a gash that ran all the way from under her armpit to her calf. The skin had separated by as wide as three inches in some places, muscle and sinew rippled as she moved. How she was still standing eluded me; I figured I could solve that problem. My sword whistled as I sliced her deep on the small of her back. If she'd ever had a tramp stamp I would have surely marred it. Then I was left to wonder if that was one of those weirder fads that had died out with my time. I guess it gave the guy something to look at while he was getting busy, not sure the need though. I'd never felt any reason to be anything more than enamored with what was already going on. Call me crazy.

The werewolf must have already been out on its last legs. As it fell, it barely gave out an 'oomph' as it collided with the ground. The next had an arrow that had caught it in the shoulder. I was looking at the protruding barb as I approached. Blood pumped out of the wound with every tortured step it took. There were another half dozen in some sort of weakened fashion that I rid of all earthly troubles, one sword stroke at a time. Now I was to the meat of the fight, the werewolves I was now encountering were fighting each other to get into better position to kill. None, as of yet, had figured out the threat to the rear. That was about to change.

I must have looked like the walking dead as they turned, a vengeful, deathly spirit come to exact my toll. I'd like to think I'd struck some chord of fear in them, but that seemed like a lot of wishful thinking on my part. In the annals of history, this won't go down as a particularly big battle, but what it lacked in size it more than made up for in ferocity. Screams of anguish were intermingled with cries of triumph and punctuated with tears of tragedy. We just needed to hold on…that was it…just a little longer. That was the gist of the battle plan: hold the fuck on. I knew that if my arms were aching, then the people on the other side of this werewolf wall had to be flagging.

The only thing we seemingly had going for us was that whoever was left, was here. There were no werewolf reinforcements rounding the bend. I gritted my teeth; shoulders aching as I slashed again. Body parts littered the ground. It looked like a Civil War operating floor. I felt a rush of heat as a claw ripped through my side, I danced away as far as I could before it could sink deep. As it was, it would need tending even with my recuperative power.

A werewolf head rocked back as a bullet struck it in the side. I couldn't be sure, but I think it was the one that had tried to take a chunk from me. Bailey was running towards me at a full tilt.

"You did not take that shot on the run?" I asked. Not that she could hear me, but the question needed to be posed.

"Last bullet," she said as she joined the fray. She was as deadly with her eight-inch blade as I was with the sword, probably more so. She jammed the damn thing so far into the throat of the closest werewolf, it came out through its back. It struggled to put its hands up to the wound. She kicked it over before it had a chance.

"Tommy?" I asked.

She gave a curt shake of her head. Her lips pressed tight.

I knew that for the impossibility that it was. It was inconceivable that Tommy could die. Nobody lives for six hundred-plus years, and then 'poof'…is just gone. I would not and – more importantly – could not accept that fact. If I lost one more tie to the past, I would be adrift in a sea of despair. Seconds became minutes as we fought. Ever-swirling, with Death as our partner; so close, he would sweep in and I'd swear I could smell the sodden earth of my burial pit.

Screw that. "If I die," I yelled to Bailey, "tell Azile I want to go out like a Viking!"

"No idea what a Viking is," Bailey replied almost effortlessly as if she were removing wax from a roll of cheese as opposed to fighting werewolves. "But you are not going to die."

If Tommy, who was bigger, faster, and stronger than me could die, then all bets were off on my particular status. I could only hope that he would somehow find his way back to his sister. There would be more than enough time to mourn later. Now, all my effort went into fighting through the Lycan wannabes and defending Azile. I could only hope it wasn't too late.

***

Tommy spotted Mike fighting. He had completely forgotten about the fire and why it hadn't been lit. Preserving one's life tended to intrude on all extraneous thoughts. He knew what Mike was asking as soon as the words blistered into his mind.

Going to have to teach him some volume control, Tommy thought as he grabbed Bailey and headed back towards the fence line. Werewolves were still making their way in, and it was all they could do to get to one of the torches that lined the street. Tommy snapped it off at its hilt and ran towards the trench. The fire was attracting unwanted attention. Tommy was carving a path; he could see the futility of being able to make enough forward progress. He quickly moved his sword to his left hand and the pitch-soaked torch to his right.

He reared back and tossed the torch as far as he could, the flame had no sooner left his hand than he felt a savage bite on his knee. The bones splintered as the animal tore through the fabric of his being. Tommy wailed in pain as the animal shook its large head back and forth. He was frozen in shock. Bailey drove her bayonet through the back of its head and then kicked it in the jaw to push it away from him.

"GO!" he screamed when she tried to grab his arm and help him. "We won't make it! GO!"

Bailey saw the wisdom in his words, but it wasn't in her to leave someone behind. They'd never be able to move fast enough together to get away. She would stay and fight with him until the end – which seemed exceedingly close at the moment. She moved out of saber range but stayed back to back with him. Werewolves closed in from all angles. There was a flash of heat as the torch found its mark. A gust of super-heated air blew past them. Werewolves close to the conflagration erupted in great gouts of flame. The chaos that ensued as burning werewolves ran into each other was the window that Bailey needed to half carry Tommy away from the melee. Tommy had taken on a sickly hue as his body did what it could to mitigate the bite and reverse the damage.

"Are you in danger?" Bailey asked as they huddled behind a broken brick wall.

"I think that goes without saying." Tommy winced.

"From the bite," she said stingingly.

"From turning? No. But the bite carries its own toxins that will make healing that much more difficult and painful. Werewolves don't have enough of the disease in them to turn anyone, but it's still enough to kill a person if they don't get proper attention." Tommy was trying to readjust his leg, every position seemed to cause more pain than the last.

"At least we stopped them," Bailey said as she peeked over the wall.

Tommy was still for a moment, his face turning white as if someone had draped a funeral shroud over him. "I never thought it would end this way," he said aloud.

"What way? You're not dead yet. BT's journals said Mike was prone to dramatics, it didn't mention you anywhere in that passage.

A small smile crept across his face. "He really is, isn't he? He's the key in all of this, Bailey. You need to protect him."

"From what?" she asked, not sure where or why this conversation was going on.

"From himself, of course. He's always been his own worst enemy."

"You protect him. I'm no one's babysitter," she said defiantly. She had meant it as a way to help stop his defeatist, dour way of thinking…not as a rebuke.

"He needs you now." His eyes rolled up a little into his head before coming back and focusing on her.

"That may be. Although I have no way of knowing how you know that. But what I do know, without a doubt, is that you need me as well."

"Ever play chess?" Tommy asked obscurely.

"I have, Tommy. What does that have to do with anything?"

"Sometimes an advantage can be gained with a sacrifice."

She liked his words less and less.

"But only if the player is deft enough to realize this. You must make him see this, he will come to a crossroads and it will be your forceful hand that will nudge him in the right direction."

"Are you saying we are merely pawns in Michael's game?"

Tommy looked at her sweetly. "No, my child," he said, struggling to get his hand to her face. "We are all powerful pieces. You, me, Azile…even Lana will play her part, but Mike is the king." He laughed, a spot of blood falling from the corner of his mouth. "Don't tell him that, though, his head is already too big."

"I need to get you to help," she said with alarm as she looked down to his ravaged knee, a puddle of blood had pooled beneath it. "Will my blood help?"

"Don't!" he said in alarm, "I would not be able to control myself. Go help Mike. When the moon has finished its damned journey, bring help back here. I promise I won't move." He laughed weakly.

"You die on me, Tommy, and leave me with that crazy man…I will haunt you to the ends of the earth."

"I look forward to it."

She had no idea the true meaning behind his words, but she did not like the way in which they were delivered. She once again rose to look up; the werewolves that had not been burned in the flash were gone. She hoped they had retreated, but she had a better idea of which direction they had headed.

"You stay here, Tommy, do you hear me?"

He nodded.

She meant spiritually. Physically, nothing short of two strong men and a litter were going to be able to move him without incurring more damage.

"Eliza?" Tommy asked.

Bailey shuddered as she moved, keeping her profile low to match the wall. She knew all about the Cruel One, and to think she was close enough that Tommy could sense her was enough to get her moving. Werewolves had taken a backseat in terms of fear – at least for the moment. She found herself pursuing werewolves, which was entirely more palatable than the other way around. She had a few bullets left – six if she had been keeping accurate count – but she wanted to save those. Also, using them would give her away.

Werewolves and Wheatonville residents choked the roadway. It looked as if the townsfolk were giving as well as they were getting. It was still an unsustainable war. The Lycan would always be able to rearm, so to speak. Those were thoughts for another time, she figured, as she drove her bayonet up and through the back of a werewolf's neck. Another was leaning up against a wall snarling at her. His leg had been chopped off at the knee. She brought the rifle to her shoulder and almost splattered his brains on the wooden wall behind him.

"Dammit," she muttered pulling the rifle down. She didn't want to get too close but she also didn't want to alert any others nearby. The werewolf was swiping with his massive paws. "How bad you want it!" She charged at him.

The thrust caught the edge of his nose, slid up the cartilage and pierced his eye; he was still before he could take an effective stab at Bailey. The rest of her journey towards the center was unencumbered with the living. For good or bad, everything that was going to take place was directly up ahead. She was distinctly aware of the passage of time and how every second she was away from Tommy was a moment lost in being able to rescue him. Even though she had known it was too late as she left him.

And there he was, the ignorant, pig-headed Michael, fighting like a demon amongst devils. Tommy was right. He was in danger, and nothing short of a miracle was going to save him. She was running towards him, rifle set securely in her shoulder. The steel sights bobbing wildly, every step changing her point of aim; left foot was the werewolf coming up behind him, right foot was Mike. Her left foot came down and she pulled on the trigger thinking she may have yanked it back a little too hard jerking her even further up and off target. If anything, it had saved Mike's life as the bullet caught the werewolf flush in the side of the head, sending a misty red spray across the throng. She dropped five more in various states of pain and death as she came up alongside Mike.

***

Bailey had afforded a clearing and I was going to do all I could to get to the doors and keep them barricaded from the carnage that would ensue if they were broken open.

"Used to love the night, the peace and quiet it afforded. Plus…no people," I said, kicking out a knee from a werewolf that had gotten too close. "Now!" I shouted. "Not so much. All of a sudden six months of sun up north sounds pretty friggin' good."

"The moon also rises there," Bailey said from directly behind me.

"Really? Buzz kill," I told her. We were getting closer, the press of flesh getting to the point where effective fighting was becoming difficult. At least, for those of us that wielded weapons, the ones with mouths as weapons seemed to be adapting to the fighting conditions just fucking fine. I'd held on to a futile hope that the Landians would make a cameo and help out, but that appeared less and less likely as more time passed and more of us died. I'd have to thank them personally if I ever got the chance.

When I finally fought my way through, I'd wished for a video camera. The look on the closest person's face as I approached was priceless.

"Yeah, and I smell just as good," I told him, making sure he didn't mistake me for an enemy. *This it?* I thought, looking upon the defenders-slash-survivors.

Laughing Man was somehow still alive and had been restocked with arrows. Someone had the foresight to place him in a roughhewn chair. He was happily firing away. I could only hope that, when I finally slid over that precipice I was continually hugging, I'd be half as effective of a fighting machine. More than once I noted that, as I cut down a werewolf, they had been tentatively turning their heads. At first, I mistakenly assumed it was their masters calling them back, but then the truth of it hit me; it was the moon…or more clearly, its descent.

Time, which is a mortal enemy to us all, had finally swung in our favor. I knew our new ally could be as finicky as hell. I wasn't going to let the opportunity slide. We were literally fighting with our backs to the wall. We had been pressed as close as we could without being on intimate terms...or at least going to dinner and a show.

"Wheatonvillians!" I shouted. It had no ring, it wasn't like 'Spartans' or 'Romans' and I wasn't even sure if it was Wheatonvillians. Seemed more like a village of bad guys than a townspeople name. What was the alternative Wheatonvillites? Even less savory. No matter, my shout had got their attention.

"I know you're exhausted, but we must press the attack! Even now the werewolves are in the process of turning back. You must not! WE must not allow them escape, for they will return!"

I knew what I was asking. In moments, the beasts before us would once again become the men, women, and children they once were. Frightened, naked, and completely unaware of what destruction they had wrought, we would still have to destroy them. There was no rehabilitation, even if we captured them; there was no chance of convincing them we were their friends and the Lycan the true enemy. Come the next full moon, the jailers would once again become meat.

In terms of speeches it was horrible but, truth be told, I was too damn exhausted to do much more than force them forward. Werewolves began the painful process of reconfiguring their beings; muzzles fell back, hair receded faster than a middle-aged man's. Razor claws were reduced to jagged fingernails. Pointed ears began to look more like a Star Trek prop (if you were alive during my era you'd get the reference, the name Spock will mean absolutely nothing to you now). Pain was etched on their features as things evolution would take millions of years to recreate were being done in mere moments.

Swords still slashed, pitchforks still poked, arrows still pierced. The werewolves were falling in droves. Some tried to retreat as a means of self-preservation, but most were stuck with limbs in mid-transformation, unable to move as the Reaper unabashedly sought them out. People faltered as the enemy began to look more like them. I had no such compunction. All I noted was that it was now easier to behead them without the thick-corded muscles around their necks getting in the way. So much had been lost, and still this stupid town thought of mercy.

"Fools!" I told them. "Do you think they will be so kind when they come back? How many of your friends…of your family members are dead?" I kept hacking away. Azile might be named the Red Witch, but I acquired the name 'Red Reaper' that night as I savagely ended their tormented existences.

"Enough!" Azile said, being supported at the doorway to the church.

My chest was heaving. If I had previously been coated with viscera, I was now my own walking pool of it. Save my eyes…they burned with a savage fury. Blood flowed around my feet as I turned to the voice.

"You would stop me?" I asked. I wanted to fight, and right now it didn't matter with whom.

"Tommy needs us." Bailey grabbed my arm.

She had been alongside my genocide. She above all others knew the wisdom in defeating our enemy when the chance arose. There could be no quarter.

Tommy, I thought.

The bodies around me now more resembled the beings they had once been. In a matter of minutes, I could finish them off alone. I weighed destroying them with going to find Tommy. I won't lie; it was a toss-up until Oggie came out of the church. He swiveled his head looking at the damage. He came up to me, somehow finding a clear spot on the back of my hand. He licked it and headed off to the main gate. That was really all I needed for the turning point. Whether they survived or not, little mattered what happened to the remnants of the werewolves. The Lycan's next attack would destroy what was left of this once-thriving community.

It wasn't like the naked people on the ground would be able to atone for their sins. This would be the first time in my history I would actually agree with the temporary insanity plea. They actually had no clue what they had done. They were as much predators as I had been the night Tommy turned me into a hunting machine. I caught fragmentary glimpses of that night, but nothing more, and it would be the same for these people. Might as well condemn the termite for eating your house. Sure, you could eradicate him, or at least try, but it wasn't like he was going to have any clue as to why you were killing him. He was doing what he had been programmed to do.

Tommy.

He was all that mattered. My walk turned into a trot, and when I didn't think that was fast enough I began to run. Oggie was still slightly ahead of me with Bailey slightly behind. Something was wrong. I could feel it in every fiber of my being. I had my line of sight slightly angled down. There were so many bodies strewn on the roadway, I had to watch my footing. It was Oggie's savage barking that got my attention first.

"No further!" a booming voice rang out.

Oggie was bristled and looked near to charging.

"Hold that diluted monster away," the Lycan said.

"Oggie, to me," I said, taking in the scene. He took his sweet time doing it, but he was unlike most of the women in my life…he actually listened.

Not more than twenty yards from me stood three incredibly large Lycan (I somehow forgot how big they were, the werewolves, who also dominated over humans, were stunted dwarves in comparison). Two were holding Tommy, more like suspending him. His leg hung at a grotesque angle and he had enough scrapes and cuts over his bare torso to look like he had gotten caught in the world's largest briar patch.

"Tommy!?" I shouted in question.

"Come no further, Old One," the Lycan that was standing in front and to the side of Tommy said.

I upraised my sword. The Lycan laughed, it was a menacing sound. His eyes glinted cold hard steel.

"This is how it ends, Mr. T," Tommy said with resignation. It looked like he had just enough energy to raise his head and tell me that.

"You have lost here!" I shouted to the Lycan.

"Have we?" he asked back. "I care not for the werewolves slaughtered here." And then he spat a large voluminous phlegm ball to the ground. "The humans even less. When Xavier finds out I have destroyed an Old One, I will become my own pack leader for this."

"Find my soul." Tommy begged.

"Humans and their airy wishes," the lead Lycan said. The other two laughed. Tommy struggled weakly against his bonds.

"I will kill you for this," I told him.

"Perhaps, Old One, but not before it is too late." He spun incredibly fast. Before I could even process what was going on, he had swung. Tommy's head tumbled to the ground.

It might as well have been my head spiraling down as vertigo threatened to drop me. Bailey gasped and reached out, holding me steady. I charged at them and they dropped Tommy's lifeless body, running back to the hole they had crept out of. I was a few hundred yards out of the town when I realized I had lost them. They had melted into the woods, and unless they were wearing reflective clothing, I'd never find them.

I howled a cry; frustration, anger and remorse were intermingled in that wail. *I failed*, I thought as I walked back. Bailey had taken off her jacket and covered Tommy's head, I would imagine so that I couldn't see the frozen expression of betrayal on his countenance.

I knelt by his body and said a prayer that I had known from my youth. I don't think I'd even got the half of it right. Oggie released a low keening as he rested his head on Tommy's chest. Something inside of me snapped there and then; that it hadn't happened much, much sooner was a mystery even to me. I stood; a wildness to my eyes.

"What are you doing, Michael?" Bailey asked with concern.

"Taking care of some unfinished business."

She reached out to stop me and missed. I put on a burst of speed she could not match. I knew what I'd find when I got there. The residents of Wheatonville were helping the former werewolves up or bandaging wounds.

"Traitors!" I screamed as I came upon them.

I meant the inhabitants of the town. I cut down anything and everything that was naked. They had no right to live while Tommy had died. Everyone fled from the ferocity and savagery I brought to bear. My sword was bathed in blood before Azile could be summoned from the church where she was tending to the wounds of friend and foe alike. I was just making her job easier.

"Don't you dare!" Azile shrieked as I pushed past her to get into the church. "They're just children!"

"They were," I told her. I brought my sword over my head and was about to bring it crashing down on the skull of the one closest to me. Azile muttered something and I found myself frozen; or, more correctly, the air around the sword seemed to be solidified as if in a block of ice. It appeared I could do whatever I wanted as long as it didn't involve my silver-gilded sword. I struggled for a moment longer.

"If you are so willing to get the blood of innocents on yourself, do it with your hands," She spat.

"Innocents?" I questioned hotly. "You keep telling yourself that when they rip your throat out. Fine, you keep your little pets." I released the sword. It hung for a few moments and then clattered to the floor. Azile kept an eye on me to see if I was going to pick it up or not. I thought about trying just to see which of us was quicker.

"I'm going to bury Tommy and then I'm leaving." I told her as I walked over to my meager pile of supplies. I grabbed my hand axe and made to leave.

"I didn't know," Azile said aghast.

"Yeah, more *innocents* did it," I told her, hoping my words would sting. It wasn't exactly the truth, but a lie was the least of my transgressions that day. "When I'm done, I'm leaving...ALONE," I added as I walked out the door.

Bailey had rounded up some shovels. She was leaning on one when I came back. She said nothing as I picked up his body and slung it over my shoulder. I bent my knees and bundled up Bailey's jacket with Tommy's head in it. I walked for hours like that. Bailey and Oggie trailing behind and thankfully silent. When I finally came across a place I thought worthy of a resting spot for him, I gently laid his body down, placing his head on his chest. We were on a small pine-covered hill that overlooked a beautiful lake, small islands the only thing breaking up the mirrored surface.

I plunged my shovel into the soft earth. Wordlessly, Bailey came up to me and began to dig as well. I knew I had found the right spot when we didn't encounter any rocks bigger than a marble and no roots thicker than a worm. The digging was easy and we got down to a proper depth in less than an hour. Bailey got out of the hole and handed me Tommy. He felt so light in my hands. I began to cry, he was one of my children plain and simple, it mattered not that he was older than me.

I thought about just having Bailey cover us both with dirt. Finally, I stood and climbed out, Bailey grabbing my hand and pulling me up. I had dug the hole slowly, not wanting to truly realize what it was that we were doing. Now I filled it in hastily in order to be done with this extremely distasteful event. Oggie pawed at the dirt mound when he saw that we were done. I thought he was going to try and get his friend back and then I noticed he dropped something in the small hole he had dug. I fell to my knees, wrapping my hands around Oggie's neck when I saw the sun glint off the foil wrapper. I covered up what couldn't possibly be there and stood.

"What was that?" Bailey asked curiously.

"Pop-Tart."

I knew she didn't have a clue what that was, but she didn't ask. I placed my hand over my heart. "Oh, Tommy, I thought I had saved you that day on the Walmart roof. Who would have known it was the other way around? I loved you like a father loves a son, and I will miss and mourn you along with the others until we are all once again reunited."

Bailey watched me silently as I spoke. She waited until I was done before she asked her question. "What now, Michael Talbot?"

"I'm done, Bailey Tynes. I can't take anymore. I'm going down to that lake, and I'm going to swim until I'm clean. Not clean on the inside, though, that, I cannot wash away."

I stumbled down the hill, my sight blurred almost to the point where I could not see. Screw sitting on my keys or getting pollen in my eyes, this was full-on crying. Bailey sat on the small beach as I sheared everything off of me. Oggie would bound into the water and out, repeating this numerous times. I left a plume of chum as I swam. Bailey was hardly recognizable when I finally stopped my swimming to see just how far I had gone. I could hear Oggie barking urgently looking in my direction. I don't think he was pleased with how far I had gone out. I turned back around; the lake still went on perhaps another mile or two. I could just keep swimming until I couldn't. Then I wondered, *could vampires drown?* Would I just be sitting on the silt-laden bottom, mourning the loss of another with only the fish and snapping turtles as company?

It was not a plan that completely lacked in merit. I

turned and began to swim back. Bailey seemed unruffled as I came out of the water naked. She had started a small fire in my absence.

"You will need clothes if you wish to hunt Lycan," she said as she tended to the flame.

"And what of you, Bailey?"

"It is my place much like BT to be by your side."

"If you remember correctly, that didn't work out too particularly well for him."

Bailey looked at me queerly. "He lived a long life, surrounded by family and loved ones, and he had an incredible tale to tell his children and then their children. Would you deny me that?" she asked.

"I would not."

"When do we start then?"

"I suppose we already have," I told her.

Epilogue – The Story of Tommy/Tomas

Tomas' mother died during his birthing. His head, which had been abnormally large, had torn the lining within her birthing canal. She had bled out on the fur and dirt floor of their mud hut in 1500s Germany. His father had never forgiven him that. If not for Tomas' sister Eliza, Tomas would have joined his mother in the afterlife. Henrick had wanted nothing to do with the baby. He had let it wail in the afterbirth for hours before he had allowed Eliza entry.

"Shut that thing up no matter what it takes," he told her in their severe sounding native language.

Eliza was five at the time. She had run in and dropped down to her mother's side. A small sob escaped as she looked upon the rapidly purpling body of her mother. A pool of blood spread between her legs, a fat cherub of a baby crying throatily. There was nothing she could do for her mother, but her brother she could love and would. They were all each other had. Henrick was a cruel man that ruled with fear, intimidation and often fists. Eliza figured her mother had probably welcomed the darkness when she saw it coming.

She grabbed the kettle of hot water the midwife had been using, some clothes and more furs. She first grabbed the baby who immediately quieted down from the contact. She cleaned him up and then swaddled him in the furs.

"What shall we name you?" Eliza asked the smiling baby.

"How about leech," her father had suggested, coming back into their hovel. "Another mouth to feed. She should have just taken the baby with her."

Eliza subconsciously shielded the baby; one never knew when an attack from Henrick was imminent. He had various trigger points some could be set off by no more than a cross look. And that was how it went for another five years, Tomas became attached to Eliza's hip, wherever the young girl went so did Tomas. From an early age Eliza knew Tomas was different, he would often warn her when father was coming home. It was safer for them to feign sleep; he was less likely to strike them although that defense didn't always work.

Tomas always knew where to find untended food. They had survived on his ability to feed them. Tomas clung to Eliza as the only mother he had ever known and Eliza had loved her brother. He was her oasis in a desert of desolation. Eliza had already started talking to Tomas about leaving; it was a fantasy of theirs. She would often times tell him of the land of dragons, where children were treated as lords and they were given sweets along with their meats.

"Is this true?" he would nearly beg her.

"Every word." She would smile at him.

Eliza's bright outlook on life began to dim when Henrick stepped over the line from physical abuse to sexual. Tomas had watched as his father forced himself upon the girl. Her first scream of pain had sent him into a fury and he had banged his small hands against his father's back. He had been rewarded with a punch to the side of the head that sent him reeling into the corner. He fell over backwards, his head slamming hard into the stone hearth. Blood had leaked out from his ears as he sat up; his thoughts became scrambled from that point forward. For a moment, he wasn't even sure who the two other people in the hovel were.

When Henrick was done, he stood, pulled his pants back up and fastened his crude belt. Eliza sobbed on the floor, blood and semen spilling from her.

"Oh, Tomas," Eliza had cried, having difficulty sitting up. When she could, she came over to him and cleaned his wound. It was strenuous for him to keep his eyes focused on any one object.

"Are you a dragon?" he had asked before he passed out.

It was a few more years before Henrick sold his

daughter to the highest bidder. He had traded her life for corn meal. Tomas had become slow, not stupid, from his father's strike. He knew he would be next. *Maybe for some rice*, he thought sourly. For a year longer he had stayed with his father, the beatings becoming more frequent as Henrick dealt with his demons in the only manner he knew how.

Tomas had slipped out in the middle of the night, but not before he made sure to relieve himself on the grain his father hoped to use for the remainder of the winter. That act alone had nearly sapped him of his courage; he wasn't sure how he was going to survive outside. Then a light came on in his head, he would not survive inside the hovel. Sooner or later, Henrick would beat him into oblivion. If he was to die then it would be with his Lizzie. He grabbed his only other set of clothes, all the dried goat jerky and struck out, unsure where he was even going.

The village was quiet this time of the evening except for the tavern where his father spent any extra time and coppers he may have had. He made sure to leave town, skirting the establishment as best he could. Life was difficult for a runaway, especially one whose thoughts were addled. He had a tenuous link to his sister. He could feel her, it was like a vast spider web and he could feel her vibrations trembling along the line. He could also feel his father's – that one he closed off as best he could, hoping that by concentrating on just his sister he would get a stronger signal. For years he had followed in her footsteps, torturously close on many occasions.

Finally, his break had come. He could see her at the end of the alleyway. He shook not only from the intense cold that blistered through his ragged garments, but also for the joy of reuniting with his beloved sister. The dark-cloaked figure she was with held Tomas at bay as he sent waves of malice radiating away. Tomas didn't dare move from his concealment behind some crates. Fear jogged through his spine. The fluid that leaked down his leg was most likely the only thing that kept him from freezing where he crouched.

Tomas noticed the man look exactly where he hid, but that was impossible, nobody could see him in this darkness. Tomas watched as The Stranger 'kissed' his sister's neck. A flash of anger welled up in him. *How dare someone do that without a marriage first!* He stood up just in time to see his sister swoon and fall. The Stranger looked back once at Tomas, laughed a small, cruel laugh, and then seemingly vanished into a darker shadow. All fear disappeared with the removal of The Stranger. Tomas ran the length of the alleyway dropping to his knees to cradle his sister's head.

Her eye's fluttered open as he cascaded her face with his tears. "Tomas? Is that really you Tomas?"

"It's me, Lizzie, it's me!" He cried. "We're finally together again! How I've missed you! Now we can be together again forever!"

"Tomas," Lizzie said sadly, stroking his face gently. "It's too late for me."

"What are you talking about, Lizzie? I'm here you're here, we're together." He wept for joy, but something evil was coming…he could feel it. His innate ability had proved an invaluable tool while he lived on the fringes of a distraught society. "What is the matter, Lizzie? You are burning up." The heat emanating from her prone form was melting the snow around her.

"You should go, Tomas." She closed her eyes.

"I can't leave you, Lizzie. We're all we have, you and me. You told me you would always look out for me. You were the only one that told me I didn't have witches living in my head." It was common in early Europe to convict the mentally challenged of witchcraft. "I love you Lizzie." Even as he said it, he could tell his sister was slipping away.

"I love you too, Tomas. And that is why you should go."

"Why won't you open your eyes, Lizzie? Please, please look at me."

Tears pushed through her closed lids. "Please, Tomas, don't look at me this way. I'm not the sister you used to know. Unspeakable things have been done to me, I found a way to right those wrongs and I took it. I will exact my revenge."

"That's not how my Lizzie talks," Tomas said, wiping his blurring eyes.

"GO!" She said pushing him away. Her eyes seemed to produce their own light as she looked at him menacingly.

"I will not!" he screamed, even though his inner-thoughts revolved around one word: 'RUN'.

Lizzie sat up. Factions warred within her. The looks she sent him fluctuated between love, sadness, and predatory awareness. Tomas kept backing up even as he shook his head in denial of what was happening right in front of him.

With an ungodly speed, Lizzie wrapped her hand around Tomas' neck. He found himself suspended six inches off the ground.

"Lizzie, please," he begged.

Lizzie pulled him in close and punched two neat holes into his exposed collar. Tomas screamed in pain.

"Lizzie, please, I love you!" His tears splashed down on her upturned face.

Some last remnant of Lizzie rose to the surface. She pulled her extended canines out of his neck. "GO!" she screamed again. "I won't be able to stop next time." She looked defeated, with her head bowed. Tomas dropped to the ground as she released her grip.

He scurried away scarcely believing the turn of events. "I love you, Lizzie. I will follow you until I find a way to fix whatever has happened here tonight."

And he had run, running until his legs burned and his chest couldn't move fast enough to pull in air. The connective string upon which she danced now hummed with electricity, his thoughts which moments before were clouded now shone as if under the brilliance of a noonday sun. He was unsure what Eliza had done to him, but she had awoken a hunger within him. A hunger for revenge, for retribution, and more importantly, for blood. He pulled the shroud from a segment of his mind he had actively blocked for close to five years. The string that connected him to his father was a cold gray thing but it moved and that was all the impetus he needed.

For three days he ran, seemingly without the ability to exhaust. He did not understand what was happening he also didn't question it. It was early evening when he returned to a home he vowed he would never set foot in again. Nothing had changed; even the bag of grain he had soiled with his fecal matter was still in the corner. A pang shot through him as he looked upon his and Eliza's bedding. It had been tossed about surely by his father in a drunken stupor, but it was still there.

He pulled one of the heavy wooden chairs away from the table and closer to the embers that burned in the hearth. He placed some logs in it to stoke a good flame. He had a cold within him that sank to the depths of his soul. He had been staring at the flames intently divining the meaning of life when his father walked in.

"Figured you'd come back someday. My stupid boy has come home," Henrick said with a cruel laugh, opening up his mouth to reveal black and rotting teeth.

Tomas stood.

Henrick had to look up, he licked his lips nervously. "Been eating well boy, since you shat on my food have you?" He moved in to strike at the boy and once again assert his dominance. Tomas flinched as Henrick struck him in the side of the head. "Hurt, boy?" Henrick spat.

"No, not really," Tomas said, placing a hand to his face. "Let me know if this does."

Tomas struck his father flush in the mouth. Blood exploded from the man's lips as Tomas' knuckles split them wide. Henrick stumbled a few steps and fell over. Henrick was a big man and never, not once in his life had someone put him on his ass.

"Good one, boy." Henrick wiped the blood from his mouth and stood back up. "You're going to pay for that, though." He pulled a long filet knife out from his waist.

Henrick charged, driving the blade deep into Tomas' midsection. All the air was forced from his lungs as he absorbed the steel. "Should have done that outside, now you're going to bleed all over the place," Henrick said, letting go of the hilt. He went over to a small cask and placed his head under the tap.

Tomas stood there wrapping his hands around the knife.

"You ain't dead yet?" Henrick asked when he was done washing the blood from his mouth. "Here let me twist that around for you a little bit." He came back over.

Tomas yanked the blade free with an audible gasp and let the knife fall to the ground.

"Too stupid to die, ain't ya, boy," Henrick said. "Should have been you I sold, then I could have kept your precious Lizzie around for entertainment." Henrick was laughing, blood spilling from his lips.

Tomas lifted up his shirt. The wound where he was stabbed had stopped bleeding, Henrick and Tomas both watched in amazement as the skin began to knit before their eyes.

"Devil!" Henrick screamed. He looked wildly past Tomas' shoulder and to the exit.

All that remained was the drying blood to allude that anything had ever happened.

"Sit, father." Tomas said evenly.

Henrick was looking around for something anything he could use to thwart the spawn of evil before him.

"I won't say it again." Tomas said with force. Henrick complied. "Why?" Tomas asked as his father finally took a seat opposite him.

"Why what?" Henrick asked belligerently.

"Why did you hate us so much?"

"I fed and sheltered you little mongrels. What more did you want?" he answered as if that was what Tomas was looking for.

"Would it have been different if mother had survived?" Tomas asked.

"Well, we'll never know will we? You and your fat head made sure of that." Henrick said with vitriol.

"I knew what I was doing when I came all the way back here, I just didn't figure that it was going to be so easy," Tomas said, rising from his chair.

"What....what are you going to do?" Henrick asked nervously.

"It won't hurt much," Tomas said as he struck, yanking his father's head to the side.

He drank the sour lifeblood from his father; not stopping even after he began to feel pieces of muscle and tendon pull up through the now empty holes. Henrick was twenty-five pounds lighter when his body was discovered. The stench of his decaying body had sent the wild dogs in the area into a frenzy as they scratched at the door trying to get in.

The tether between brother and sister intensified over the years, it became a game of cat and mouse, although in this version the mouse was stalking the much more dangerous cat. Eliza was aware of the bond they shared and allowed her brother only enough access to it as would keep him on the leash. It wasn't that she enjoyed the connection but rather the cruelty of always staying one step ahead of him. She could feel his disappointment when he came agonizingly close to catching her.

What Eliza was not aware of, was that, as Tommy's powers grew, so did his ability for clairvoyance. He could see things that made no sense, but that had a purpose and would play a much greater role in events to come. He did not know why he saw those things, but he felt compelled to act on them.

Western Front 1918

"Who the bloody hell are you?" Crackers asked as Tommy slid into the trench next to him. Crackers was covered in mud and blood, he was almost indistinguishable from the grime that enveloped him, his hands no less filthy. When Tommy came upon him, the man was scooping some sort of beef hash out of his helmet with those same hands. The food was intermixed with flies, lice, dirt, and gore.

"I'm Tommy. Looks good," Tommy said sarcastically, looking at the helmet.

"Get your own." Crackers pulled the helmet out of range.

"I already ate," Tommy replied subconsciously wiping away any blood that might be around his mouth. He had visited the enemy lines first before coming to find Crackers. He had spent three days riding hard to get here today. He had dropped two mounts along the way. He had not understood the urgency with which the power had directed him here but he also knew that he could not fail.

"You new?" Crackers asked in between mouthfuls. He had the social graces of a two-year-old, he talked while he chewed and also smacked his lips.

"Far from new." Tommy smiled.

"Uniform looks new," Crackers said, touching the lapel and leaving a smear of something better left unidentified.

"I had to run a message back from the lines, got one in the rear."

"Lucky bastard, you are. I've got more critters living in my britches than I care to count." And with that phrase he began to furiously scratch at his crotch. "Got sores on my arse and lice the size of lobsters crawling around my balls!" Crackers laughed.

A whistle sounded off in the distance. "Oh shit." Crackers said plopping his half-full helmet onto his head."

"What's that?" Tommy asked. Crackers looked at him strangely and warily as he gripped his rifle.

"Thought you said you weren't new?" Crackers asked.

"Not new to the Army...new to the trenches."

A great grin split Crackers face, his teeth preternaturally white in contrast to the rest of him.

"Well ain't you in for a treat then. That was the warning whistle."

"Warning whistle?" Tommy asked completely at a loss.

"Yeah, a warning to how many of us are going to die!" Crackers laughed. "Next blow and we crawl out of this perfectly good trench and run across all that open, barren, muddy ground. Alst the while, Germans are sitting in their fancy hidey holes shooting at us with machine guns, it's a riot!"

"You're kidding right?" Tommy asked.

"Watch this," Crackers said as he leaned in close. He scrambled up over the top and out in to the open.

"Bloody hell, Crackers! Where in the blimey fuck are you going?" a voice shouted over to Tommy's left. Tommy thought it was his sergeant-in-arms.

"Visions suck sometimes," Tommy said as he grabbed his helmet and rifle and followed after Crackers.

"Who the hell is that? And nobody blew the bloody whistle yet," the officer shouted. The end of his statement was punctuated with the loud long blast of a whistle. Men screamed as they emerged from their trenches running pell-mell towards the German lines. Crackers had a good twenty or thirty-foot lead on the rest of his mates, with Tommy closing in fast.

The Germans watched in casual amazement as the British teamed out of their side of the battlefield and streamed towards them. Tommy watched as soldiers on the other side took one more drag from their cigarettes, or one more forkful of food before they primed their weapons and let loose a deadly volley of lead. Sheets of the projectiles were being sent down range. War cries became screams of the dying. They had not covered more than half the distance to their goal when the retreat whistle was sounded.

"What the hell was the point?" Tommy asked as he saw the British soldiers that could, begin to turn around and head back to their side. They're exchanging bodies for bullets, that's all they're doing. It comes down to who is going to run out of what first. Tommy was saddened at the needless loss of so much life. He had passed up Crackers at some point and had intended to stay right on his back as a protective cloak as they retreated. As he spun, Crackers passed him by still going forward.

Crackers had become silent, a look of anger and determination etched in the dirt of his features.

"They sounded the retreat," Tommy said, struggling to catch back up.

"To hell with the bloody retreat," Crackers replied. "I'm getting this over one way or the other. I'm sick of that whistle. Next time I hear it I'm going to shove it up his ass. He blows, good men die. And for nothing, that's the quick of it…for bloody nothing. We run, sometimes the krauts let us get halfway, sometimes when they're feeling a little pissed off they only let us get about a quarter of the way before they cut us down, then the whistle blows so we can go slinking back to our diseased little holes. Don't see those bastards trying to get over here."

Dirt clods began to fly in the air all around Crackers and Tommy as more and more guns began to train on them. They were rapidly becoming the only targets available on the frozen bloodied and muddied killing fields. Tommy got in front of Crackers; the force from the rounds as they impacted Tommy sent him back into Crackers. The pain was damn near immeasurable, but still he was able to clutch Crackers and bring him down with him.

"Stay down, you damned fool," Tommy said as Crackers tried to squirm out from under him. A few more rounds bounced their way with another catching Tommy in the leg. Tommy winced.

"You're still alive?" Crackers asked incredulously. "I'm so sorry. Do you have any messages on you that you want delivered?" Crackers asked sincerely.

"You really think you're going to make it out of here to deliver one?" Tommy asked.

"Sure…why not?"

"Well, because you're about twenty meters away from a trench filled with Germans who would say otherwise."

"Oh them. I bloody well plan on killing them. I came here with four of my best friends, Lumpy Vales, Henry Smith, Wendall Renton, and even the limey bastard Cray O'Malley, loved them all like brothers. They're dead…every single one of them. The bloody fucking whistle did it just as much as the krauts. But I can't kill the whistle blower, can't do that. I get shot as a traitor and bring shame to my family. The funny thing, though, I just make it across this little line nothing more than a fly shit on a map and I can kill everything and everyone I see and I'll be a hero. War is strange."

Tommy agreed. "First, we stay here for a while, quiet. And when the night comes, we'll exact some revenge for your friends."

"You going to make it that long?" Crackers asked. "You got shot up pretty good."

"Barely scraped me," Tommy told him.

Crackers wanted to tell him that he'd seen the blood sprays and the approximate locations of the shots, and they weren't of the fleshy wound variety. But he'd play along for now, a nap was exactly what he needed; and if it gave him a respite from the cries of dying men around him then that was just an added bonus.

The night was cloudy and dark as onyx. Crackers had to blink a few times just to make sure he hadn't gone blind sometime during his sleep.

"You still with me, Tommy?" Crackers asked softly, not expecting a reply. Not unless ghosts could talk…and those he didn't believe in. He'd made a pact with his mates that if any of them died, they would haunt the others just for the hell of it, and he'd yet to see any of their ghostly mugs. He was startled a bit when Tommy responded.

"Still here."

"Able to move?" Crackers asked.

"Can I convince you to head back to our side?" Tommy asked.

"As dark as it is they'd be just as likely to shoot us as the krauts. No, I'll take my chances on this side. Plus…we're closer," Crackers said as he began to silent crawl.

"Ever heard of a plan?" Tommy hissed behind him.

"Heard of it, ain't never used one," Crackers replied. Tommy could see Cracker's teeth as the man had turned to smile at him.

"Apparently. You need to stay safe, you play a much larger role in world events." Tommy said.

If Crackers heard he didn't respond, all that mattered to the man at the moment was the here and now. He couldn't worry about a future he didn't think he'd be around to see.

Periodically, flares would go up on both sides and Tommy and Crackers would halt their progress until the eerie fluttering light gave out. They crept closer, if another flare were to go up they would have no choice but to rush the Germans, and they were too close to be anything but an approaching enemy.

Crackers slid over the small berm quietly, making absolutely no noise as he dropped into the German trench. Tommy's foot came down on the edge of an upturned helmet sending it skittering off on the wooden planks inlaid on the bottom of the trench.

"*Haben sie eine zigarette?*" (Do you have a cigarette?) Crackers asked, trying to cover Tommy's noise

"*Wer ist das?*" (Who is that?) the German asked back.

"Death," Crackers said before he started shooting.

Pandemonium broke out inside the German trench. Nobody knew who was shooting at whom. Germans spilled more of their own blood with friendly fire than Crackers could have ever hoped for. Tommy ripped a Maxim machinegun from the rapidly cooling hands of the dead German who had been wielding it. A stream of fire shot out from the barrel as he swept it back and forth, harvesting men like a farmer harvested wheat.

He moved slowly North up the trench firing in short bursts. Crackers was watching their back, constantly grabbing new German guns.

"This is the life," Crackers said in between rounds.

"What?" Tommy asked, hardly believing Crackers words.

"Look at this place. They actually have a floor and they have these dugouts in the back where they sleep. There's food and supplies everywhere. This is like the Ritz"

"Ever been to the Ritz?" Tommy asked, looking quickly for more rounds. Germans kept coming around blind corners almost too many to keep up with.

"No," Crackers replied.

"This isn't like the Ritz," Tommy said before firing another burst.

When the British realized the Germans were in the midst of some confusion, the whistle blew in quick succession. Soldiers roared out of their holes hopeful that this time their bayonets would finally drink their fill of German blood, a debt owed many times over.

"Bloody whistle. I swear, right after they pin a medal on my chest for this, I'm going to shove it up that blower's arse. Right now we're in a bit of a pickle," Crackers said. "As soon as those soldiers come in here...they aren't going to ask questions."

Flares shot up on both sides, the faces of British soldiers were illuminated in various forms, some in utter terror, others exhilaration, determination, and a dozen other variations and combinations. Tommy waited until the soldiers were within twenty meters or so.

"Now we hide," he told Crackers.

"I'll do no such thing," he told Tommy. "Hey! What the bloody hell?" Crackers shouted as Tommy lifted him easily off the ground and shoved him into one of the German sleeping cut-outs. "I suppose you want me to buy you some sweets now that we're sharing a bed?" Crackers asked.

"Shut up, you fool," Tommy said, quickly digging at the dirt with his hands to get them further into the recess. Within a few moments they were another two or three feet deeper into the ground, nearly invisible to anyone who might notice.

"Now I guess we just have to hope no one tosses a grenade in here," Crackers said calmly.

"Hadn't thought of that."

"Want some dried meat?" Crackers asked, shifting around until he could get to one of his pockets. "I'm not really sure what it is…could be goat…maybe horse. Hell, knowing the guy I traded with, it could be rat," he said as he began to chew.

"You're eating dried rat?"

"Maybe," Crackers replied. "I'm starving."

As the fighting raged through the night, Tommy made sure Crackers lay where he placed him. The British had finally made some headway that night. They would give it back in less than two weeks at the expense of fifteen hundred lost souls, but it had been a victory nonetheless. Crackers had been sent back to England to receive that medal he had talked about. However, he did not get a chance to fulfill the second part. The whistle blower had caught a bullet in the mouth. The ironic part of it was that the whistle had deflected the shot, but the marble had come loose and lodged in his throat, closing off his airway and killing him before anyone could get it loose.

Tommy melted into the crowd, his uniform discarded when he had completed what he had set out to do. Crackers was up on the stage, cleaner than Tommy ever imagined he could be, a wide, gap-toothed smile plastered on his face.

"...in honor of your achievement while facing down the teeth of the enemy The British Royal Army awards you, Reginald 'Crackers' Talbot, with this, the Imperial Gallantry medal."

And with a complete lack of military decorum Crackers grabbed the side of the general's face and planted a kiss on it much to the ruckus enjoyment of those assembled.

Talbot-Sode #1

During Inuktuk's telling of the Landians history I drifted back to the first time I had killed a man. I was a kid; old enough to vote for the shithead that sent me off to a foreign land, but not old enough to legally obtain liquor. Strange that it was alright for me to kill someone, but not drink whiskey to forget about it. I had always thought the book, *1984* by George Orwell, was full of shit. How big could the government be that they could control all the transfer of information? Surely those people would be able to find out that they were constantly being fed lies. How wrong I was.

A division of Marines, myself included, had been sent to South Korea in an effort to quell the ranting politics of a dictator throwing a tantrum. Shots would constantly ring out, from both sides; at the time, only the Koreans were involved. We were strictly told that if we weren't specifically shot at, we couldn't join in. Never understood that shit. I had to wait for some itchy-trigger-finger asshole to take a shot at me before I could do anything. So if I was lucky and he missed, then, and only then, could I fire back. *Bullshit* seemed to be the general word of the day when that order came down.

Bobbie-fucking-Chen was his name, I'll never forget it. Not sure if you could possibly know the difference, but that is not a Korean name. Chinese, to be specific. Unbeknownst to us, the Chinese, in direct response to the Marines landing, had sent four divisions of Chinese regulars to bolster the lines of North Korea. Typical Chinese overkill. China back then was like the big brother of North Korea; kind of despised the little fuck and thought the crazy shit he did was just asinine, but he sure as hell wasn't going to let anyone else fuck with him, if you get my point. How the higher ups missed four divisions rolling into town is beyond me – my conspiratorial ass will always believe that they did know, and that we were merely pawns in a much bigger game.

If we were to get slaughtered, then that would give the allies all the impetus they needed to go in and shut the little tyrant up once and for all. We had satellites, spy planes, CIA agents on the ground, and a sympathetic North Korean populace that would do all in their power at the penalty of death to let people know what was going on, and yet the US Government would feign ignorance to any knowledge of the Chinese build up. Is it any wonder where my mistrust comes from? Luckily this isn't some socio-economic-political rant, I was closing in on nineteen, and I had no clue what any of that stuff meant. I trusted the guy next to me, and the weapon I held in my hands; that was about it.

We were far enough away from the barricades and fences that the North Koreans couldn't get off a decent shot, but close enough for them to realize we were still there. I constantly felt like we were being watched. We did combat drills all day, whether in the searing heat or the torrential rain that seemed to dominate that shitty little corner of the world. I don't know what the fighting was all about; the only thing that wanted to be there were the encephalitis-carrying mosquitoes. We'd been there a few weeks and the abject terror of potentially being thrust into a war had kind of worn off. We were settling in for the long haul. Cards, when off-duty and four hour guard duty shifts during the night, was the norm.

My partner Corporal Quentin Johnson and I had just lost a particularly close game of Spades and we went out of our Quonset hut to get some air and talk about the game. I had fifteen or so minutes before my shift started, and I was trying to convince Quentin he should take my shift.

"Come on, man, if you hadn't of played on suit and pulled my queen out we could have won," I told him. "The least you owe me is to take my fire watch so that I can sleep my anger off."

Quentin lit up a smoke.

"Gimme one," I told him when he didn't even respond to my words. He lit my Camel unfiltered, tasted like shit, but better than the bile that was going to replace it in a few minutes. I took my first drag and was about a half a hitch away from coughing my lungs out.

"You hear that?" he asked, placing his hand on my chest – I guess to shut me up.

And I had. Sounded like large birds shooting overhead. Not the cries, but rather the flow of air whooshing over large wings. He poked his head back in the barracks; most of the guys were out like a light considering it was somewhere around three in the morning.

"Get up! Get your rifles!" he shouted.

We were all kids; and you know, if you're a parent, that waking one of us up in under a half hour is a damn near impossibility…that is, of course, unless the threat of death is a real possible consequence for sleeping in. It was under a minute, and every swinging dick in that barracks was outside, M-16s at the ready. Most not completely dressed, all had boots on, though.

Some were looking around wildly. Quentin had them all shut up, even the ones grumbling that if this was a drill they were going to piss on his bunk. The general alarm had not been sounded, not so much as a firecracker had gone off. I was a moment away from thinking I had imagined it when the world turned on its side, or rather, I did as the concussion from the explosion tossed me on my ass. Sirens wailed, lights blazed, flares were popped off. Multi-colored tracers were flying up from anti-aircraft positions. Giant gray birds floated overhead, I didn't know it then, but they were gliders, gliders big enough to carry a couple of paratroopers who were even now making their rapid descent on our position.

When they realized they'd been spotted, they began to drop grenades to clear a landing zone. You know the expression 'raining cats and dogs'? Pissed off Pit bulls and crazed, carnivorous cats would have been ten times more preferable to what was falling from the sky that night. I watched as a Marine was nailed in the head with one of the dropped bombs. He had just fallen to his knees from the strike when the explosion ripped his head off. He stayed kneeling longer than seemed possible given the circumstances. The body finally fell forward, smacking wetly against the ground. That vision more than anything is what finally got me moving. Couldn't hear anything except a nerve-damaging ring in my ears but I could see just fine and we had almost been completely caught off guard.

Grenades were striking and rolling off the sides of the Quonset huts blowing holes in the thin metal as they did so – at least three had struck ours. If not for Corporal Johnson's quick thinking, more men would have died that night. Most, if not all, of our forces were trained upwards for obvious reasons, but something just didn't feel right. I can't imagine the North Koreans putting all their eggs in one basket, even if the country was so damn poor that they only could afford one basket. Didn't seem right.

We would later learn that Chinese engineers had created tunnels almost a mile in length. They would eventually tie into the existing infrastructure sewer lines that the South had created. Back then, the monitors weren't as sophisticated, and they had dug them down deep enough so as not to be detected anyway. While our forces were pointing upward, finally inflicting some damage on the invaders, the second part of the invasion was unleashed. Manhole covers behind us were moved, and troops flooded out of the sewers like water-logged rats, and with the same mean, shitty disposition.

Gunfire chattered behind us, most didn't think anything of it because of its location, and that the bastards were even using M-16s as opposed to their normal firearm – the AK-47. The heavier staccato sound of the AK would have given them away a lot quicker. I shouted to those around me and pulled their gazes downward. We found some cover and began to lay some suppressive fire back at them. It was like they didn't care or something, it was their single mission in life to return back to the country they had just evacuated as they came running right back into the stinging teeth of the bullets we fired.

I remember distinctly my heart hammering so hard I thought for sure it was going to jump out of my throat. I couldn't control my breathing enough to get off a well-aimed shot. Bullets were whining by, some striking the Quonset hut I was using as a shield. Above everything that was going on, the machineguns, the small-arms fire, and the grenades, I heard men…just the men. Some in deep-throated war cries, others merely crying for help and the most disturbing were the ones that were wounded and crying out for their mothers. I learned the North Korean and Chinese words for 'mother' that night. *Uhm-ma* and *mu-qing*, respectively. Seems no matter how different we think we are from each other, we're pretty much hard-wired the same.

I made more than one man cry out for his *uhm-ma*, but only so that I wouldn't have to, not because I hated them. The first, well, he's the one that haunts me some hundred and seventy years later. I had emptied my magazine; ducked back down around the corner of the hut and reached into my cargo pocket, grabbing my last remaining magazine. At the time, we were told to carry only one extra. Going forward, I would make sure to carry five times what was authorized, but right now I had to make it through the night. My bayonet was by my bunk which right now might as well have been in Boston. I had my knife strapped to my side. I truly hoped it didn't come down to that, hell, the only reason I wore the thing was because I thought it looked cool. I was eighteen, tell me you didn't do shit because it was cool, or at least you perceived it that way. I can bet that girl Henna didn't think peeling rubber in her folks' driveway was cool. Or that crap-tastic tattoo your buddy did on your arm…bet you thought that thing was AWESOME! Let's face it, as young men, we do a lot of stupid stuff we think is cool. But, when I strapped that knife on, it was never with the intention of getting close enough to the enemy to actually use it. I was thinking it was a much better deterrent.

I heard footsteps approaching even as I shoved the magazine in its well. The words they spoke might as well have been from another planet they were so foreign. My heart, which I figured was already getting ready to explode, might just stop. I can't imagine any muscle being able to work that hard and not just up and fail. I wondered, for a flash, if it would feel like a charley horse when it quit. I stood so quickly with adrenaline-fueled legs that I nearly hopped. I poked my head around the curved corner of the hut. Three men were coming my way, they were looking around wildly, and I would imagine just as scared as I was, but I didn't see it that way at the time. I brought my rifle around and pulled the trigger…nothing.

No loud bang, no force into my shoulder as the round exploded out, and definitely no enemy falling as it caught my high-speed offering. What I figured was a jam was merely the fact that I had never pulled back the charging handle on my rifle, thus putting a round in the chamber. The funny part about it (okay, not truly funny, I guess just a bad expression) but the funny part about it was that not a one of them realized I was there or that I had attempted to fire on their position. Two of the men were looking back towards where they had just come and the third was now coming up to my corner. I had ducked back down and was about to do emergency procedures on my rifle to get it firing, I did not have the time, and they would certainly hear the noise.

And then I got pissed, I'd be fucking God-damned if I was going to die with a useless rifle in my hands. I stood, flipped the clip on my knife, and quietly slid it free from its sheath. The brown of a Chinese boot just became visible as I brought my right fist up to right under my chin, the blade pointing outwards – otherwise that night would have really sucked for me. I flexed my elbow out as hard and as fast as I could. The Chinese soldier's eyes got huge as he watched my black metal blade swing towards him. He was ducking down to his left and simultaneously bringing his rifle up. My blade clipped off the top of his front sight post slowing me down marginally…and that was it, the tip of my blade pierced his forehead.

My arm shivered from the force of the strike. His eyes crossed for the briefest of seconds to try and focus on the steel that was even now scrambling his thoughts. The weight as he fell pulled my arm down, almost making me lose my weapon. I yanked it free, somewhat stunned at how little blood there actually was. I had been kind of expecting it to spurt out like a geyser. Quentin and another Marine had come up behind me and quickly dispatched the two remaining enemy soldiers.

"Hard core, man," Quentin said to me after he checked the soldiers to make sure they were dead. I had pulled my knife free, wiping it on Bobbie-fucking-Chen's uniform. "Right in the forehead, fuck that must have hurt. You alright, Talbot?" he asked.

Right there and then the world took a hard left turn, I wasn't sure if I'd ever be right again. But I nodded to him, seemed the right thing to do. I'd kill more men before the night was through and many more before the veil of death will enshroud me; but like any first, he would linger in my thoughts. I searched his body quickly, grabbing what I had originally thought was Intel and shoved it into my pocket. I would forward it to someone with shiny shit on their collars as soon as I found any of them. Probably riding the whole thing out at the Officer's Club.

The element of surprise was long past, but the forces attacking us were winning by sheer numbers. If not for our battleships parked on the peninsula's doorstep, we would have been screwed and overrun. Rounds whistled overhead, the ground shook with each impact. The North side of the line was getting hammered into the Stone Age. I waited for their response, figuring missile strikes would be incoming at any moment. They never did; all I can figure is that they didn't want to escalate to the next level. They had given it a shot, and when it fell short, they decided to cut and run. I don't know, it made no sense to me then, and still doesn't. They were winning.

The sun was coming up by the time we drove the yellow devils back underground or for the truly unlucky ones into the ground. Not that I cared at the time – or could even tell – but most of the paratroopers were North Korean and the men coming up through the sewers were Chinese. Media on all sides had completely quashed the notion that anything extraordinary had happened that night. The thirty-two Marines and eighty-six South Koreans that had died were apparently due to a training accident. A troop transport Marine helicopter had collided with a Galaxy transport plane that had been taking the South Koreans on a training exercise in Japan – that was the official report.

The two hundred and seventy-four North Koreans and Chinese that died that night were never reported, at least not in papers I had read. It was like they had fallen into a black hole never to be heard from again. What did those regimes tell the grieving families? Anything? Probably nothing. Probably told them they never had a son, and if they wanted to live out the rest of their natural lives they'd never talk about the mythical boy again.

We were on high alert that entire next day and night. I was straddling the line of wanting to fall asleep and thinking I would never be able to do so again. The army finally came in and relieved us, five divisions. Never seen so many men holding a rifle in my life. I think I slept a full twenty-four hours straight. Time had been severely skewed for me during this time frame; surreal, I guess, would be the appropriate descriptor. I wasn't quite sure how I felt. As humans, I'm fairly convinced that we are hardwired with the ability and want to kill other men. Only as a means of self-defense, I'm not saying all Hannibal Lecter-style. But morality, religion, common decency, civilization, they all scream with *Thou Shalt Not Kill*. I got some commendation for killing Bobbie-fucking-Chen, couldn't even begin to tell you where it ended up. Never seemed right that his life boiled down to a combat ribbon. I could bet he felt the same.

Sorry…digression. So there I am sleeping off the effects of a major adrenaline rush, and I start coming up from the depths of my tiny death with this thing poking me in the side, couldn't get comfortable to save my life. I finally moved enough to where I could reach my hand into my pocket. I pulled out this notebook that was about six-by-nine. What I had thought was Intel was actually Bobbie-fucking-Chen's journal. No biggie, who among us can read Chinese? Only it's not in Chinese, it's English and the handwriting is meticulous. Seems my first kill went to school in Chicago. He was going for his doctorate in Engineering when his government had called him back to die uselessly at the hands of a troubled teen.

He was twenty-six and actually had a fiancée back in Chicago, not sure what his parents were going to think of Lillian Fraser…didn't sound Chinese to me. I read that entire journal. Probably simultaneously the smartest and most stupid thing I had ever done in my life. I got to know Bobbie, his dreams, his hopes, his love. But on the flip side, it gave dimension to a nameless, faceless enemy. I think I could have more easily forgotten about that night if not for the journal; but then, should I really have been let off the hook that easily? It's important to know that the person you are killing is indeed human. Bobbie-fucking-Chen was the reason I started writing journals, I figured if someone were to kill me I would want them to know who I was. Kind of a guilt hand-off if you will.

I went to see Lillian on my next leave, almost eighteen months later when I got rotated back to the mainland US. She lived in a brownstone apartment in downtown Chicago. I thought long and hard about what I was going to say if she would even talk to me. I figured it would be a slap followed by a litany of accusations, curses, and tears. It was a cold Wednesday when the cab dropped me off by her apartment – forgot the rest of the world was on a different schedule. I loitered around the front of her building for a good five hours before I finally saw her walking down the sidewalk. Bobbie-fucking-Chen's drawings did her no justice. She had long, blond hair, looked like worked gold with the sun setting behind her. From this distance I could see a sadness in her features even when she smiled and talked with some of her neighbors as she approached.

    I had thought out an entire speech. I said not one word of it as she came within three feet of my location. She said nothing to me, my dress greens probably not stirring any kind of patriotic musings in her. She went past and I let her. She had gone up most of the five stairs leading into her building. I had turned and was berating myself for being such a coward.

    "You knew him didn't you?" she asked.

    I spun, thinking she couldn't possibly be talking to me. How could she know?

    "Not really," I said. "Not at first anyway."

    "You were there the night he died, the night the government denied anything happened?"

    "I was," I told her.

    I couldn't tell her much more than that without potentially putting myself in judicial harm. If I so much as breathed a word of what happened, I'd find myself in Leavenworth and I had no desire to make small rocks out of big ones for the rest of my life. I dipped my head, I wanted to confess, I wanted her to absolve me of his death. I approached her; my hands were trembling. She looked like she wanted to dash into her building and I couldn't blame her. I handed her his journal. She took it, her eyes never leaving my own.

"He loved you, and I'm sorry," I told her.

She took the notebook from me, her hands beginning to tremble as if the book was the source of the shaking. I turned and left. She didn't say anything else. I could only hope the words he wrote would give her some measure of solace and perhaps closure, although, the only thing that would ever make it right was if she could hold her love again. I found a bar close by. Didn't even have to show my fake ID. I let a bunch of the patrons buy me free drinks; enough so that I could attempt to wipe the stain of events clean from my mind. Alas, I never did find an elixir potent enough to do it. I tried…I tried really hard. Bobbie-fucking-Chen would haunt me all of my days.

Talbot-sode #2

Figured I'd expand on Mike's couch fiasco at the age of 16.

I grabbed up my stuff and jammed myself between the couch and the wall. Heather had stuffed her things under the couch and pulled the throw blanket over herself.

"Hey, honey, what are you doing all bundled up?" her father asked. He was a cop and I'd had more than one run in with him. He'd forbidden his daughter from dating me; I should have silently thanked him, that just made me all the more desirable to her.

"Don't feel too good," she told him.

"You do look a little flushed," he'd replied, coming over I think to feel her forehead. "That's why I came home early, don't feel too well myself. I think something's going around."

"You should go lie down," Heather said. I could hear the desperation in her voice, I hoped he couldn't.

"Nonsense, misery loves company. I'll go brew us some tea," he said.

Some might think this would be a perfect opportunity for escape. No such luck, the kitchen had a knee wall which gave a full view to the living room – fucking open floor plans. We were both stuck, Heather had more reason to be where she was, but she couldn't get up naked, that would surely raise red flags with her father.

"Great," Heather said, trying to add some cheer.

"Let me turn the heat up, it's a little chilly in here," he told her.

It was then I realized my entire backside was pressed up against the radiator. I could hear the pops of expanding pipes as hot water began to find its way to the register.

"You have got to be kidding me," I lamented.

"You say something?" her dad asked.

"Just clearing my throat," she told him.

Dad Killington put on the television, and for two hours I got to listen to how lions were the kings of the savannah. At one point, her Dad asked Heather if she smelled chicken, pretty sure that was my ass frying. Then the party really began to swell as Mom Killington came home and started dinner.

"I have to pee so bad," Heather muttered, when her dad went into the kitchen with her mother.

"Yeah, well I need about a gallon of aloe for my third degree burns. Not going to be able to sit for a friggin' week."

She laughed and quickly turned it into a cough for effect.

"Are you sure you're alright to go get this stuff?" Heather's mom asked her husband.

"For my women…anything." A few moments later I heard his car start and he pulled away.

"You've got about fifteen minutes, Heather. I suggest you get dressed and get Mike the hell out of my house."

I felt the blood drain from my soul. "Oh, shit," I muttered.

"I'm going into my bathroom to freshen up and then I'm going to pour myself a huge glass of wine and pretend this never happened," she said.

I needed all of a minute and a half to pull my clothes on, even over my singed ass. I was halfway home when Mr. Killington drove past. He glared at me as he went, probably would have arrested me for something if he hadn't been coming back from an errand. I waved and smiled. "I'm doing your daughter," I said as I kept smiling at him.

I hope you enjoyed the book. If you did please consider leaving a review.

For more in The Zombie Fallout Series by Mark Tufo:

Zombie Fallout 1

Zombie Fallout 2 A Plague Upon Your Family

Zombie Fallout 3 The End....

Zombie Fallout 3.5 Dr. Hugh Mann

Zombie Fallout 4 The End Has Come And Gone

Zombie Fallout 5 Alive In A Dead World

Zombie Fallout 6 Til Death Do Us Part

Zombie Fallout 7 For The Fallen

The newest Post Apocalyptic Horror by Mark Tufo:

Lycan Fallout Rise of the Werewolf

Fun with zombies in The Book of Riley Series by Mark Tufo

The Book Of Riley A Zombie Tale pt 1

The Book Of Riley A Zombie Tale pt 2

The Book Of Riley A Zombie Tale pt 3

The Book Of Riley A Zombie Tale pt 4

Or all in one neat package:

The Book Of Riley A Zombie Tale Boxed set plus a bonus short

Dark Zombie Fiction can be found in The Timothy Series by Mark Tufo

Timothy

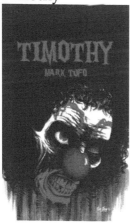

Tim2

Michael Talbot is at it again in this Post Apocalyptic Alternative History series Indian Hill by Mark Tufo

Indian Hill 1 Encounters:

Indian Hill 2 Reckoning

Indian Hill 3 Conquest

Indian Hill 4 From The Ashes

Writing as M.R. Tufo

Dystance Winter's Rising

The Spirit Clearing

Callis Rose

I love hearing from readers, you can reach me at:

email
mark@marktufo.com

website
www.marktufo.com

Facebook
https://www.facebook.com/pages/Mark-Tufo/133954330009843?ref=hl

Twitter
@zombiefallout

All books are available in audio version at Audible.com or itunes.

All books are available in print at Amazon.com or Barnes and Noble.com

Printed in Great Britain
by Amazon.co.uk, Ltd.,
Marston Gate.